PRAISE FOR *The Best Laid Plans*

"Realistic, funny, and honest."
—HUNTLEY FITZPATRICK, AUTHOR OF *MY LIFE NEXT DOOR*

"Fresh-voiced and heartfelt, this debut pairs irresistible friends-to-lovers tension with vital questions of first love. It's a witty, welcome entry in the rom-com resurgence."
—EMILY WIBBERLEY AND AUSTIN SIEGEMUND-BROKA, AUTHORS OF *ALWAYS NEVER YOURS*

"An authentic, hilarious, and heartwarming debut, *The Best Laid Plans* is the pitch-perfect rom-com you've been waiting for!"
—KASS MORGAN, *NEW YORK TIMES* BESTSELLING AUTHOR OF THE 100 SERIES

"A laugh-out-loud, sex-positive story about love, lust, and complicated female friendship. Keely's voice is spot-on and her trials and tribulations are funny and relatable to anyone who's ever been a senior in high school."
—LIZ LAWSON, AUTHOR OF *THE LUCKY ONES*

"Filled to the brim with heart, *The Best Laid Plans* is a raunchy and hilarious quest to get it on— and all of the hijinks along the way."
—ASHLEY POSTON, AUTHOR OF *GEEKERELLA*

Also by
CAMERON LUND

The Best Laid Plans

Heartbreakers and Fakers

CAMERON LUND

RAZORBILL

RAZORBILL

An imprint of Penguin Random House LLC, New York

First published in the United States of America by Razorbill,
an imprint of Penguin Random House LLC, 2021

Copyright © 2021 by Cameron Lund

Visit us online at penguinrandomhouse.com.

Library of Congress Cataloging-in-Publication Data is available.

ISBN 9780593114940

Manufactured in Canada

1 3 5 7 9 10 8 6 4 2

Design by Maggie Edkins
Text set in Cartier Book Std

To the friends who have seen all the worst parts of me

and love me anyway

NOW

IT TAKES ME A SECOND to realize I'm not in Jordan's bed.

My head is pounding—a throbbing ache at my temples—and before I pry open my eyes, I'm struck by how bright the light is on the other side of my lids. I reach a hand out, expecting to feel Jordan's warmth beside me, envisioning his smile, the crooked tooth that only makes him cuter. I've been waiting half my life to wake up next to Jordan Parker.

Instead, my hand touches what feels like grass, wet with morning dew. That's when I open my eyes. Because I'm not in bed at all. I'm on a lawn chair in Jordan's yard.

I scramble to sit up, and as I do, a wave of nausea rolls through me, my stomach twisting. I'm not sure whether it's from the alcohol still coursing through my system, seeping out my pores like sweat, or whether it's from the knowledge that Jordan and I did not sleep together last night, in any sense of the term. That somehow I ended up on this chair and I can't exactly remember how I got here.

I stumble to my feet, noticing then that my shoes are missing, the hot pink high-tops Olivia and I bought together last week. We'd wanted to match. When you match with somebody, it proves to the rest of the world you're important; you're part of something. And everyone wants to be part of Olivia.

Now both of my shoes are gone, one foot totally bare, the other covered in a slimy wet sock. My knees are bruised, but I don't remember falling. Actually, I don't remember much of anything. Dinner with Olivia and Katie at the place downtown with the endless breadsticks and the waiter that never cards; piña coladas and margaritas and daiquiris, because the best drinks are the kind you can take pictures with, that make it look like you're on vacation and make everyone else on Instagram jealous.

I remember leaving dinner, arms thrown around each other's shoulders, laughing so hard in the Uber it felt like I might pee. Then later, dancing to Lana Del Rey in Olivia's room, helping her apply the perfect smoky eye. The feel of Jordan's arms around me when we got to his house, the way his cheek felt scratchy against mine; the smell of him, something earthy and exciting, a thrilling reminder of our plan for later.

But the rest of it is a blur. How did I get out here on the lawn? And why didn't anyone bring me inside?

I pull my phone out of my pocket—thank god I haven't lost it too—and check the time. It's nine a.m., which isn't as late as I'd usually sleep after a party, but isn't that early either. I must have been out here for hours. I don't have any texts, which is unusual. In the mornings, my phone is typically buzzing like crazy—conversations happening on every app about the night before. *Did you see Brett and Darlene making out? How drunk was Katie? You looked so hot last night. Love ya, babe. Love ya love ya love ya.* But right now, it's quiet, the screen darker than it's been since sixth grade, back when I was still Pukey Penelope. Back before Olivia discovered me.

I can't help the buzzing fear that something is wrong. Because if everything were normal, I wouldn't be out here. There's something I can't remember, something I'm pretty sure involves Olivia. I can feel it in my gut. And I'm scared of what she might say.

Olivia has always had a way of telling the truth to your face and making it sound like a kindness, her dazzling smile tricking you into thinking she's on your side. *Maybe next time, don't be such a sloppy mess. Girls like us are better than that.* It's just I'm not usually on the receiving end of it—not since we became best friends. These were comments meant for Katie, who's always a little too eager and embarrassing; for Myriah, who cries in school over bad grades; for Romina, who always ditches us to hang out with the guys. No, I'm always on Olivia's good side, the one she laughs about it with later.

But maybe I'm overreacting. I probably told my friends I was heading home and then couldn't get a ride or something. I bet this chair just seemed like the best option at the time. When I go inside, everything will be totally normal. Olivia will be asleep on the L-shaped couch with Katie, grumbling and hungover, but happy to see me. *I knew you wouldn't disappear before breakfast sandwiches!* she'll say, laughing and unpacking the eggs and cheese and muffins we bought yesterday to prepare for today's hangovers. Jordan will be upstairs in his room, the bed with the fresh sheets he washed just for us, because last night was meant to be special. Our first time.

Jordan and I officially started dating last December, but I've been in love with him for years. He finally asked me to be his girlfriend right before winter break, and then Olivia was dating Jordan's best friend, Kai, by Christmas. I love that we got boyfriends at the same time, and even though Kai is one of the most annoying people on the planet, I deal with him for Olivia's sake.

Last night was supposed to be perfect—the final night of our junior year, the first day of summer, officially seniors, the ones in charge of everything.

Now I'm not so sure.

I'm still in my junior class shirt, the one we all wore to school yesterday so everybody could sign them. Some of the signatures are smudged now, the Sharpie running from the wet grass. My hair is still in its twin braids, same as Olivia's, hers blonde to my brunette. I don't want to see my face. I'm sure it's a disaster. I really went for it—full contour, highlight, brows. I wanted to look like the kind of girl Jordan would be proud of. I'll have to run to the downstairs bathroom to clean up before I see him.

Raising a hand to shield my eyes, I turn toward the house. Sun roasts the back of my neck, the heat of it making me dizzy. I squelch through the damp grass in my sock to the sliding glass door that opens up to the TV room and try to pull it open, but it's locked. Peering inside, I see Katie asleep on the couch in a position that can't be comfortable, one foot on the floor, an arm thrown above her head. I knock on the window, and she startles awake. When she sees me, a wave of emotions passes over her face—first a smile, then a grimace, finally settling on confusion, her eyebrows knitted together, frown lines on her forehead that are sure to cause wrinkles. It makes me nervous.

It makes me even more sure something is wrong.

She stands up from the couch, coming over to me, dodging piles of trash—cans, red cups, spilled chip bags—that have become a maze on the floor. Katie's got these unruly black curls that are almost bigger than she is, and right now, they've tripled in size from her night on the couch. She unlocks the sliding door and pulls it open, just barely, not enough that I can fit inside.

"Penny," she says, almost a whisper. "What are you still doing here?"

"What do you mean?" I say. "Come on, Katie. Open the door."

She glances behind her. "I really think you should go."

"But this is my boyfriend's house." Even right now—even feeling like this—I can't help the little burst of pride that blooms inside me as I say it. Katie claims to have a boyfriend too—a guy named Matt she met at summer camp and never stops talking about—but none of us have ever seen a picture, so we're not sure he's real. "You can't block me from Jordan's house, Katie. That doesn't make any sense."

Katie presses her lips together in a tight line. "I'm trying to help you." And there it is again—the buzzing in my chest. Something went horribly wrong last night, and Katie knows what it is.

"I guess I spent the night on the lawn?" I try to put a smile in my voice. If I can pretend this whole thing is funny, then maybe everything will be okay.

"I thought you went home," she says. "After everything that happened."

"Katie, what happened?" My stomach clenches. The nausea is worse now, and I'm sweating in earnest, the sun on the back of my neck unrelenting.

"Penny, you should leave."

This isn't how things work with Katie and me. I'm usually the one in control, the one on the better side of the door.

My brother once told me that popularity wasn't real, that I should stop worrying about something that doesn't matter. But he's a guy, so of course he doesn't get it. I told him I could rank every girl in our class in order. Olivia is number one, obviously. I'm number two, and Katie is number three. Darlene is number fifteen, because even though she's weird, people still hang out with her to buy weed. Sarah Kozlowski, who doesn't wash her blue hair—who pricked her finger once in biology so she could study her own blood under the microscope—is number fifty-six. Dead last. It's not something that's ever really talked about; everybody just knows. It's important to know your place in the world. It gives you a road map of how to act— who to be friends with, who you're allowed to date, who you need to avoid at all costs.

"Katie," I say again. "Please let me into the house."

"Fine." She sighs heavily and pulls open the door wide enough for me to squeeze by. Inside, the hot summer air is trapped with the stale stench of trash and sweat. There are other people in the room, I realize. Danny Scott is asleep on the other side of the couch, and Romina and Myriah are curled up on an air mattress in the corner.

"Thanks," I say to Katie. "I'm gonna get cleaned up. I feel like roadkill."

"You *look* like roadkill," she says back, which I should have expected. She shakes her head, pausing before she adds, "Are you okay?"

"I'm fine. I love the fresh air." I know I sound ridiculous, but

I can't make any of this a big deal. Not if I want the story to go away.

I'm about to walk into the downstairs bathroom when I'm stopped in my tracks by a familiar voice. "What the hell are you doing here?"

Olivia has just appeared at the top of the stairs and she's looking at me like I'm the enemy. Her blonde hair is out of her braids—so that we no longer match—and her skin is fresh and dewy; Olivia's hangovers don't show on her face. She's still in the same junior T-shirt as I am, and I can see my message for her there, right over her left boob: *love you forever*. I want to read it to her, make her remember I'm the girl who put it there only yesterday.

"Hey, Liv," I say, forcing out a laugh. "You'll never believe where I slept last night."

"I don't care where you slept." She folds her arms, looking down at me with a sneer.

"Oh . . . okay," I say, still hesitant. "Should we start breakfast?" We've made breakfast sandwiches at every sleepover since middle school, and even though our sleepovers have now turned into parties, we would never let the habit die. Maybe right now, the sandwiches will make everything better—will smooth over whatever went down last night.

"So you're just gonna pretend you don't remember?" Olivia puts her hands on her hips, and I know that eggs will not magically fix anything.

"I *don't* remember, Olivia. I mean, I remember parts of last night, but if we got in a fight or something, I'm sure it wasn't a big deal." My voice is really wavering now, and my nose starts to itch as I hold in the tears. Katie sits down on the end of the couch, watching us with big eyes. The others are waking up now too—Danny yawning and pulling out his phone, Romina and Myriah laughing quietly, whispers back and forth like the hiss of snakes. I can't cry, not in front of an audience.

"How convenient for you," Olivia says.

I rack my brain, trying to think of anything I could have said to offend her. But everything yesterday was so *fun*. It wasn't a real school day—the teachers dismissed us early because we were all so hyped up on summer. We gathered in the field to sign each other's shirts, but Danny had sneak-attack pelted us with water balloons, and soon it was all-out war—Olivia and I teaming up on Jordan and Kai and dropping balloons on them from the second-story stairwell. Then we'd gone home and dried off and gotten ready to go out, laughing and dancing around in her room. Olivia had been excited about Jordan and me. She'd looked up silly sex tips online—the ridiculous ones from *Cosmo* that I swear no one has ever tried in real life. We'd read one that suggested throwing a handful of pepper into the guy's face while in the act and died laughing so hard Olivia fell off the bed. I'd brought a little pepper shaker to the party with me as a joke and when I showed her later, she'd screamed.

Whatever happened to ruin all that must have been bad.

"If I said anything that hurt your feelings," I say, "I'm sorry."

"You're sorry," Olivia repeats, her voice flat. "Well, that changes everything."

"Where's Jordan?" I start walking up the stairs, pulling off my sock when it squelches into the carpet. Whatever went down between Olivia and me, I know Jordan will take my side. I need him to tell me that everything is going to be okay.

"Why would you care?" Olivia laughs, but there's no humor in it, and suddenly I'm terrified. Is this all about Jordan?

"Liv, what are you talking about?" My voice catches, and I have to clear my throat. "I love Jordan."

She steps to the side, blocking me from passing. Jordan's room is across the hall at the top of the stairs. I can see the bumper stickers on the door: KEEP TAHOE BLUE, BOB MARLEY, SANTA CRUZ BEACH BOARDWALK.

"Oh really? Did you think about him at all last night?" she asks. "No, wait, you can't remember anything."

"You don't live here," I say, dread pooling in my stomach at her words. "Let me talk to him."

She pauses and then smiles. "Okay. Let's talk to him. That sounds fun."

She steps aside, and I walk past her and up to the door. I push it open and then there he is, lying on the bed, a sheet twisted around his bare torso, dappled sunlight shining through slits in the closed blinds. He's beautiful—tan skin and clean, hard lines. I'm not the only one obsessed with Jordan—we're all half in love with him. I'm just the lucky one who actually got him.

"Jordan," I say, coming into the room and sitting down on the edge of the bed. I glance behind me and see Olivia hovering in the doorway, watching. There's a peal of laughter from downstairs, someone telling someone else to "shut up." I want to close the door. I want Olivia to leave. But I want to fix things with her, so I don't say anything.

"Jordan," I say again, tapping him lightly on the shoulder. He groans, shuffling around under the sheet, and then jerks awake, his eyes flashing back and forth between Olivia and me before settling firmly on my face.

"Penny," he says in a gust of air. "What are you still doing here? I thought you went home last night."

"No, I . . ." I trail off, not wanting to fill him in on the rest of the details. I'm holding my breath, waiting for something else to go wrong. "I'm so sorry about last night . . . if something happened." I don't know what I'm apologizing for, but it seems like the right thing to do.

"Penny doesn't remember anything," Olivia says, taking steps into the room. "She has *amnesia*."

"I just drank too much." I turn back to her, the tang of the piña coladas, margaritas, and daiquiris still sharp and sweet in the back of my throat.

"You were a mess." Jordan sits up, and the sheet falls down around his waist.

"I know," I say. "I know, and I'm sorry." *Are we okay? Do you still love me?* That's what I really want to ask. Jordan has always been too good for me, our relationship so tenuous.

"Come on, Penny," Jordan says. He reaches out like he's going to take my hand for a second and then pulls back, clearly mad at himself for doing it. "This is seriously unfair. You do something fucked up, but you don't remember it, so then you don't have to feel guilty?" His words cause a flare in my stomach, the feeling like I've lost control of my car on the freeway.

"What happened, Jordan?" I'm trying to keep my voice steady. "I love you." How can I make him believe it? I repeat the words in my mind, like I'll be able to imprint them on Jordan's heart. *I love you, I love you, I love you.*

Olivia sits down next to me on the bed. "Well, maybe you should have thought about that before you made out with my boyfriend."

"What?" For a second I think Olivia must be joking. It's a well-known fact that Olivia's boyfriend, Kai, and I don't get along.

And besides that—I would never do anything to hurt Olivia.

But then, there's a flash of memory—I'm leaning into Kai, my hands in his hair, a feeling of want pooling in my stomach. I instinctively shake my head to make the image go away. It's not a full memory, not exactly, just a flicker of feeling. It's like what we learned last year about Plato's cave; I can't see the image, just a shadow of the image reflected onto the wall.

"Do you need me to repeat it?" Olivia asks.

"Jordan." I turn to him. "I didn't. I wouldn't do anything with Kai. I don't even *like* Kai."

"Olivia walked in on you guys kissing," he says. "In the laundry room."

And I know it's true. I can see the basket of folded clothes upturned on the floor, can feel my back pressed against the washing machine, can remember leaning in to kiss him, trying to convince him I wasn't that drunk, him pulling away. It's all there in my memories—a horrible movie reel of terrible decisions.

No no no no no. It doesn't make any sense. Last night was supposed to be special. I'd been planning it for weeks. Why would I ruin that? Why would I ruin that with Olivia's *boyfriend*?

"I'm . . . sorry," I say, my voice weak. I know *sorry* doesn't cover it. I know there isn't anything I could actually say to make this better. I'm the worst person in the entire world.

I remember lying with Olivia on her bed last night before the party, the conversation drifting from Jordan and the questionable *Cosmo* sex advice over to Kai. "I just can't figure him out right now," she'd said, unsure. "I feel like we're drifting apart."

"What if you stuck an ice cube down his pants?" I'd suggested with wiggling eyebrows, referencing one of the stupider tips we'd read.

"Yeah, that'll win him over." She'd laughed and then we'd moved on, like the conversation hadn't even happened. And I'd made everything so much worse. She'd been upset about things with Kai and instead of being a good friend, I'd *kissed* him.

"I think you should probably leave," Jordan says now. "I don't really want to do this anymore."

"Do this like . . . this conversation?" I ask softly. "Or, like . . . *us*?"

"I mean, I don't think we should be together."

I feel bile rise at the back of my throat, tears stinging the corners of my eyes. I have to get out of here before anything gets any worse. I can't cry in front of everyone. Worse—I can't throw up. Pukey Penelope will *not* be making another appearance. I've worked so hard for this, to be here in Jordan Parker's bedroom, best friends with Olivia Anderson, to finally be a girl everyone else wants to be—a girl with friends who make her feel like she matters.

There's no way they'll still want to be friends with me. I wouldn't want to be friends with me.

"Did anything happen last night with you and Olivia?" I ask Jordan, working at a hole in his sheet with my fingernail. It's the question that's been nagging at me, a sliver of unease in the back of my mind. It's the way her hand is still on his shoulder, how she's sitting on his bed like she belongs there. This problem with Jordan is fixable—I know I can get him back, so long as Olivia hasn't gotten to him. In a competition against Olivia, anyone would lose.

"Anything going on with me or Jordan is none of your business," Olivia answers. "You lost the privilege to know anything about us when you stuck your tongue in Kai's mouth."

"I'm sorry," I say again, even though I know it's not enough. "I don't know why I kissed him. It doesn't make sense. I love you guys." I shake my head, trying to clear the memory away, like if I can forget it happened, everyone else will too. I know that's why I couldn't remember it when I woke up. It was self-preservation.

My mind flashes again to the way Kai's hair felt between my fingers, his hands on my back before he pulled them away. I wish I could make this all his fault, but I know it's not. He'd tried to stop me, but I'd kissed him. And I'd *liked* it. That's the worst part.

Because besides the horrible fact that he's with Olivia, there's also this: Kai ruined my life in elementary school. And yeah, maybe we grew up and were forced to hang out, but I've never quite gotten over it.

According to chaos theory, a butterfly flapping its wings can cause a tornado all the way across the world, events flowing outward like ripples on the surface of a lake. All of this started when Kai moved to our town from Hawaii in fifth grade—Pukey Penelope, my friendship with Olivia, falling for Jordan; all the moments of my life built one upon the other.

And this right now? This is the freaking tornado.

"I have to go." I stumble out of the room and down the stairs, holding my breath so the tears don't fall.

I can hear Olivia's footsteps behind me. "Yeah, get out!" Her voice is sharp as a knife, her words twisting in my gut. Katie's eyes are wide, mouth hanging open. Romina has her phone pointed in my direction, and I see the light that means she's recording. Soon my misery will be posted all over social media. Soon the whole school will know what I did.

I pull open the screen door and race out into the yard,

Olivia right behind me. The sprinklers are on, and I run through them, the cold water shocking me awake. My bare feet squelch through the grass and then I'm on the blacktop, tar burning hot from the sun, and running down the driveway. It's not until I'm out onto the street, around the corner, where I know Olivia can't see, that I start to cry.

THEN

JUNIOR YEAR–SEPTEMBER

I WAKE UP EVEN earlier than usual the morning of the first-day-of-school pep rally so I can take the necessary million years to get ready. Each grade was assigned a color for the day— green for the freshmen, blue for the sophomores, red for the seniors, and black for us. Whichever grade has the most school spirit gets a Friday off at the end of the month, so it's going to be war.

My friends decided to go all out—lots of dark eyeliner and fishnets that will probably get us in trouble with Principal Hanson but are totally worth it. I laid my outfit out on the floor the night before—a black Thrasher T-shirt and a pair of pleather pants I transformed into shorts. I went to the touristy thrift store by the lake for accessories—I even got a pair of those Madonna gloves from the eighties to complete *the lewk*.

"You're actually wearing that shit to school?" my brother, Sebastian, grumbles when he sees me. Olivia is coming to pick us up since there is no way she would ever leave me to die on the bus with the freshmen.

"What's wrong with my outfit?" I glare at Seb. He doesn't know the hours I spent on YouTube learning how to sew a perfectly straight hemline.

"You're breaking about thirty dress code rules." Seb is wearing all green, but not in a way that looks purposeful. Not like he means it. He's got a Redwoods High School baseball cap backward on his head, ears sticking too far out the sides. I've got the same ears, which is why I can never ever wear my hair in a ponytail.

"Dress code rules are meant to be broken. Is Mom still here?" I ask, although the question is unnecessary. There's a ten-dollar bill on the counter for each of us for lunch money, a sticky note with a smiley face on it indicating she's already left for work. I crumple the note and throw it into the trash, tucking the money into my pocket. I know it's stupid—that in the grand scheme of things, it really shouldn't matter. It's just I was kinda excited to show this outfit to my mom.

But I should have known better. She's a nurse at a rehab hospital, and they're stupidly understaffed, so they're always calling her in at crazy hours. Sebastian and I are used to fending for ourselves—lunch money on the counter, frozen pizzas and ramen noodles, little notes with smiley faces that are supposed to be suitable fill-ins for an actual human parental presence.

A horn *beeps* outside, and I grab my backpack from the closet. "Come on, Liv is here."

Olivia has a green punch buggy, and Seb punches my arm as soon as we get outside, which I should have expected because it happens every time we see her car. But somehow I'm still caught off guard. "Ow!" I say, pulling my arm away and thwacking him back.

Olivia rolls her window down and lifts her sunglasses to perch them on top of her shiny blonde head. "Could that be my best friend, Penelope Ann Harris, or has a beautiful supermodel angel taken her place?"

"Are you saying I'm not usually a beautiful supermodel angel?" I ask, all faux-offended, and climb into the front seat of her car.

Olivia laughs, deep and scratchy. She's got a low voice for a girl, but it works for her. She's pretty much the embodiment of a sexy war-era lounge singer draped across a piano. "Actually, I misspoke. You are *all* devil today, girl."

"Back at you." Olivia is dressed almost exactly the same as me. She's in a huge vintage AC/DC T-shirt that goes down to her mid-calf, matching fishnets, and big black combat boots. People are generally scared of Olivia even when she's wearing her standard flouncy dresses and floppy hats. Today, in this outfit, no one will fuck with her.

"I need you to do my makeup when we get to school," Olivia says. "I need your winged liner skills. I tried to do it myself this morning, and I looked like a wet raccoon." She turns around and eyes my brother. "Hi, Sebastian. No *good morning* for me?"

Seb's face immediately flushes pink, and he clears his throat. "Good morning." Like every other living, breathing straight male on the planet, my brother has a huge crush on Olivia. And she totally knows it.

"Don't be gross," I say. It was okay when Sebastian was still a little kid, but now that he's growing up—now that he actually looks like a boy who could date her—the teasing feels a lot weirder.

"I'm just being nice." Olivia gives me a toothy grin. "Sebastian and I are friends. Aren't we, Seb?"

His eyes light up. "Yeah, if you say we're friends, we're definitely friends."

"But don't worry." Olivia turns to me. "I would never replace you, Penny. You're the spicy tomato soup to my extra-sharp Vermont cheddar grilled cheese."

This is a game we've played for a while. It started back in eighth grade with fairly normal combinations: *You're the milk to my cookies, the Kendall to my Kylie, the Batman to my Robin.* But over the years the comparisons have gotten a lot more creative as we've run out of ideas. Making it strange and specific is part of the fun.

"You're the fashionably ripped fishnets to my badass combat boots," I say, wiggling my foot in her direction.

"Oooh, very on brand for today." She grins.

At times like this it's easy to forget that Olivia and I haven't always been close—that I spent all of elementary school alone with my nose in a book. But those days are behind me. All that matters is we're here now; we've found each other and we won't let go.

Olivia knows everything about me: how my dad left when I was little—the way I sometimes like to pretend he doesn't exist so I don't have to think too hard about how a guy could do that to his own kids. She knows how mad I get sometimes when my mom is pulled into work, how much it sucks when she uses her limited free time to go out on dates instead of hanging out with Seb and me. Olivia has been there with me too many times—

big bowls of Easy Mac at the kitchen counter—when my mom comes home with some dude she'll only see for a night, introducing him to us like he actually matters.

"What do you think Jordan is gonna say when he sees your outfit?" She turns to me again, waggling her eyebrows. Another thing Olivia knows: all the details of my lifelong debilitating crush on Jordan Parker.

I flush, embarrassed because Seb is in the car, but also because this is a natural reaction I have every time Jordan's name is brought up. I'm in love with Jordan for all the obvious reasons—he's tall and fit and amazing at basketball with dimples that are actually soul-crushing. But for the not-obvious reasons too. He's just so *nice*. A guy like Jordan doesn't have to be one of the good ones; he could be a huge douchebag and everyone would probably still worship him. So every kind gesture feels like it matters even more.

"Jordan isn't going to notice my outfit," I say quietly.

"There is no way anyone could not notice your outfit," Seb grumbles from the back seat. "You look like a baby prostitute."

Olivia spins around in her seat—a dangerous feat considering she's still driving the car—and glares at him. "You know, I take that as a compliment, Sebastian. You're saying she looks like a strong, independent entrepreneur who celebrates her sexuality." Then she turns back to me. "And believe me, Jordan will notice."

When we get to school, Olivia pulls into her spot under the shady tree toward the back of the lot. It's not *technically* her spot—we don't have assigned parking at RHS—but everyone knows Olivia's green buggy, and they know to keep space cleared. It's just one small example of Olivia's power—people probably don't even know they're doing it; she just gets away with things mere mortals can't. To be honest, if I weren't always reaping the benefits by carpooling with her, this would probably be supremely annoying.

Seb unfolds his too-tall body from the car and pulls his backpack onto one shoulder. "You gonna sit with me at lunch, Olivia?" he asks with a smirk as he walks away. "I mean, if we're friends and all."

"In your dreams, freshman!" Olivia shouts at him, laughing.

"Will you please for the love of all that is holy stop flirting with my brother?" I shut the passenger door a little too hard. "He is like five years old."

"It's harmless," Olivia says. "Come on, I want to take some shots of you before first period. Got to commemorate our win today."

"We haven't won yet." The truth is the seniors usually win the extra day off, which is completely unfair considering they get out for the summer a whole month before we do anyway. Even so, I feel good about our chances. These outfits took work.

Olivia pulls her camera out of her bag as we walk, skirting around the side of the building to the expanse of grass behind school. There's a soccer field back here, a baseball diamond, and some old tennis courts slightly overgrown with weeds.

"Tennis courts?" Olivia asks, leading me there before I've answered. The weeds are looking especially plentiful this morning, which Olivia has said is part of the charm. She likes the combination of the chain-link fence with the overgrown grass: industrial meets natural. We take photos here a lot.

Olivia is Very Serious when it comes to her camera—she

only uses real film and pretty much lives in the old darkroom after school. Once she's developed a photo at least three times to find the exact right exposure, she'll scan it and put it on Instagram. We've got a photo series going, which she's dubbed the Tennis Court Kids—black-and-white shots of all our friends posed back here like we're on some album cover from the nineties. I do what I can with hair and makeup, but Olivia has a gift.

We snap a few pictures, and then the bell rings in the distance, signaling we're about to be late. Since it's the first day, we're meeting in the gym for the pep rally before homeroom.

Olivia tucks her camera lovingly into her bag, and then we sprint back across the field, joining the crowds of people swarming down the hallway toward the junior locker area. There's a banner proclaiming a JUNIOR BLACKOUT hung across the ceiling beams taped up by the kids that got here early, black balloons strewn about the floor, black streamers twisted around columns. And everyone is wearing all black too—black hats, black leggings, black boots, with smudged football stripes across their cheeks. It's amazing.

But then my eyes catch on a singular white T-shirt, its wearer nonchalantly pulling a book from his locker, ignoring the chaos behind him. Kai.

"*Are you kidding me?*" I say, more a grumble under my breath than to Olivia. Of course Kai Tanaka would ignore the pep rally, would think himself above showing even a little bit of school spirit. "He's the only one who didn't dress up."

"Who?" Olivia asks. She walks over to her locker to put her camera away and I follow. We got to pick our lockers last week at orientation, so most of our group's are in the same corner.

This means that every time I stop by my locker between classes, there is the exhilarating and terrifying possibility of running into Jordan. But it also means I have to deal with *him*.

"Kai." I nod my head over to his stupid white T-shirt, and Olivia calls out: "Hey, Tanaka!"

Kai looks over at us, shutting his locker.

"*No*," I say, swatting Olivia's arm. "Don't call him over here. I'm not in the mood for—"

But it's too late. He's grinning and heading in our direction, and soon he's right in front of us. Olivia and Kai have been friends ever since he moved here and I don't understand why. He's the kind of person who always has to make a stupid joke when things get too serious, who doesn't care about anything that matters, who talks to fill space that doesn't need to be filled.

"You never texted me back last night," Olivia says, pouting.

"Yeah, I fell asleep partway through the episode." He shrugs. "Her British accent is so soothing, and every time she starts talking about the cupcakes, I—"

"So do you just not give a shit?" The words are out of me before I've thought about them.

Kai turns to me. "About who wins the Bake Off? Of course I do."

"No, about who wins the pep rally!"

He chews on his lip for a second and then laughs. "Um, yeah, for sure. I most definitely don't give a shit about the pep rally."

"It would have taken you like three seconds to pick out a black T-shirt."

"Oh, lighten up, Penelope," Kai says. "If I want a day off school, I can skip. Why are you so pressed?"

"You can't just . . . cut class all the time, Kai. That's not how this works."

"It's not a big deal," Olivia says, ever the mediator between us. "Come on, you still need to do my eyeliner."

And I know she's right. *I know* it's not a big deal. I can't control how other people act, can't force them to take things seriously. But I can't let it go. Because it's not just the T-shirt. It's a million little moments built upon each other: all the times Kai has told me to "lighten up," the way he always makes fun of the effort I put into things—as if the act of caring is something to be ashamed of.

Before this, it was last year in Mr. Simon's English class, when Kai and I were partnered up for a project and despite my incessant pestering, he'd written his share of our poem *twenty minutes* before it was due.

It's when I didn't get any cards in my Valentine's Day box in fifth grade, and instead of ignoring it to make me feel better, Kai pointed it out to everyone; when I came to school with the flu and threw up all over myself and Kai said: "It's Pukey Penelope!" and the name followed me down the hallway for the rest of the year. *Pukey Penelope smells like barf. Don't let her touch you.*

So yeah. Maybe this white shirt isn't a big deal to everyone else, but it is to me.

"This doesn't make you cooler than everyone," I say. "Just because you're not dressed the same."

Kai laughs and rolls his eyes. "Yeah, I could *never* be cooler than you."

"Even if you don't want the extra day, the rest of us do." I pull the black Madonna gloves a little tighter on my hands. "Besides, I actually think dressing up is fun. You should try it sometime."

"So I can look as fake as you do?"

I'm about to lunge at him when Olivia steps between us. "Children, please. Tanaka, settle down with the insults. Today is supposed to be a happy and momentous occasion, and I don't want my two besties fighting." She boops me on the nose and then spins around and boops Kai's nose too. "You are both perfect in your own ways."

"No, don't encourage her," Kai says with a maddening grin. "Penelope already thinks she's perfect."

"I just don't get you," I say, speaking to him over Olivia's head. That's the thing about being almost a foot taller than her—she may be strong, but I'll always have the height advantage.

"I don't see what's so hard to get," Kai says with an infuriatingly indifferent shrug, like he's not even bothered by this conversation at all. That's when I see Jordan approaching from down the hallway behind him, and my response shrivels up on my tongue, my mouth a dry husk.

He's smiling that megawatt Jordan smile, holding an old boom box up on one shoulder with AC/DC's "Back in Black" blaring from it. He's got tall black knee socks below his shorts, two black football smudges across his cheeks. Of course he does. Jordan always goes all in.

"Hey, Jojo!" Olivia says when he reaches us, leaning in to give him a quick hug. We took that love language quiz last year and Olivia unsurprisingly got *physical touch*—she's always draping her body around people, pulling us into hugs, tapping us on the nose. Jordan holds up a fist for Kai to bump and then brings it in my direction too. I tap my fist against his, reveling in the brief moment of contact when his skin is on mine. I can feel the flush of heat to my cheeks indicating I've gone completely red. From a fist bump. Pathetic.

"'Sup, Harris?" He nods, and I nod back, hoping he doesn't notice the color of my face. "I like your outfit. Very cool." He waves a hand over the whole of me, and I am trying not to freak out about the fact that he is maybe kind of checking me out.

"Nice gloves," Kai says to me. "Are you trying to look like a Victorian woman who just killed her husband?"

"They're eighties," I say. "Not Victorian."

"Michael Jackson, right?" Jordan asks, and I die a little inside because that is so not an association I want him to make with me.

"It's supposed to be Madonna?" I say, my voice lilting like it's a question. I clear my throat and try again. "Madonna. It's supposed to be." Great. Now I sound like Yoda. For the millionth time, I curse the fact that Jordan Parker turns me into a puddle incapable of human speech.

"Don't you like *my* outfit, Jojo?" Olivia asks, with a spin.

"You fishing for a compliment, Anderson?" Jordan smiles, showing off his dimples. "You know you're a dime."

"And don't you forget it."

The second bell rings, indicating it's time to head to the gym, and we pour down the hallway, black shirts coming from all directions.

"So, you gonna wear those gloves all day?" Kai asks from beside me. Olivia and Jordan have fallen in step ahead of us, and with the crowd, I can't really move up next to them.

So I'm stuck with him.

"I was planning on it, yes. Why is that a concern of yours?"

"I dunno, seems like you wouldn't be able to text with them on."

"I'll manage, thanks."

"It's just, you know, you're usually always on your phone."

"Jealous?" I ask, turning to him. "You know, when you're fun to be around, people actually text you to hang out."

Kai laughs then—loud enough that both Olivia and Jordan turn back and glance at us with confused expressions. "You? Fun to be around? That's hilarious. I didn't know you were capable of making jokes, Penelope."

"*Ha ha*," I say in a sarcastic tone. "Just because I don't turn everything into a joke doesn't mean I'm not fun."

"Yeah, when I look back on high school, that's how I'll remember you. Penelope Harris. She was so much *fun*."

I hate to admit it, but his words sting a little bit. I want to be above it. I don't want to let stupid Kai Tanaka keep affecting me. Still, I know I could be more fun. I know I could loosen up a bit, try to care less about things, but who is this boy to think he knows better about my own life than I do?

Besides, it's not like Kai knows me the way Olivia does. He wasn't there all those times we put on her old dance costumes—sequined leotards and pink cowboy hats—and shimmied around the living room. He wasn't there the night we mixed frozen strawberries in a blender with her parents' whiskey and ended up calling everyone in school.

He doesn't know that side of me. He only knows the me that's constantly on the defensive. The truth is, the reason I suck so much when I'm around him is just because he sucks *more*.

"Don't act like you know me," I tell him.

He shrugs. "You're right. I don't know you because you're exactly the same as everyone else." He motions between my combat boots and Olivia's, our matching black tights, and waves his arms in the general direction of every other person around us—the sea of black T-shirts.

"It's spirit day," I grumble. "That's the whole point."

We round the corner into the gym, and I use the opportunity to move away from him. My legs are a little bit longer than his, so I take the biggest, most aggressive strides I possibly can and push my way up toward Jordan. I've always been a fast walker, have never understood the concept of strolling, or god forbid, *moseying*. I am a girl with places to be.

I let myself daydream briefly of two Septembers from now, speed-walking to my first college class at UCLA, where Olivia and I are planning to go together. If Kai was moving slowly in front of me, I would push him out of my way. Maybe dump a coffee on him for good measure. The vision fills me with a special kind of warmth as we enter the gym.

Until I look to my left and Kai is still there. I was so sure I lost him, but he's like a cockroach. He just won't die.

"What are you smiling about?" he asks, nudging me gently with his elbow.

"I was thinking about dumping coffee on you," I say.

"You daydream about me a lot, Penelope?" He grins. "I'm flattered."

"It wasn't a daydream," I answer. "It was a nightmare. You are my sleep paralysis demon."

The noise of the gym is deafening—a sea of colors all around the bleachers as each of the classes enter, trying to one-up each other on school spirit. I hate to admit it, but the seniors are definitely going to win. Their section is bright red—red cowboy hats and ribbons and T-shirts. One of the soccer players, Gabe Pinkerton, is dressed like Moses in long red robes with a huge fake beard and staff. There's another guy dressed in a full Spider-Man costume, a mask covering his face so I can't even tell who he is. Everyone has whistles and tambourines and cymbals—anything to make noise.

"See?" I shout to Kai so he can hear me. "The seniors are going to beat us. They actually *care* about spirit day."

"I know," Kai says. "It's so sad, isn't it?"

I roll my eyes and turn away from him, finding our friends in the juniors' section. They're all waiting for us—Katie laughing with Danny Scott, Myriah and Romina sitting close and whispering about something. When they see us approach, they all turn in our direction, making room.

"Parker, my man!" Danny says, raising his fist for one of those complicated bump-handshake things that guys do. Jordan takes a seat next to Danny, and I try to maneuver so I can slide in beside him, but then Kai is there, taking the spot that was supposed to be mine. Typical.

Olivia shoots me an apologetic look, and then sits on the bench in front of Jordan. I decide to sit next to Myriah and Romina because I do not want to spend another second near Kai Tanaka.

"I heard Luke Stevens wanted to ride in on a horse," Myriah is saying, referring to one of the seniors. "That would have been amazing, but the school wouldn't let him."

"Where the fuck would he get a horse?" Romina says, then turns to me. "Nice outfit, Harris. You are a vintage queen."

"Thanks," I say. "You look awesome too." Romina shaved the side of her head in an old-school Skrillex way sophomore year after a particularly bad breakup with her girlfriend Harper. Her parents freaked out—they're Persian and can be strict—but she knew if they could get over the fact that she's gay, they would get over the hair.

Right now, she's in this amazing dark red lipstick—like she's a vampire—with her hair twisted up into a million little buns. "Ugh, I can't wait until college so I can get my nose pierced." She sighs. "I feel like a nose ring would have made this so much better."

"You look beautiful either way," Myriah says. She reaches out as if to squeeze Romina's knee and then pulls her hand away before it makes contact. In complete contrast to Romina, Myriah is in one of her black ballet leotards, her wavy light brown hair held back by black butterfly clips. She has tiny black hearts dotted like freckles across her cheeks.

"Only you would be able to find black butterfly clips," I say, and she smiles, reaching up to touch one of them.

"She has butterfly clips for every occasion," Romina says.

"I like what I like," Myriah says. "Butterfly clips are cute. Even these little goth ones."

"I think Myriah might *actually* be made of cake," Romina says to me.

Myriah frowns. "Is that a good thing?"

"Duh," Romina says. "Everyone loves cake."

It's funny that Myriah and Romina are best friends because in a lot of ways they're so different. But they've been close since elementary school—back before anyone knew Myriah would grow up to become a gentle, soft-spoken horse girl, and Romina would become a person who generally hated most gentle, soft-spoken horse girls. But they just fit. And ever since Myriah came out as bi last summer, they've become inseparable. *We spent all of fourth grade obsessing over Kim Possible,* Romina joked to me once. *I should have seen the signs.*

"I saw you talking with Tanaka," she says now, leaning closer to me with her voice lowered. "You guys gonna pound it out or what?"

My whole body shudders at Romina's words. "Did you just use the phrase *pound it out*?"

"Ride the Pound Town Express." She grins. "A one-way ticket to Pound Town."

I roll my eyes. There's a common theory among our friends that Kai and I are secretly into each other or something—that all our fights stem from displaced passion and one day we'll fall in love. But sometimes an annoying guy is just an annoying guy.

"Ewwwwww," Myriah whines, pushing against Romina's shoulder. But then she giggles. "They wouldn't go to . . . Pound Town," she hesitates on the words, tripping over them. "They would *make love*. A one-way ticket to Falling-in-Love Town."

"Doesn't have the same ring to it," Romina says.

Myriah thinks for a second. "Lovers' Lane?"

"Soul Mate City," Romina answers.

I give them my best *are you done?* face. "I'm not going to be taking any train rides with Kai Tanaka to any destination."

"Oh, come on," Romina says. "Your sexual tension is insane. If you guys would hook up already, we could all move on with our lives."

I feel myself flush with heat, can tell my cheeks have turned a spectacular shade of scarlet. Because before I can help myself, I'm thinking about it. Kai may be the absolute worst, but he's got this power—that effortless cool I hate so much, but which seems to make all the other straight girls in our class love him. And yeah, he has high cheekbones, a wide smile, black hair that flops down into his eyes. I guess his face is objectively attractive, even if it's extremely punchable.

I shake my head, embarrassed to have been complimentary to Kai, even inside my head. If he knew what I'd been thinking, his ego would grow so monstrous it would crush cities.

"Would you keep it down?" I say, trying to shush her. Kai and Jordan are both *right there* on the bench in front of us, like four feet away.

"She's not denying it," Romina says with an evil grin.

"I don't like Kai like that," I say. "I like . . ." I trail off, nodding my head to where Jordan is sitting. He's too close for me to possibly say any of this out loud.

"Yeah, we know," Romina says. "Penny is madly in love with Jordan." And *oh my god*, her voice has not gotten any quieter. It feels like it's ricocheting off the walls of the gymnasium. It's so loud in here right now, practically vibrating with school spirit, but I swear her words have carried above all of it. It feels like everybody around us can hear.

I risk a glance to my right to where Jordan is sitting, and notice with horror that he's looking at me. Our eyes meet, just for a moment, and then he turns away, flipping around to laugh at something Danny is saying.

Did he hear what Romina said? *Does Jordan Parker know I have a crush on him?*

And then it gets so much worse, because Kai is looking at me too. If Kai heard, he'll use this against me for the rest of our lives. This will be more ammo for him, another thing to throw in my face. *Penny is madly in love with Jordan.*

31

And obviously Jordan doesn't like me back.

"Romina," I say, her name a gasp. My stomach is churning like maybe I'm about to be sick.

"Relax." She shrugs. "No one heard."

"Maybe it's a good thing if someone heard?" Myriah reaches out and squeezes my hand. "How are you and Jordan ever going to get together if you don't make a move?"

"I don't . . . I can't . . ." I sputter, not able to find the right words. Because she's right. I'm so terrified of Jordan, so scared to talk to him, that there's no way we'll ever get together unless I can get over it. But I can't imagine opening myself up to anybody like that. If you show someone interest, you're only giving them an opportunity to reject you.

It feels so much safer living in the daydreams inside my head.

"You gotta go for it," Romina says. She motions vaguely in the direction of Jordan and Kai. "One of those boys is gonna get you in trouble this year. Good trouble. I can feel it."

NOW

I CALL SEBASTIAN AND WAIT on the side of the road for him to come pick me up. It's embarrassing having to ask a favor from my little brother, but I don't have much of a choice. Our town is spread out, houses buried between the trees, *neighbors* only a relative term. It's hard to walk anywhere unless you have a gallon of water and a tent.

Seb pulls up twenty minutes later, and I take a few deep breaths, wiping at my face before pulling open the door of our mom's Toyota. He just got his permit, which means technically he's only supposed to drive if there's an adult with him in the car, but I'm so glad he's here.

"You look like shit," Seb says, and then when my face crumples, he changes tactics. "Whoa, please don't cry."

"I'm fine." I take another deep breath. It feels a bit like I'm choking every time I inhale.

"Um, where are your shoes?" He pulls the car out onto the road, hands gripping the wheel so hard they're turning white.

"Do you want me to drive?" I ask instead of giving an answer.

"I got it," he says, and it's probably for the best. There's a chance I might still be drunk. "Do you . . . want to talk about it?" I love him for trying so hard, but I don't want to dump all my emotional baggage on my brother.

"Everything's fine," I tell him. "Can you just take me home?" All I want is to sleep for a million years in a real bed.

"I think Mom's actually home for once," he says. "We'll have to sneak you past her. No way she can see you looking like this."

"Seb, do you ever drink?"

He turns to me briefly before fixing his gaze firmly on the road. "This . . . feels like a trap."

"You shouldn't," I tell him, running a finger over the bruise on my knee. "People do stupid things when they're drunk."

It's crazy how one terrible, drunken decision can unravel relationships that took forever to build—thirty seconds canceling out five whole years.

Memories of Olivia flash in my head before I can scrub them away, sickening reminders of everything I've lost. Giving each other silly makeovers in eighth grade, wearing giant sunglasses and feather boas and dancing around her room to old Miley Cyrus songs. The trip we took with her parents to LA, sitting front row at our first big musical, how we promised each other we'd both end up there together when we grew up—her as a famous fashion photographer and me as her assistant. *I need you there with me*, Olivia told me once, the two of us lying out on sandy towels at the lake. *You're my muse.*

And Jordan—thinking about him feels even worse. When I think of Jordan I think of his hands—how we always laughed because his fingers were so much longer than mine when we pressed our palms together. Lying for hours on the floor of his tree house, talking about nothing and everything at the same time. How excited we were to spend senior year together, the days spread out endlessly before us.

I had so many plans.

I watch the trees pass by on either side of the car, bright green in the sun. It's officially the first day of summer, a day that was supposed to feel magical. I'm mad at that other girl, the one I barely even remember being. I'm not the one who did this horrible thing. It was her. If I can hate her, maybe I won't hate myself.

When we get home, Seb gets out of the car first and looks around before coming back and opening my door. "Okay, so the good news is that Mom is upstairs," he says. "But the bad news is she's not alone."

That's when I notice the other car in our driveway. My mom probably had a date last night, and I do not want to see the grisly aftermath. I learned years ago it's better to slip by unnoticed than to have to deal with these awkward, one-sided conversations. And today, when I'm looking and feeling like this? Definitely not gonna happen.

"Let's hope they're preoccupied," I say, and Seb sticks his tongue out.

"Gross."

We creep quietly up the path to the front door, and I can hear a low rumbling of voices coming from an open bedroom window, my mom's high, clear laughter and something lower and distinctly male.

"That's not even her real laugh," I say.

"There's no way this guy is actually funny." Seb opens the front door so quietly it makes me wonder if this isn't the first time he's snuck in or out. To me, Seb will always be spilled Cheerios, lost front teeth, smelly gym shorts, and fuzzy pajamas, not the almost-grown-up he is now. I hope this story about me doesn't get around to him, but I know it will. I just don't want him to think I'm a horrible person like everyone else.

We both tiptoe into the hallway, and Seb takes off his shoes. I don't have any shoes to take off, so I slip by him in my bare feet. The house is bright and sunny and smells like coffee. It's so normal, the sight and smell of any other summer morning, and it makes my chest ache. I want so badly for last night not to have happened, to have woken up in my bed and come down to this same house as the girl I was yesterday.

"You run upstairs," Seb whispers. "I'll get us some coffee."

"You're a baby," I whisper back. "Babies don't drink coffee." But then, "Thanks." He's being sweet, helping me sneak in like this. I step quietly down the hallway, turning the corner to the stairs, and then stop short because my mom is right there. She's hand in hand with her date, both of them frozen in place. The irony is not lost on me—my mom trying to sneak someone out of the house while I'm trying to sneak back in.

She straightens, clears her throat. "Penelope, hi. You're home!" She seems to remember the man behind her then. "This is Frank. He was just leaving."

"Hey, sport," the man says, like I'm five years old. I watch my mom's eyes roam over me, finally noting all the parts that aren't quite right. I still haven't seen myself in a mirror, but I know I must look terrible.

"What happened?" she asks.

"Nothing happened, Mom. I just didn't get any sleep."

Seb rounds the corner then, two mugs of coffee in his hands, and my mom turns to him. "Wait, Sebastian—were you driving? You know you're not supposed to drive. You're too young."

"Seb just picked me up from Olivia's," I say. My mom doesn't know that Jordan's parents were out of town last night at a work conference. Actually, my mom doesn't know that Jordan exists. I mean, she knows who he is—our class is tiny, and we've all been together since kindergarten. But my mom doesn't know about Jordan and me, that we're a *we*—or, I guess, that we used to be. We don't really talk about that stuff. I usually just tell her I'm staying over at Olivia's, no matter where I go, and she never questions it.

Things used to be different once. Before she went back to school and got her nursing degree—back when she still had time for us—we were always together. When I was little, I'd follow her around the house, chattering about some drama or other from my elementary school classes, who had been mean to me that week, who had pushed who on the playground. But somewhere along the way, we grew apart. Somewhere along the way, I stopped being a priority.

Now she lingers in the doorway for a moment. "We'll talk about this later, okay, baby? I'm really late for work. But I want to hear about your night." Then she grabs her keys from where Seb has left them on the hook, ushering Frank past her and out the door. "We'll talk when I get home, I promise."

I'm used to these kinds of promises, and I know she means them when she makes them, but we both know the truth is she'll come home after I'm already asleep and she'll be too exhausted from work to chat even if I weren't. But maybe it's for the best this time. I don't know how I could explain to her that I kissed Olivia's boyfriend when I don't even know how it happened myself.

"Go to work," I say, because I know she needs to believe I'm okay before she leaves. "Everything is fine."

"Okay, baby girl. I left some money on the counter for you guys. Make sure you buy some veggies or something healthy this time. What kind of medical professional would I be if I let you both live off pizza?"

And then she's gone.

I head upstairs and into the bathroom, turning on the shower as hot as I can get it. I want to burn last night off my skin, peel back the layers until I'm someone else. I wait for the water to heat, and that's when I finally look in the mirror.

My immediate thought is: *Jordan saw me like this.*

I look like I'm melting, mascara running down my face in tracks. I pull my hair out of its braids, my hand catching on a tangle the size of a dead rat. Usually, I'm pretty. I know I am— it's the only way I could have possibly overcome who I was in elementary school, probably one of the reasons Olivia first started being my friend, although there's more to it than that now. I have big lips, eyes that are usually bright blue when they're not red-rimmed from crying. I've always thought it was strange to like my face and know that half of it came from my dad, a guy who I can only remember from pictures. At least he gave me one good thing.

I'm not as pretty as Olivia, but that's not surprising. She's half Swedish and half Italian, a combination that makes her naturally blonde and tan and curvy. I'm a little too tall, a bit too skinny, weirdly pale and flat and gangly in all the ways Olivia is not.

I get into the shower, letting the hot water roll down my back. I examine myself, looking for more clues about last night. Besides the bruises on my knees, I don't look bad, and once I wash my hair, I barely seem any different at all. Outside, everything looks fine. It's inside that feels like a mess.

It's hard to believe anything happened with Kai. I have this theory that a kiss lingers on you, that you can feel it on your skin the next day, proof of what you've done.

Right now, I just feel nothing.

I pull on my softest pair of sweatpants and climb into bed, curling up under the covers. The sun is beaming through the window, so bright it hurts my eyes, so I pull the shutters closed. I could stay here under this blanket for two whole months, I realize, only crawling back out when it's time for school. Maybe by then, everyone will have forgotten.

I could pretend I'm traveling, that my mom took Seb and me on some amazing trip—South America, or Iceland, or Greece. People fake Instagram posts all the time.

But that would never work.

I click on my phone and stare at the picture on my lock screen. It's of Jordan and me from Christmas this past year. He got me a blue Gonzaga baseball cap to match his own, and I'm wearing it proudly, beaming at him. I swipe and delete the picture, feeling the loss of it like a stomach punch.

Then I finally do what I've been dreading: look for any posts about what happened last night. Evidence I'm officially over. Romina has posted the video, my mascara-streaked face for the world to see, Olivia chasing me down the stairs and screaming, "Get out!" It has thirty-two likes. There are dozens of comments underneath, and against my better judgment, I scroll through them. It's so enthralling, watching my own destruction, and I can't stop looking, like I'm passing a wreck on the freeway. Wow, did you hear what Penny did? That makeup is so tragic. Are Kai and Pukey Penelope actually a thing?

My stomach clenches at the last one. I thought I had made everyone forget that nickname, thought I had become untouchable. I should have realized how precarious it all was.

I keep scrolling, hoping I might find something that will spark a few more memories and dreading it at the same time. Myriah posted a story, and I tap through it. There we all are in Jordan's kitchen, wasted and laughing in our matching junior-class shirts. There's Olivia and me dancing on the countertop. I don't remember how we got up there. There's Romina kissing Danny's cheek, Katie with a milk carton on her head. It's all vaguely familiar, like it happened in a dream or a past life. Then there's one of Jordan and Olivia. He's got an arm around her waist and her shirt is bunched up so you can see the flat, tan skin of her stomach. Looking at them together makes my chest feel like it's splitting open.

I click on the next picture and grow cold. Kai and I are beside each other on the couch, faces close together. It's clear he's saying something to me, probably only leaning in close so I can hear him over the noise of the party, but in this picture, it looks like we're about to kiss. There's a funny feeling in my stomach as I stare at it. I know how this will look to everyone else.

I have to text him. I have to find out what's going through his head—if he's as confused and regretful as I am.

I find his number and type. Can we talk?

He answers right away. Do you want to come over?

I've hung out in Kai's barn before—watching movies on the crooked old TV, playing games of flip cup and beer pong on his picnic table, spin the bottle back when we were in eighth grade. But I always tried my best to avoid him. I've never been inside his house. I've never been alone with him.

But I want answers.

I'll be there in twenty.

NOW

I PARK THE CAR IN KAI'S DRIVEWAY and step out into the hot afternoon sun. It's even warmer now than it was this morning, the kind of summer day meant for picnics, hikes, and swims in the lake. The weather doesn't know it should be dark and miserable like my mood.

Kai's mom answers the door. She's a tiny Japanese woman with a round, friendly face, black hair thrown up on top of her head with a banana clip. I met her once before at a terrible birthday party Kai had at the lake in middle school—I was only invited back then because she'd wanted him to include the whole class. This was back before I had any friends, and when I'd arrived, setting down the copy of *Lord of the Flies* I'd brought as a present, Olivia had placed a hand on top of her soda. *Careful*, she'd warned everyone, *or she might puke in your drink*. I'd run to the parking lot to cry, and Kai's mom had been there to comfort me with pizza and a hug. I wonder now if she remembers me.

"Penelope!" she says with a smile, and I'm relieved she does. "What a nice surprise. It's so great to see you again."

"Actually, it's Penny now." I've tried to distance myself from the name Penelope ever since Kai's nickname. I don't like reminding people of that dark time in my life.

"Of course." She opens the door wider, ushering me inside. "You look just the same. Always such a beautiful girl."

"Thanks, Mrs. Tanaka." Her words feel like a hug right now, one I desperately need. I glance down at my bruised knees, hoping she doesn't notice them. I've put on a bit of makeup, trying to cover up the tired effects of last night. I want to look like the girl Kai's mom still thinks I am. It's crazy how parents can be so oblivious to everything. Kai's mom has no idea what happened between her son and me last night. She doesn't know he has a habit of consistently ruining my life.

"Oh, please," she says. "Call me Mari. If you wouldn't mind taking your shoes off—we're a no-shoes house."

"Sure," I say, reaching down to untie my sneakers.

It's quiet inside, the humming of the refrigerator the only sound. I like the way the house is decorated—huge patterned rugs, bright paintings on the walls. And there are more plants than I've ever seen inside a house before, tall, leafy trees and succulents in colorful pots by the windows. It looks like his family brought a bit of Hawaii here with them, a little piece of home. I hate that I like it. I don't want to like anything about Kai, even his stupid tropical house.

"Kai is in his room," Mari says. "I can call him for you."

And then he's bounding down the stairs, taking them two at a time, and when he's right in front of me he stops short, almost tripping in his attempt to slow momentum. He's disheveled, brown pants cuffed at the ankles, a black soccer team T-shirt so old it's worn a few holes.

There's that flash of memory again—bringing him toward me, crushing my stupid traitorous lips against his, and him pulling away. The shame of it all makes me want to fold in on myself. The embarrassment is twofold—it's the fact that I kissed him and the even worse fact that I'm pretty sure he told me to stop.

He stuffs his hands in his pockets. "Hey."

"Um, hi." I feel a bit like I might puke again, which absolutely cannot happen. I take a deep breath to calm myself.

"Do you want to go up to my room?" He pulls his hands out of his pockets and cracks his knuckles. "Or, like . . . maybe not. Would that be weird?"

I don't know if I want to be in his room, a place with a bed and a closed door. But I also don't want his mom to hear us talk. "It's fine," I say. "Wherever."

"Okay, cool." He turns around and walks back up the stairs. I guess I'm supposed to follow. His mom is still watching us with a sweet mom-look on her face, like she wants to get us drinks or make us a snack or something, but that is so not what this is.

"Thanks, Mari," I say, following Kai. "It was nice seeing you again."

"You're welcome anytime, Penny."

We walk into Kai's room and he shuts the door. It feels a bit like being in an enemy lair. It's nothing special, typical boy stuff: a guitar in one corner, poorly taped pictures of surfers on gigantic life-threatening waves, dirty laundry strewn on the floor. He's got the same *Endless Summer* poster as Jordan, and I wonder if they got them together. Still, I look around, soaking it in, like all these little pieces of him are clues that might help me destroy him.

He kicks a pile of laundry under the bed and sits down. Then he stands back up and pushes his desk chair in my direction, patting the seat like I'm a dog. I roll my eyes, but sit anyway. I don't want to follow his instructions, but more than that, I don't want to sit next to him on the bed.

We look at each other for a minute. I feel like I'm trying to read his mind. I wish I could see into it, could play his memories back like in that episode of *Black Mirror*.

"So," he says. "Last night was . . . weird, huh?" He smooths his fingers down his pant legs.

"I don't know if *weird* is the word I'd use." I cross my arms.

"Did you get home okay after everything? Jordan kicked me out, so I couldn't stay over, obviously. I got a ride home with some of the soccer guys and then felt like an idiot for leaving you." He smiles faintly, as if everything is okay. How can he treat this like it's something worth smiling about?

"No, I didn't get home okay," I say. "Spent the night on a lawn chair, actually."

Kai's face turns red. "Are you serious?" He stands and takes a step toward me, holding out his arms like he might try to give me a hug, but then thinks better of it and sits back down. "I'm sorry. You could have called me."

"It's fine." There's no way I would ever ask for Kai's help with anything. "I survived the elements."

"I can't believe they didn't bring you inside, though. That doesn't seem like Jordan."

"It's not his fault. He thought I left."

"Oh." He cracks his knuckles again. "So did you guys talk everything out, then?"

"He broke up with me. If that's what you mean."

"Oh, fuck," Kai says. He runs a hand down his face. "This is all so messed up. This wasn't how any of this . . ." He trails off, shaking his head and looking down at the navy blue rug. "Have you talked to Olivia?"

"Did you guys break up last night too?"

He pauses for a minute, chewing his lip. "Well, yeah. We're done, obviously."

"I'm sorry." Even though I don't like Kai, I still feel like a horrible, destructive person for ruining his relationship.

"No, it's not your fault."

"But I . . . kissed you. Right?" The words make my face flame with heat. It is so strange to be talking about this.

"I kissed you back," he says. "We're both equal-opportunity assholes here, okay?"

It's weird that he's being so nice to me. I'm not used to it. I feel like this peace offering between us is made of glass—that at any moment it will shatter, shards scattering all over the carpet at our feet.

But right now, we're on the same side.

"I just feel bad that I came between you guys."

"I mean, it's not . . . Wait." Kai chews on the side of his fingernail. "What can you remember about last night?" He takes out his phone and starts tapping it against his palm.

"I don't know," I say, looking down because eye contact right now feels excruciating. "I remember kissing you, I think. We were in the laundry room. And then . . ." I strain, trying to make the memory sharper—Olivia opening the door, the sound of her shouting. "Olivia saw us. I think she was crying." The thought makes me sick, and I shake it away.

"Oh," he says. "Okay." He keeps tapping the phone against his palm. *Tap-tap-tap.* I want to grab it out of his hands to make him stop. It's like he always has an incessant need to make noise.

"What happened, Kai?" I know we kissed, but what I don't understand is *why.* That's what I'm really asking: *How did we get here? Why the hell did I kiss you?*

"You got sick," he says. "I found you throwing up in that little bathroom off the side of the laundry room."

I wince at his words. Of all people to find me puking. He probably ran and told everyone about it—that's why they're all calling me that name again. It's hard to breathe all of a sudden, and I know I'm going to cry. "You could have kept it to yourself." I'm mad he escaped the party last night—that he didn't have to deal with any of this morning's repercussions. I had to live through everything twice.

"I was trying to help you. I cleaned you up, got you some mouthwash."

"Yeah, and then you told everyone you saw me puking."

He narrows his eyes. "I don't know where you're getting that idea from."

"Where do you think?" I snap. The tears are falling now because I can't hold them in as I think about how this morning was supposed to feel, my future with Jordan brighter than ever. I hate that I'm crying in front of Kai. I look so weak.

"Hey, that's not what happened. I don't call you that stupid name anymore, you know. This isn't middle school."

"Yeah, instead you just call me fake and shallow, which is *so much better.*" I cross my arms.

"Come on, that's not what this is about." He smiles again, and I don't understand it. "Besides, you can't hate me *that* much based on the way you jumped my bones last night."

"I did not jump your *anything*." The tears have stopped now, replaced by buzzing, red anger. This is so typical. Kai has never bothered to care about anything else in his life—why would he care about this?

"You wanted me." He is full-out laughing now, his eyes twinkling. "You can admit it."

"This isn't funny," I say.

"It's a little funny." He reaches out like he's actually going to touch me.

I scoot farther away from him. "No. It isn't. We messed up, Kai. What were we thinking?" Olivia and Jordan. Our two best friends. It doesn't make any sense. "I wouldn't cheat on Jordan," I say. "Especially with you. I don't even like you."

"Thanks," he says, glancing up at me and then returning his gaze back to the rug. "You've been pretty clear about that fact, Penelope." I narrow my eyes at his use of my full name. It feels like an insult, even though it's my name, a part of me. But Kai is the only person who always insists on using it. "You can say what you like," Kai continues, "but the fact is you *did* cheat on Jordan. You kissed me because some little part of you deep down wanted to, and I guess I wanted to kiss you back. Although I have no idea why, considering you're the most obnoxious person on the entire planet."

"Oh, get over yourself," I say, throwing my hands in the air.

"We can't change what happened," Kai says. "Sue me for trying to be a little lighthearted about it. We can't change the past. So what's the point of worrying about it? Some of us don't like to spend our entire lives in a constant state of panic. Some of us like to make jokes and laugh about the shitty situations we can't fix."

"Are they really jokes when you're the only one laughing?"

"Yes!" Kai says, standing up. "I don't care if I'm the only one laughing. At least I'm laughing. I'm trying to lighten the mood, Penelope."

"Okay, well . . . darken it a little! My entire life is ruined, Kai. Olivia isn't talking to me anymore. I threw away everything I had with her, everything I had with Jordan, all because of you? You're not worth it."

Kai isn't smiling anymore, thank god. He's chewing his bottom lip again, staring down at the carpet. There's another knuckle crack. "Wow. Okay," he says.

"I don't know why I even came over here," I say, standing abruptly. I thought maybe talking to Kai would explain everything—that somehow he might have the answers. But I don't feel better at all. I feel so much worse.

"Yeah, me neither," Kai says, standing too. "Apparently I ruined your entire life."

"That's what I said." I walk back out into the hallway.

"So this was a huge mistake," he says.

"Obviously." I spin around to shut the door in his face, but I'm too slow, and before I can reach out, he slams it closed in mine first.

THEN

JUNIOR YEAR–SEPTEMBER

"WE SHOULD PRANK-CALL the boys," Katie says, sprawled out on Olivia's bed. It's the first Friday of the first week of school, and we're having a girls' night—celebrating the start of junior year with Korean face masks, nail polish, and Disney movies.

Olivia has a TV in her room—something my mom has never allowed—and right now there are icicles shooting out of Elsa's hands as she twirls around the screen. But we're barely watching.

Olivia likes to pretend she's too cool for cartoons—she's explicitly stated that Disney movies are for middle schoolers—but I've caught her singing *The Little Mermaid* under her breath enough times to know she's secretly into them too. Sometimes it's like Olivia puts on this front like she's older than all of us, as if she's our sophisticated babysitter teaching us the ways of the world.

The truth is, I'm older than she is by three months.

"No way," Olivia says. "Prank calls are for middle schoolers."

Katie looks stung, but lets it roll off her back, pasting a smile on her face. It's past midnight, and we were all supposed to be asleep hours ago because Olivia has a dentist appointment in the morning. But we don't care. Myriah and Romina are on the air mattress on the floor, and we've piled a bunch of couch cushions for Katie. She'll eventually move down there—everyone knows Olivia and I always share the bed.

Olivia's room is amazing—painted a deep purple, twinkling fairy lights crisscrossing the beams on the ceiling. The walls are covered in photographs she's taken, the pictures of all of us down on the tennis courts, poses that look like stills from a magazine. There's a particularly beautiful one of Jordan staring down at me from above her bed, and I can't help but turn away from his gaze. Even a picture of his smile gets me all flustered. It's pathetic.

"Well, I'm bored," Katie huffs. "We should do something more fun."

"I have an idea," Olivia says, her eyes sparkling. "Penny, give me your phone."

"Why mine?" I grip my phone a little bit tighter, but then Olivia holds out her hand and I give it to her anyway.

"You have Sarah K's number, right? From back when you were weird?"

My cheeks flame at her comment. We don't usually talk about the way things used to be. It's an unspoken agreement among all of us.

"Yeah, I have her number, but I don't, like . . . use it or anything."

I used to hang out with Sarah Kozlowski sometimes back in

elementary school. We'd sit together at lunch when I wasn't eating in the library, protected by a barricade of books. She was the only girl everyone hated more than me because someone saw her pick her nose on the bus and eat it. The fact that Olivia still remembers that friendship between us is so embarrassing.

"Perfect." Olivia grins. She scrolls through my contacts and then enters Sarah's number into her phone and starts typing.

"Show it to me!" Myriah squeals. The air mattress makes a farting sound as she sits up, and we all burst out laughing. Olivia turns her phone screen to us.

> Hey Sarah, it's Kai. I got your number from Penny.

"Stop," I say. "Don't drag Kai into this."

It's a stupid lie anyway. I don't have Kai's phone number. I don't have Jordan's number either, but that's because I'm too scared to ask. Olivia has everyone's number; she's not scared of anything.

"Too late," Olivia says. "Already sent."

She types again. I think you're so hot. Maybe we can hang out sometime?

"She's not gonna buy it," Romina says. "She's not stupid."

"She'll buy it," Olivia says. "No way a cute guy has ever texted her. This is like Christmas freaking morning."

"I think she's Jewish," Katie says. "Remember? My mom made me invite her to my bat mitzvah because our moms are, like . . . friends or something."

"Not important, Katie," Romina says.

"I don't like this." Myriah leans forward. "This is mean. Besides, what if she already has Kai's number? Or yours, Olivia?"

"Sarah Kozlowski does not have my number," Olivia scoffs. The phone buzzes in her hand, and then she screams. "Oh my god, she texted back!" She holds it out for us to see.

Um, okay dude.

"Boring!" Katie says.

"Wait, she's still typing." Olivia holds a finger out, shushing us.

You know I have a boyfriend though.

We all scream.

"No way!" Olivia says. "This is too good. Sarah K does not have a boyfriend. She is totally lying."

"Maybe she does," Myriah says. "We don't know her that well."

"Why do you hate her so much?" Romina asks Olivia.

"She's a nose picker," Olivia snaps.

I have a nagging sliver of guilt somewhere in my stomach, a bubbling anxious feeling that won't go away. Olivia has always had a dark side—I know from experience. But when she likes you—when she's on your team—she would do anything for you. And the days she used to turn her bite on me are so far in the past it's like they barely even happened at all. I'm afraid if I say something—if I remind her of who I once was—that girl could come back.

There are only two options, and every girl knows them: you can side with the Olivias of the world, or you can side with the Sarahs. And survival is key. Being on Sarah's side would mean losing everything—all my friends, my place at the lunch table, the friendly shouts in the hallways, and the weekend plans. It would mean becoming Pukey Penelope again.

So I keep quiet.

"Ugh, you guys are no fun," Olivia says. "Fine. Whatever. I have another idea." She sits up straighter on the bed, fluffing the pillows behind her. I don't like how easily she's moved on from this Sarah thing—like it barely even registered on her morality radar.

"We should make resolutions for the year," Olivia says. "Like, pretend it's New Year's Eve. Let's figure out how to have the best fucking junior year ever. Actually, hold on." She stands and joins Myriah and Romina on the floor, sitting next to them and crossing her legs. "Let's all sit in a circle."

Katie and I join her, and then we're all sitting cross-legged beside the air mattress. Elsa is still singing loudly about letting it go, and Olivia grabs the remote, pausing the movie so we're plunged into silence.

"Wow, that's so much better."

"I love *Frozen*," Myriah says. "You guys think you're too cool for everything."

"Elsa is hot," Romina says. "She's a queer icon. But she's so *loud*."

"Hush, children," Olivia says. She stands up and grabs a tall candle off the top of her dresser. It's got the Virgin Mary on it, but with Lady Gaga's face. I gave it to her for her birthday last year. "We've got to light the sacred candle."

It feels suddenly like we're in a coven, like we're witches about to bring someone back from the dead.

"Okay," Olivia says. "Myriah, you first. What's your resolution?

Tell Gaga your desires and she'll make them come true."

Myriah brings her hands up to her long hair, braiding it absentmindedly. She's in a lavender silk PJ set, matching top and bottom. Myriah is the only person I know who actually wears matching pajamas. I think she's secretly eighty years old.

"Okay, so I really want to get a better part in *The Nutcracker* this Christmas. I always get stuck in the ensemble." She lowers her voice to an almost whisper. "I really think I could be the Sugar Plum Fairy."

"Fuck yeah, you're such Sugar Plum material," Romina says. "It's in the bag."

"Also, I want to finish my college apps."

"Slay those apps, girl!" Romina says.

"And, um, kiss someone." Myriah's hands stop braiding, and now she's holding on to the braid like it's a lifeline. Her cheeks are bright pink.

"Just kiss them?" Romina leans a little closer.

Myriah lets out a breathy, nervous laugh. "Okay, I want to take them to Soul Mate City."

"Who?" Katie asks. "Who do you like?"

"Yeah, you're holding out on us," Olivia says. "Is it a girl from your dance studio?"

"It's no one!" Myriah says, the words a little too high in pitch. "I don't like anyone."

"Okay, well, I want you guys to finally meet Matt this year," Katie says, referring to the boyfriend who seems to be allergic to social media.

"Oh, fuck off," Olivia says. "Matt isn't real."

"Yes, he is," Katie says. "He just doesn't like getting his picture taken."

"Sounds like he's hiding something, if you ask me," Romina says.

"Are you sure he doesn't have a girlfriend?" Myriah says gently.

"Yeah, he has a girlfriend," Katie snaps. "*I'm* his girlfriend."

"If you insist," Olivia says. She turns away from Katie, the conversation closed. "Romina, spill."

Romina looks down at her fingernails, which were once painted brown and are now horribly chipped. But that's just Romina. She's pretty much the only one of us who can get away with dressing like she doesn't care and still make it look purposeful. My nails are always perfectly groomed, expertly painted to match whatever outfit I've planned.

"Okay, I've got some shit with my parents to sort out," she says. "I've got to get them on board for New York."

"I know they'll let you go," Myriah says.

"It's not about letting me go, though." Romina shrugs. "I'm moving there after school either way. It's about them forgiving me for it." Myriah reaches out and squeezes Romina's hand, just for a second.

"Okay, well, I'm going to get my Instagram up to one hundred K," Olivia says, and the moment is broken. "The one for my photography, not my personal one. Okay, well, maybe both." She laughs. "I mean, I probably could."

Sometimes when Olivia says things like this, I can't help but feel a small twinge of jealousy. I want to be the type of person who is so sure of herself, who knows who she is so securely that she doesn't ever worry about it.

I worry about it so much.

"Penny?" Olivia says. "How about you? What's your perfect junior year? Say it over the sacred candle."

And suddenly I'm stuck. I mean, I think I know what I want: for all of this to stay the same, to always be this girl on Olivia's floor, finally surrounded by a circle of friends. I want my mom to understand me, to be around more. But I feel like I can't say any of these things to them. They're too personal, too much a part of me.

I look down at the flickering candle, at Lady Gaga's steely expression, and then glance up behind Olivia and see Jordan's picture tacked to the wall right over the bed. I want to be the kind of girl deserving of Jordan's attention, to be brave enough to finally talk to him. And yeah, maybe this candle isn't magic and Lady Gaga isn't actually going to make all our junior-year dreams come true.

But she might.

"I want Jordan Parker to fall in love with me." I say it right at the candle, my voice clear, and then look up and meet Olivia's gaze. She narrows her eyes, just slightly.

"That's your biggest wish?"

"I mean, yeah . . ." I say, hesitant.

"We all wish Jordan were in love with us," Katie says.

"I don't," Myriah and Romina say at the same time.

"Okay, well, most of us who are into dudes," Katie says. "But what about Kai, Penny? We want you to have his babies."

"I want Jordan's babies," I say. "I mean, no, wait."

"We all know you're into Jordan, Penny," Olivia says. "I just didn't realize it was your, like, biggest biggest wish."

"Oh, and your biggest wish is more Instagram followers?" I challenge.

"Okay, fine. Touché." Olivia leans forward and blows out the candle. "You know what we should do? Prank-call the boys."

NOW

I FIND JORDAN THE NEXT DAY at the Upper Crust, the sandwich place downtown where he works. He hasn't answered any of my texts, so I know I have to approach him somewhere he can't avoid me.

He's behind the counter preparing someone's turkey on rye when he looks up and sees me. His hands, which were moving expertly over the condiments only seconds before, freeze in midair.

"No," he says. "I don't want to hear it."

"Jordan, please." I walk a few steps over to the counter.

He actually backs away from me. "I don't want to do this here."

"I just want to talk to you. You're not answering my texts."

"Yeah, because you"—he lowers his voice to a hiss—"you messed around with my best friend." Plastering a smile on his face, he drops the sandwich he's working on into a plastic bag and holds it out to a man on my left. "Here's your sandwich, sir. Have a crusty day!"

The man takes it and leaves the store, glancing back at me and narrowing his eyes. I know he heard what Jordan said about me.

"That slogan is terrible," I say.

"I didn't write it," Jordan answers. "It's from corporate."

"Can we please talk? When do you have your break?"

"Fine." Jordan pulls off his hairnet. "Meet me around back."

"I didn't mean to do anything with Kai," I tell him when he walks out the rear door into the parking lot. We're out by the garbage cans, and it smells horrible, sharp and acidic. It's a fitting smell for a conversation like this one. "Jordan, I love you." My voice cracks.

"Yeah, then why did you?"

"I don't know." It kills me that I can't answer him, that I can't find the right words to say to make this all better, to explain a decision I barely even remember making.

Jordan fiddles with the strings of his apron. "You know what last night was supposed to be."

"I know," I say. "I was excited."

"I waited months for this, Penny. Did I ever pressure you? You told me you wanted to wait, and then the same night we're gonna go for it, you kiss my best friend. Like . . . I have nothing to say to you."

"It was nothing," I say, my nose stinging again like I'm going to cry.

"I have to get back to work." Jordan tries to brush past me, slipping his hairnet back onto his head.

"It didn't mean anything," I try again.

He spins back around. "I mean, why should I believe that, though? This isn't the first time you guys have hooked up."

I'm floored by his words. I try to speak, but I can't get any sound to come out. What the hell is he talking about?

"What?" I gasp out finally. "Kai and I have never."

"What about the freshman camping trip? The boathouse. Didn't you guys . . ." He trails off, presumably at the confused expression on my face.

"No," I say. "That wasn't anything. Wait," I say, angry again for a whole different reason. "Did Kai tell you something happened?"

Jordan sighs. "No, I just . . . figured."

It would almost be funny if it weren't so horrible. I know exactly what moment he's talking about. Freshman year, we were all sent on a camping trip as some sort of silly class bonding activity. Olivia and I weren't paired in a tent together, so we'd decided to sneak out in the middle of the night. She'd hidden a bottle of wine in her duffle bag and told me to meet her and the boys in the boathouse.

At five minutes till midnight, I zipped open the flap of my tent and crept past the campfire we'd spent the night circled around, roasting marshmallows and listening to ghost stories that suddenly felt a lot more real in the quiet darkness. I snuck through the circle of chaperone tents and headed toward the lake. The boathouse was down on the pebbled beach where we'd spent all afternoon doing team-building activities like we were ten years old.

I was the last to arrive. When I creaked open the door, Olivia was sitting on a sheet on the floor, drinking straight from the wine bottle. Jordan and Kai were on either side of her. It smelled like mildew, and there was a thin layer of dust coating the floors, the windows, the racks of old kayaks and canoes.

"You made it," Jordan said, his smile bright even in the dark. Warmth pooled in my stomach because of course I was already embarrassingly obsessed with him back then.

"Now we can't have a threesome," Olivia said to the guys, pouting. She was obviously joking, but the comment still made me nervous. Her hair was thrown up in a messy bun on top of her head, a look we all started calling *the Olivia* back in sixth grade.

I sat down next to Jordan, immediately aware of how close he was to me—his knee, the bare skin of his arm, his long fingers only a few finger lengths away. It was dark enough that I could have stretched out my hand to touch his and the others wouldn't have been able to see. I was on high alert, buzzing with possibility. The air felt electric.

Olivia held out the wine in my direction. "Drink up, girly."

I had never tried alcohol before, but I took a sip of wine anyway, trying to be brave, choking a little when I swallowed.

"Let's play a game," Olivia whispered.

"Spin the bottle?" Kai suggested, and Olivia whacked him on the shoulder.

"No way, Tanaka. That's just asking for an orgy."

"Never have I ever?" I asked, and then immediately regretted it. I hadn't ever done anything, not really, and I wasn't so sure I wanted to admit it to any of them. Especially Jordan. "I'll start," Jordan said. "Never have I ever had an orgy." We all laughed, bubbling with nervous energy.

"Oh man, last summer was wild," Kai said, taking a long swig from the bottle.

"Yeah right." I shoved him so that some of the red wine dribbled out the side of his mouth and onto his neck, like he was bleeding. "You could never find more than one girl to hook up with."

"Ouch!" Jordan said. He raised his hand to high-five me, and I felt like I was flying. It was just the right insult at just the right time. I felt cool and funny and unstoppable. Our hands smacked together, the sound loud enough that we all *shhhhhh*'d and erupted into more giggles.

We found out Kai had smoked weed, Jordan had called a teacher *Mom*, and Olivia had shoplifted. Soon, we were all a bit tipsy, laughing louder than we should.

"Penelope hasn't done anything," Kai said, wiping his mouth with the back of his hand. He gave me the bottle. "Have you even lost a turn yet?"

"That's not my name," I snapped, taking the bottle from him as forcefully as I could. I had been taking small sips in between rounds, hoping nobody would notice. It's a delicate balance being a girl. Is it worse to have done too much or nothing at all? I wanted to be somewhere in the middle, safely ordinary.

"Have you ever been kissed?" Kai leaned closer to me. His black hair was all pushed up on one side, like he'd been sleeping on it. I didn't like that he was bringing this up in front of Jordan. I could still feel Jordan's warmth right beside me, the energy radiating off him. There was a bird outside, a ghostly howl over the water, the sound of waves lapping against the shore.

"None of your business," I said.

"So you haven't."

I turned to Jordan, my eyes straying down to his lips of their own accord, then back up to his face. Turning back to Kai, I saw he was looking at me, his expression a challenge.

"So what if I haven't?" I said, aware as I was saying it that he'd probably make fun of me for the rest of time. But I didn't want to lie. If I lied and they saw through it, that would be way worse.

"I'm cold," Olivia said suddenly. She was in a strappy cami-sole, and I could see goose bumps on the skin of her arms.

"Why didn't you bring a sweatshirt?" Kai asked.

She ignored him and turned to Jordan. "I'm gonna go grab one. Come with me?"

"I can go with," I said, feeling cold all of a sudden too.

"No offense, but you could not protect me from the Smiling Man."

"Come on, you don't believe that stupid story Hanson told." Kai groaned.

"He could be out there!" Olivia stood up, pulling on Jordan's arm. "Come on."

Jordan brushed his hands off on his pants, shrugging and smiling like he thought Olivia was being stupid, but that he also thought it was cute. I pressed my fingernail into the palm of my hand, creating a little half-moon in my skin. It was true—Jordan was the biggest of all of us by far, already tall with a six-pack at fourteen. I'd have picked him to protect me if I were scared too, and not just because Kai probably would have fed me to a mon-ster and laughed while it chewed. But I was worried that wasn't what this was about.

I tried to make myself relax. Olivia knew I liked Jordan. We'd talked about it a million times.

"We'll be right back," Jordan said. Olivia pulled open the creaky door and they left.

Kai and I sat alone together on the sheet for what felt like forever, the empty wine bottle overturned between us. I pulled at the sleeves of my sweatshirt, staring down at the floor. There was a spider crawling toward the edge of the sheet, and I watched it stop and change directions, creeping away into a hole in a floorboard.

"Well, this is fun," Kai said after a while.

I tore my gaze away from the floor and looked at his face, glowering. "They'll be back in a minute."

"Sure."

"I don't have to entertain you," I said. "Look at your phone."

"No signal." He tapped his hands on the floor, a beat that sounded vaguely familiar. "Jingle Bells"? I glared angrily down at my lap. Everything was backward. The night wasn't supposed to have gone like this. I hated that I was there with him, hidden away in the dark, a moment that was supposed to have been with Jordan.

Kai kept tapping, the sound of it like a migraine.

"Can you stop?"

He tapped louder, adding a beat with his mouth, lifting one hand up to become a snare drum, his tongue the crash of a cymbal.

"Seriously," I said. "Shut up."

"I should've known you hated music, Penelope," he said. "Completely heartless."

"You're gonna get us caught." I leaned forward and brought my hands down on top of his on the floor, holding them in place. He stopped moving, his hands under mine, and I didn't pull away for some reason. The room was quiet, and the tapping had stopped, and the bird howled again out on the lake, like it was crying. I could smell the wine on Kai's breath, and I didn't know how he'd gotten so close.

And then we heard the sound of Olivia's voice outside the door, and I lifted my hands and pulled away from him, crossing my arms and bringing my hood up like I was trying to become invisible. I didn't know what had just happened. It was like I forgot for a second who he was and who I was, who we were to each other. I had never touched a boy's hand before, at least not one who wasn't related to me, and the feel of skin against skin had made my brain fuzzy. That and the wine.

"What was that with Jordan last night?" I had asked Olivia over the platter of cantaloupe at the breakfast buffet the next morning. "You know I like him."

"Of course." Olivia had smiled and tapped me on the nose. "I wanted to get Jordan alone so I could talk to him about you. I was only telling him how great you are."

There's always been something slightly off about that night, something I've let time cover over. But I didn't realize until right now what it was.

"You really thought something happened with me and Kai that night?" I can't believe how incorrectly Jordan had read the situation. This entire time we've been together, he's been under the assumption that Kai got to me first.

It makes me feel . . . weird. Was that what made him pursue me in the first place? Did he only want me in some competitive dude way because he thought I'd been with Kai? The thought is too uncomfortable, and I shake it away before it can take root.

"Well, yeah," Jordan says. "I thought . . ." He trails off, and we both flinch when we hear a voice from inside the shop: "Parker, you're five minutes over on your break!"

"I liked *you*," I tell Jordan. "I've always liked you. We snuck out that night so that you and I could be together. And then I got stuck with Kai."

Jordan squeezes his eyes shut for a second. "I gotta go, Penny. I'm sorry. I have to get back to work."

And then he's gone. The screen door to the sandwich shop slams angrily behind him.

I leave the Upper Crust and walk back toward my car. Everywhere I look there are signs of Jordan—layers upon layers of memories reminding me of everything I ruined. Down the street is the convenience store where he once took me to get Popsicles. There's the row of parking meters he jumped over on a dare. Across the street is the park bench we sat on once while waiting for his sister, when he let me play him my favorite song from the musical *Waitress*, each of us using one of his AirPods. And there, out of the corner of my eye because it hurts too much to look at it head-on, our tree; the one he once said resembled me— long-limbed and delicate and beautiful.

I can't spend all summer feeling like this.

There's a senior trip to Disneyland planned in August, something the school does every year to celebrate the incoming senior class. We did stupid fund-raisers and car washes all last year to raise money for it, and I've been dreaming of this trip ever since Jordan and I got together: fantasies of us strolling hand in hand down Main Street, taking cute pictures in front of Sleeping Beauty Castle. I already made us each sets of ears—simple black felt ones for him, the fancy rose-gold kind for me.

Now the thought of the trip fills me with anxiety. I picture myself in the single-rider line for Splash Mountain, my old group of friends walking past and laughing. If Jordan isn't talking to me by August and my friends are still ignoring me, I'll probably have to stay home.

With a sigh, I turn away from my car and see the sign for Scoops, the old ice-cream shop I used to be obsessed with as a kid. There's a flier taped to the door—horrible Comic Sans font and frayed corners. Scoops is hiring.

Suddenly, I have an idea. Since Jordan works right next door, if I take this job I'll be able to keep track of him—have more opportunities to try to convince him we belong together.

Also there's this: I want to keep busy in case no one invites me to anything for the rest of the summer.

I push the door open and duck inside. There's a little jingle of a bell as I enter, and then I'm hit with the sugary smell, so sweet it makes my teeth ache. The walls are a pastel lilac color—my favorite—and the cool air inside the shop immediately makes me feel better. Scoops is a classic tourist spot, and already this morning there are several people inside—families with towels and armfuls of children on their way to the lake.

I approach the case with the colorful assortment of ice-cream flavors. There's a yellow sand bucket filled with applications on the counter, a cup of sparkly seashell pens, because everything in our small town is ancient and still done on paper; I bet Scoops doesn't even have a website. I grab one of each and am about to walk them over to a corner table to fill them out when a head pops up from behind the counter, a girl straightening from where she's been bent over scooping ice cream. Her frizzy blue-streaked hair is currently hidden under a cap, but pieces of it are still curling out around her face, fighting desperately against the humidity.

I clench the application in my hands, wondering if I can quickly turn around, back out of the store before she's noticed me. But it's too late. Sarah Kozlowski narrows her eyes and then turns away, handing a cone of mint chocolate chip ice cream to the kid at the register.

My mind flashes again to the time she pricked her finger in science lab so she could study her own blood under the microscope, how one of the boys made some joke about studying her period blood next and we all laughed and gagged; that time Olivia texted Sarah pretending to be Kai and I did nothing to stop it. Looking at her now, it all makes me feel a bit queasy.

The kid hands Sarah a large stack of quarters and scampers away with his ice cream, and then we're alone at the counter.

"Are you lost?" she asks, tucking a blue curl behind one ear. It immediately bounces back into her face.

"What?" I'm caught off guard.

"Forget it." She holds the ice-cream scoop out to me like a weapon. "What can I get for you?" And then she sees the application in my hands.

I fight the urge to hide it behind my back. I feel weird about working with Sarah K after how we've all treated her. But I don't want to let Sarah control me either. I don't want to back away from her, let her run me out of this shop from my own shame. And if this job brings me one step closer to getting back with Jordan, it's all worth it.

So I lift the application up where she can see it. "How about a job?"

She turns away from me, busying herself by straightening

things around the cash register—a stapler, a tape dispenser, a box of paper clips. "We're not hiring, actually."

"Pretty sure you are," I say, waving the paper.

She picks up the stapler and clicks it a few times in her hand. "Fine. Fill out the form and stick it in the bucket. The Comic Sans is ironic. Just FYI." *Click click click.* "I thought . . . never mind."

"What?" I sit down at one of the tables and begin filling out the form.

"I thought people like you didn't get jobs."

I snap my head up from my paperwork and look at her. "What's that supposed to mean?"

"Your crowd. Doesn't Romina drive an Escalade?"

My *crowd.* Her casual use of the word stings, because I'm not so sure I'm part of a crowd anymore. My phone has been silent for two days. No one has reached out to see if I'm okay. And it's not like they all mysteriously broke their phones and have no service, because all those pictures and comments on social media have been pretty freaking loud.

Still—despite all of that, I don't like Sarah's implication about my friends. Olivia has never worked, but Romina teaches cello to the kids at the elementary school, and I'm pretty sure Kai coaches soccer. And then there's Jordan, only a few blocks away at the Upper Crust. My mind flashes to him now, picturing him behind the counter, looking so stupid and adorable in his hairnet. I realize I'm grimacing and take a deep breath before answering.

"I'm doing my own thing this summer." I have no idea if Sarah has witnessed my demise online, if she even has social media. For one brief moment, I let myself be tempted by the idea that Sarah knows nothing at all, that spending all summer with someone who still thinks of me as the real Penny, as the Penny from before, might be just what I need. But then she ruins it.

"Because you're in love with your best friend's boyfriend."

"That's none of your business," I snap.

"Whatever." She puts down the stapler and picks up a rag and a spray bottle of glass cleaner.

"And Kai and I aren't in love," I add. "We kissed—that's all. I hate him." My whole body tenses. "Wait, is that what people are saying?"

"I thought it was none of my business." Sarah smirks. "But . . . if you hate the kid and made out with him anyway? You're even worse than I thought."

"It wasn't—I'm not—" I sputter, but there's nothing I can actually say in response. She's right.

"I'm only saying." She sprays the glass case and starts to scrub. "Maybe you should just let people believe it. Everyone forgives a good love story."

NOW

I SPEND THE WHOLE NEXT DAY attempting to distract myself, trying to think about literally anything other than the total and complete destruction of my social life. But it's pretty hard to ignore.

Danny Scott is having a cookout by the lake for his birthday, and if the night of Jordan's party hadn't happened, I would be there too: Mike's Hard Lemonade bought by someone's older brother, burgers smoking on the grill, Olivia and me giggling and checking out the shirtless guys in the water. The image of it hurts because it's so easy to imagine. The summer I might have had.

Instead, I spent the day vacuuming my room and organizing my bookshelves by color. I watched a YouTube video to learn how to crochet and took the kit I got for Christmas down out of the closet. I thought about making a scarf, but the fact that it's summer and a beautiful day made it feel especially pointless.

Now the sun is just starting to set, painting my walls in golden light, so I know everyone must have been at the lake for hours, swimming and tanning and doing other fun summer activities people can do when they haven't drunkenly destroyed all their friendships.

I check my phone for the millionth time, opening Instagram and flipping over to Olivia's personal account. She's posted a picture with Katie, Romina, and Myriah, all of them looking beautiful and sun-dappled in their bathing suits. It feels just like it used to back when I was still a little kid, sitting on the hill at lunchtime watching all the other girls have fun without me—back before the day everything finally started to get better.

It was at Kai's thirteenth birthday party—the same terrible day I'd run away from Olivia in tears. It was unusually hot, and I'd worn the wrong thing: a big sweatshirt and leggings, oversized and ugly compared to Olivia's crisp white shorts, Katie's yellow sundress. I'd felt even more like I didn't belong.

After Kai's mom had called my mom to come pick me up, I'd wandered into the visitor center bathroom to hide and then stopped short because Olivia was already in there. She was standing by the sink, and when she turned to me, I could see she was crying.

"Sorry," I said, because it was instinct. Even if it was Olivia, it still sucked to see someone upset. Her eyes were big and wet, and she was looking at me with what could only be described as terror. And then I saw why. There was a huge red stain on the bottom of Olivia's white shorts.

"I . . ." she said, wiping at her eyes with her manicured hands. "It just happened."

"Oh," I said, like an idiot, coming into the bathroom and closing the door behind me. I hadn't gotten my period yet, but I knew what it was like having unwanted bodily functions in public.

"You're probably so happy." Olivia turned away from the mirror, looking at the back of her shorts, and her face crumpled.

"What?" I had my hands out in front of me, like she was a wounded animal and I wasn't sure if she was going to attack.

"Well, aren't you gonna go tell everybody?"

I realized this was it. This was the moment that might save me. If Olivia went back out to the party in her stained shorts, it was going to be just as bad as when I puked. Worse maybe. Kai would give her a horrible nickname of her own. Olivia's period would make Pukey Penelope go away.

"You can take this." I untied the sweatshirt from around my waist and held it out to her. She tilted her head to the side and studied me for a second, like I was a science experiment she didn't understand. She was still so beautiful, even with her face full of tears.

She grabbed the sweatshirt, tying it quickly around her waist. "Thanks, Penelope."

"Penny," I corrected.

"Penny," she repeated. "I like it."

After the party, it all changed. Olivia invited me to sit with her at lunch, and then amazingly, my nickname went away. Suddenly, everyone at school was calling me Penny. Keep your friends close and your enemies closer, they always say, and that's exactly what Olivia and I did. And soon we weren't enemies at all.

There's always been this underlying layer to our friendship—the fact that it was built on a moment I could have used to ruin her and instead I'd saved her. She'd been horrible to me only an hour before, but I think when I didn't stoop to her level, she respected me for it.

Except now I've betrayed her after all.

I can't keep hiding out in my room, hoping for this mess to go away. When you make a mess, you clean it up. You vacuum the dirt off the rug. You fix things until they're better. I need to fix our friendship. And I need to fix things with Jordan.

I have to go to this party.

I park my car on the side of the road, behind everyone else's, and then take the path through the trees down toward the water. Ordinarily, I wouldn't drive here because I'd be drinking, but I don't plan on having anything tonight. Just the thought of it, after everything that happened, makes my skin crawl.

The path is dark, so I pull out my phone for a flashlight. But I've done this walk a million times. It's where we usually hang out when there's a weekend no one's parents are gone. All the cars on the side of the road make it kinda obvious, but the path to the water is long enough that the cops never bother to walk it.

The beat of the music from somebody's speaker gets louder as I approach, and I can hear laughter, drunk and relaxed. There's a firepit, glowing now that the sun has fully set, a grill, and a beer pong table someone carried all the way down here last year. Some camping chairs are propped in the sand, along with some soggy cushions that have probably been here since our parents were our age.

I stand on the edge of the path, too nervous to walk out onto the beach. All I can think about is the video Romina posted, Olivia's angry comments below it, the way my phone has been silent for days. I don't know how they're going to react when they see me, and I brace myself for the worst.

I walk over to a folding table piled with a thirty rack and some sticky red cups, reaching for a beer, and then putting it back down when I remember I'm not drinking.

Danny sees me then. He's big and hulking, would be a football player if our school had a team, but he's so drunk he looks unsteady, a tree blowing in a strong wind. "Hey, Penny!" he says. "Penny for your thoughts!"

"Hey, Danny," I say. "Happy birthday."

"Where have you been all day?"

I'm about to answer him, make something up, when the smile on his face fades and I see he's remembered. "Oh," he says. "They're all talking about you. Olivia's piiissssed." He draws the word out, his voice raising in pitch.

I wonder then if Kai is here—if he was brave or stupid enough to show his face too. "Have you seen Kai?" I ask.

Danny smiles, raising his eyebrows. "You and Tanaka, eh?" He takes a long sip of beer. "I support it. Let's switch everything up."

"Not me and Kai," I say. "I'm with Jordan." I realize my mistake and correct myself, the act of it physically painful. "*Was* with Jordan. We just need to talk it out some more and then we'll get back together."

"I dunno," Danny says, taking another slurp of beer. "I always thought you and Tanaka would hook up one of these days. You've got Han and Leia vibes." Danny has been obsessed with Star Wars since third grade and sometimes still wears embarrassing novelty shirts to school.

"It was a mistake." I stuff my hands into my pockets, scanning the beach for Olivia or Jordan, but it's too dark to make out anyone's figures.

"Whatever," Danny says. "He's down there in the water if you want him. Been here all day." He motions vaguely in the direction of the lake, and I can just make out a shadowed silhouette that looks like Kai standing with a few other guys. *Of course he's here.* Why would Kai ever let a small thing like cheating on his girlfriend get in the way of a party? He was probably splashing around in the water all afternoon while I was stress-vacuuming.

Danny burps, crushing his beer can and throwing it down into the sand. "I'll see you later, Penny." He musses the top of my head with his bear paw hand, and as he lumbers away, it hits me. *Danny isn't mad.* Danny is talking to me, not treating me like I'm some social pariah.

But maybe he's just too drunk to hate me.

Still, it feels good. It gives me hope that I'll be able to make this better.

I take a step toward the fire, scanning the shadowy figures in the distance, and then turn back to the woods in time to see Myriah coming toward me from behind a tree. We both look at each other for a second, do that thing where we try to decide if we should pretend we didn't see each other.

"Um, sorry," she says, taking a hesitant step closer. "I was just . . . peeing."

"No, you're fine," I say, taking my hands out of my pockets and then stuffing them back in. "It's okay. Go for it."

"No, I already did." This is all so awkward. I don't want Myriah to be mad at me—if dear, sweet Myriah with her butterfly clips and her pink daisy-print bathing suit hated me, it would break my heart.

But then she smiles. I feel like I can breathe again.

"How is everything?" she asks, tentative. I can tell she's searching the beach behind me—like she's afraid we might get caught together.

"Are you allowed to talk to me?" As soon as I ask, I want to suck the words back in. I don't want to say anything that will push her away.

"I won't tell if you won't," she says. "Are you okay? I'm sorry I didn't text you, or, like . . ." She trails off. We both know why she didn't text me.

"It's okay," I say. "I get it."

"Can I just say something?" She takes a cautious step toward me, her voice quiet. "I mean, maybe this is super messed up—and don't tell Olivia—but the truth is . . . all of us think this is kind of romantic."

I actually laugh out loud. Of all the things this crazy horrible situation from the last few days has been, romantic is not one of them. "How?"

Myriah chews her lip. "Well, I mean, you and Kai falling in love." I blink at her for a few seconds, not answering, and she continues, "Well, you are, aren't you? I know you're a good person, Penny. Obviously, you wouldn't do something like this unless you had a good reason. And maybe you and Kai went about things in a messy way, but you're meant for each other."

I know I should answer her, but my words feel stuck in my throat. How can I possibly tell Myriah that she's wrong—that I kissed Kai for no good reason; that this isn't the romance she wants it to be; that no, actually, I'm not a good person after all?

I think back to what Sarah Kozlowski said to me the other day at Scoops: *Maybe you should just let people believe it. Everyone forgives a good love story.*

My friends have been rooting for Kai and me to get together for as long as I can remember. They're not mad because they think this is all some twisted, romantic happy ending.

They think this is a love story.

"You're right," I say. "Yes. Kai and I have been fighting our feelings for a while now, but it was getting harder and harder to resist him."

Myriah smiles. "I knew it."

"We have those Han and Leia vibes, you know? I know it's all wrong, but I can't help it. We were written in the stars."

Myriah sighs. "Soul Mate City."

I am fully aware of the hole I am digging myself into as I speak. At this point I might as well bury my whole body in the sand of this beach and suffocate. If Kai finds out what I said, he's going to kill me. And Jordan—*Jordan!* Jordan will think he was right about the boathouse all along. He'll think I've been lying to him.

But I don't want to be the terrible person they'll think I am if they find out the truth. I like the kindness in Myriah's eyes too much.

"We should tell everyone," she says. "Do you want me to talk to Olivia? Maybe she would understand if—"

"No!" I say, the word a little too loud. "No, I'll handle it." I don't want Myriah spreading this information all over the beach. I have to find Kai—need to talk to him before he hears my stupid lie from anyone else. Maybe we can fix this. "I'll be right back," I tell Myriah, heading toward Kai's shadowy figure standing in the surf with a group of guys from the basketball team.

He's bouncing a hacky sack on his foot when I charge up to him and grab his arm. The hacky sack falls into the wet sand with a *splat*. There's a chorus of annoyed groans around me, but I pull him away from the group before they can protest.

"Ow," Kai says, tugging his arm from me as we walk back up the beach toward the table of beers by the tree line. "That was obnoxious, even for you."

"I did something bad," I say.

"Well, yeah, that's been established." He smirks. "You want a beer?" Kai nods toward the table behind us. I don't want a beer from Kai. Really, I don't want a beer from anyone.

"I'm not drinking."

"Yeah, you probably shouldn't."

It feels like a jab. As if he has any right to judge, considering he drank too much at Jordan's party too.

"Actually, a beer sounds good." I grab one out of the cardboard container and crack it open. It's warm and flat, so I know it's probably been sitting in the trunk of someone's car for months.

"Fine, Penelope. Do what you want."

"I don't need your permission."

"Clearly." Kai laughs, but there's no humor in it. "So who did you kiss this time?"

"Nobody," I say, clenching the edges of the can so hard it dents. "Just you, unfortunately." I take another unpleasant sip. "But don't you think it's weird, I dunno, how *cool* everyone is being about it?"

"What do you mean?"

"Like I showed up here tonight fully expecting that everyone would claw my eyes out. But they've all been . . . friendly. I mean, you were just playing hacky sack with all those guys! Those were Jordan's teammates, Kai. Those guys should hate you."

"Who I hook up with isn't any of their business, so—"

"It's because they think we're in love!" I hiss at him.

Kai's face goes bright red. "Where did you hear that?"

"You've been getting all the same comments for years, haven't you? Everyone joking that we're secretly pining for each other. Before I got with Jordan, I mean, even *after* I got with Jordan—the jokes never stopped." I let out a barking laugh. "Our friends have been shipping us."

Kai lifts a beer off the table and then sets it back down. "Fuck. Yeah, it's been relentless."

"That's why they're being so nice. They think we're together."

"So maybe we should get together," Kai says, cracking his knuckles.

"What? No!" I squeeze the can in my hand a little too hard again, and some beer spills out the top.

"Not for *real*, Penelope," he says with a harsh laugh. "But . . . we could pretend." He runs a hand through his hair, takes a deep breath. "I mean, this is our lifeline, right? If we get together, we're not the assholes who cheated on our significant others at a party for no reason. We're not cheaters who threw everything away for one stupid night. We're cheaters who fell in love. People might forgive that."

"Everyone forgives a good love story," I say, echoing Sarah's words from the other day. "But what about Jordan and Olivia?"

"If they see us acting all disgusting and happy together, they'll be jealous, right? Jordan will want you more than ever."

"I don't want Jordan to think I've been lying," I say, because really that's the most important thing. If we go through with this plan, what will Jordan think of me?

"Olivia is competitive," Kai says. "You know that's true. If she sees you with me, she'll want me back just to take me away from you."

I don't like that he's made my friendship with Olivia sound so cruel, like everything between us is one big chess match. This isn't *Game of Thrones*. "Olivia is my best friend," I say. "Don't minimize that, Kai."

"And *he's* my best friend," he says. "And Olivia too. You're not the only one going through this. You're not the only one who lost something."

I feel myself softening a bit at that. Because he has a point—in all of this, I've been so caught up in my own heartbreak, I kind of forgot Kai was dealing with some heartbreak too.

But it's too risky. There are too many variables, too much that could go wrong. "I don't think this is a good idea." I don't want to help Kai, and I don't want his help. "Let's just go talk to them, okay?" I take a few steps closer to the fire, walking down the beach and scanning for an overly tall Jordan-shaped shadow. Kai follows behind me.

And that's when I see them.

Jordan is on one of the camping chairs, long legs spread out in front of him, and Olivia is sitting on his lap. She's leaning in close, hair falling around him like a curtain, and they're *kissing*.

I abruptly stop walking and Kai bumps hard into my back. It feels like I've been hit, the shock of it stealing my breath. I'm in a horrible nightmare and soon I'll wake up and it will be the first day of summer, and everything will be how it was supposed to be: Jordan beside me in his bed, that morning-after grin, our perfect senior year laid out in front of us.

I knew this might happen. Of course it might. Olivia and Jordan are both attractive people with broken hearts. Why wouldn't they comfort each other with their mouths? It just hurts because I know it's my fault. I was wrong before—*this* is the horrible moment all those ripples of bad decisions have led up to. *This* is the tornado.

Olivia pulls herself away from Jordan and notices me, and there's a smile on her face, triumphant. *I win*, it says. I came here to apologize, but that smile makes me want to run away. It makes me feel like this is unfixable. It makes this whole thing feel like a game I'm currently losing instead of a fight with my best friend.

Jordan looks at me, pressing his lips together in a tight line. At least he looks a bit guilty.

"Who invited Pukey Penelope?" Olivia smirks.

"Olivia," I say, her name like an open wound. I want my best friend back, the one who laughs so hard at my jokes she sometimes snorts soda out of her nose. The one who threatened to punch Gabe Pinkerton in the face last year when he told everyone I had a flat ass. The one I was going to move to LA with to start our new lives. The spicy tomato soup to my extra-sharp Vermont cheddar grilled cheese.

But I know how much I must have hurt her. I don't know if there's any way to make things better.

"If you're planning on sitting with us," Olivia says, "don't. I have nothing to say to either of you."

"Oh, is this your fire?" Kai sits down on a log directly beside her. "I didn't realize you built it. Did they teach you that in Girl Scouts?"

"You're one to talk about setting fires," Olivia says.

I'm still hovering on the outside of the circle, afraid to get too close. My gaze meets Jordan's, and he quickly looks away.

"Can we just talk about this?" Kai says.

"I trusted you." Olivia's voice is quiet, and it sounds more fragile than I've ever heard it. "I trusted both of you. I'm done talking about it."

I take a step closer, joining the circle. "I'm sorry, Olivia. I wasn't thinking. I care about you both so much." I fix my gaze on Jordan, and he looks away again. I've become a person he can't even look at.

"See, that's what I don't get," Olivia says. "You're *always* thinking. You overthink literally everything." I can see the hurt in her eyes hardening into anger, and I brace myself for impact, ready for whatever terrible words I know are coming my way. She takes a few steps closer to the fire. I can see the flames reflected in her eyes. "Do you actually care about me? Like for real? Or do you just, I don't know, like me for what I can give you? You try so hard to get people to like you, Penny, but they don't, do they? Your dad left. Your mom is never around. Honestly, Jordan is better off without you."

This is what she wants, I realize, this public humiliation, this admission she's better than I am in front of everyone. And even though I probably deserve it, Olivia bringing my parents into this hurts.

I'm about to reply when Kai interrupts, his words so loud and out of place that we all go quiet. "I'M IN LOVE WITH PENELOPE!"

"What?" Olivia and I ask in unison. Everyone on the beach is facing us now—Danny's beer can frozen halfway to his mouth,

Romina and Myriah whispering behind raised hands. "I knew it," Katie says. Myriah grins, gives me a discreet thumbs-up.

"Fuck," Kai says, running a hand through his hair. He shrugs, an embarrassed smile on his face. I can't tell if he's faking the embarrassment or the smile, but I know he's faking everything else. "I just . . . That's what's happening here, okay?" He tucks his hands in his pockets, looking down at the ground like he's some ashamed schoolboy. "It's all my fault, all right? I'm so sorry, Olivia. But don't blame Penelope. This isn't her fault. I kissed her because I'm in love with her. And now you all know."

He's laying it on a little thick. But maybe this is the best way. Olivia and Jordan don't want us back—they've got each other. And I can't watch them together without something to show for my awful mistake. I need Kai. And he needs me. It won't have to be forever. Just long enough to save face, to make everyone forget about our mistake, to show our friends they're right: we're not horrible people. All I can hope for is that Kai is right—that maybe seeing us happy together will make Olivia and Jordan realize they want us back.

"Well," Olivia says. There's a small smile on her face that is honestly more confusing than everything else. "Then I guess it's all sorted out."

"This is so messed up," Jordan says. "If you were in love with my girlfriend, you should have told me. I would have . . ." He cuts himself off. He would have what? I don't want to think about the end of that sentence. I don't like this assumption that I'm someone—something—the boys can claim or trade. Like I don't have a say. "How long has this been a thing?" Jordan stands up, coming face-to-face with Kai.

I'm trying to read his expression, his body language, figure out what his reaction means, how it relates to his feelings for me.

"I don't know," Kai says, running a hand through his hair. "Like kinda forever?"

Jordan's fists are clenched, his shoulders rigid. Is he jealous? Is this working?

"Jordan, please," I say at the same time Olivia says: "Jordan, sit back down. It's not worth it."

And he does. He turns away from Kai and goes back to Olivia, sitting down next to her in the beach chair. She snakes an arm through his, pulling him close. Like she owns him.

Fine. I can play this game too.

I take a step closer to Kai. And then I take his hand in mine and fold myself into his arms like I belong there.

NOW

"SO ARE YOU GUYS, LIKE ... together now?" Olivia is laughing, and the sound of it mixed with the smoke from the fire, the warm beer sitting heavy in my stomach, and the clammy feeling of Kai's hand is making me slightly dizzy. The look that comes to Jordan's face makes me feel like I might cry. His mouth is open and his forehead wrinkled, but it's his eyes that get me—they look betrayed. Like maybe I've just made everything worse.

But he's with Olivia now. Isn't he?

Kai's arm tightens around me, and I try not to flinch. "Yeah," he says. "We're together."

"This is so epic!" Danny holds up a hand for Kai to high-five, and when Kai doesn't let go of me, Katie swoops in, smacking her palm against his.

"I'm getting out of here." Jordan stands so abruptly he accidentally knocks over his chair. "I don't need to see this shit." He turns and walks quickly back toward the path in the trees, pulling his hoodie up over his head. I want to chase after him, but I know I can't.

Olivia sighs heavily, her smile gone. She stares at Kai for a minute, her eyes narrowed, and then she flips around and scampers up the beach after Jordan. Olivia isn't supposed to be the one who gets to comfort him. This is all wrong. I watch as they disappear into the trees, my heart in my throat.

Once they're out of sight, I try to wriggle out of Kai's arms, but he holds on, nodding toward all the other people who are still sitting around us in the camping chairs, watching intently. I need to get out of here. I want to be alone, want to stop touching Kai, want to be somewhere I can process everything that's just happened.

"I need to get home," I say, trying to unclench my hand from Kai's, but his grip is like a claw.

"Okay, let's go."

"No," I say. "I mean, I'm leaving."

"Babe," he says, leaning in closer to me. "Let's get out of here together."

I don't like that he's calling me *babe*. It's what Jordan always called me, and the sound of it stings. And I know couples leave parties together all the time, but the implication that we're going to hook up again makes me uncomfortable. With Jordan and Olivia gone, pretending like this feels so strange, like we're performing a play without an audience. Still, I know with the way news travels around school, we have to keep this up in front of everyone or we'll be caught in the time it takes to send a text.

"Fine." I squeeze his hand harder and start pulling him up the beach. "Let's go home."

Kai turns around, saluting the rest of the partygoers with his free hand. "See ya later, buddies. Happy birthday, Danny!" He's still so cheerful and it infuriates me. I keep dragging him away and he stumbles a bit in the sand.

Once we're on the path under the cover of the trees, he finally lets go of my hand. I stretch my fingers, rubbing at them to bring back circulation. Kai takes his phone out of his pocket and turns on the flashlight as we walk.

"Oh my god," I say. I feel electric all of a sudden, alert from the *wrongness* of everything. "So we're doing this. Are we actually doing this?"

"Yeah," Kai says. "I mean, yeah. There's no turning back now."

Kai is right. We can't take back what just happened—can't unsay the words we said. The only way out of this mess is through it. We just have to stay together for long enough that it feels realistic, and then we can break up.

"But we . . ." I pause, trying to think of the best way to phrase it. "Do you think we'll be able to pull this off? We don't really . . . get along." The only thing worse than faking this would be getting found out.

Kai laughs softly, the flashlight casting shadows on his face. "It'll be okay. I'm a good actor."

We walk in silence for a few minutes, and then soon we're at the trailhead, where all the cars are parked. Jordan's car is gone, but Olivia's green buggy is still here, and I feel a swooping sickness as I realize that means they left together.

"Let me drive you home," Kai says. "You've been drinking."

"I had a beer."

"That's a beer more than I had." His words feel like a criticism again, and it makes my skin prickle. Still, I follow him to his car. A part of me wants Jordan to see my car parked on the side of the road tomorrow morning when he brings Olivia back for hers. A part of me is that petty.

Once we're driving, I turn to him. "So, we should probably have some ground rules."

"Okay," he says.

"Like, I just think this all happened so suddenly and I want to talk about it."

"Okay, let's talk."

"Okay," I say. "Well, you're not really saying anything."

He glances at me with a wry smile. "You're doing enough talking for the both of us, babe."

I bristle at the word. "Don't call me that."

"What's wrong with *babe*?"

I pause for a second—it feels too personal to tell Kai the truth. But the thing is, he already knows what's wrong—if he stopped thinking about himself for just a minute he would remember all the times he's heard that word come out of Jordan's mouth. "Jordan calls me that."

The road is dark and winding, thick trees lining either side of the car. There are no streetlights out here by the lake, but we've all driven these roads so many times we have them memorized. Kai is drumming his fingers against the steering wheel even though there's no music. It strikes me then how alone we are—just the two of us on a dark road in the middle of nowhere. I'm not sure why I got so easily into this car with Kai after what happened between us at the party.

"All right," he says after a minute. "Then what can I call you? Sweetie? Shnookums?"

"Anything besides *babe*." I don't want this thing with Kai, whatever it is, to ruin the memory of what I had with Jordan.

Those memories are special; they're real. This game we're playing right now is just that: a game.

"My precious?" he asks, and I swat his arm.

"Not that either."

"Okay, so what are the rules?" he asks. "How long are we doing this for?"

We're on a busier street now, a few scattered houses and stores: all places that remind me of Jordan. I have to turn away when we drive by *our tree*. We pass the Upper Crust on the left, and I think back to the horrible conversation I had there with Jordan just yesterday: the sharp, acidic smell from the dumpsters as he told me he didn't want to be with me, how pathetic I felt to be turned away. The memory makes something in my stomach tighten. This thing with Kai has to work.

"We just have to stay together long enough to get us out of this mess."

"Long enough that it feels believable," Kai says.

"Then we stage a big fight. Something loud and messy and heartbreaking." Before I can stomp it down, the image is in my head again: Jordan and me in front of Sleeping Beauty Castle, his arm around my back, kissing me like I'm the only girl in the world. "Disneyland!" I say. "At the senior trip. I need to be back with Jordan by then. I've been looking forward to it all year."

"Of course you have," he says. "How cute." His voice does not sound like he thinks it's cute.

I scowl at him. "This is our best chance. And if I don't get Jordan back, well, then . . . at least we'll still look less terrible in the eyes of our friends." The idea of not getting Jordan back is too horrible to think about, and I push it away.

"Aw, you always look terrible in *my* eyes," Kai says.

"Can you not make jokes like that at a time like this?" I say. "You're making it really hard to pretend I like you."

"You *don't* like me," Kai says, leaning closer. "You *love* me."

"Just because you said you loved me doesn't mean I'm going to say it back."

Kai barks out a laugh. "Ouch, Penelope."

I think about my conversation with Myriah, how quickly she had assumed Kai and I were in love. I'd told her we were meant to be, that we were written in the stars. But *love*? That word feels a little too much to say out loud.

"Well, you could have been more subtle about it," I say. "Instead of shouting it out to the whole beach." We're in my neighborhood now, houses spread out between the trees, redwoods casting long shadows across the road.

He laughs again, a harsh, unfriendly sound. "I was trying to help you."

"Yeah, well, now I'm stuck with you!"

"I'm stuck too, Penelope! You're not exactly a picnic. You think that was fun for me? Proclaiming my love to you like in some Shakespearean tragedy? That was scary as shit. I went out on a limb for you. All that stuff Olivia said. I just . . . I wanted her to know someone cares about you."

His words make me feel like I'm going to cry. It's the fact that he's only saying it to be nice. That Olivia is right. I don't want Kai to have real feelings for me—that's not what hurts. What hurts is that he's the only one who stood up to Olivia, and he was telling a lie.

"If I say I love you back, it might push Jordan away." There's a mosquito bite on my thigh, and I dig my fingernail into it. "I want him to be jealous, not hopeless."

Kai pulls into the driveway, turning off the engine. It's so quiet in the car all of a sudden that I can hear my ragged breathing as I try to stay calm.

"Fine," he says. "You don't have to say it. You don't love me. I get it."

"Well, obviously I don't love you."

"Okay, so rule number one: you don't have to say you love me."

"Rule number two," I say. "No kissing."

"What? But we've already kissed."

"Yeah, and look how that messed everything up. If we kiss again, we'll probably set off a nuclear winter or something."

"Fine," he says. "No kissing."

"It's for the good of the planet."

"We're environmentalists."

"Rule number three," I say. "You have to apologize for Pukey Penelope."

"But that name is so much *fun*," he whines.

"*Kai.*"

"Fine. You know I'm sorry about it. I was a stupid kid. I didn't think it would be so *catchy*."

"Rule number four," I say. "If either of us wants out at any time, we're done."

"So the second dreamy Jordan gives you a dreamy smile. Got it."

I bristle at his words. Of course he would try to get one last barb in; even though we're on the same side right now, we'll never really be a team. "If you're going to be mean like that, I'm not doing this."

"Okay, how about this?" he says. "Rule number five: we stop hating each other."

"I don't know about that one," I say, opening the door. "You're way too easy to hate."

"No kiss good night?" he asks.

I slam the car door in his face.

NOW

KAI AND I TEXT LATE into the night, trying to hash out the details of the plan. We confirm we're going to stage our big breakup at Disneyland—somewhere memorable so the story will travel fast.

How about on the top of Splash Mountain? I suggest. It's more of a joke, really, because I don't want to go on a water ride that will force me to be soggy when I'm supposed to be celebrating my eventual freedom from him.

But when Kai refuses, it makes me want to go through with it, just to be combative. You'll never get me on anything that high up, Penelope, he says. It's barbaric.

Kai explains his theory that it's possible for the logs you sit in to flip upside down and plummet you to your death. He won't listen to the laws of physics.

Maybe that's a reason we can break up, I suggest. Because you'll refuse to go on that ride with me.

Maybe, he says. Let's workshop it.

But until then, we have lots more to figure out. We make a tentative plan to have dinner one night at his house, taking lots of pictures of ourselves cooking, which I know may end in bloodshed but will be worth it for the gram. And next weekend is the Fourth of July. We're all supposed to be spending the night at Romina's family cabin on the other side of the lake. Kai and I need to go there together, have to show up as a united front, as if spending an entire night with each other isn't going to be a nightmare.

We've got to carpool to the cabin, I text him. And we have to be sickeningly adorable together.

Sickening sounds about right, he says.

We have to touch each other a lot.

Unfortunate.

And say nice things about each other.

Torture.

I'm serious, Kai!

I know, he says. I will rave about your beauty in front of Jordan, okay? Don't worry.

The thing is, we can make all the plans in the world, but I

don't actually know if we're still invited. I text Romina to find out, crossing my fingers that maybe our scheme and Myriah's thumbs-up on the beach will mean everything is fine. Are we still on for the 4th of July?

The three dots appear indicating she's typing; then they disappear. She's taking her time formulating a response. Finally, they appear again and her text comes through. Well now that Olivia and Jordan are a thing, it's not as weird, right? If you guys are down, it's cool. Lots of new couples!

I stare at the words on the screen: now that Olivia and Jordan are a thing. Before I can help it, I'm picturing them together at the cabin, snuggled up under a quilt on the couch, making out beneath the fireworks, frolicking together in the stupid water, taking adorable sun-drenched photos.

Well if all the couples are going, I text back, biting hard on the inside of my cheek, Kai and I wouldn't miss it.

The next morning, I get an email from Scoops saying I've been offered a job, and they want me to come in and start training. I'm surprised for a second that Sarah didn't throw my application away—if I were her, I would have tossed it the moment I left.

It feels great to have a new purpose: this plan with Kai, and now the job. For the first time in days, I'm feeling tentatively optimistic.

I take my time getting ready in the morning, watching a video on YouTube to learn how to do a crown braid. If I can channel some of my energy into looking my best, maybe I won't have to think so much about how screwed up last night was.

Then I hear voices downstairs—my mom laughing a little too loudly about something—and my stomach sinks. There's another guy here.

I'll just have to sneak past them. I'm especially not in the mood to pretend right now—not when I'm currently faking everything else in my life.

I tiptoe down the stairs, climbing deftly over the one that creaks, and make my way toward the front hallway. The voices are coming from the kitchen, and when I get to it, I try to run past, but my mom calls out to me.

"Penelope, come meet Steve!" *Steve.* It's such a middle-aged-man name. I can picture him immediately—probably balding or divorced with three kids. My mom is still in her thirties. She's way too hot for this.

I go into the kitchen and there he is. I'm not far off. He's wearing a jacket and a white button-down, and although he's got a full head of hair, it's going a little gray. Mom is at the counter pouring some coffee, and even Seb is here too, sitting at the table, eating forkfuls of pancakes. When he sees me, his eyes widen in a *help me* expression.

"Steve made pancakes," Mom says.

"Hey, kiddo!" the man—Steve—says like I'm a child.

"I'm not hungry," I say. And then, "I'm going out."

I turn away from the kitchen and head toward the front door. I really don't want to play happy family with some guy my mom probably won't ever see again. And I don't want to watch her pretend everything is okay with all of us—this charade with Steve as if we usually eat breakfast as a family instead of grabbing coffee to go on the way to wherever else we'd rather be.

I escape outside, letting the screen door slam shut behind me. Then I realize the car is missing. All that's parked in the driveway is a black Ford Focus that must belong to Steve. I can't believe I completely forgot Kai dropped me off last night. The car is still at the lake. It's too long to walk to Scoops, and also way too hot already. There's heat radiating off the driveway, so the air almost looks like it's shimmering, and it's only ten a.m. Today is going to be brutal.

There's a creaking behind me as the screen door opens, and my mom is standing there. "Been wondering where my car went. You're lucky I don't have work this morning."

"I got a ride with someone last night," I say. "Sorry. I'll bring it back."

"Well, maybe Steve could take you. It would give you two a chance to get to know each other." She turns and calls, "Steve!" behind her and he appears in the doorway before I've had the chance to object.

"I don't want to get to know him," I say.

"It's no skin off my back," Steve says with an infuriating smile. "We could all go together. Where's it parked?"

"No," I say, and then feel a little guilty when I see Steve's smile falter. But there is no way I am getting into a car with him. "A friend is coming to get me, okay? It's fine. You can finish breakfast."

"Penelope," Mom says with a tired smile. "We'll talk about this later, okay?"

"I bet we will."

My mom and Steve disappear back inside, and I realize with a painful lurch that there's no one I'm on good enough terms with to ask for a ride. Well, if Kai and I are—whatever we are, then he can come get me. He's the one who forced me not to drive last night anyway.

My car is still at the lake, I text him.

He responds a few seconds later. Yeah, and?

I growl and punch a reply into my phone. Yeah, and you're taking me to get it.

So pushy, he replies. But then: Be there soon.

A few minutes later, his Jeep pulls up my driveway. He's got a pair of Ray-Ban sunglasses perched on his head, a green T-shirt, and swim trunks patterned with whales.

"Hey, crumpet," he says as I climb in. "Miss me already?"

In the time I've been standing in the sun, my makeup has practically melted off my face, and I'm self-conscious about all the places sweat is pooling on my body. But there's no way I was going to go back inside to Mom and Steve.

"Just drive," I say for an answer. He laughs and accelerates, and then we're zooming down the street. The wind feels so good, like finally I can breathe again.

"You're in a chipper mood this morning," he says, his voice flat.

"Yeah, well, I had this crazy dream that you and I were dating."

I think again of Jordan's face as I took Kai's hand, how he stormed off into the dark and Olivia followed him. Everything about last night is so messed up.

"You're always having dreams about me," Kai says.

"Don't get too excited," I say.

We cruise through town then back down the winding road toward the lake. It really is a beautiful day, now that we're driving. I catch a glimpse of the water through a break in the trees, and it's sparkling and silver in the morning light. I'm so relieved to be out of that house, away from Mom, even if it means I'm here with Kai.

"You're quieter than usual," he says after a pause. "Are you having doubts about the plan?"

"Obviously, I have doubts about the plan," I snap back at him, and then I feel bad. He's actually trying to be nice. "And it's my mom."

"What Olivia said to you last night was way over the line," he says.

I let out a bitter laugh. "Yeah, it was. My mom means well. Things between us are just . . . complicated."

"Complicated how?"

And for some reason I tell him. Maybe it's because he was the one who stood up for me last night when Olivia was tearing me down.

"My dad left when I was two," I say. "Right after Seb was born. And I don't think she's ever recovered."

My dad was a guest lecturer at the university where my mom got her degree—much older than she was when they met and, it turns out, already married. She didn't know until it was too late. And once his wife found out, he bailed on us completely. Major dick move.

"She always talks about how he was the love of her life," I continue. "Even though, it's like—how could you love someone who does something like that to you? I want her to grow a backbone, you know?"

"I don't know," Kai says. "My mom has a backbone, and I'm not sure it's any better."

I turn away from the lake and look at him. "Your mom is amazing."

I feel myself flush as soon as I've said it, because even though it's true, it's too honest, too vulnerable, and he might tease me for it.

"Did I ever tell you why we moved to the mainland?" he asks.

"No, we didn't exactly . . . hang out much back then." I think back to the first time we talked, on the playground in the winter of fifth grade a few days after Kai arrived. I had actually liked him at first—had actually thought we were going to be friends. I was still quiet and invisible and lonely back then, spent most of my time at school reading—the Song of the Lioness, Harry Potter, Lord of the Rings. I liked series, stories I could sink my teeth into, characters that could stay my friends for as many pages as possible because I didn't have any friends yet in real life.

We'd all noticed Kai immediately. January in our part of California doesn't exactly get that cold, and he showed up in a full snowsuit, like that kid from *A Christmas Story*—puffy coat and pompom hat. It was so embarrassing. It made me like him more.

A few days later, he talked to me. "How come you're sitting over here all alone?"

I didn't notice him walking up to me on the playground because I was so absorbed in my book. When I looked up at him, I blinked a few times, adjusting to the brightness of the real world. He had a knit Patagonia beanie pulled low over his black hair, not the embarrassing pompom hat from his first day; already he was learning to blend in.

"I'm reading."

"Oh." I liked the sound of his voice. It was well-rounded, like he'd probably be a good singer. "You're not gonna play tag with everyone?"

He motioned behind him to where Olivia, Myriah, Romina, and Katie were running around on the field. I could see Jordan in the distance standing at the top of the big slide with Danny Scott. I didn't want to tell him I wasn't invited to play, so I shot his question back at him. "Well, how come you're not over there?" I pointed to Jordan and Danny.

Kai shivered. "Too high up."

"The big slide is not even that high."

"Everything is too high up," Kai said. "Even the little slide."

"You're scared of the little slide?"

"You won't tell anyone, will you?" His face went a little pink, like maybe this wasn't the first impression he was trying to make.

"Nope, it can be our secret."

"Cool." He sat down next to me on the bench. "What are you reading, anyway?"

I was reading *The Giver*, and I held it out to him. "It's about memory. It's this world in the future where nobody can remember anything."

He turned the book over in his hands and looked at the back. "Is it good?"

"Yeah. Do you want to borrow it? I've already read it before. Like three times."

"Really?" He pulled the book a little closer into his chest. I'd never seen someone else treat a book like it was a precious object. Usually, the other kids in class threw them, ripped and broken, into the bottom of their backpacks, complaining loudly about how they hated to read. "I'll bring it back," he said.

And for the first time since elementary school started, I'd had a glimmer of hope. All I'd ever wanted was a friend—a real one, who wasn't just a character in one of my books.

Then we all learned that Kai moved here from Hawaii, and suddenly everyone came at him with questions: Do you know how to surf? Have you hiked a volcano? Did you ever swim with sea turtles? He became the center of attention so quickly, became the coolest, most interesting kid in our class and stayed that way. From then on, he'd ignored me—until, of course, he'd made up the nickname that had ruined everything.

Obviously, Kai never returned my book.

"My dad is still back on Maui," he says now. "He cheated on my mom with his fucking assistant. It's a small town, and everybody knew."

We're at the lake now, and I see my car parked up ahead. Kai pulls up next to it. Olivia's car is missing, which fills me with both relief and dread. A part of me wanted them to catch me alone with Kai. Another part felt sick at the thought of seeing them together.

Kai turns off the car and faces me, continuing his story. "Then my mom decides she wants a divorce. So they split, but we're still on this small island and everybody knows, and everyone is giving her these awful, pitying looks everywhere she goes. So she just has to get out, get as far away from there as she can."

"Your mom was brave to leave like that and go somewhere totally new."

"I mean, I get why she had to do it, and why she took me and my brother with her, but it made everything so much harder, you know? I had to leave all my friends and my dad and my community behind, and I know it's so unfair to be mad at her for it because my dad is the one who did something fucked up, not her. But I kinda wish we could have stayed there. I wish she could have forgiven him."

"I'm sorry," I say. I'm surprised he's telling me all these details; sharing a story that's so personal.

"Tommo and I have always tried to, like . . . parent-trap them," he says with a laugh. "We fly back to Maui to visit my dad and try to convince my mom to come with us, but she never will. She hasn't been back to Hawaii since."

"That's messed up," I say. "I mean, Hawaii is her home."

"Yeah, I'm so mad at my dad for taking Maui away from her. But sometimes I wish she wasn't so stubborn."

Now that the car has stopped, it's hot again, the sun beating down hard on the back of our necks. The leather seat feels slippery beneath my bare thighs. I know now is the time to get out of the Jeep, but for some reason I don't want this conversation to end. It feels good to talk about this. It feels good to know that someone else is going through something similar to what I am.

"My mom always brings guys home," I say. "There was a guy there this morning. He made pancakes. That's why I was in a bad mood."

"Yeah, pancakes are disgusting." He smiles so I know it's a joke.

I sigh, fanning myself with my hand. "It's just—I'm not opposed to my mom dating, or even hooking up with guys, even though it's gross. It's just frustrating because she brings them home, tries to play nice with me in front of them, and then she pushes them away."

"That's fucked," he says.

"I know." I'm completely melting now, sweat dripping off me in the grossest of ways. I've got to get out of the car. "Anyway, thanks for driving me back here." I climb down out of the Jeep.

"Hey, wait," he says. "Aren't we swimming?"

"What?"

"It's hot as shit out right now. We're at the lake."

"I don't have a bathing suit."

"Skinny-dipping?" He wiggles his eyebrows.

"I'm not getting naked in front of you and all of the innocent people down on that beach."

He laughs. "It was worth a try." But then he unbuckles his seat belt and jumps down out of the Jeep. "Come on. Just go in your clothes."

I tentatively touch the crown braid I spent so long making this morning. It's already wilting, flyaway hairs frizzing around my face from the humidity. I look down at myself. I'm wearing a pair of jean shorts and a black tank top and my nicest bra—the one I bought at a fancy boutique in LA when Olivia and I took that trip there with her family. It's not the kind of bra you submerge in the lake.

Besides, I'm already late for my first day at Scoops. And I don't want to spend any more time with Kai right now than I have to.

"I have to go," I say, opening the door to my car. "I have to be somewhere."

Kai sighs. "Your loss, Penelope."

"Sorry." I don't know why I say it. It's just that the look of disappointment that flashes across Kai's face makes me feel for a second like I'm disappointed in myself too.

THEN

JUNIOR YEAR–OCTOBER

THE PARKING LOT AT school is too small to fit everyone's cars, so if you're running late, it only makes everything worse. It's early October—a month into school—one of those perfect crisp fall days where you can taste the air. But I've been circling the lot for five minutes and I'm already ten minutes late for homeroom.

I decide to give up and drive out onto the winding road that wraps around campus, looking for street parking. Unfortunately, driving isn't my strong suit, and parallel parking even less. I've been trying and failing to park in the same spot for another five minutes when Jordan walks by and knocks on my window.

At first, I don't want to roll it down. I wonder for a minute how tinted the window is, if he can tell I'm the one inside, the one so pathetic she can't even park her car—so frazzled about being late she's near to tears. But then I remember the stickers my mom put on the bumper—FLORENCE'S GARDEN EMPORIUM, CO-EXIST, MICKEY MOUSE. Jordan knows this is me. Besides, you don't turn down a chance to talk to Jordan Parker, even if you're at your worst.

I roll down the window.

"Everything okay, Harris?" He grins wide, leaning into his arms on the roof of the passenger side. I can see his muscles through his T-shirt.

I hastily wipe my eyes. "I'm so late. And I can't park this stupid car."

"You want me to try?"

At first I want to tell him no. I don't want to be the silly girl who needs a boy to rescue her. But the idea of Jordan Parker inside my car, his hands on my steering wheel, is too tempting to turn down.

"You don't mind?" I ask, stepping out of the car.

"Nah, I'm a pro."

He slides into the driver's seat and motions for me to climb back in on the passenger side. But once I'm seated and he's behind the wheel, he doesn't try to park the car. Instead, he puts it into drive and cruises down the street, away from the school.

"Wait," I say. "Where are you going?"

"Let's do something fun," he says. And then he turns to me and his beaming smile wipes any doubt from my mind, dries the protest right off my tongue. I don't care that I'm officially cutting class, that it could hurt my chances of college, that I am technically being kidnapped. Because I have waited my whole life to be in Jordan's passenger seat, someone worth cutting class with, someone boys find pretty enough to take on adventures.

I don't know why I've caught his interest right now—if it's because he's specifically interested in me at all, or if I'm just a girl with a car, an opportunity for something more interesting than school. But I know I look good today. Since it's the start of the year, we're all still trying our hardest. Everything we do now in these first months sets the tone for the entire year. I've been watching makeup tutorials all summer—learned how to contour from YouTube, how to make my nose look smaller and my cheekbones look sharper, how to overline my lips so I look like an Instagram filter in real life. And maybe Jordan has finally noticed.

He parks the car in town, right in front of Scoops, and then climbs out, running around to the other side to open my door. I've never had someone open a door for me, and it seems so romantic. Suddenly, it feels like we're on a date.

"You want some sorbet?" He nods toward the sign. "Whenever I'm upset, I always get sorbet."

"I'm not actually upset," I say. "I just can't park."

"Still," he says.

It turns out Scoops is closed at eight a.m., so we go to the corner store instead and buy Popsicles, taking them down by the edge of the lake. I'm anxious the whole time—about getting caught, about someone asking why we're not in class, or seeing one of my mom's friends out running errands. But the thought that we're doing something bad makes it even more fun. Being with Jordan right now feels dangerous.

"I can't believe it's still so hot," Jordan says, licking his arm where a drop of Popsicle has dribbled down to his elbow. "I'm ready for winter."

"I can't wait for Halloween." Halloween is my favorite holiday. I love getting the chance to dress up, spending days putting together a costume and taking pictures of cool makeup looks. Except usually I get too embarrassed to wear a costume to school.

"I like Thanksgiving," he says. "My family is huge. All the cousins and aunts and uncles and everybody comes over, and it's, like, complete mayhem. Mashed potatoes everywhere."

I grin at his description, picturing a bunch of mini Jordans running around. It sounds so different than the quiet Thanksgivings I'm used to at my house: my mom, Seb, and I eating Chinese takeout in front of the TV.

"No mashed potatoes for me, though," Jordan says. "I'm lactose intolerant. It's grisly. Like absolutely rank."

"Gross," I say, but I'm laughing because I can't help it. Sometimes it's unfair that guys can make jokes about disgusting stuff and we'll still think they're hot no matter what. I could never make a joke about stomach issues to a guy.

"Your family sounds fun," I say instead, changing the subject back to better topics.

"They're the best." He breaks his Popsicle stick in two, spinning the pieces around in his hand. "My parents are so in love, it's sick." He laughs, sticking his tongue out in a disgusted way. "You ever seen your parents make out? I guarantee mine make out more."

"Oh," I say, feeling my face flame. There's just so much to get into. I don't want to bring the mood down, admit to Jordan that I don't know my dad—that I've seen my mom kissing different men over and over again. This is the first real conversation we've ever had, and I don't want to ruin it. So instead, I nod. "Um, yeah. My parents are always kissing too."

"So gross, right?" Jordan laughs. Then after a moment: "How come we never hang out, Harris?"

"We do hang out," I answer, and it's true. We go to the mall with our friends, to the lake and mini golf, and sometimes parties in Kai's barn. But obviously we don't talk. Olivia is always there, taking charge, speaking for me because I'm too shy around Jordan to speak for myself.

"Nah, but not like this. You're pretty cool, you know that?"

My phone buzzes then, and I see a text from Olivia. Where the eff are you?!

Jordan and I got popsicles, I text back, and it makes me feel so powerful.

We return to school then, walking through the doors together just in time for second period. We go our separate ways, him to English and me to bio, but that moment we're together in front of everyone is enough. If everything we do right now sets the precedent for the rest of the year, then I am officially the girl who cut class with Jordan.

This is the coolest I've ever been.

NOW

WHEN I GET TO SCOOPS, Sarah is waiting for me.

"You're late," she says, and I check my phone to see it's five minutes past my given arrival time.

"Sorry," I say. "I had to get my car from the lake. So where's the manager? I'm supposed to be training."

"I'm the manager." She puts her hands on her hips.

I stare at her for a second, trying to make sense of everything. Why would Sarah have picked me for this job? Maybe I was the only one who applied. It's not like Scoops is a place people are dying to spend their time.

"What?" she asks when I still haven't said anything.

"Nothing," I say. "I'm just surprised. Don't you hate me or something?"

"Honestly, Penny, I don't think about you that much. Go put your bag in the back room and grab an apron."

We spend the next hour going over everything I'll need to know. Sarah shows me how to use the cash register. She points out which flavors are the best and which ones to avoid at all costs (although having grown up on Scoops ice cream, I already know), and the proper technique to make the perfect scoop, round and fluffy and perfectly centered on the cone.

By the end of the hour, my arm is sore.

"One last thing," she says, bringing me over to the storage freezer in the back room. "Never ever order a banana split."

"What, why?"

She opens the freezer door and I see three giant clear tubs of what look like they were once bananas, but appear to have frozen into a congealed black lump. It's like a rotten block of banana ice.

"We're not allowed to throw them away," Sarah says. "I swear there is mold in here. Best to avoid it."

At around noon, the store gets busy. I can feel the sun blazing hot through the windows, and I'm glad to be inside in the air conditioning. I wonder briefly if Kai ever went for that swim in the lake. I'm not sure I would have gone alone if I were him. I always feel awkward doing things by myself, like all the strangers around me must be watching, thinking I have no friends.

I picture myself at Disneyland again, waiting alone in a single-rider line and feel the shame of that moment so fiercely I have to lean my head on the cold glass of the ice-cream case.

"Um, everything okay?" Sarah asks.

I pull back. "It's just hot."

"Yeah, this summer is scorching." She pauses for a second, as if debating whether to continue. "Hey, do you remember that summer in fourth grade when we did the Olympics?"

I do remember. That was a brutal summer too, maybe even hotter than this one. My mom had gone on a trip somewhere and she'd left me at Sarah's house for a few days. We'd set up sprinklers in her backyard, filled a kiddie pool from the hose, and invited all the neighborhood kids over to play summer Olympics. Sarah and I pretended we were from countries all over the world, speaking to each other in different accents. "You should hang on to Sarah," my mom said later when I told her about the accents. "She's weird—the weird ones always become the most interesting adults."

I'd had so much fun that summer, but then when we went back to school in the fall, things changed. Sarah had been caught picking her nose and I had become the girl who puked, and instead of turning to each other for comfort, it was like we'd both tried to distance ourselves—too afraid some of the other's humiliation would rub off on us. Then Olivia and I had miraculously become friends, and I'd left Sarah behind, thankful to finally become one of the lucky ones.

"Can you still do a British accent?" I ask now.

"Ay, I reckon I've gotten even better at it," she says in a full accent, a voice that sounds remarkably like Captain Jack Sparrow. Then she immediately turns red and spins away from me, busying herself at the cash register.

I know Olivia would make fun of her in this moment. The thought comes to me surely and immediately that what Sarah has done is shameful and embarrassing and I should feel bad for her. But something stops me from saying anything. Maybe it's because I've felt that way about myself for the past week.

So instead I answer her back in a British accent of my own. "Pip pip, cheerio."

She turns around and laughs. "You were always terrible at accents."

"Hey!" I'm suddenly indignant, but I can't help but laugh too because I know she's right. "Okay, fine. So maybe I'm not destined for the stage."

"Eh, as long as we don't do *My Fair Lady* next year for the musical, you'd be fine. Your Eliza Doolittle would cause ear bleeds."

"Come on, Dover!" I shout in the worst accent I can muster. "Move your bloomin' arse!" It's a famous quote from the show and I don't know what compels me to say it so loudly.

"Fuck, that was horrifying," Sarah says, tucking a blue strand of hair behind one ear. "If you ever use that voice again, you have to eat a freezer banana."

"I'm not going ten feet near a freezer banana," I say.

"That's what you think. Newbies always have to make the banana splits. Them's the rules."

"I'm allergic to bananas," I say, which is a total lie and we both know it. But Sarah lets it slide. It's so weird to be joking around like this, to actually be having . . . fun with the person I've tried the last few years to avoid. I can't help but worry that Jordan or somebody else will walk by and see us together, that if I'm caught laughing with Sarah, it'll only make everything else in my life worse.

"Seriously, though," Sarah says. "You should help out with the musical next year."

"No way," I say. I love listening to show tunes, but being in a show? Hard pass. "I don't do theater."

"You just quoted classic Rodgers and Hammerstein. It kinda sounds like you do." She pauses. "Anyway, I've seen those annoying photos Olivia is always posting. Like, god knows I try to avoid them, but they're everywhere. The tennis court shit? You're actually really good in front of a camera."

"No, I'm not," I say, turning red. "I just do that to help her. She's an amazing photographer, but I'm not, like, actually talented."

Sarah pulls out her phone and flips through it. "Get over yourself and take a compliment, dude. Okay, like this one . . . oh, fuck." She stops scrolling and then flips her phone around so I can see it. "Sorry, this just popped up." There's a picture of Olivia and Jordan on Olivia's Instagram. He's smiling with his eyes closed tight and Olivia is kissing his cheek. It hits me like a punch to the gut.

Sarah flips it back around and reads the caption. "'When this guy smiles, he becomes the sun.'" She looks up at me. "Wow, that is the stupidest shit I've ever heard."

Olivia was always posting pictures like this with Kai when they were together, writing captions she thought were deep— snippets of song lyrics, nonsensical phrases meant to intrigue, clues other people were supposed to spend their time decoding. Once, she posted a picture of Kai with just the whale emoji and we all spent days trying to figure out her message.

It hurts that she's doing this same thing again, but with Jordan.

"Are these idiots together now?" Sarah asks. "What about you?"

It's sweet of her to ask, and I'm surprised there's a small part of her that seems to actually care about my well-being. I'm not sure I would have asked if our situations were reversed.

"Yeah, they're together." Suddenly, there are tears in my eyes. I really don't want Sarah to see the emotion on my face. "It's no big deal," I say, hoping the hitch in my breath doesn't give me away. "I'm dating Kai now."

"The Kai who you . . . hate?" Sarah asks, an eyebrow raised.

"Oh, is that what I told you?" I wipe my nose, blink, try to force the tears back in. "I must have been confused. Kai is my boyfriend."

I'm in the bin candy aisle at the local market the next day when I bump into Myriah.

"I should have expected you here," I say. Myriah is obsessed with bin candy. Whenever she's upset about something, she always buys herself a big bag. The fact that she's here now means something must be wrong. "Is everything okay?" I ask.

She picks up the pair of plastic tongs and reaches into the sour strawberries. Myriah is vegan, so she's done her research. She knows which candies are acceptable (Sour Patch Kids) and which to avoid at all costs (gummy bears). "I'm okay. Of course I'm okay. Why wouldn't I be okay?" Her face has gone bright red.

"Myriah," I say. "You can talk to me."

"Are you coming to the cabin this weekend?" she asks.

"Yeah, Romina said I could still come, so . . ." At the mention of Romina's name, Myriah's face turns an even darker shade of red.

"Okay, good." She looks behind us, peeks over the edge of the shelf to make sure no one is around and eavesdropping. Whatever she's about to tell me, she clearly doesn't want an audience. "So, um . . . I didn't tell you the other night because, well, you had your own issues. But . . . Romina and I kissed at Jordan's party."

Of all the things I was expecting her to say, this wasn't one of them. But it is the best kind of surprising. "Wait, that's amazing," I say.

"Is it?" she asks.

"Of course it is!"

"I think I really, really like her." She eats a sour strawberry. "I mean, I *know* I really like her. And I think she likes me. But it's such a cliché, right? The two of us. I don't want her to think I like her *just because* we're the only two queer girls in the group, and, like . . . even though we both like girls doesn't mean we automatically like each other—that's not how it works. And I'm just scared to ruin our friendship, you know? I really don't want to mess this up. Besides, I'm so different from Harper."

Romina dated Harper McNulty for all of sophomore year—Harper, who she met at her cello lessons, who collected dead animal skulls and crystals and had tattoos of wildflowers up and down her arms. Harper, who is the complete opposite of the ball of sunshine that is Myriah. But there's a reason they broke up. For how cool we all thought Harper was, she also never wanted Romina to hang out with us, used to get jealous and clingy anytime Myriah was around.

"Have you told Romina how you feel?"

"No, she thinks I like this girl at my dance studio, because I am a pathetic coward."

"You guys will work this out," I say. "You're not Harper. You're Myriah, and that's so much better." I feel horrible then that she's letting me in on this secret, sharing her true feelings with me when I've been feeding her lies. But I can't tell her the truth about Kai. It would ruin everything.

"Thanks, Penny." She puts the plastic tongs back in their holder. "I'm so glad I could talk to you. You're such a good friend."

"I wouldn't go that far," I say, and she bursts out laughing.

NOW

I WAKE UP RIDICULOUSLY EARLY on the Fourth of July, filled with so much anxiety I can't sleep. Kai is coming to pick me up at ten thirty so we can drive to Romina's cabin together, and the predawn hours of the morning feel endless. I know Kai and I sorta faked it at Danny's campfire on the beach, but that was for like five seconds. This will be the first time we'll have to really fake it. Our first big test. And I'm nervous.

Do you think this is a good idea? I text him, before realizing he's probably still asleep. Maybe they don't actually want us there.

He responds a few minutes later. You should stop worrying so much about what everybody else thinks.

I toss my phone onto the bed, suddenly buzzing with anger. How dare Kai tell me how I'm allowed to feel. I grab my phone again and start typing and erasing messages, trying to figure out how to phrase what I mean to say: Are you seriously suggesting . . . of course I care about . . . I can handle . . .

In the end, I don't send anything, and I know Kai can probably see the three dots on the screen as I waffle. Instead, I grab my little red suitcase out of the closet and start throwing clothes into it. I bought a red checkered bathing suit and a pair of bright red heart sunglasses a few months ago, back before this whole mess started. And I want to wear them. I want to take cute pictures, need Jordan to see me in my bathing suit and realize what he's missing out on.

I think that's what makes me maddest of all. I'm not angry with Kai—not really. I'm angry with myself. Because he's right. I do care what people think of me. I care what Jordan thinks of me. I want to go to the cabin so, so badly. More than I want to be there, though, I want them all to *want* me there—for Olivia to be excited when I pull up, like nothing has changed.

Like I didn't ruin everything.

But that's why we're doing this. The only way to get my life back to normal is to put on a brave face and play nice with Kai and rock that bikini like I always planned.

So I text him. Fine. See you later, asshole.

I'm in the kitchen making peanut butter and jelly sand-wiches—I debated not making one for Kai, but decided I'm not cruel enough to starve him—when my mom pads in.

"You're up early." She reaches for the coffeepot. "Don't usually get to see you before work."

"Yeah." I press two slices of bread together and drop them into a plastic sandwich bag. "A bunch of us are going to hang at the lake today. I'm spending the night at Olivia's, okay?" My usual line.

"Well, that sounds fun," she says, filling the pot with water and scooping out some coffee grounds.

"How are things with Steve?" I ask, just to see the look on her face. She turns on the coffeepot and sighs, and then when she looks up at me, she's actually smiling. Like, really smiling. Not the I *ditched him after one date* grimace I was expecting.

"Steve is wonderful. He's such a sweetheart. I'm feeling really good about this one."

"Oh," I say, trying to match her smile. I don't know why I feel so mixed up. "Well, that's good, then."

"I really like him." She ties her hair back into a bun. "Listen— I have to run. Still have to get dressed, and everything has been crazy this week at the hospital. I'll see you tomorrow morning, okay? You'll call if you need anything?" And then she turns and dashes out of the room, back up the stairs.

I know I should be excited that I can get away with going to parties like this so easily—it should feel great to be this free. But a part of me wants her to stick around longer, to ask a few more questions: *When will you be home? Will Olivia's parents be there?*

Most moms would have time for that.

Kai is always late for everything, so by the time he pulls up at eleven thirty, I'm about ready to kill him.

"Let's get this over with," I say, slamming the door to Kai's Jeep when I get in.

He's dressed for the occasion—a pair of red-and-white-striped swim shorts and red sunglasses. We didn't even plan it, and we're matching. It's disgusting.

I want to change into something different, but I know our matching outfits look good. If we want to pull this off, we have to look like the kind of couple who does cute stuff like this—the kind of couple Jordan and I used to be.

You guys always look the same, people used to say when we'd walk down the hallway hand in hand, both of us dark-haired and taller than everyone else in our matching Gonzaga hats. I liked wearing Jordan's number on game days, felt so special that everyone knew we belonged together.

It feels weird re-creating all these memories with Kai.

"Ready to show off our blossoming love?" he asks, grinning.

I throw the extra sandwich at him and am satisfied when it hits his chest, hard. "Ready as I'll ever be."

Kai grabs the sandwich. "Wow, you made this for me?" He's smiling wide, like he's genuinely pleased.

"It's poisoned," I say just to annoy him.

Kai takes a left off my street, and soon we're cruising through town. "Speaking of poison," he says, turning to me. "Next Saturday work for that dinner? I might have accidentally mentioned something to my mom, and now she wants to help us cook."

"Kai," I say, a warning in my voice. "Does she think we're dating?"

"That was the whole point, wasn't it?"

"Fine," I agree. "But I don't like the idea of lying to her." Even though we're lying to everybody else, the idea of Kai's mom getting the wrong idea feels just a little bit worse.

We take another left, and then we're on the winding road that will bring us all the way to the other side of the lake. The cabin is tucked away in the trees, in a remote area with hardly any cell service. It makes it feel like we're in a scary movie. *I would turn back if I were you.*

"This isn't all some big ruse for you to murder me, right?" I ask Kai.

"Nah." He smiles. "That would be way too predictable. It's always the boyfriend."

His use of the word *boyfriend* jolts me, even though I know that's technically what he is in this crazy alternate universe we've found ourselves in.

"If anyone were going to do any murdering around here, it would be Olivia," Kai continues.

"I mean, I guess we would deserve it."

"She's a little scary sometimes," Kai says, and I'm surprised. It's weird that he wants to be with her—that he's trying to get her back—but can make comments like that.

"But you still like her, though," I say, turning toward him.

Kai clears his throat, drumming his fingers on the steering wheel. It takes him a second to answer. "She and I go way back. I would do anything for Liv, you know?" He turns to me and shrugs. "She's just . . . intense. You know that better than any of us."

"*Intense* is a good word," I say, chewing my bottom lip.

"And she's astonishingly hot," he says with a full grin.

"But there's more to it than that, right?" I turn down the music on the stereo. "I mean, we're not doing this whole plan—trying to get you guys back together—just because you think she's hot, right? It has to be deeper than that."

I'm feeling protective all of a sudden, even though I know Olivia doesn't need it. Out of anyone I've ever met, she can take care of herself. But I will fight any guy who tries to use her, that only wants to be with her for her looks. Just because Olivia said those horrible things to me at the campfire doesn't cancel out our years of friendship. I poked the wasp's nest by kissing Kai, so it's my fault I got stung.

"Of course there's more to it," Kai says. "She's Olivia. When she's mean, she's mean. But there's just something about her.

When she likes you, you just . . ." He trails off, and I try to fill in the words for him.

"Feel like you matter, right? Like you're special."

"Yeah. It's like . . . sometimes it's hard to say no to her. I just feel this stupid need to make her happy."

"Me too."

It's weird to be talking about Olivia like this with Kai. It's always been the other way around—late-night talks with Olivia and me on her bed, whispers about their first date, the stupid texts he sends her, how amazing he is at kissing. But I need to remind myself we're in the Upside Down now—this is my new normal.

"Okay," Kai says. "So then tell me what you like about Jordan."

"I'm not gonna tell you that." I bristle at his words. "That's personal." I know I'm being a hypocrite, but I can't help it.

"Oh, so is that how this works?" His tone is still light, but I can tell he's annoyed with me. I would be annoyed with me too. But the truth is I don't know quite what to say. Obviously, Jordan is hot—astonishingly hot, to borrow Kai's words—but that's not why I love him. The reasons I love him are too small on their own—the dimple on his right cheek when he smiles, his perfectly shaped eyebrows, the way he actually got kind of into the musicals we listened to together, how it felt when he pointed at the oak tree in the sidewalk downtown and said it was *ours*. But added together they form the whole of him, the whole of us—Penny and Jordan. The honest answer is that I love Jordan because I've always loved him. I wouldn't know how not to.

"He's a really good person," I say instead.

"Of course he's a good dude. He's my best friend." Kai takes a turn onto a back road, and the ride turns bumpy. Dust clouds us from the open sides of the Jeep, and I wave my hand in front of my face. "But fair is fair," Kai continues. "I want to hear why you like him. There are lots of good dudes out there."

"Are there?" I counter. "I don't know very many."

"Okay, our dads not included."

"Ha," I say. "I forgot I told you about that."

"Actually, my dad just invited us all to come stay with him at the end of the summer," Kai says. "Including my mom."

I sit up in my seat and bring my legs up under me, Kai's request about Jordan mercifully pushed aside. "Really? Is she gonna go?"

"My brother is flying back there from Auburn and he keeps asking my mom to come too. Trying to get the whole fam back together. But she refuses to go. Says she doesn't want to pretend everything is normal because then my dad gets away with how he treated her, you know?"

"I kind of love that," I say. As if I could stan Kai's mom any more.

"Yeah, she's pretty great," Kai says. "Sorry for the wild subject change. I don't even know where that came from. You're just kinda . . . like . . . the only person I've ever told this to. That's weird, right?"

It's very weird, and yet somehow it's not. Sure, Kai and I might not always get along, but in all the ways I would ever seek to destroy him, I think he knows this is sacred. This weird connection between us—our shitty families—is a place we've drawn a truce.

"I think my mom is in *love*," I say, remembering our weird interaction in the kitchen.

"That's awesome!" Kai says. "I'm happy for her."

"Is it?" I stare out the window. "I don't know how I feel about it."

"Is it the pancake guy?" Kai asks. "Think about all the pancakes you'll get out of this."

"I guess so," I say. "Thanks for the optimism." I turn back to him. "This doesn't mean that I'm ever going to start liking you."

He laughs, harsh and abrupt. "Wouldn't dream of it. You're the most stubborn person I've ever met. Don't see you changing your mind anytime soon."

"I'm sorry, I'm the most stubborn? Have you ever met yourself?"

"Pumpkin, you are a million times worse than me."

"Don't call me Pumpkin."

"You're right, wrong holiday. I should keep this Fourth of July–themed. How about Popsicle? Corncob? *Weiner?*"

"If you call me Weiner, I will actually jump out of this moving vehicle."

"Don't hurt yourself, *Weenie.*"

"I swear I will jump."

"Weenie, no!" It almost sounds like he's calling me sweetie, which makes the whole thing even more annoying. I am so frustrated I want to strangle him, but for some reason I can't stop laughing.

He turns the Jeep down Romina's long driveway, and then we're there, her cabin tucked into the trees in front of us.

"This is it," Kai says. "Showtime."

We jump out of the Jeep and start gathering our things together and then Kai grabs my hand. I try to pull away, but he holds tight, a smile plastered on his face. "They're watching us." He motions toward the front of the cabin, and sure enough there are five heads visible through the front window. I feel my stomach tighten with nerves and keep my hand clenched in Kai's, and then paste on a matching smile of my own. We can do this. Make them jealous. Show them what they're missing. *Everyone forgives a good love story.*

I repeat the words in my head as we walk up the driveway, gritting my teeth to keep the smile on my face. The front door opens and then Jordan is standing there, arms folded. When I see him, it occurs to me suddenly that I successfully avoided answering Kai's query earlier: *Tell me what you like about Jordan.* Relief floods through me, but then just as quickly is replaced with something else, something sharp around the edges.

Because I don't know why the answer was something I was trying so hard to avoid.

THEN

OCTOBER–JUNIOR YEAR

WE ALL DECIDE TO DRESS like the boys for the Halloween dance. This requires lots of preparation the day of, texting back and forth to make sure they bring their favorite clothes to school. It doesn't matter that we won't look sexy in our costumes, because wearing the boys' clothes is more important than that: it marks our territory. *These are our boys*, it says. *You can't have them.*

We're at lunch sorting through everything, the boys pulling sweatshirts and hats and flannels out of their backpacks and scattering them all over the table. Everyone wants to dress up like Jordan—to be the *most* special—but it's kind of understood that Olivia will get his clothes. Olivia is always the chosen one.

Kai pulls his signature beanie off his head and kisses it before setting it down on the table. "All right, who wants it? You guys take good care of my baby."

Romina picks it up and hands it to me, her lips quirked. "Penny should dress like you."

"Yeah, that would be hilarious!" Katie says. She grabs Danny's Manchester United jersey off the table and holds it up. "I can be Danny because my boyfriend, Matt, loves this team."

"Oh, Matt loves this team?" Olivia says, laughing. "What else does Matt like?"

"I swear he does!"

"I wish I could look up all of Matt's interests on Instagram." Olivia sighs. "But I guess he doesn't have one."

"Matt thinks social media is rotting our brains and shortening our attention spans and is going to destroy humanity," Katie says. "That's why he doesn't have one."

"Or it's because he's secretly married." Olivia smirks.

"What if he's got a secret identity?" Romina asks. She's still holding Kai's hat, and she tries to hand it to me.

"I'm not dressing like Kai," I say. "I have standards."

"Wow, Penelope thinks she's too good for something," Kai says with a grin. "What a surprise."

"Fine," I say, grabbing the hat forcefully out of Romina's hand and pulling it onto my head. "But if this flies off and ends up in the girls' bathroom, it's not my fault."

"No way!" he says, trying to pull it back off my head, but I duck out of his reach.

"It's windy today!" I squeal. "I can't help if it flies off my head!"

Jordan has a signature hat too, his blue Gonzaga baseball cap, from where his sister attends college. It's slightly worn down, frayed on the brim, because it goes everywhere with him. We all obsess over that hat. He takes it off now, and Olivia reaches for it. He doesn't hand it to her.

"Actually, I thought Harris was gonna be me." He holds the hat in my direction.

I just blink at him for a second. Does Jordan actually want me to wear it?

"We already decided our costumes," Olivia says, smacking her gum and reaching out her hand. "Hand it over, Parker."

He hesitates. "Penny should be me. She's taller. It makes more sense." He holds the cap out to me, like an offering. It does make more sense, from a costume perspective. It's just—Olivia not getting what she wants feels wrong, somehow, like the proper order of the universe has been all mixed up.

But I want to dress like Jordan more than anything.

I peel Kai's hat off my head and take Jordan's instead, pulling it firmly into place. "I mean, if Jordan wants me to wear it . . ." I glance to Olivia.

She looks back for a second and then shrugs. "Sure, whatever."

There's a fizzing in my chest at the feel of Jordan's hat on my head, like my veins are filled with champagne. This hat is a part of Jordan, the part he displays to the world, something special. I feel powerful in it, like I can be as confident and important as he is.

A small part of me worries for a second that Olivia will be mad, but I brush that part away. She knows how I feel about Jordan. She should be happy for me. I watch as she grabs Kai's sandwich off the table and takes a bite, shoving him with her shoulder, and I know everything will be okay. Everything always works out how it's supposed to in the end.

We get to the dance last so we can make an entrance. We want to give the rest of the school a moment to miss us, to wonder where we are, to think the dance is dull because we might be somewhere better.

Katie's sister bought us some hard lemonade and strawberry kiwi Smirnoff Ice—drinks that will smell more like sugar on our breath instead of alcohol in case a teacher decides to check. "Monster Mash" is blasting as we walk in, and mostly everyone is hanging out on the sides of the gym because there's no possible way to dance to that song and not look incredibly stupid. I'm still wearing Jordan's hat, along with his basketball jersey and a pair of Sebastian's gym shorts. Olivia has Kai's flannel shirt tied around her waist and is wearing his favorite black soccer T-shirt. Kai has a tiny tattoo of a wave on his wrist, and I drew it there for her with eyeliner.

Katie is wearing one of Danny's Star Wars shirts, her long curly hair tied below her chin as if she's got a beard. Even though Danny doesn't have any facial hair, it was too funny not to do.

I scan the room to see who else is here, and that's when I find Jordan. He's dressed as a fireman, in red pants and suspenders with a big plastic red hat. He's got a white T-shirt on under the suspenders even though the costume would totally look better if he were shirtless, but it's a school dance after all. I know if we all go back to someone's house afterward, the shirt will come off. Jordan never wastes an opportunity to flaunt his abs, for which I am forever thankful. When he sees me, he breaks into a huge toothy smile, and I walk right up to him.

It's weird—in the past I've always been too nervous to approach Jordan, to actually talk to him like we're equals. But the fact that I'm dressed like him changes everything. I'm confident this time that he wants to talk to me too. As Jordan, I'm the most popular boy in school, and I feel like it. And maybe it's just the sugary alcohol buzzing through my veins, but I like this confidence more than anything. This must be how Jordan feels all the time.

"You look familiar," Jordan says when I reach him.

"Do you think I pulled it off?" I give him a full spin so he can check out the costume from all angles.

"You're even better-looking than usual," he says, and I feel like a million sunbeams are bursting through my chest. "This is your favorite holiday, right?"

"Yeah," I say, so immeasurably pleased that he remembers the conversation from our Popsicle adventure. "I like making costumes. Doing makeup looks and stuff."

"Oh yeah. I remember your pep rally outfit. That was dope." He waves his hand over my body. "Not a lot of prep work with this one, though."

I finger the seam of his basketball jersey. "No, well. I thought about trying to re-create this really cool *Little Mermaid* look I found online. Like with seashells and sequins and a hot glue gun . . ." I cut myself off, realizing I'm rambling and Jordan probably doesn't care.

"That would have been legit." He grins. "But I like that you're dressed like me." He reaches out and takes my hand and we do a funny step-touch dance for a second, because it's all we really can do to "Monster Mash."

I realize I have no idea where the rest of the girls went, that I wandered over to Jordan without them. Usually, I feel naked, exposed without the barrier they build around me, but right now it doesn't matter.

The song switches to something we can dance to finally, all thrumming bass, and everyone runs out onto the dance floor. Jordan pulls me into the crowd, his hand still in mine. Our group is right in the middle of the floor, and we're right in the middle of that, in the eye of the hurricane. But I'm not looking at anyone else. They're just shapes and colors around us. There's nothing in the world except Jordan and me.

He pulls me to him so that my back is pressed up against his front, then leans his head down to my neck, whispering into my ear.

"Feels weird dancing with myself."

His breath tickles my neck. I turn slightly so I can respond, and suddenly my lips are only a few inches away from his. I can smell alcohol on his breath, the faint burn of cigarette smoke, and the spearmint gum meant to cover it all up. I forget what I was planning to say because all at once my brain and my mouth have completely malfunctioned.

Jordan threads his fingers through mine and pulls our clasped hands around me so that he's hugging us both—hugging two Jordans in one. His hips press into me and I lean back tighter against him and I feel like I'm bursting open, like every moment of my life until now has been building up to this. This is what it means to be alive. This is the whole point.

There's a tap on my shoulder, and I open my eyes. I didn't realize I had closed them. It's Principal Hanson. I already know what she's going to say before she says it, so I break away from Jordan automatically, feeling the loss of his touch like a physical ache.

"Keep it G-rated, please!" Hanson puts her hands on her hips. "You too!" I turn to where she's looking, expecting to see Olivia and Kai in a similar embrace, but it's Romina and Myriah. They break apart with an exaggerated eye roll. It's weird, actually—I thought Olivia would have been right beside me, but

I don't see her or Kai anywhere. They're not in our circle at all.

I scan the crowd and finally spot them. They're still by the door to the gym like they haven't even bothered to come into the dance yet. Kai is leaning against the wall, arms folded, and Olivia is whispering something into his ear.

And they're both staring directly at me.

NOW

"I'M NOT GONNA PRETEND I'm happy you guys are here," Jordan says. He hesitates for a second as if deciding whether he's actually going to physically block our entrance, but then moves aside. I don't know what to say to make it better, to make this all less awkward. I don't know how we're possibly going to get through a whole night like this. Luckily, Kai answers before I have to.

"I know, man. This whole thing is fucked. I really am sorry."

"Yeah," Jordan says. "Whatever."

Romina appears then, a big flannel shirt over her black bikini, what looks like half of a grilled cheese in one hand. "Our star-crossed lovers have arrived," she says, taking a big bite of her sandwich. She steps back and makes room for us to enter fully into the house, the screen door slamming behind us. "People have mostly claimed places to sleep, but don't worry, there's still one room left."

She walks deeper into the cabin, and we follow her inside.

"We don't need a room," I say at the same time as Kai says: "Hope our room is private." And I shove him hard in the ribs.

Romina walks us down the rickety stairs and into the musty bottom floor. There are a few couches down here, but mostly it's sports equipment—bicycles, paddleboards, an old canoe that looks like it might sink to the bottom of the lake if anyone tried to use it. Clearly, this is where things come to die. It's fitting she's putting us down here too.

There's a room off to the side, and she leads us through the door. I hold my breath as it opens and then am so relieved to see a bunk bed pushed against one wall. I can't believe my luck. *Two separate beds!* And no one down here to witness us using them. If Kai thinks I'm going to squish into one bed with him just to prove a point, he's going to be severely disappointed.

It's twin-sized, with colorful pastel-colored *Frozen* sheets— Elsa on the bottom bunk and Anna on the top. Apparently this is the kids' room. I imagine Jordan and Olivia up in the master bedroom—a king-sized bed, epic views of the lake, nothing musty and buggy and made for children—and feel a little sick to my stomach. But this is our place now. *At least we're still here.*

"I'm surprised no one else claimed this creepy room," Kai says. "So nice of them to leave it open for us."

"Sorry about the bunk beds," Romina says. "But you guys can definitely share the bottom bunk if you want. Or the top, if that's how you like it, Penny." She wiggles her eyebrows.

I ignore Romina's joke and walk into the room, dropping my little red suitcase. "This is perfect."

"Okay, now that you guys are finally here," she says, "we're going to take out the boat."

"Your dad's okay with you driving it?" I ask.

"I got my boating license last summer," she says. "But maybe, like . . . don't mention it to him next time you see him? I'll meet you upstairs, okay? I'll let you two have some alone time first." She narrows her eyes at us suggestively, and then twirls around and heads back up the stairs.

To be honest, being out on a boat with everyone sounds like a nightmare. I'm nervous about seeing Olivia, how it will feel to watch her with Jordan while I pretend to be all into Kai. And trapping us all together in the middle of the lake is going to make things worse. This is setting itself up to be the biggest nautical disaster since the *Titanic*.

Kai shuts the door. "So, should we break in the bed?"

"Gross. The fact that I am even sharing this room with you instead of going out to sleep on one of those couches is a choice."

"You know you can't sleep out there. It'll look weird."

"Clearly." I lift my suitcase and drop it down onto the bottom bunk, right on top of Elsa's face. "I'm taking bottom."

Kai doesn't answer right away, just chews on his bottom lip. "Actually . . . I was hoping maybe I could have it?"

"Don't you know anything about being a gentleman, Tanaka?" He drums his fingers against the side of the bed, and I notice he's not smiling. And then I remember. "Oh. Are you . . . Is this a heights thing?"

"I know it's stupid," he says. His cheeks are red. "Like, obviously, this child-sized bunk bed is, like . . . not going to hurt me, but still. Don't think I could fully fall asleep up in the air." He's looking down at the ground instead of at me.

I know I could tell him tough shit, could use this as payback for all the ways he's wronged me, but I don't think I have it in me. I don't want to be mean just for the sake of it.

"Okay, no, it's fine. You can take the bottom." I pull my suitcase off the bed and then climb up the ladder with it, trying to haul it onto the top bunk. It's way too heavy, though, and Kai has to help me with it.

"Thanks," he says. "Um, what do you have in there? We're here for one night, Penelope."

"I needed a few outfits just in case. You don't know how cold it's going to get!" What I don't mention is the blow-dryer, the curling iron and straightener, the ring light, and the three pairs of boots. Boys never know how much work we put into looking like we don't try.

"This is supposed to be rustic." He rolls his eyes. "This is a cabin. We're in the woods. You can't chill out for one night?"

"You know what?" I say, poking at his chest. "Boys always say they like girls who don't wear makeup, but it's not true. If I didn't wax and moisturize and shape my eyebrows and all the other stuff you think is *so* fake, you would judge me."

"All right, Weenie, you do you." He takes a step back. "Should we go boat?"

"Ugh, remind me why I'm putting up with you?"

"Because we're in love," Kai says. "Let's go."

I unzip my suitcase. "I have to get ready."

"You got ready this morning."

"I get ready several times a day."

Kai sighs dramatically. "Fine. I'll meet you up there." Then he leaves the room.

"Wait," I say, but he's already gone. I don't know why I say it;

it's not like I enjoy his company. I wouldn't want him watching me recurl my hair, making snide comments about how high-maintenance I am or something. That would be even worse than being alone.

When I get upstairs, the house is empty. It's quiet, just the low hum of the refrigerator, the ticking of the GONE FISHING clock on the wall. There's a creepy deer head hanging over the fireplace, and I can't help the feeling that it's judging me. The deer knows how messed up this all is. He can see right through me with his glassy deer eyes.

"This isn't my fault, okay?" I say, and then realize with a lurch that I am actually speaking out loud to a dead deer. I have become the girl who talks to roadkill. Luckily, there's no one else around to witness it.

Where is everybody? It hits me then with sudden clarity: they probably left. They took the boat out onto the lake, and nobody remembered I was still getting ready downstairs. Would Kai have left me like that? Even if we're supposed to be in love?

But then I hear faint laughter from outside and head to the window and there they all are at the docks. I'm filled with such relief that I'm a little embarrassed and I glance back one more time at the deer as I leave, hoping he can't tell what I was thinking.

"Yo, Harris! Get your ass down here!" Romina shouts, and I scamper down the stone steps and over to them. It's the whole crew. Romina, Myriah, and Katie are untying the boat from the dock. Danny is there too, shirtless and lying out in the sun. And then there's Jordan and Olivia. They're on the cushioned seats at the back of the boat, his arm around her, holding her tight. It reminds me of the first time he held me like that, at the Halloween dance—how I knew in that moment my life was changing.

"Hey." Kai is next to me suddenly. "You ready?" He puts his arm around me and leads me onto the boat, sitting us down on another bench. He pulls me close to him, so that we're mirroring Olivia and Jordan. "All good?" Kai asks, his voice lowered, like he can tell I'm feeling a bit mixed up about everything. I take a deep breath and try to relax.

Kai's arm might not be Jordan's arm, but it's still an arm. To be honest, it still feels kinda nice. Secure. I like having somebody to lean against while the boat rocks. "All good," I say back to him.

"You were right, by the way." His voice is louder now, clearly meant for an audience. "The wait was worth it. You look so good."

Even though I know it's not a real compliment, my cheeks still burn, and I'm embarrassed by how pleased it makes me. It's nice to feel like my efforts aren't going unnoticed. I went for a 1940s look—bright red lipstick and pin curls—because I thought it went well with the whole America theme.

But then Olivia ruins it. "So are we just supposed to be okay with hanging out with them?"

"Jump off the boat if you don't like it," Kai says.

"Everyone chill," Romina says. "Actually, you know what? I want to say something before we leave." We all stop talking and look at her. "I just think it would be really, like, *modern* if we could all put aside our differences and be friends. This is actually really cool, you know? I'm thrilled for Olivia and Jordan for getting together." At her words, I can't help but look across the boat at the two of them holding hands and my stomach clenches. "And to my little problematic babies, Penny and Kai," Romina continues, and I whip my head back to her. "Cheers to finally getting your act together. We've all been waiting for this day for literal years. And yes. You both went about this in the worst way ever, and we can all agree that it was fucked up, but now everything is how it's supposed to be, right?"

"Fine," Olivia says.

"I guess," Jordan says.

"Wonderful." Romina smiles. She backs the boat away from the dock, and we're off.

Myriah crawls over to us then, trying to keep herself steady as the boat moves. I watch as she brushes past Romina, almost crashing into her and then jumping out of the way.

"Hi," Myriah says, sitting down next to Kai and me. She's wearing a giant floppy sun hat and pulling off a burgundy one-piece bathing suit like she's made for it. The look is very distinctly un-Myriah. "I'm so glad you're both here." She lowers her voice. "It's been so *awkward*."

"What's been awkward?" Kai asks. "I mean, besides the fact that Penelope and I are desperately in love."

I shove him with my elbow. "Not now."

"I can't just turn off my love for you," Kai says. "It's an eternal flame."

"Okay, yes, so is mine, but Myriah and I need to talk."

"She won't even look at me," Myriah says. "And I'm wearing her favorite color. I even did my nails!" She holds her hand up to show off black nail polish that looks completely out of place with the sparkly daisy ring on her hand.

"Oh," Kai says. And then: "Ohhhhh."

"You should just be yourself," I say. "You don't have to fake who you are for Romina."

"How did you two know you were meant for each other?" She asks, her eyes wide and hopeful. I'm distinctly aware of the fact that Olivia and Jordan are across from us, very likely within hearing distance. I chance a look at them, and both their heads snap away right when I do.

"Um," I say, unsure how to answer. Kai and I never prepared for a question like this. And it's not like our origin story is very romantic, even if this *were* real—we drunkenly made out at a party. Not really something to celebrate.

"It's all about chemistry," Kai says.

"Believe me, I never expected this to happen," I say truthfully. "I mean, Kai is the most annoying guy I've ever met."

"Annoyingly *attractive*, you mean," Kai says.

"Yup, but somehow through all that annoyance, I . . ." I trail off, trying to think of a way to explain it that feels real, that doesn't hurt Olivia even more. "Friends are supposed to be the most important thing. I betrayed my best friend for a guy and I'll never forgive myself." I glance at Olivia and see her back has gone rigid and she's staring down at the floor. "But Kai and I . . . we just get each other. We're more similar than we realized." The truth of the words surprises me.

"I've been wanting you to get together for years," Myriah says. "You're my OTP." Then her cheeks go pink. "I mean, but not like this, of course." It makes me feel a little guilty. Myriah is too pure for this world, and on top of every other horrible thing I've done, I hate that I'm still lying to her.

We spend the next few hours cruising around the lake, exploring little coves and circling tiny islands. I've lived by this lake my whole life, but I've never seen it from this angle. My family doesn't own a boat, obviously. The only other time I've been out here was on a school fishing trip in third grade where I ended up crying anytime someone caught a fish. Not my best moment.

But this actually isn't so bad. The breeze feels nice in my hair, the sun is warm on my skin, and if I close my eyes I can almost forget for a second that my ex-boyfriend and my best friend are cuddled up together across from me.

"We should take a picture," I say to Kai. "We don't have any yet." If we want this thing to seem natural, we should be doing all the same cutesy stuff I did with Jordan. And right now, on this boat in our stupid matching outfits . . . well, if I actually liked a boy, I would want to post this. He leans toward me and I hold up my phone and snap, then upload it, trying to think of a silly caption, something that will tell the world how okay I'm doing, how fine I am with all of this.

Is there anything better than a hot boy on a boat? Loving this summer already. I add Romina's joke hashtags: *#somelakeithot #noparents.* There. Appropriately happy. I am a fun girl with a fun life. If I can believe it, then maybe everyone else will too.

Romina drives around the back of one of the little islands and then parks in a cove so we can swim. "You guys all need life preservers," she says, throwing foamy orange monsters at all of us. "I'm serious!"

"I'm not putting this on," Olivia says. I don't blame her. If I had Olivia's boobs, I would never want to cover them.

I take a life preserver from Romina and hesitantly slip it over my chest. I feel stupid immediately—it's probably the least flattering thing a person could ever put on their body—but I don't want to rock the boat, no pun intended.

Next to me, Kai straps his own life vest on too, and then turns to me with a big smile. "You look adorable."

"Shut up," I say, shoving him angrily with my shoulder, forgetting for a second how in love we are.

"I mean it!" He reaches out and gently tugs on one of the straps, tightening it for me, then brings his hand up to my face, tucking a strand of hair behind my ear. "There. All set."

I know he's just playing this up for everyone else on the boat, but at the feel of his palm against my cheek, I suck in a short breath and my face flushes with heat. I don't know why I'm having such a stupid reaction. It's probably just because it feels nice to be complimented like this. Even if I know deep down it's all bullshit.

"Thank you," I say, smiling.

"Now you really do look like a pumpkin." He grins. "But you're *my* pumpkin."

"I won't be your *anything* for long if you keep calling me a pumpkin," I say, and then press my lips together, because this is so not how I'm supposed to be acting. *You're in love.* I repeat the words inside my head, a mantra, so that I won't forget them. "I mean—you're so hilarious and you look so cute. Um, good job being you." I smile at him, trying to pretend that whatever words came out of my mouth made any reasonable sense. It's just that saying nice things to the worst person on earth isn't the easiest.

I glance over to where Olivia and Jordan are sitting and am disheartened to see they're not even looking at us. Olivia is buckling up Jordan's life vest, standing above him and leaning down for a kiss. It makes me feel like I'm going to cry.

"Wow, thank you for that detailed and beautiful compliment," Kai says, laughing. "Love you too."

He must see some look on my face because he stops laughing, his smile fading. I try to smile back at him, but it doesn't work. "Hey," Kai says softly. He glances over at them and then back at me. "Hey, let's just go in the water, okay? Let's go for a swim."

I shake my head. "I can't."

All around us, people are getting up, laughing and shrieking and jumping off the side of the boat. I watch as Jordan and Olivia stand up and jump into the water together, holding hands as they fall. We're alone on the boat now, everyone splashing and playing in the water around us. All I want is to be back at the cabin, curled up in that creepy children's bunk bed with all the cobwebs, as far away from all this as possible. I don't know why I thought any of this was a good idea.

"You can," he says. "Let's get in the water."

But he doesn't understand. My pin curls and red lipstick can't get wet. Kai doesn't get the hours that went into my hair, my makeup, how afraid I am to wash everything all off, to let anyone see the real me underneath.

"Just go without me," I say.

"No way," he says. "If you stay on the boat, I stay on the boat."

"You don't have to." I feel bad that I'm taking away from his fun, which doesn't make any sense considering I've pretty much wanted Kai to suffer for my whole life.

"Nah, the jump is kinda high up anyway."

"Okay," I say. "Thanks." Somehow I don't really believe him. I know I'm holding him back. But I'm weirdly pleased he's staying with me, even though it's probably just to keep up appearances. He's trying to be a good boyfriend after all.

"But one of these days, I'm still taking you skinny-dipping," he says, laughing. And just as fast as they arrived, all of my positive feelings toward him are washed away.

THEN

JUNIOR YEAR–OCTOBER

JORDAN SENDS ME a picture right after the Halloween dance. It's of his face, and he's drawn purple horns on his head, green fangs with blood over his ridiculously perfect smile. Monster Smash? it says, and then there's a winky face.

Nothing in my seventeen years on earth has prepared me for this text. I'm in the back seat of Romina's car, pressed up against Olivia. Olivia is the only person I know who actually likes to sit in the bitch seat because she says it means she's in the center of all the conversations and won't miss out on anything. Katie is on her other side and Myriah is up front (Myriah is always up front when Romina drives), but when my phone buzzes in my pocket and I see the message from Jordan, suddenly I'm not in the car at all. Everything disappears around me, fades to black, and all I can focus on is the way my heart feels like it's stuck in my throat. This isn't a simple message. This took time. Jordan thought of me long enough to draw me a picture, to send me a stupid joke—*a kinda sexual joke*—which means he thought about me and sex in the same brain wave, at least for a second.

But then I realize with a sinking feeling that he probably sent this to all of us. It's likely not meant for me at all. I nudge Olivia, who is laughing, leaning forward talking to Romina about something.

"Did Jordan just send you a pic?"

"What?" she asks. "Probably." She pulls her phone out and lights up the screen and I wait, holding my breath, like somehow this is the most important thing. There's nothing there. "Why, did he text you?" Olivia asks, stuffing her phone back into her purse. I show her the picture. Katie leans forward. "Oh my god, that is so flirty!"

"Who, something from Matt?" Myriah turns around.

"No, Jordan just, like . . . propositioned Penny!"

"It's for sure a joke," I say, flushing.

"Is it a joke?" Romina asks. "Or does Jordan want to make sweet, sweet monster love to you?"

"Jordan loooooves you," Myriah says, spinning around in her seat to face me and fluttering her eyelashes. "Will you let me plan your wedding?"

"Like Jordan would ever get married," Olivia says with a sharp laugh. "He's never with the same girl long enough."

"Accurate," Myriah says. "And Penny is gonna marry Kai, anyway."

"It's stupid," I say, even though it definitely isn't. It's just that I don't want to let myself get too excited. "I thought maybe he sent it to all of us."

"Nope, that one is all you, girl," Myriah says.

"We saw you guys dancing together." Katie has a habit of

talking with her hands when she gets excited, and right now they are fluttering like crazy in Olivia's face. Olivia swats them away.

"The whole school saw," Romina says. She turns down the music like this is serious business. "Kai told me that Jordan has a thing for you, actually."

"What?" Why would Kai be talking about me with Romina?

"Yeah," she says, "just now as we were leaving. I was outside smoking and Kai came and found me—you know how he always calls me out on it, but whatever. He was getting on me about the cigarette, and then we were talking about the dance, and I don't know, he said something like, 'Jordan is having a good night.' He said it's clear Jordan is into you."

"Sounds like Kai was just guessing about that," Olivia says. "Like he *thinks* Jordan might be into you. Not that Jordan has told him anything."

"I don't know, dude," Romina says. "Sounded pretty factual to me."

I'm the closest stop on our way home, and when the car pulls up to my house, I say my goodbyes and then run inside and up to my room. I can't wait to be alone. I want to text Jordan back, but I don't want four other voices in my ear while I do it.

What even is the monster mash anyway? I hold my breath until he texts back almost a minute later.

> Well, when a mommy and daddy monster love each other very much . . .

I send him the laughing/crying emoji. And then: A graveyard smash. I mean, it's totally a song about creepy sex, right?

I canNOT believe I just texted the word *sex* to Jordan. But he started it. That means he wants this; he's enjoying this flirting as much as I am.

Graveyards not your thing, Harris?

Definitely not my thing.

Then what is your thing? he asks.

You, I want to say. Jordan is my thing, has always been my thing, has always taken up about 75 percent of the space in my brain. But instead, I type out something much better, something that will make him work for it: Guess you'll just have to find out.

NOW

WE HEAD BACK TO THE HOUSE once everyone gets cold, all wet and shivering and bundled up in towels. The sun is starting to set, painting the lake in pinks and golds. It's just the kind of summer moment I know I should remember when I'm old—all of us young and beautiful and tired out from the sun, the warm twilight breeze in our hair.

But I feel like shit.

Kai stayed true to his word and sat next to me on the boat all afternoon, but honestly it only made me feel worse. I don't know what's wrong with me. How is it so easy for everyone else?

Sometimes I feel like everybody around me is living their life without really trying, like they all just naturally know the right things to do or say. I have to think about every move I make and analyze the consequences.

Jordan and Olivia were wrapped up in each other on our way back to the shore—literally wrapped together under one big beach towel—and they barely looked my way at all. Clearly, whatever Kai and I are doing isn't working. We have to step up our game, be more convincing, do something to shuffle the pieces on the board.

I pull him around the cabin when we get back, out of the way in the trees so no one can see us. "This isn't working."

"We don't know that yet," he says, shrugging. "It's still early days."

"They barely even looked at us the whole afternoon." There's a pine needle in my hair and I reach up and try to pull it out, but it doesn't help. "They were too busy gazing longingly into each other's eyes."

Kai is quiet a minute. "Okay, but maybe . . . I mean, sometimes the Not Looking means more than you think."

"What does that mean?" The pine needle is still stuck in my hair, and I drop my arm, frustrated. Kai reaches out and extricates it for me.

"I just think . . . they're probably purposefully not looking at us. It's a good thing. It means they're bothered."

"I still think we need to step it up."

"Yeah, how so?" He smirks, and I want to shake the grin off his stupid face.

"Don't look at me like that."

"Like what?"

"Like you think this is funny."

His grin widens. "My bad, *Weenie.*"

"*Ugh.*" I groan and push him away from me. "Everything is always some big game to you, isn't it? This is my life, Kai. It isn't a joke." Except lately, it certainly feels like one.

His smile falters. "You're right. I'm sorry. Would it help if I told you I use shitty humor as a defense mechanism?"

"That's not an excuse," I say. "You can't just be mean to people and then say it doesn't count because you were trying to be funny."

"When am I ever mean?" Kai asks, and I let out a harsh laugh because I actually think he's serious. Like he actually doesn't know how condescending he is. How can he be so blind to his own faults? I'd love to live in a world with such an undeserved high opinion of myself.

"Um, a certain Pukey Penelope comes to mind," I say.

I can still feel the pain of the humiliation like it's fresh. I'd had the flu but decided to come to school anyway because it was Valentine's Day and I'd wanted to be festive. We decorated cardboard boxes in Mrs. Epling's class with glue sticks and lace doilies, tiny pieces of confetti shaped like hearts. We spent the morning sticking cards into the boxes, and then opened them after lunch. Olivia's was, unsurprisingly, bursting open; she already had boobs, and everyone had noticed. She and Katie were giggling about something, lollipops in their hands, their lips stained artificial red. Jordan had a lollipop too, and I watched as he and Olivia clinked them together like they were toasting, which meant part of Jordan's mouth had now touched part of Olivia's. It sent a burst of jealousy through me and the symptoms from the flu came back hot and fast.

My breath was coming in short spurts as I reached into my box. There was a roiling in my stomach, my vision blurred, and when my hand found nothing, I thought at first it was the flu playing tricks on me. But then I looked inside, and sure enough, it was completely empty.

"No way." Kai took a step forward. "Penelope didn't get any Valentines."

Everyone was looking at me. I locked eyes with Jordan and had to look away, staring down at my feet instead. "How on earth?" Mrs. Epling came over, long skirt billowing. "You were all supposed to give Valentines to everyone in the class. That was the rule. Penelope, are you sure?"

I was furious with Mrs. Epling. How could she come up with an activity like this? How could she let us make pretty boxes and put them on our desks and expect everyone to actually follow her stupid rule?

And then, instead of an answer, I vomited all over myself—all over the pretty lace box on my desk, all over my bright red shirt with the sparkly heart. It was everywhere and it smelled disgusting.

"Holy shit!" Mrs. Epling said before she could stop herself.

"Ewwww," Olivia whined.

And then Kai: "It's Pukey Penelope! Don't let her touch you. She's contagious."

In front of me now, Kai winces. "I told you I was sorry about that."

"Just because you apologize for something doesn't cancel out the fact that you did it."

"I know." He sighs. "But I can't take back the fact that I said it. All I can do is apologize. And no matter how many times I do, you're still going to hate me forever."

"Yes," I say.

"What about the rules?" he asks now. "Didn't we agree to get along?"

"You just make it so difficult."

"Okay, well, how do you suggest we step this up?" He cracks his knuckles, all business. "You said you didn't want to kiss me or say you love me, so I don't really know how we can be more convincing."

"I'm not kissing you," I snap.

"I know," he says. "I'm disgusting and you would never."

"I'll think of something else." And then I have an idea. I pause for a second and then run my hands through my hair, trying to muss it up a bit. It's already a little windblown from the boat, but I want to make it look like someone has been running their hands through it. "They're gonna wonder where we are."

"I think they've probably made some educated guesses."

"Let's give them some more clues."

He follows my lead and runs his hands through his hair too, messing it up so it's standing on end. Laughing, he reaches down and grabs a handful of leaves and pine needles and drops them on his head.

"Ew, stop. I wouldn't make out with a dirty forest person."

"You were overcome with passion," he says, grinning. "You pulled me back here and pushed me to the ground. I would have leaves in my hair."

"There are spiders on the ground," I refute. "I wouldn't do that. I pressed you against that tree."

"Okay," he says, taking a step back and leaning against the tree behind him. Then he reaches out and takes my hands, gently pulling me closer to him. For some reason, I let him do it, taking the final step to close the gap between us so our bodies are almost touching. We're close enough to kiss, if we wanted to. Which we don't, obviously.

"So what happens next?" Kai asks, his voice low. "After you push me against the tree."

"Okay." My voice is breathy. "So then I run my hands through your hair. Like this." I slide my hands around the back of his head, running my fingers through the strands of his hair. It's soft, would be gloriously silky if not for the leaves he just dumped there.

"Me too," he says, and then he cups his hands around my head too, the feel of his fingers a delicious tingle. He plays with my hair, running his fingers through it, leaving it the kind of messy that only a make-out session could produce. Well, a make-out session or . . . this.

We're so close together that I can feel his breath on my lips, and for a second I'm tempted to close the distance and finish this. I'm reminded suddenly of Jordan's party—that flash of memory, a kiss in the laundry room, still fuzzy around the edges.

But kissing Kai right now would be crazy. We're not even in front of anyone. If I were to ever kiss him, there would have to be an audience; it would have to be because Jordan and Olivia were watching.

So I take a step back, putting space between us. "We should head inside."

There's a distant burst of thunder, and I know we have to get to the cabin soon. The air smells electric, like the kind of summer storm that crashes in for an hour and then disappears, leaving everything wet and torn apart.

Kai shakes his head and blinks a few times, as if waking up from a daze. "Um, yeah. Okay."

"I think our story is pretty believable." I turn around and start to walk back through the trees toward the cabin, but then I stop short. "Oh no." I bring my hand to my mouth, pressing my lips to my palm. When I pull back I'm horrified to see an imprint there, two bright red lips. *Oh no, no, no.* "My red lipstick."

"What about it?" Kai asks. "It looks nice."

I show him my palm. "Ugh, every girl knows you never wear red lipstick if you're expecting to kiss a boy. I'm such an idiot."

"Well, yes," Kai says, and I glare at him. "But to be fair, you weren't planning on kissing anyone."

"Yeah, but it's a giveaway! If we were dating for real, I would *not* have worn this color. I would have been making out with you all over the place." I turn around to look at him, his mussed-up hair, the leaves on his head, stuck to his shirt. He looks thoroughly kissed. He's just missing the most important detail.

"You would have this lipstick all over your face if I had actually pushed you against that tree."

"So put it all over my face," he says, shrugging.

I dig through my pockets hoping somehow I'll find the lipstick hidden somewhere in my shorts—that maybe I can just apply some of it on his lips. But I know it's not there. I can picture it sitting on the bathroom sink on the first floor, right where I left it.

There's another rumble of thunder, closer this time.

"Hey, it's okay," Kai says. "Let's just drop it. I don't want you to feel like you have to—"

But I don't let him finish. I close the space between us and kiss him before I can change my mind. It's not a real kiss, just a quick press of my lips on his, just enough to leave my mark on him. My heart is pounding from adrenaline. I can't believe I'm doing this. I feel wild, out of control, like the kind of girl who acts impulsively, who kisses boys she hates.

I pull away and then leave another quick kiss on the side of his mouth and then, bringing my head lower, kiss the soft skin of his neck. Kai sucks in a sharp breath.

When I pull back, I can see I've left a trail of red lipstick marks. Perfect.

Kai's eyes must have closed because I watch them slowly open and look at me with surprise. "Um, that was . . . unexpected."

"You look much better now," I say, my voice shaky. I'm trying to sound calm and collected even though my heart is beating wildly in my chest. "You look properly ravaged."

"I *feel* properly ravaged," he says. The wind has picked up a bit, and it's making his hair look even messier.

"That wasn't real," I remind him. "That was just because of the lipstick." I turn away from him and walk back toward the cabin, glad he can't see the flaming red of my cheeks. I feel the first drop of rain on my arm and know we have to hurry if we want to get inside before we're drenched.

"I know," he says, following quickly behind me.

"I just don't want you to get any ideas," I say. "Don't forget the rules."

"I know the rules," he says.

I start to run then, through the patch of trees and around to the front of the house. We get to the front porch right as the clouds open up above us and the rain pours down. I'm screaming—because of the rain drenching my skin, but also because it feels good to scream. I need to release some of this anxious energy inside me.

I mentioned the rules for Kai's sake, but I know I'm the one who needs to keep herself in check. The rules are there for a reason. They're to keep this whole thing under control, to keep us from spiraling out into uncharted territory. They're to keep me from getting hurt.

And I know what just happened between us was so *not* a part of the rules. I can't let it happen again. I don't know how it happened at all.

THEN

JUNIOR YEAR–NOVEMBER

TEXTING JORDAN BECOMES a regular thing. He sends me snaps in the morning on the way to school, shoots me stupid pictures from soccer practice. Every time my phone pings, I'm filled with a giddy rush of nerves. I can't believe Jordan is *talking* to me. I can't believe Jordan is talking to *me*.

"So he really likes you or something, huh?" Olivia asks with a playful shove of her shoulder. We're at Starbucks after school, sitting out at the little wrought iron tables on the sidewalk. The air is getting crisper now—it's partway through November—and it smells like fall. My coffee is warm and comforting and delicious. I am a pumpkin spice bitch, and I have no shame.

"We're just talking," I say. "It's nothing official."

"Do you think he's talking to any other girls?" Olivia takes a long, slurping sip of her drink, and when she pulls back there's a bit of whipped cream on her nose. Of course I've wondered who else Jordan is talking to, but hearing Olivia actually say the words out loud makes it a real possibility, and my stomach churns.

"I mean, probably, yeah. He's Jordan Parker."

"I saw him give Annie Chen a ride home after practice the other day. You know, that sophomore who's in our journalism class?"

I feel a little short of breath at her words. Like, obviously, Jordan and I aren't exclusive, so there's nothing I can say or do here. I have no rights on who he spends his time with. But still— Annie Chen is *so pretty*. "Was she watching practice, you think?"

"Who knows?" Olivia answers. "I stayed late in the darkroom, and then I went over to the field to say hi to the guys and Jordan was leaving with her. Kai said she was all over him."

"Well, I'm used to that." I take another sip and try to let the pumpkin spice and the perfect day soothe me. "It's fine. We're not together."

"It's so annoying, though," Olivia says. "Whoever dates you better treat you right or I'll kill 'em. Jordan isn't good enough for you."

I feel my cheeks warm at her compliment and bump my shoulder against hers, sweater to sweater. "C'mon, Liv, you know that is so not true."

"I'm just looking out for you. Jordan is *our* guy. Those sophomore bitches need to stay away."

"You're right," I say. "Thanks."

"I'll always look out for my girl," she says, tipping her cup to me. "My best friend deserves the whole freaking world."

"You're the dollop of whipped cream in my pumpkin spice latte," I say with a smile.

"What's a dollop? Isn't that like an old-timey sexy lady?"

"That's a trollop." I laugh. "You're one of those too."

"Well, then you're a strumpet."

"That one sounds like a cookie. Do you think Starbucks sells strumpets?"

"We should ask them."

"Definitely. Love you, Liv." I feel so mixed up inside, so many different emotions fighting in my chest, but there's one thing I'm sure of. Olivia will always have my back. And she's someone you want on your side—someone who will rage and fight and scratch out the eyes of your enemy just because you ask her to.

"Love you too."

NOW

KAI AND I TUMBLE THROUGH the screen door, and everyone is there in the living room, giving us the kinds of looks that make it very clear this step of the plan worked like a charm.

Jordan is leaning back on one of the couches, Olivia next to him. When they see us burst through the door in a crash of thunder—laughing and tousled and damp—Olivia narrows her eyes and then shifts a little so she's sitting in Jordan's lap. It's an obvious move, and it actually makes me feel a little better. It's proof she's jealous, that pressing my red lips to Kai's was actually worth something.

"Holy shit, did you guys get caught in a tornado out there?" Romina asks.

"Kai, my man," Danny calls out. "Did you get attacked by a bear?"

Kai wraps a wet arm around my shoulder and pulls me into him, placing a quick kiss on the top of my leaf-strewn head. "A very cute bear."

Olivia groans. "Well, I think it's trashy."

"Liv, that's not fair and you know it," Jordan says, squeezing her arm. She glances at him and he stares back at her, and something passes between them unspoken. I don't like it. You have to be close with someone to do that.

"Matt and I would never have sex in the woods." Katie taps her phone against her palm.

"We didn't have sex." That's not what this was supposed to be.

"This was only a glorious make-out sesh," Kai says, following my lead. "She pushed me against a tree."

"You've got lipstick all over your face," Myriah says.

Jordan presses his lips together in a tight line. "Penny, you never used to kiss me when you did your makeup like that." I can't tell from his tone how he's feeling—if he's jealous or just confused—but his words stir something in me.

Olivia smacks him on the arm. "Don't talk about that. It's weird."

"Guess I'm too irresistible." Kai grins.

I want to tell him he's being annoying again, but I keep my thoughts in check. Instead, I try to think of something nice to say. "Just couldn't keep my hands off him."

I flash Kai a winning smile and he beams down at me and *we are so good at this.*

We spend the next few hours getting showered and changed and ready for the night. Romina makes us quesadillas on the stove (the cabin isn't stocked with food, and it seems all she bought on her grocery run was a giant bag of vegan cheese and various carbs to accompany it), and then we all eat them with our hands, standing in a group around the kitchen island.

The rain doesn't let up at all—instead it gets worse, bright flashes of lighting, booms of thunder that shake the rickety walls of the cabin. At one point there's a boom so loud the deer head on the wall actually moves and we all scream, thinking it's come alive or might crash down to the floor.

"Well, there go any plans for fireworks," Myriah says. "Happy Fourth of July."

"I mean, this is kinda the same thing, right?" Romina says with a shrug as there's another crash overhead. Myriah is on one of the couches, curled up on a blanket, and Romina is sitting on one of the bar stools all the way across the room. It's body language that makes it clear they still haven't sorted anything out.

"I wanted to have a campfire." Olivia pouts. "We could light the fireplace maybe?"

"No way," Romina rushes to answer. "I have no idea how that thing works."

"Well, this sucks." Katie folds her arms over her chest. "We're, like . . . trapped inside all night with nothing to do. I wish Matt were here."

"Do your parents have anything to drink?" Olivia asks, rummaging through the cupboards.

"No," Romina says. "I mean, yeah, they do, but we can't drink it. They would notice."

"But they don't come here very often, right?" Katie follows Olivia's lead and starts looking. "We could probably find someone to replace it before they come back. My sister could get something."

Olivia finds it then—some bottles of wine in the back of the pantry, and she picks one up, wiggling it back and forth in excitement. She pouts again, using her babiest baby voice, pretending to make the bottle of wine speak to us. "Pleeeease, Romina. Let them drink me. Your parents won't notice, and I bet I've been in this pantry for years."

"Ugh, okay, fine." Romina starts laughing and then opens the silverware drawer and hands Olivia a corkscrew.

Olivia twists open the bottle of wine and everyone cheers, and I'm a little annoyed. I still don't want to drink, and I guess I never really noticed until this summer how much we all depend on alcohol to make a party fun. I wish we could just hang out.

But I can't say any of this out loud.

Romina gathers some glasses out of the cabinet and then pours each of us a bit of the wine. I take the glass but don't drink it.

"I have an idea," Olivia says, a wicked grin spreading over her face. "Let's play truth or dare."

"No way!" Katie whines. "You're gonna make me do something stupid."

"Hell yeah," Danny says, finishing his cup of wine in one big gulp.

"Get over yourself, Katie," Olivia says, and then she heads into the living room, sitting down cross-legged on the rug. "Everyone get in a circle. It'll be fun."

"I don't know," Jordan says, but he still follows her. "This might be a bad idea."

"Bad ideas are the best kind of ideas," she says, waggling her eyebrows at him.

I'm with Jordan on this one—this sounds like it could only end in disaster. I don't want Olivia daring me to do anything, not when she's mad at me. I don't know what kind of crazy ideas she might come up with. And I don't want to admit to any truths either, especially when Kai and I are right in the middle of the biggest lie.

But then everyone is circling around Olivia on the floor, and I'm dragged over there with them. I don't know how to say no when everyone else is saying yes. I can't be the only one who doesn't play. Not when my position in the group is so precarious.

But I feel a little sick.

Kai sits down next to me in the circle and gives my knee a comforting squeeze. He took a shower after we got back inside, so the lipstick marks have been scrubbed from his cheeks, the leaves and dirt washed out of his hair. He's still got the lipstick kiss on the side of his neck, though. When I asked him about it, he shrugged and told me he liked that one.

"You good?" he asks now, leaning close to me so that no one else can hear. "We can make up some excuse. Go have another breathtaking make-out sesh in the room if you want to bail."

But I shake my head. "No, it's fine." I don't want to be the kind of girl who runs away. Besides, I want to keep my eyes on Jordan. It's better to know what he's up to than to wonder about it from downstairs.

"Okay, I'll start," Romina says. "Katie, truth or dare?"

Katie looks at her hesitantly, wrapping and unwrapping a curl of hair around her finger. "Um, dare, I guess."

Romina thinks for a minute. "Okay . . . I dare you to microwave some cheese and then pour it onto Danny's chest and lick it off."

We all scream.

"Ewwwww," Katie shrieks. "No way!"

"That is the foulest thing I've ever heard," Olivia says. "Romina, your mind is a filthy place."

"Guilty as charged." Romina grins.

"I'm not doing it," Katie says.

"You said dare, Katie, you have to." Olivia shrugs, her voice calm.

"Do I get a say in this?" Danny asks. "I mean, I totally want her to do it. But just checking."

"She has to," Olivia says.

"Ugh, fine. You suck." Katie stands up and then grabs the bag of cheese from the fridge, sprinkling some into a bowl and microwaving it for fifteen seconds. Soon a delicious cheesy smell fills the room. We all watch as Danny takes off his shirt, waiting for the bowl to cool, and then Katie tenses, hesitating for a second before she pours it out onto his chest. Then we all scream and cover our eyes as she licks it off. It's weird, and gross, and I feel a little bad for Katie, because I can tell by the way she's chewing on her bottom lip and staring down at the rug that she didn't want to do it.

But Olivia is too persuasive.

"Okay, Olivia," she says pointedly, once we've all calmed down. *"Truth or dare?"*

"Dare," Olivia says. "Obviously."

Katie's eyes are glittery with mischief. "Okay, I dare you to kiss Kai."

I suck in a sharp breath at her words, anxiety pooling in my stomach. I shake my head, trying to snap out of it.

Olivia lets out a harsh laugh. "What the hell? I'm not doing that."

"You made me do mine!"

"But he's my . . . he and I . . ." It's weird to see Olivia sputtering like this, so flustered and out of control. "Fine," she says, and then she crawls across the circle to Kai. My heart is thumping wildly in my chest and I don't know why. I know they dated for like six months, but I still feel weird about it. He's supposed to be *mine* now, and even though it's fake, this still feels wrong.

Kai glances at me and we lock eyes, and then Olivia is right in front of him, so he pulls his gaze from mine to hers. "Hey," he says to her quietly.

She chews on her bottom lip. "Let's just get it over with."

And then they're kissing, softly and gently, the kind of kiss that looks practiced. It's tender and comfortable and even though they've been snapping at each other for the past few weeks, I can tell they care. There's something between them still, something this lie between us can't take away.

Or maybe our lie is making them stronger. *Good.* That was the whole point. I shouldn't have let myself get carried away earlier out in the trees. Because this kiss is a reminder of what this is all about—why we're doing what we're doing. Kai is only helping me because he wants Olivia back.

And once he and Olivia get back together, then everything will be normal again. Jordan will be free to fall back in love with me. So when everyone starts cheering and laughing and clapping as they kiss, I do too.

It feels like a million years, but finally they pull apart, faces flushed.

"That was the hottest thing ever," Romina says. "I'm screaming."

Kai sits back down next to me, and I can't look at him. I'm

too aware of his arm next to mine. I can tell he's looking at me, though, that he's probably trying to say something, but I keep staring at the floor. I don't know what is wrong with me.

And then Olivia jolts me out of it.

"My dear, sweet Penelope," she says, and I tear my gaze up from the floor to look at her. She smiles, her teeth pointy like a shark's. "What'll it be? Truth or dare?"

"Um . . . truth," I say, after a long pause. I don't know which is more dangerous. But I'm afraid picking dare might lead me to someplace I'm not comfortable. At least with truth, I can lie.

"Interesting choice," she says. "Okay, let's see." She pauses, letting the tension build. "Who do you like more? Jordan or Kai?"

There's a hush around the room, broken by Katie, who is giggling quietly behind her hand. I feel the air sucked out of my lungs at her words. How the hell am I supposed to answer this question? What is the best move? I don't want to ruin this plan with Kai, but I don't want Jordan to think I've forgotten him.

"You don't have to answer," Kai says, and I turn to him thankfully, but then I can't help it and my eyes find Jordan. He's looking right at me, chewing on his bottom lip, and when I see him I want to kiss the worry off his face. It's supposed to be Jordan sitting next to me in this circle, supposed to be Jordan giving my knee a comforting squeeze.

"Um, yeah, she totally does," Olivia says.

"If I had to lick hot cheese off Danny's chest," Katie says, "Penny is not getting out of this one."

"*Vegan* cheese," Danny says, "which is even worse."

"I . . ." My voice trails off, because I'm too confused, too panicked. "I don't know."

"That's not an answer." Olivia leans forward, her hands pressed into the rug.

"Well, maybe that's how she honestly feels," Myriah says. "Emotions are complicated."

"No," Olivia says, her voice sharp. "Pick one."

"Which one is the better kisser?" Katie takes a sip of her wine and laughs.

"Do you actually like Kai or is he just a rebound?" Olivia asks.

"Hey, lay off her," Kai cuts in.

"You just don't want to hear the answer." Olivia smiles, and I notice her teeth are stained red.

"She only has to answer the first one," Myriah says. "Don't be unfair."

"This isn't cool, Olivia," Jordan says finally.

"She cheated on you," Olivia says. "I don't know why you're always defending her."

There's another loud *crack* of thunder overhead.

"Leave her alone, guys," Romina says. "This is supposed to be fun."

"Jordan or Kai?" Olivia repeats. The words swim in my head, and I'm dizzy from them, even though I haven't even had a sip of wine. Jordan or Kai? Jordan or Kai? Jordan or Kai?

"I don't want to play." I jump up and stumble out of the circle, and before I can think about the implications of ditching the game, I leave them and head down the stairs. I don't even care that it's still pouring rain, that it's dark and creepy down there in the storm. All I know is I've had enough of Olivia. I don't want to sit there and just take it. I'm so done.

This whole time, despite all of Olivia's mean comments, I've been so *sure* I wanted Olivia to forgive me. I wanted things to go back to exactly the way they used to be: Olivia as my best friend, Jordan as my boyfriend. I did a terrible thing—I was the one to destroy our friendship—so I've felt I deserved her anger, that I needed to feel the pain of every wound.

But for the first time I'm not so sure. I've been so spoiled all these years to be Olivia's best friend, because it meant I got only love and attention from her and none of the bite. I thought I would do anything to be her best friend again. But maybe I'm better off without her.

I close myself in the bedroom and stare in the mirror over the dresser. The girl that looks back at me is pale and tired and trying so hard to look like she isn't. Her hair is still damp from the shower, her lips painted red again, her cheeks glowing with highlight. She's pretty enough. I just wish she were braver, and stronger, and tougher. I wish she were confident enough to say what she felt instead of wrapping herself up in a big lie.

There's a soft knock on the door, and I yell at it. "Go away, Tanaka!" I so don't want to deal with him right now.

But then the door cracks open and I'm surprised to see Jordan's face instead. "Um, it's not Kai, actually. Can I come in?"

I straighten, trying to calm myself, bringing my hands up to twist my hair into a more pleasant shape. "Um, yeah. Yeah, come in."

Jordan enters and closes the door softly behind him, and then we stand awkwardly, looking at each other. I'm so instantly aware that we're in a bedroom alone together, that there is a bed only a few feet away from us. There isn't really anywhere to sit in here except for on the bottom bunk, and I think we both know instinctively how weird that would be. So we stand. Jordan lifts my hairbrush off the dresser and starts playing with it, his hands distracted.

"Does Olivia know you're down here?" I ask, and he shrugs.

"Olivia can deal."

"She'll be mad," I say.

"Just wanted to see if you were okay."

"I've been better."

"Me too," he says. "That was weird when they kissed earlier, right?" He fiddles with the hairbrush. It's so strange that Jordan and I are together in this, playing the parts of two people who just watched the people they're into make out. I've been dying to get Jordan alone, to try to convince him I've made a mistake, and now here he finally is. And I don't know what to say.

"They still like each other," I say, wondering how Jordan will take it. Kai has been so over the top about his love for me, I don't know if it's the best idea.

"Yeah." Jordan shrugs. "Well . . . when you break up, sometimes you can't turn those feelings off right away." He takes a step closer to me. "Like, your head tells you to get over it and move on, but your heart says, *Fuck that.*"

"They have too much history." I take another step closer to him. We're only about a foot apart now, so close I could reach out and touch him, but I don't. There's a spark of tension between us, the air in the room crackling with it. "They like each other even though they shouldn't."

"Yeah, I mean, you try to be angry, but . . . you still care."

"I don't know," I say. "I feel like I'm always angry about everything."

"Yeah?" Jordan takes a step back and the tension breaks. "Okay. Got it."

We look at each other for a while longer, the silence stretching unbearably between us. There's too much to say, and I don't know how to say it. I don't want to say the wrong thing and mess this up. Suddenly, I'm back in his tree house, lying down on the floor and looking at the stars through slits in the ceiling. I'm riding piggyback on him down the sidewalk, holding tight around his shoulders so he doesn't drop me. We're studying together in his kitchen, pulling faces at each other when his parents won't stop making out. I should be able to talk to him about how I feel. It's just—we usually spent most of our time together kissing, and now that we can't do that, I don't really know how to act.

"Cool," he says. "Well, I'm gonna go back upstairs."

"Okay," I say softly. "I'll see you up there."

He reaches out and squeezes my arm. "Okay."

My heart folds in on itself then, a dying thing. Because even though the word he's saying is *okay*, it sounds a little too much like *goodbye*.

THEN

JUNIOR YEAR–NOVEMBER

IT'S FRIDAY OF THANKSGIVING break when Jordan finally invites me to hang out.

I've spent the last two nights cooped up in the house with Seb, bored out of my freaking mind. There's a wreckage of leftover Chinese takeout boxes scattered on the kitchen counters, old *Friends* reruns looping on the TV. Jordan's text comes right as I'm starting to feel like I'm becoming one with the couch.

Have you ever seen a Hallmark movie? he asks. I think I am actually in pain.

Not watching football, then? I text back.

He sends me a picture of Kai and Olivia on a sofa, pizza slices laid out in front of them on the coffee table. Olivia has her middle finger up and pointed at the camera.

These two won't let me. They're holding the TV hostage.

I'm annoyed at first that Olivia is hanging out with Jordan without me. But based on the picture, the twinkle lights strung up behind them on wooden slats, I can tell they're in Kai's barn, so I understand why he didn't invite me.

Olivia loves hating on those movies, I respond, trying to pretend I'm fine about everything. You'll never drag her away.

And then the text that changes everything: You should come over. Put me out of my misery, Harris.

And so it is. My mom drops me off at Kai's house an hour later—once I've changed my outfit three times and curled my hair. I want to look good, but also natural. Like this is how I look all the time. Like I didn't just eat twenty-five pounds of Chinese takeout.

Kai's barn isn't really a barn anymore, although I think it was built for horses back before his family owned it. Now it's a mix between a storage shed and a hangout space. There are a few lumpy couches, some piles of blankets, a plastic folding table we sometimes use for flip cup, and an old TV, crooked on its stand. Kai told us once that his mom let him keep it out in the barn when it broke. There are always tons of bugs, and it's pretty drafty, but it's still a great spot to hang out.

Except for the fact that Kai is always here too.

I push open the creaky barn door and see them. Jordan is sprawled sideways on one of the couches, his long legs stretched out on the cushions. Olivia is on the floor beneath his feet, knees crossed, sipping out of a can of Coke. Kai is on the other couch, facing me, so he notices me first.

"What are you doing here?"

"Jordan invited me," I say, defensive.

Jordan and Olivia turn away from the TV then and look at me.

"I needed reinforcements," Jordan says. He rearranges his body and clears an empty spot on the couch next to him. "Harris, save us! Please tell these guys that literally any other channel would be better than this one."

"Kai doesn't have Netflix because he lives in 1995," Olivia says. I walk hesitantly into the room. I wish I could feel more confident, take my place on the couch next to Jordan like I belong there, but there's so much with this situation that could go wrong. Sitting next to Jordan is terrifying, but sitting next to Jordan at Kai's house is even worse.

Still, I take a deep breath and do it anyway. The couch shifts as I sit down and I fall into Jordan, touching him all the way down from our legs up to our shoulders. I try to rearrange myself—I don't want to make it seem like I'm trying too hard to get with him—but that feels weird too, so I stay still, my cheeks flaming so hot I feel like I might combust.

But then he makes everything better because he wraps his arm around me and pulls me closer. "This movie is the *worst*," he says, voice low.

"That's the whole point." Olivia rolls her eyes. "The point is to hate it and love that you hate it."

Jordan turns to her. "I don't get that, though. Why purposefully put yourself through something you hate? That's enjoyable to you guys?"

"Aw, you're so *wholesome*, Jordan," Olivia says, a teasing tone. "It gives off the illusion that you're actually nice."

"Hey," Jordan says. "I *am* nice!"

Olivia lets out a barking laugh. "Sure, Jan."

"What is this movie, anyway?" I ask.

"Okay, so she's this powerful executive in the big city," Olivia says, sitting up straighter, her eyes gleaming. "And the guy owns a Christmas tree farm in Vermont. But her company wants to knock down his farm and build a ski resort on top of it."

"They've played that Joni Mitchell song like three times already," Kai says. "About paving paradise."

"'Big Yellow Taxi,'" I add, before I can help it.

"Right." He smiles. "And oh god, they're both *so* white. They're, like . . . *podcast* people. *Prius* people."

"*Ed Sheeran* people?" I add. Kai laughs, and I'm unexpectedly pleased.

"So of course they hate each other," Olivia continues. "But in the end the spirit of Christmas will bring them together and she'll quit her job or some bullshit because obviously women can't fall in love *and* be CEOs at the same time."

"See, I don't get that either," Jordan says.

"What, feminism?" Olivia asks.

"Not that," Jordan says. "This plot is stupid. In real life you don't fall in love with the woman who is going to plow your Christmas tree farm."

"I mean, I'd be pretty into someone plowing my farm," Kai says, and my eyes roll back so far in my head I feel like they might get stuck there.

"Like, people don't go from hating each other to falling in love. It's unrealistic." Jordan shifts so his body is pressing even closer to mine and my breath catches.

"It depends," Kai says. "It depends why you hate them. Like if the reason is something you can forgive."

"There's a difference between, like . . . *real*, true hate, and just being mad," Olivia says.

Jordan looks at me. "What do you think, Harris?"

I can barely think having him this close. "I think love is complicated." Even saying the word *love* in front of Jordan makes me feel like I'm going to die from embarrassment.

"Well, I think this movie is torture," Jordan says.

"Is our company *that* horrible, Jojo?" Olivia asks, pouting.

"Well, now that Harris is here, things are looking up." Jordan squeezes my shoulder, and I can't help the butterflies that erupt inside me at his words.

"Ouch, Parker," Olivia says. She stands up from the floor then and sits down next to Kai on the other couch. Olivia and Kai have been spending more time together lately, and even though I don't understand why anyone would willingly spend time in his presence, this whole thing feels *right*. The four of us are meant to be here like this, two power couples on two couches, everyone in their rightful places.

I wonder briefly where the others are tonight—Katie and Myriah and Romina. I feel lucky that I'm special enough to be in this room, that an hour ago I was just like them, but now Jordan's arm is around me and I'm *somebody*.

We sit for a while and watch the movie, but I can barely focus on what's going on. On-screen, the characters sled and skate and kiss under a sprig of stray mistletoe—accompanied by sarcastic comments from Jordan—but all I can think about is his arm around my shoulders.

I can hardly breathe as Jordan's fingers start running up and down my arm, fiddling with the soft flannel of my shirt. Then he moves his hand lower, finding the gap in between my shirt and jeans, tickling the bare strip of exposed skin. I feel like I'm on fire, and before I can help it I suck in a quick breath.

This makes Jordan laugh—I can feel the shaking of his shoulders—and he purposely tickles my stomach again, drumming his fingers against me. Then he leans down and whispers.

"Cold? You've got goose bumps." He pushes up my sleeve, and I see he's right—tiny dots cover my skin, my hair standing alert.

I shiver. "Yeah, it's chilly in here." And yes, it's drafty in the barn, but these goose bumps are all Jordan. He grins back at me in a way that means he knows it.

"I'll keep you warm," he whispers. "Just get closer."

I give in to it then—my aching need to be as close to him as possible—and lean against his chest, melting into his body like we're one. The arm around my side pulls me tighter, and this is the closest I've ever been to a boy in my life. The fact that it's not just any boy, but *Jordan Parker*, makes me feel like I'm flying.

I'm staring straight ahead at the TV screen, trying to pretend everything is normal, that I've been in this position a million times. I don't want Jordan to notice how much I'm freaking out. Can the others tell I'm freaking out? I glance quickly over to Kai and Olivia, just to make sure, and see they're not paying any attention to me at all. Kai has his arm tight around Olivia, and she's leaning against him, her head snuggled on his shoulder. They're both staring intently at the TV, watching the movie like I'm watching them.

I wonder if inside they're freaking out too—if we're all pretending to calmly watch this movie but internally flailing.

Then Jordan brings a hand to my chin, turning and lifting

my face toward his, and all other thoughts fly from my mind. Suddenly, he is kissing me, warm and soft and thrilling. All I can think about is how lucky I am—how Jordan could have picked any girl in the entire school to kiss, but he wanted *me*.

And so we kiss, over and over again, together under the twinkle lights, and I fall a little bit more in love with him.

NOW

THE STORM RAGES on for the rest of the night, and it definitely feels like we're in a horror movie. I mean, the thunder and lightning, the dark forest, and the lack of Wi-Fi are all scary, but the rest of it is scarier: snuggling with Kai on one couch, Olivia and Jordan snuggling on the other.

Watching them kiss is more terrifying than any storm.

Luckily, the game of truth or dare ended while I was downstairs, and when I came back, Romina had switched on a playlist and everyone was up and dancing, jumping on the couch cushions, Khalid drowning out the sound of the rain. Weirdly, the cheese thing may have worked, because Katie and Danny are dancing a little too close, laughing and whispering to each other in a way that Matt wouldn't like if he were real.

Eventually, thankfully, everyone decides it's time for bed, and I extricate myself from Kai's limbs and the couch and head back to our room. There is one positive to this night: the glorious fact that Kai and I won't have to share a bed and no one will even know. These bunk beds are a salvation.

I reluctantly change into the tank top and shorts I wear to sleep—Olivia and I bought matching silk boxers last year at Urban Outfitters—and I'm a little self-conscious about the fact that Kai is going to see me in them. It didn't occur to me when I was packing. I should have brought something long-sleeved and shapeless and made of wool. Something fit for a nun.

"You wear that to sleep?" Kai says when he sees me. He's in a gray T-shirt and boxer shorts and I feel a little weird about it. I know they're pretty much the same thing as regular shorts, but technically they are underwear.

"No," I say. "Close your eyes."

"Fine. Why don't you just shut off the light?" I watch as Kai puts a hand over his face, shielding his eyes as he peels back the Elsa comforter and crawls into the bottom bunk.

"I will. Your boxers are going to give me nightmares." I flip off the light switch and the room goes dark. I try to find my way back over to the bunk bed, but it's pitch-black. I trip on something sharp and metal that feels a lot like the curling iron I may or may not have left lying on the floor.

"Ow! Dang it!"

"All good over there?" Kai's voice comes out of the darkness.

"Yes," I hiss. "I'm fine. Go to sleep."

"Did you just say *dang it*, by the way? Are you in kindergarten?"

"Why are you still awake?"

"Because you're stumbling around so loudly."

"I'm not being loud. You're the one still talking." I find my way over to the ladder on the side of the bed and start to climb. There's another big crash of thunder above us. The rain sounds extra loud down here, the *plink plink* of dripping water. I don't know how I'm ever going to sleep with the storm above me and Kai below me. I bet he snores.

"You better not snore, Penelope," Kai says. "I'm a light sleeper."

"In that case I'm going to snore as loud as I can," I snap. I climb into my top bunk, pulling back the sheets, and that's when I feel it. The side of the mattress is *wet*. "Are you freaking kidding me?"

"There's that kindergartner again."

"What the *fuck*, Kai? Is that better?"

"No need to swear. What's wrong?"

"Ugh, my bed is all wet." I hear the dripping sound again and look up to the window. It's still mostly too dark to see, but I can tell what's happening. "There's a leak."

I hear rustling then as Kai sits up. "Wait, really? I don't feel anything down here."

"It's coming from this window. The whole side of the mattress is wet."

There are some more sounds down below me. "Oh yeah, it's dripping down the wall. There's a puddle on the floor."

"Is your mattress wet?"

"Nope, dry and cozy."

"Switch with me." I turn back around and try to climb back down the ladder.

"No way. I'm not going up there."

I resist the urge to kick my feet out as I'm climbing down the ladder, in case I can make contact with his stupid face. Then I'm back on the ground. "Okay, well, then I'm taking your bed and you can sleep out on the couch."

"Why should I take the couch?"

"Because you're a gentleman."

"We're in love, remember? They'll think it's weird if we don't sleep in the same room."

I stumble over to the door and flip on the light, then squeeze my eyes shut at the sudden brightness.

"Ouch! A little warning next time?" Kai whines.

"Don't be a baby."

I open the door and peek out into the main room of the first floor, trying to assess the situation. I'll sleep out on the couch if I have to, and then set my alarm to wake up before everyone else. That way no one will catch me out here. But then I notice a shape slumped onto the cushions, dark curls spreading out under a blanket. *Katie.*

I shut the door. "Katie is on the couch."

"We can share my bunk," Kai says.

"I would rather sleep on the floor," I say back immediately. But of course it's not true. The floor is tiled, the ceramic cold and hard under my feet.

"There's plenty of room," Kai says, but obviously there isn't. It's a children's bunk bed. The mattress was built to fit one child—not two seventeen-year-olds.

I flip off the light so we're plunged back into darkness. I don't want to have to see the look on his face when I make this choice. "Okay, fine. Move over."

There's more rustling as I hear Kai make space for me. I come back over to the bed and then slide under the covers next to him. And he's right—it is dry and cozy in here and so, so warm. I can feel the heat radiating from his body, and I angle myself so I am practically hanging off the other side of the bed from him— as far away as I can possibly get. But I can still feel him right next to me—I'm too aware of his body less than an inch away.

"Don't touch me," I say.

"Pen, I gotta move a bit closer. I'm getting into leak territory over here by the wall." Kai shifts, and then I can feel his shoulder, the side of his arm against mine. I turn away from him, trying to curve myself so we're not touching, but it makes it worse because suddenly my back is flat against his chest, and we are snuggled up together like two freaking turtledoves.

"You're touching me," I whisper.

"There's no space," he whispers back.

I know I have to give in, just let the snuggling happen, because spooning with Kai will be way more comfortable than hanging half off the bed and onto the floor. It's the only way I might actually be comfy enough to get some sleep. So I take a deep breath and then let myself relax, melting against his chest.

"Can I put my arm around you?" Kai asks. "It's floating in the air right now."

"Okay," I say, and so he does, setting his arm down on me and pulling me closer to his chest, his hand resting lightly against my stomach. And it's actually kinda nice. We fit together perfectly, lined up in all the right places, and I would never admit it to him in a million years, but I'm comfortable. I think it just feels good to have someone to cuddle with, even if it's not Jordan.

"Is this okay?" Kai's face is right against my shoulder, and when he speaks I can feel his lips brush my skin.

I nod, but then realize that maybe he won't be able to feel it, so I whisper, "Yeah, it's okay."

"I can try to move if—"

"You don't have to move."

The rain patters above us, and I close my eyes, trying to fall asleep, but I'm still so aware of how close we are, how it feels to be pressed together. The hand on my stomach begins to move then, soft, fluttering fingers that find the gap of skin between my shorts and my top. I suck in a sharp breath and they freeze.

"Don't stop," I reassure him, the words like an exhale I didn't plan for. I want to take the words back, but then his fingers move again, sliding under my top so his hand is pressed right onto my skin, and it feels so good I keep quiet. *Kai Tanaka is touching me. Why am I letting him touch me?*

I shift a bit then, straightening out my legs, and his legs follow. My feet find his, and then they are sliding on one another, our legs tangled together. Before I can help it, I press myself back against him, like my body has betrayed me. His hand is still tracing fluttering circles on my stomach, and then I feel his lips on my shoulder. They leave a light kiss there, so soft I think I might be imagining it.

And for some reason, all I want to do is turn around so that I'm facing him, shift so his mouth is lined up with my lips instead of my shoulder, but I can't let that happen. So I lie right where I am, willing my body not to move without my approval.

We stay like that for a while longer, and I squeeze my eyes closed, trying helplessly to fall asleep. But I'm so awake, so tense, so aware of the feeling of his fingers.

"Kai?" I say at last, my voice barely above a whisper. "You still awake?"

He nods against my shoulder. "Mm-hmm."

"I'm sorry about not swimming earlier." I don't know what makes me say it. It's just that lying here in the dark, I feel like we're cocooned from the real world. Like this is the kind of place to be honest.

"You don't need to apologize for that," Kai whispers.

"I feel like I ruined your day."

Kai's fingers stop moving for a second. "I had fun with you up on the boat. If I wanted to swim, I would have."

"You're just saying that."

"Don't worry about me," he says. "Life is too short to waste the whole thing worrying."

"I can't help it." I pause for a long time then, listening to the rain, deciding how truthful I really want to be. "I just want everyone to like me."

But he doesn't answer. His hand has stilled, and I realize he must have fallen asleep. I close my eyes and listen to the rain, and finally, eventually, I drift off too.

THEN

JUNIOR YEAR–DECEMBER

"KAI ASKED ME TO BE his girlfriend." Olivia pulls a bright pink knit hat—complete with a fluffy pompom—over her head, and makes a kissy face at herself in the mirror. We're at the mall, trying to take advantage of the last few shopping days before Christmas.

"Oh my god!" I answer, dropping a hideous penguin sweater back onto the rack. "Wait, when?"

Olivia pulls the hat off her head, her smooth blonde hair still perfectly wavy beneath. "Last night."

"That's amazing!"

Jordan and I became official on December twelfth, which means he has been my boyfriend for ten whole glorious days. He took me here for our first date and we went ice-skating on the little rink they set up in the middle of the mall, drinking peppermint hot chocolates and clutching on to each other to stay warm—like we were characters in our own cheesy holiday movie. It was the single most incredible night of my entire life, and I feel bad because I know I haven't been able to shut up about it. So I'm thrilled now that Olivia has a boyfriend too. We can be annoying and in love together.

And I knew this was coming. Ever since our Hallmark movie marathon over Thanksgiving break, Kai and Olivia haven't been able to stop loudly flirting with each other at all hours of every day.

We leave H&M and automatically head in the direction of the promised land—aka Sephora. We came here to the mall because I wanted to pick out a Christmas present for Jordan, but what do you buy for a boy you've only been dating for ten days? I kind of want to make him something, but I don't want to scare him off.

It's much easier to try on free makeup samples instead.

Mariah Carey's "All I Want for Christmas Is You" blasts us for what feels like the tenth time in the past hour, and I wrap my arm through Olivia's, pulling her closer to me as we walk. "Okay, so spill the deets. Tell me everything."

She pauses for a minute, chewing on her bright-red-stained lips. "Okay. So, we were in the barn. He lit a bunch of candles."

"That sounds like a fire hazard."

"I'm trying to tell you my romantic story and you're worried about if the candles are dangerous. Classic."

"That barn is old! Lots of dry wood."

Olivia looks at me for a second. "Well, sure. Okay, you're right. They weren't real candles, they were those little light bulb ones. Anyway . . ."

Olivia stops midsentence as we walk into Sephora, and then pulls me over to one of the little mirrors. She grabs a shimmery, wintry-looking cream shadow and starts dabbing it on her lids.

"Anyway . . . what?" I nudge her to continue the story. I don't really get why she's being so cagey about this. When Jordan and I got together, I FaceTimed Olivia immediately, explained the entire conversation to her word for word so we could decode it. That's what I want to do now.

Maybe this act is because of my history with Kai. But my friendship with Olivia is more important than that. I would never say anything rude about Kai now that they're together. I mean, at least not out loud.

She screws the top back onto the pot of eye shadow and sets it down. "All right, so you know how he and I have been friends for years? So we were watching a movie and Kai, like . . . couldn't stop talking about how amazing I am. He was like . . . 'You are a literal goddess and I am obsessed with you, you smell amazing, you're the hottest girl I've ever seen.'" She picks up a tube of highlighter and tests a bit on her wrist.

"He said all that?" I ask, a weird, uncomfortable flutter in my stomach.

"Yup. And he was like . . . "'You're the last person I want to talk to before I go to sleep. I just want to be with you, and when you know you want to be with someone, you want the rest of your life to start as soon as possible.'"

"Isn't that . . . *When Harry Met Sally*?" I ask, turning to her hesitantly.

"What?" She laughs, then drops the highlighter back down on the shelf with a clatter. "Oh yeah. I mean, that's the movie we were watching."

Of course Kai would quote some movie at her instead of coming up with his own original thoughts. He'd actually have to care about something for more than three seconds to put any effort into trying to impress her. "Wow," I say, and then realize I'm grimacing. I try to smile but know it probably looks more like I'm constipated.

"Are you okay?" Olivia asks.

"Oh yeah," I say. "Yeah. I think it's adorable."

"He's a fucking dreamboat," Olivia says. "And the world's best kisser. It feels right, you know? Like we've been friends forever and now we're finally together. It's totally meant to be."

"And just in time for Christmas!" I say, clutching her arm. "I'm so excited we got boyfriends together."

Olivia squeezes my arm back. "We are thriving."

NOW

WE ALL PACK UP AND head out early the next morning, cleaning everything so well you can barely tell we were at the cabin at all.

Kai and I woke still wrapped in each other, and I jumped up and quickly got dressed, leaving him alone in the bed like I was never there. If I don't bring up the fact we were spooning, maybe I can pretend it didn't happen.

Now we're headed back to town, sleepy and content and sun-drenched. I'm weirdly calm being in this car with Kai, more relaxed than I felt on our way here. This feels like my spot now— this passenger seat with the imprint of my sandy feet on his dashboard. Before I can help it, my mind flashes to an image of Olivia sitting here last year, on her way to school, or some party, or down a quiet road to hook up. The image makes me a bit queasy, and I shake my head, trying to force it away. I don't like the thought of Olivia here. I don't like the idea that this was her spot before it was mine. But I don't want to think about what that means.

"Mind taking a detour?" Kai makes an abrupt left, driving us down a bumpy back road before I can answer him. "There's someplace I wanna show you."

"What kind of place?" I lean forward, folding my feet up under me.

"You'll see."

We drive for another forty minutes or so, and then the air around us changes—I can smell the musty, brackish scent of salt, and wind whips through the open edges of the Jeep. We turn a corner and then there it is, spread out before us—the ocean.

We must have backtracked. The beach is an hour from home, the other direction from Romina's cabin. I don't get the chance to come here much, what with school and all. Besides, the water is usually too freezing to swim. It's a NorCal beach, thick fog and mossy cliffs, whitecaps frothing in the distance.

"If you squint real hard, you can see Hawaii," Kai says, pulling the Jeep into a lot and parking.

"Hardy har har," I say, hitting him on the shoulder.

"Okay, so not really." He grins and jumps down out of the car. "This place still kinda reminds me of home, though. Even if it's super different." I follow down after him, folding my arms around myself to keep warm. "There's a sweatshirt in the back, if you want it." Kai reaches in and tosses me something soft and fleecy and I pull it on gratefully.

"Do you come here a lot?" I ask as we walk over to the sand. I strip off my sandals and he does the same, and we walk together out onto the beach.

"Yeah, the surfing's okay here. Nothing like home, but it doesn't completely suck."

"Do you miss home?"

"Not as much anymore. All the time when I was little, though."

"That's why you got this." I reach out and grab hold of his wrist, turning it over gently and running my finger down the little wave tattoo inked there.

Kai sucks in a breath. "Yeah."

I'm immediately self-conscious I grabbed his arm, that I touched his skin without thinking about it first. I'm reminded of his fingers on my stomach last night, the fluttering feeling of bare skin against bare skin. I still feel so awkward about it now that we're in the light of day.

Yet for some reason, I don't let go of his wrist. I run my finger over the tattoo again, like maybe I can feel the ink in his skin. "When did you get this? Don't you have to be eighteen to get a tattoo?"

"Got it from a buddy of mine when I was fourteen. A bunch of us from home got them one summer when I went back to visit. My best friends from growing up."

It's surprising to think about Kai having a life back in Hawaii. I was always so caught up in the jealousy I felt when he moved here—how he so quickly became a part of the popular crowd, became one of the kids everyone circled around only a few weeks after he first arrived. It never occurred to me that he must have felt homesick, that he was forced to pick up his whole life and move because of his dad's affair. I guess I never really thought about everything he left behind.

I'm still holding on to his wrist, and I let it go, embarrassed.

He pulls his arm back and cracks his knuckles, shaking his hands out, almost like he's trying to shake me off him. There's a flare of hurt in my chest, something that feels a lot like rejection.

"So," he says. "This beach is kinda my spot." He scratches his nose. "I, uh . . . well, I come here usually when I need to be alone. When I need to think and recharge."

The rejection in my chest fizzles out, replaced by something warmer. "Kinda far for a thinking spot," I say.

"Nah, the drive is part of it. Just throw on the surfboard, blast some music, and zone out. Then come here and let the waves get rid of everything else."

I'm unexpectedly flattered that Kai chose to bring me here. I don't know why he'd want to show me something so personal.

But then I realize *I do get it*. Because even if we'll never completely get along, we understand each other in some small way. I know what it feels like to have a family you want to escape, to have a parent who makes you so angry sometimes you just want to blast music and drive and let the waves beat the feelings out of you, let them wash away the anger until you're all clean.

"Thanks for showing me this," I say. It's the only way I can think to let him know that I understand. "I feel . . . honored."

He scratches his nose again and laughs, and I'm worried I've gone a bit overboard.

"It's nothing," he says.

"It's not nothing." And then I reach out and take his hand, my arm moving before my brain has time to catch up. I'm *mortified*, my face instantly flushing, and I want to let go, but then he threads his fingers through mine and holds tighter. I have no idea what we're doing. It's just that my fingers kinda liked the feeling of his wrist, or maybe I just wanted to comfort him in some way, show him I understand everything he's going through.

It doesn't have to mean anything. People hold hands all the time. Still, I squeeze his hand and then let go, stuffing my hands into the pocket of my sweatshirt so they won't get any more ideas.

"My mom used to do that," Kai says, his hands reaching for his pockets too.

"Do what?" I burrow my toes into the sand, like maybe I can dig a hole big enough to jump into and bury myself.

"Squeeze my hand," he says. And *thank god*, it actually makes me feel a bit better. I was only comforting him, like a mom would. "It was our thing," he continues. "When I was little. She used to squeeze three times. Said it meant I *love you*."

And then suddenly I'm mortified again. I start coughing for no reason, anything to keep from having to respond to him.

Kai turns to me, his eyes wide. "Not that that's what you were doing or anything. I mean, I wasn't implying that you, like, *loved me*."

"Obviously not," I say.

"Okay, good."

"We hate each other, remember?" I'm laughing as I say it, like it's a joke, and I wonder briefly when it started to feel that way, like something I'm not serious about.

"Yeah, you're the worst," Kai says back, and it strikes me that he doesn't sound serious either. For the first time, being with Kai actually feels . . . *nice*. But nice is dangerous. Laughing at Kai's jokes won't lead anywhere good. I can't let myself get too comfortable.

When I get home that night, Mom isn't there. There's a twenty-dollar bill on the counter, a note for us to use it to grab some dinner. I find Seb in front of the TV, eating a Cup O'Noodles with a plastic fork. "Thought we could just eat trash and split the twenty," he says.

"Okay," I say. "Where's Mom?"

Seb shrugs. He's watching some weird anime thing, and apparently it's too hard to tear his eyes from the screen. "I think she got called in," he says, taking another slurp of noodles. "Or maybe she's with Steve."

There's that uncomfortable ache in my stomach again. It's weird—I've always been so annoyed by the way my mom jumps from guy to guy, have always assured myself I wanted her to settle down, but now that she seems to have found someone she likes, I don't really want to hear about it. I thought I just wanted my mom to be happy, but maybe it's more complicated than that.

I head into the kitchen and make myself a bowl of Cheerios, bringing it back into the living room and sitting next to Seb on the couch. "Of course she's with freaking Steve."

"I like Steve," Seb says, surprising me. "We all hung out a little bit after you left that day to get your car. He's an arborist, actually. Like, really into trees. He moved here to study the redwoods. I think it's cool."

"Dad was a scientist too," I say. "I guess Mom has a type."

"Yeah," Seb says. "At least her type is smart, nerdy guys and not like . . . garbagemen."

"I don't know, our dad is kind of a garbage man."

"True," Seb takes another slurp of noodles. "But I think you should give Steve a chance. Mom seems really happy."

"I wouldn't know because I haven't seen her in days," I say bitterly.

"She's trying to find someone," Seb says. "Sometimes that

takes time. You'd be a lot happier if you stopped being so stubborn about it."

I think of Kai's mom then, who is still so angry she refuses to go back to Hawaii. I want to be as strong as she is, but at the same time, I don't want to miss out on *my* Hawaii, whatever that is.

I tilt my head, studying Seb. "Okay, maybe you're not a baby. That was surprisingly mature."

He grins. "I already know Olivia is the right one for me, though."

"And then you ruined it." I shove him with my shoulder. "Don't be disgusting."

"Just give it a few years," he says. "Once we all graduate and come back home for Thanksgiving or something, she'll fall in love with me."

"I am both proud and terrified of your confidence," I say.

Seb laughs and takes a big bite of noodles. "Actually, speaking of . . . I heard you have a new boyfriend." I guess the news has traveled down to the sophomores already. That means everyone in school probably knows Kai and I are . . . together.

"Shut up."

"You're dating Olivia's ex, aren't you?"

"Not really," I say. "I don't know, it just happened."

"So does that mean Olivia is single now?" He grins at me, and I whack him with the couch pillow, forgetting about the Cup O'Noodles until it's too late and disaster has already struck.

Later that night, I'm up in my room watching *Beauty and the Beast* on my laptop and planning my outfit for the Disney trip. I made a yellow Belle T-shirt—simple except for these puffy ruched sleeves (you're not allowed to wear real costumes at the park or you go to Disney jail). I'm going to wear it with my Mary Janes and these rosebud earrings I found at the thrift store. I even sewed a cute face and handle onto my backpack to turn it into Mrs. Potts.

I've just put on a lavender sheet mask, the feel of it cold and soothing, when my phone buzzes.

Do you think I should get glasses? It's Myriah. Romina used to always love when Harper wore her glasses.

Don't you have perfect vision? I answer.

I'll be eighteen in four months. Sometimes eyesight gets worse in old age.

She's your BEST FRIEND, I type back. Just. Talk. To. Her.

I thumb over to Olivia's contact info before I realize what I'm doing, about to type a message to her, when I remember. I'm hit with a wave of sadness. In my old life, she would have been right here beside me, a matching sheet mask on her face, the two of us walking Myriah through this situation together.

The phone buzzes again, and I glance at it, expecting another response from Myriah, but the words on the screen surprise me:

Feels so great to have a whole bed to myself, Kai says. I flush with heat despite the mask, because even though he's joking, I'm immediately thinking back to how it felt to have his arms wrapped around me. How great it felt to *cuddle* Kai Tanaka. Cuddling is even more dangerous than laughing.

I spend a good six minutes trying to decide what to say back. You liked sharing your bed with me, I type, nervous. What am I doing?

Anything for you, my sweet munchkin.

Is a munchkin a food group? Or have your horrible nicknames expanded?

A munchkin is a tiny donut. I can go back to "weenie" if you want.

I will murder you.

What are you doing right now? Kai asks. I debate whether I should tell him the truth—whether I should pretend I'm being an intellectual and reading *War and Peace*—but I decide to be honest. I'm doing a sheet mask and watching Beauty and the Beast.

Oh right, you and your Disney.

We should wear matching sets of ears on the trip so we look like a real couple.

Absolutely not. If you ever see me in Mickey Mouse ears, please set me on fire.

Yeah there's nothing worse than being festive and bringing people joy.

You bring me no joy, weenie.

Don't worry, you can break up with me soon. Typing out the words gives me a funny feeling in my stomach. For the first time, the idea of breaking up with Kai doesn't fill me with relief. The truth is, I *like* texting him. And if we break up—if we get back with Jordan and Olivia—I don't know if we'll be able to keep doing this.

I stare at my phone as Kai types and deletes. And then: Let me see the sheet mask.

No! I type back. Absolutely not. Sheet mask privileges are for friends.

We're friends now, aren't we?

It all makes sense, then. *That's* what this is. That's the feeling I couldn't place, the word I've been searching for. Kai and I have stopped biting at each other's throats, and instead we've been having real conversations about the things that matter. *Kai and I have become friends.* It's why I'm scared of breaking up—I don't want to go back to fighting all the time. Being angry has always been so much work.

So I hold up my phone and take a selfie of my sheet mask, making a kissy face at the camera, and send it to him before I can change my mind.

You look like you're from the Purge, he answers immediately, and I send him the middle finger emoji in response.

THEN

JUNIOR YEAR–JANUARY

JORDAN SHOWS ME his tree house on a Friday night in January, after we've been together for four weeks. I tell my mom I'm studying at Olivia's, and Jordan's parents are out together at a movie, so we're all alone. It feels more magical this way—like we're lost from time—like this is a moment meant only for us.

It's cold, colder than most other January nights, so we bundle up in sweaters and jackets from the hall closet. I wrap myself in Jordan's mom's ski parka, and he carries a stack of blankets out to the tree house so we can wrap ourselves up in them too. He lights a little fire in the camping stove, and we pour hot chocolate packets—the kind with the mini marshmallows—into mugs.

"It's like we're camping," I say, taking a sip of my drink. It's too hot and it burns my tongue.

"I wish we could spend the night out here."

"Your parents will be back soon."

"They'll probably be a little late. They always stay through the closing credits so they can make out."

He laughs and I stick my tongue out. "Gross."

"It's sick."

The truth is that even though we joke about it, I think it's cute how in love Jordan's parents are, that they can't keep their hands off each other like they're still a couple of teenagers. Secretly, when I see them I think of my future with Jordan. I want to be the type of old people who still make out in the movie theater.

"I listened to that musical you told me about," Jordan says. "*Hadestown*? It was dope."

"You really liked it?" It's been my mission to share my love of show tunes with Jordan ever since he asked me what *Dear Evan Hansen* was and I discovered he was obtuse.

"Who knew Broadway was actually good?" Jordan takes a sip of his hot chocolate and a mini marshmallow sticks to his nose.

I reach my hand up and wipe it away. "You have a thing."

"Thanks, babe."

At his use of the word *babe*, my heart starts fluttering a million miles per hour in my chest. No one has ever called me that before. It's so crazy that only a few months ago I was terrified to touch Jordan, terrified to speak to him. And now that he's mine I can casually wipe a marshmallow from his nose.

"You're welcome," I say back, feeling warm inside.

Olivia used to tell me about Jordan's tree house—she came over here once when we were freshmen and Jordan's older sister threw a party. Olivia had been one of the few non-seniors in attendance, and she'd told us she had climbed up the ladder in the backyard with Jordan and Kai and they'd all shared a joint and talked about aliens and the infinite unfolding of the universe. I remember I had felt funny when she told me about it, so many conflicting emotions at once. I was horrified about the joint, which I knew must have come from Kai, but so jealous that she'd had a moment like that without me. It's not like I wanted to be there—Kai and the joint wouldn't be worth it—but I was hurt I hadn't been invited. I'd found out about the party Monday morning at school like the rest of the freshmen.

But I'm here now. I'm the one in Jordan's tree house, the one he set this all up for. I'm the one he just called *babe* for the very first time.

He puts his mug down and leans toward me, claiming me in a kiss. I set my mug down too, worried I'll spill it, and as I do, Jordan lays me down, climbing over me and pressing me into the blankets. I am immediately aware of every single nerve ending in my body, can feel every inch of my skin for the very first time in my life.

Jordan threads his hand through my hair, pushing himself against me. Then he brings it lower, touching the soft skin of my neck, and then lower still to my belly. He pulls his mouth from mine and looks into my eyes. "I think I love you, you know that?"

Suddenly, I can't breathe, but in the best kind of way. "I love you too," I say back, feeling my face break out into the world's most impossibly huge grin.

"Good," he says, smiling to match mine, and then he kisses me again, his hand finding its way under the giant parka to reach my bra.

"Wait." The word's out of me before I've decided on it. There's a part of me that wants Jordan to keep going, that never wants him to stop, but there's another part that doesn't want to rush things. There are already too many firsts tonight, and I want to bask in them, want every first with Jordan to be a crisp and clear memory I can look back on and savor for the rest of my life.

"You sure?" he says, his hand still cupped there. "We have like an hour at least till my parents come back."

"Can we just talk instead?" I move so that his hand slides off me, sitting up slightly and propping my body back on my elbows.

"I looked up the lengths of all the movies when they asked me for a rec, and I suggested the one that was three hours." He sighs, but flips his body over so he's next to me, propped up on his elbows too.

"So that means we have three hours to talk." I smile at him. "Will you tell me you love me again?"

"Sure. I love you."

"I love you," I say back. "I love you, I love you, I love you." I could probably fill three hours with that. There's a gap in the wooden ceiling, and I look up. Above us, it's started to snow.

NOW

WHEN I GET TO WORK a few days later, Sarah is already there, scrubbing down the tables with a rag and a bottle of disinfectant.

"Help me sweep the floor before we open," she says, nodding her head in the direction of the storage closet. I grab the broom and come out to meet her.

"It already looks pretty clean," I say, starting to sweep.

"Oh, are you the expert?" she asks. "Did you get promoted to manager?" I roll my eyes and keep sweeping. I'm tired—wiped out from everything that's happened—and spending time with Sarah only makes me more on edge.

We work in silence for a few minutes and then Sarah breaks it. "Sorry, I didn't mean to snap at you."

I'm surprised she's apologizing. I kinda thought part of her might enjoy having this power over me—payback for all the years Olivia has tormented her. I would totally get it if she wanted to boss me around like some evil dictator. Force me to eat freezer bananas.

"It's okay," I say, giving her a weak smile. "Long weekend?"

She sets down the bottle of disinfectant with a loud *thunk*. "So long." She pauses, like she's deciding whether she wants to tell me more. Then she plows on. "My band had a show on Saturday night and then the venue refused to pay us because some guy threw up on one of their speakers. But, like . . . that wasn't *our* fault. Some guys just can't hang."

I'm staring at her, and it takes me a second to realize my mouth is hanging open. There is so much about what she just said that I don't know how to process. I always thought Sarah hung out by herself on the weekends like I used to back when I had no friends, hunched over her laptop watching old seasons of *Doctor Who* or something.

"You're in a band?" I ask once I have properly stopped gaping. "I didn't know that."

"I mean, you don't really know anything about me, do you?"

"I guess not. I mean, not since we were ten."

"I've changed a lot since then." She tucks the disinfectant and rag into a cupboard below the cash register as I finish up my sweeping. "Can you flip the sign for me?"

I scoop the dirt into the dustbin—Sarah was right, the floor *was* kinda dirty—and then dump it into the trash. Then I walk over to the front door and flip the sign around to OPEN. "Okay, well, what instrument do you play?" I ask, joining her behind the counter and pulling on my custom Scoops baseball cap.

I remember our fourth-grade music class—Sarah in the back of the room with her clarinet, disrupting constantly with sharp, ear-piercing squeaks. I was up front on the keyboard with Katie, giggling when she giggled. I feel bad about it now and wonder if I should say anything. But I don't want to remind her.

"I play the bass," she says. "And the synth. We're kinda space-age electro pop."

"Whoa, that's cool." I have no idea what most of those words mean, let alone put together, but it does sound cool. It sounds very *un*-Sarah Kozlowski. "I just . . . I mean, no offense, but, like, who else is in the band?" I'm not trying to be rude, but Sarah is always alone at school. Always. "I've just never seen you hang out with anyone. I thought you didn't have any—"

"I have friends, Penny." Sarah lets out a harsh laugh. "Just because all the people at RHS suck ass doesn't mean I don't have a social life."

"Fine," I say. "Sorry." I know it sounds crazy, but it actually never occurred to me that anyone could have a life outside of Redwoods High. I mean, everyone I've ever hung out with has been someone from school—someone I've known since I was six years old. I didn't realize I had any other options. "So what's the band called?"

"We're the Disco Cats. You may have seen our fliers around town? There are cats on them, like, flying through galaxies." She sounds hopeful when she says it, and I want to tell her I've seen them, but I definitely haven't. I would remember something that weird.

"No, sorry."

"Well, maybe you could come to a show sometime? I mean, if you're interested. There's one at Java Town on Friday night." And there it is between us—an olive branch. Sarah is offering me her friendship, and I could reach out and take it if I wanted.

Maybe she isn't so bad. Maybe she's actually . . . kinda cool? I mean, not the kind of cool that means anything in high school. Not the kind of cool that will get you invited to the right parties, that will open up the right lunch table, earn you a place in the best group chats. But still, she's interesting. That counts for something.

But I can't do it. If I start hanging around Sarah K, this whole mess I've gotten myself into will only get worse. I'll never get my friends back, will never get Jordan to fall back in love with me. Not if they find out I went to see a band called the Disco Cats.

"I can't," I say. "I'm busy Friday."

Sarah chews on her bottom lip. "There are other shows. Other Fridays."

"I'm busy every Friday," I say, and then feel awful.

"Got it," she says, and then after a long pause. "You know, I was actually starting to believe you were different."

Her words are sharp, like they're meant to be an insult, and I'm surprised at first how much they hurt. But Sarah doesn't get that I'm not like her. I don't want to stand out.

"I'm not different," I say, and for the first time the words don't feel right. "I'm just like everybody else."

"Yeah," she says. "I figured that one out."

THEN

"GUESS WHAT KAI SAID to me the other day." Olivia and I are walking arm in arm like always out of biology on our way to lunch. She's wearing a big floppy felt hat like she's at Coachella instead of the gym-sock-stink hallways of our high school.

"Um, that you are beautiful and amazing?" I tease, nudging her shoulder with my own. Olivia is at that annoying point in her relationship where she literally never shuts up about Kai. It's February now—almost Valentine's Day—and the hallways are decorated with pink construction-paper hearts and red streamers. I know the boys are probably going to get into some cute competition to see who can get us the best presents. I mean, they have to know we're going to compare.

"Basically"—she leans in closer to me—"he told me he can't even believe I'm real. He feels like he's won the lottery."

"Wow," I answer, a lump in my throat. "Jordan says I'm hot, but . . . nothing like that."

"Well, you *are* hot," she says. "My best friend is an eleven."

"If I'm an eleven, then you're a twelve."

"*Duh*, Penelope. My hotness is infinite. I contain multitudes." She's giggling, quoting this poem we read last month in English class, and I know she's joking, but I feel stung by the casual way she's just announced she's hotter than I am.

Sarah Kozlowski walks by us then, her nose buried in a book, and she shifts out of Olivia's way without even glancing up from the pages. She's got her blue hair tied up on top of her head with a pen, and there are ink smudges all down the back of her neck.

"Oh my god, it's so sad, isn't it?" Olivia says to me in a mock whisper. She's trying to be quiet, but I know Sarah can probably hear her. "Valentine's Day must be the *worst* when you don't have any friends."

I don't know whether or not Olivia remembers my own terrible experience when we were kids—if the memory of my empty box has faded with time. I hope so. I don't think she'd be saying this to me if she could remember that moment in the same painful, visceral way that I can.

"Yeah," I say, glancing back at Sarah. There's so much I want to say to Olivia, but I don't know how. "It would suck."

"She's been single for seventeen years." Olivia giggles. "I bet she's never even kissed anyone. She probably just sits alone in her room crying and looking at pictures of our boyfriends on Instagram."

"It's so sad," I say as Sarah turns the corner. I can't help but think about how a few months ago—until Jordan invited me to hang out on Thanksgiving—I hadn't kissed anyone either. But I don't want to remind Olivia of that.

"Some girls get all the luck in life, ya know?" Olivia says.

"Kai is the lucky one," I say, grinning, "to be with a twelve like you."

"Hell yeah, he is," she says. "But I'm lucky too."

We walk into the cafeteria and our friends are waiting for us—Myriah and Katie with a messy stack of pink and red construction paper laid out before them, scissors in hand. Romina is between them, ignoring the arts and crafts and listening to something on her headphones. Kai and Jordan have folded a piece of red paper into a table football and are flicking it back and forth at each other.

"I mean, look at him," Olivia says to me as we approach. "Isn't Kai the hottest, coolest, most amazing guy you've ever seen?"

Jordan smacks the paper too hard and it hits Kai in the face, and Kai laughs and pretends to fall backward out of his chair.

"He's going to hurt someone," I grumble, because it's the best answer I can give.

"Hey, babe," Jordan says with a big grin as I slide into the seat across from him. His long legs are stretched out beneath the table, and I stretch mine out too so I can tease him by running my foot along his. We have perfected the art of footsie. "You gonna make me one of those?" He nods toward the pile of papers, half of which have fallen haphazardly onto the floor.

"I already made you something better," I say, and it's true. I spent weeks pressing flower petals between the pages of heavy books in my room, laying them out in a mosaic pattern on a poster board in a way that looks like Jordan's jersey number. I've been so antsy to give it to him, but a part of me is worried it's going to be a little too extra.

"Yeah, what are you gonna give me?" He leans closer, lifting an eyebrow, and the tone of his voice raises goose bumps on the skin of my arms. I know what he wants me to give him—I know what he's implying—but I'm not ready.

"Not that," I say, my voice soft. "Not yet."

He shrugs and backs away. "What? I was talking about chocolate chip cookies. The kind you made for that bake sale last week."

"Cookies give you gas," Kai says, smacking Jordan's arm. He turns to me. "Please, for all our sakes, don't make him cookies."

"Maybe don't tell me what I should do," I say, folding my arms.

"Wow, my mistake," Kai says flatly.

Katie slams a purple marker down on the table. "Ugh, I can't get it right!"

"What are you making?" Myriah puts down the scissors and inspects Katie's paper. "What does that say? Is that a . . . cabbage?"

"It's supposed to be an anatomical heart." Katie folds her arms. "Matt loves science."

Jordan leans closer. "Well, you've made the ventricles way too big. This heart has a pretty serious disease."

"You could just turn it into a cabbage," Myriah suggests. "Does Matt love cabbages?"

Romina pulls her headphones partway off, patting Myriah's hand. "Myr, nobody loves cabbages."

"Matt said he had this huge surprise for me, and I want to give him something nice back," Katie says.

"I swear to god if you don't take a picture of this boy on Valentine's Day and send it to us, I will officially think he's a ghost," Olivia says.

"Can you have sex with a ghost?" Romina pulls her headphones all the way off now, setting them down on top of a stack of lace doilies. "Like, do you guys think that's possible?"

"He's not a ghost!" Katie says.

"You could one hundred percent fuck a ghost, though," Olivia says. "Katie, what if he's a Revolutionary War soldier?"

"Probably not likely in California, though," Jordan says.

"Or what if *you're* the ghost?" Romina says, smirking. She makes an exaggerated *ooooo* noise until Katie threatens her with the scissors and Myriah tells everyone to settle down, and I think for the millionth time how lucky I am to be here—at this table, but also here with my friends and my boyfriend, right in the middle of it all. I love these people so much. And yeah, maybe Valentine's Day is about romantic love, but it's about this too.

"So, Jordan," Olivia says, leaning over the table toward him. "Where are you taking my best friend for Valentine's Day?" She picks up a pair of scissors, running her hand over the blade absentmindedly.

Jordan wraps an arm around me, pulling me closer, and I feel giddy. At this point, Jordan could probably gift me a hug for Valentine's Day and I would still be thrilled.

"Oh," he says. "Um, I was gonna make her some . . . spaghetti. I mean, that's all I really know how to cook, but—"

"Kai and I love spaghetti," Olivia says. "Don't we?"

Kai laughs. "It's a top-five food for sure."

"Wait, what if we did a double date?" Olivia picks up a piece of construction paper and starts cutting it into a heart shape. "I mean, not if you don't want us to. I wouldn't want to interrupt. But wouldn't that be so much fun?"

I don't want her and Kai to join us, to crash whatever romantic night Jordan has planned for me. But I don't want to shoot down Olivia's idea, not when she seems so excited and her eyes are so sparkly.

"Yeah, you guys can come if you want," Jordan says. "But bring some paper plates. I'm not doing your dishes."

Jordan's mom has Jordan's dad pressed against the refrigerator, kissing him in a way that is starting to feel like the start of a creepy old-person porno. I don't know if I should look away.

I'm sitting next to Jordan on one of the stools around the kitchen island, and I take his hand, squeezing it in what I hope he'll understand is a *help me* grip.

Finally, his mom pulls back and turns to us. Her red lipstick is smudged all over her face. "So sorry about that, kids. This man is so handsome I can't help myself."

"She's a tiger!" his dad says with a toothy grin.

"Could you guys maybe not maul each other in front of my guest?" Jordan asks. "Or, like, preferably ever?"

His dad winks. "It's Valentine's Day, son! If there's ever a time to show our love, it's tonight."

"We think it's so sweet you've invited your girlfriend over for a special romantic night." His mom straightens her dress—this killer red A-line that I am obsessed with—and fluffs her dark hair, heading toward the front door. "We won't be out *too* late. Well, maybe a little bit late. Your father has a surprise for me!"

"Your mother loves surprises!" his dad says, pulling on his suit jacket. They're clearly going to a fancy place, one with little tables and candlelight and waiters who let you try sips of wine before you order. I can't wait to go on a real date at a place like that someday.

If Kai and Olivia weren't coming over, we could have tried

to re-create that here—maybe decorated the dining room with twinkle lights and lit candles and played soft accordion music. But it won't feel the same. I should have told them not to come. I don't want Kai here to ruin another Valentine's Day. But sometimes it's hard saying no to Olivia.

"Okay, we'll see you little lovebirds later!" Jordan's mom says, and then she blows us a kiss and they both leave.

"Thank god that's over," Jordan says once the door shuts. "I swear this holiday turns them into hormonal monsters."

"I think it's sweet," I say, considering my own mom.

"It's not sweet. It's atrocious." He stands, plugging his phone into the aux cord on the counter. "Hold up, I have something for you." He shuffles through the songs, and then "All I've Ever Known" from *Hadestown* starts playing.

"You did not," I say, my face breaking out into the widest smile.

"Did too," he says. "It's a Valentine's Day Broadway playlist. Just sent it to you."

My phone vibrates, and I open his text and see the playlist there. I still can't believe Jordan's gotten into musicals, that he's kind, and smart, and so freaking beautiful he takes my breath away.

The door bursts open then—no knock—and Kai and Olivia come in.

"Honey, I'm home!" Kai shouts, and the moment is ruined, the cozy atmosphere built from the perfect song destroyed.

"Yo, we're in the kitchen!" Jordan says. He hits a few buttons on his phone and the Broadway music is quickly replaced with Post Malone, the transition jarring. Olivia comes into the room and spins, showing off her outfit. She looks incredible, obviously, in a tight red skirt and black off-the-shoulder top.

I look down at my own outfit—I went simple and elegant in a black dress—and feel sharply self-conscious. But then Olivia makes me feel better, like she always does. "Who is that sexy Victoria's Secret model angel, and what has she done with my best friend?"

"Thanks, Liv. You look so amazing."

"You're a work of art," she says. And even though I don't want them here, even though I want this night to be just Jordan and me, it's hard to be annoyed with her in moments like these.

But Kai, on the other hand . . .

"So, were you too lazy to plan a Valentine's Day of your own?" I say, turning to him. "And that's why you had to crash ours?"

"Yeah, I guess I wanted to spend this night with people who make me truly miserable." He grins at me. "Or just the one person, really."

I look at him in his stupid green T-shirt—because of course he wouldn't dress up for the holiday—and grimace.

"Double dates are way more fun than single dates," Olivia says. "Thanks so much for inviting us, Jojo."

Jordan wraps his arm around me, bringing me in tight. "I know you two love to fight with each other, but it would be cool if my girlfriend and my best friend could get along, ya know? Can we just make some spaghetti and get over it?"

So we make some spaghetti and get over it. And it's actually kind of fun. Jordan puts on his dad's apron—a cheesy one that says KISS THE COOK—and dumps the pasta into the boiling water.

I heat up the sauce, and Kai manages to make garlic bread without burning down the house.

Then we sit down to eat, and it's time to exchange presents. Olivia gives Kai a waxing kit for his surfboard, and Kai gives her the world's most gigantic teddy bear. He brings us out to the driveway to surprise her because the bear has been hiding all night in the back of his Jeep under a bunch of towels.

Finally, it's my turn. I'm so nervous to give Jordan his present. My heart feels like it's going to explode from my chest as I hand over the large silver paper–wrapped frame.

"You got me a thing?" he says, taking it.

"Um, I made it, actually." It's embarrassing exchanging presents in front of the others, especially because this one means so much.

"You made me a thing?" Jordan smiles and then rips the paper open. "It's flowers."

"It's your jersey number," I say. "See? It's a twenty-three."

"Oh," Jordan says, and then there's a long pause while I wait for him to continue. Why isn't he saying anything else? My cheeks grow warm. I can feel the weight of all three of their stares, sense immediately like I've done something wrong.

When the silence has gone on unbearably long, Kai cuts in. "This is really fucking cool, Penelope."

"Don't make fun of me," I snap at him.

"I'm not. You're, like . . . super talented." The compliment is so earnest, so out of place from Kai, and I'm surprisingly pleased.

"Thanks, babe," Jordan says finally. "It's dope."

"Okay, your turn," Olivia says to Jordan.

"My turn, what?" Jordan asks, setting down my present for him on the table.

"To give a present to Penny."

"Oh, I already gave it to her," he says.

"You did?" I feel giddy with possibility, trying to remember if he secretly handed me something in class, snuck something into my backpack when I wasn't looking.

"Yeah," he says. "That playlist I sent you."

"Oh," I say, deflating. "Oh, right."

I glance down at my phone again and look at the Broadway playlist. There's no text in the message. No *I love you*. Just the Spotify link. I thought I'd be thrilled with just a hug from Jordan, but it turns out maybe I wanted a bit more. Suddenly—before I can stop myself—there's an image in my mind: I've made a present for Kai instead and it's just the two of us here together eating spaghetti alone. It's so crazy, so unthinkable, that I feel myself flush with horror.

"Thanks," I say to Jordan, forcing a smile. "I love it." I take a deep breath, risking a glance over at Kai and Olivia and then looking back at him. "I love you."

Jordan grins and ruffles my hair, looping his arm around my neck. "Back atcha, babe."

NOW

A FEW DAYS LATER I'm standing anxiously in front of
Kai's front door. We made that stupid plan to cook dinner tonight, and while a part of me is feeling an overwhelming desire
to bail, another part of me is actually a little bit excited. Now
that we're friends, taking pictures cooking together might actually be fun.

I borrowed my mom's car and drove myself over here, telling
her I was headed to Olivia's. Just because Kai's mom thinks he
and I are dating doesn't mean my mom has to know anything
about it—there would be too many questions there, too much I
wouldn't be able to explain. Plus, Steve was with her. *Hey, kiddo,*
he'd said as I left. *Sure you don't want to stay and play Monopoly?*

I decided to dress up a little—a yellow sundress and strappy
sandals, a cream-colored sweater to cover my shoulders. Even
though this thing with Kai is fake, I still want to look good.

Kai opens the door, and I notice he dressed up for this a bit
too—he's got on a pair of brown khakis rolled at the ankles and

a navy blue shirt with buttons down the front and an actual collar. He looks nice—*handsome.* The word comes to me before I can tell myself not to think it. I shake my head, trying to make the thought go away.

"Hey," I say casually, walking into the front hall. The house smells amazing—like garlic and tomatoes.

He steps aside to let me pass. "Hey, Lemon Poppy Seed Muffin."

"Now you're just reaching."

"But those are delicious!"

"So are you saying I'm delicious?" It strikes me that I'm flirting with him again, and I press my lips together so I will stop speaking immediately.

"Is that Penny?" A voice comes from the kitchen and then Kai's mom appears. She's smiling wide, her hair thrown up in a messy bun. She's got on a colorful flower-print dress that matches the vibrant patterned paintings on the walls, a bright green chef's apron tied over it. "Welcome! We're so excited to have you here. Kai has told me so much about you."

"Mom," Kai grumbles.

"Oh, hush," she says. "I can't tell your beautiful girlfriend that you talk about her?"

I blush at her comment, reaching down to take off my sandals.

"God, leave a little mystery or something," he says. He heads back into the kitchen and we both follow. Kai takes a seat at one of the stools around the kitchen island, and I take his lead, sitting down next to him. His mom ties her apron tighter and begins to stir something on the stove.

"Thanks for inviting me over," I say to her. "I love your house."

"Thanks, Penny," she says. "I'm a bit of a collector. I ran a gallery back when we lived on Maui, actually. When I see art I like, I have a really hard time walking away."

"She has a bit of a problem," Kai says in a teasing tone. "She'll buy random paintings from Goodwill. She went to one of my art shows when I was a kid and asked if she could buy some other kid's project! Not even *my* project. Some random project she liked better."

She taps the spoon on the edge of the pot. "That is some major revisionist history, Kai. Of course I liked your painting best. Why else would it be in the place of honor?" She uses the spoon to point at the wall above the couch, where there's a framed blocky painting of a blue whale.

"Wait, you made that?" I ask, getting off my stool and walking to the couch to get a better look. "I didn't know you painted."

"Mom, it's like you're actively trying to embarrass me." Kai covers his face with his hands.

"Of course I am," she says. "That's what mothers do best."

"It's really good." I reach my hand out as if to touch the canvas and then pull back.

"It's not," he says. "I was like eleven when I made that."

"Well, then it's even better." I turn back to him. "How come you never told me you're an artist?" I realize the question doesn't make sense as soon as I ask it. Until recently, I've never really made an effort to find out anything about Kai's life. I've never wanted to know.

"He's being shy, but he's extraordinarily talented," Kai's mom says. "I'm an art teacher now over at the elementary school. Not many eleven-year-olds can paint like that."

"Can I see anything else you've painted?" I walk back over to join him on the stools.

"No," he says. "It's private."

"But I'm your giiiiirlfriend," I say, batting my eyes at him and pouting my lips. If we're gonna go through with this charade, then I'm going to take advantage of it in all the ways I can.

"Don't be a douchebag, Kai," his mom says, and I burst out laughing. "Show the girl your art."

She turns back to the stove, facing away from us, and Kai glares at me.

"Don't break your mom's heart," I whisper with an evil smile. "Show your beautiful girlfriend your art."

You're evil, he mouths back at me. "After dinner, okay?"

"Yay!" I clap my hands together, happy I've won this battle. But there's more to it too—I really do want to see his other paintings. I want to get this honest glimpse of him, peel back the layers to see who he really is underneath all the puns and defensive jokes.

"I do art sometimes too," I say. "Well, not real art, but . . . I like making crafts. Sewing clothes and doing makeup and stuff. I watch DIY videos on YouTube."

"That certainly *is* real art," Kai's mom says. "Anything you put your heart into is art."

"Oh boy, don't get her started," Kai says.

"It's true!" she counters. "Art is a state of mind. Penny, you should look into taking some classes."

"We have a studio at school, actually. Olivia is really into photography, so she stays after a lot and works in the darkroom."

"Olivia?" Kai's mom asks, and I wince. I cannot believe I

brought up his ex-girlfriend's name in his house with his mom. I don't want her to be reminded of Olivia—of all the ways I'm different. Of all the ways I don't measure up.

"Olivia from school," Kai says. "It's nothing."

"Well, you could look into other art classes too," she continues. "There are some wonderful classes available at the university that are open for all ages. I could talk to some of my contacts there if you'd like?"

"Um, sure," I say, breaking into a smile. "Thanks, Mrs. Tanaka."

"Mari," she corrects again. "And of course! We've got to nurture that creative instinct of yours." She turns back to the stove, stirring, and as I watch her, I feel unexpected tears sting at the corners of my eyes. I take a deep breath, trying to calm down. I can't cry right now. It would be so embarrassing and ridiculous and out of place. It's just—this is how I wish it could be with *my* mom. I know she loves me, I know she means well, but I want her to show it. I want her to talk about signing me up for art classes and cook me nice dinners on the stove instead of spending all her free time with her boyfriends and leaving me money for takeout.

"You okay?" Kai asks from next to me.

I nod, pressing my hands into my eyes for a second, and then smile at him. "Yeah. It's all good."

"Okay, cool. Good. Well, your mind is about to be blown. My mom's food is insane."

"Actually, can you start chopping me some onions, Kai?" his mom calls over her shoulder. She looks at me with a smile. "I can't chop the onions. It always makes me cry."

"You're just a big softy," Kai says lovingly.

"Yes, well. That's true too."

"I can help," I say, jumping up out of my stool. "Actually, wait." I dig my phone out of my bag and hold it out to her. "Can you take some pictures of us?" I forgot for a second that was the whole reason we planned this dinner in the first place.

"Of course!" Mari says, setting down her knife.

I pick up one of the onions and step closer to Kai, holding it out between us in a way that's supposed to look pensive, like we are contemplating what to cook.

"What . . . are you doing with that?" Kai asks, putting his arm around me.

"We're supposed to look like we're cooking."

"We could just cook instead of pretending to cook."

"Then the pictures won't look right," I say. Mari snaps a few photos while we strike different poses. She hands the phone back to me, and I look through the photos, relieved to get this whole thing over with so we can go back to having fun. "Hold on," I say, bringing the phone back up. "You should kiss my cheek." I take a picture as he does, his lips tickling the soft skin there.

"That one's better than the one with the onion," he says. I post it, quickly typing out the cheesiest caption I can think of: Feel so special cooking dinner with Kai. How did I get so lucky? I add six heart emojis to really drive the point home. Then I turn back to him. "So what are we cooking, anyway?"

"You mean what are we pretending to cook?" Kai asks. "We're making chili rice. We wanted to make you something local style. I thought about doing kalua pork and going, like, *full* Hawaiian, but I don't really know how to cook that. Also, there's no good pork on the mainland. It's a fucking travesty, actually."

"*Language*," his mom says. "We have a guest. But he's right. It is a travesty." She turns around to face Kai. "You'll just have to take her back to Maui sometime. Show her a real meal."

"I'd like that," I say, and I don't know what is wrong with me. Like, yeah, maybe we're friends now, but we're not the kind of friends who take trips together. We would probably murder each other within five minutes if we ever sat together on an airplane. I would likely pull open the emergency exit just to get away.

"I could show you the house I grew up in," he says. "I had a tire swing. Tommo and I used to fight like crazy over that thing."

"You and your brother were monsters," Kai's mom says. "You would fight over everything."

"He'd probably like you," Kai says to me. "He'd love that you put me in my place all the time. He was the *serious one*," Kai says, lowering his voice as he says it, as if they're bad words.

I remember Tom—barely, from before he graduated. He was a few years older than us, but everyone knew who he was. He was the star of our baseball team and kind of a big deal.

"He's at Auburn now, right?"

"Yup," Kai says, and then, surprised, "how did you know that?"

"You told me. I'm a good listener."

"Kai doesn't want to go to college," his mom says. "He wants to travel the world and surf and make art. It's a dream life, but it doesn't pay the bills."

"Wait, really?" I ask. "I didn't know that." It's never occurred to me to not go to college. Olivia and I have dreamed of UCLA for as long as I can remember. It's the plan. Or at least, it *was*. "But you have to go to school. That's . . . I mean, that's what people do."

"Maybe I'll go," Kai says. "I just think eighteen is too young to figure out what you want to be for the rest of your life."

"Now, that I agree with," Mari says. "But I want you to get an education. I want you to have the best life you possibly can. An education opens doors."

"I know," he says. "If I find something I'm passionate about, I'll get the loans and I'll do it. But I don't want to do it for the sake of doing it."

I don't know how to answer him. I don't get how Kai can roll through life like he doesn't care—how things seem to always work out for him anyway. That's not how it goes for me at all.

The rice cooker on the counter beeps, and his mom removes the lid, using a big wooden spoon to make the rice nice and fluffy. Little puffs of steam are billowing out the top, and it smells delicious. She scoops rice into three bowls and then brings them over to the pot of chili on the stove.

"Wait," I say. "I just realized what you said. What is chili rice? You're mixing the rice and the chili together?"

"Don't make that face," Kai says, dipping a ladle into the chili and pouring it onto the rice. He sprinkles some cheese on top and hands me the bowl. "This is the only way to eat chili. Whatever else you've been taught is a lie."

"Corn bread is the only way to eat chili."

"Hell no." He laughs. "Try it."

"Okay, fine." I mix it all up with my spoon and take a bite. And yeah, it's so much better this way.

"You like it," Kai says. "I can tell."

I swallow my bite and smile. "Okay, fine, yes, this is amazing." I turn to his mom, clutching the bowl in my hands like it might disappear. I'm pretty sure I've turned into the heart-eye emoji. "You're a wizard."

She laughs. "I like her. You've picked a good one, Kai."

• • • • • •

We eat dinner together out on the porch, the night air warm, surrounded by the chirping of crickets. When the meal is done, Kai and I help his mom collect the bowls and wash them in the sink. I grab a towel and start drying, but his mom shoos me away.

"I can take care of this," she says. "You two go have fun."

"But you cooked," I say.

"It's my treat." She takes the towel out of my hands and waves it in the direction of the doorway. "Now go spend some time together. And keep the bedroom door open!"

The truth is that going up to Kai's room, hanging out in there like we're a real couple—it feels weird. Down here in the kitchen, we're with his mom, we're putting on a show of our relationship. But there's no reason for me to be over here and in his room.

"Come on," he says. "I can show you some of my terrible paintings."

"Well, in that case," I say, and then follow him up the stairs.

Kai's room looks the same as it did a few weeks ago, the morning this all started. I remember how nervous I felt back then, how I was searching the walls for clues to destroy him. But I don't feel that way now.

I look around with fresh eyes, noting the little details that are all Kai. There's a postcard with his name hanging over his desk, Japanese characters painted beneath the English letters. His bed is made, navy-blue sheets tucked neatly into the sides. And there—sitting on his pillow—a worn whale stuffed animal I didn't notice before, frayed and falling apart. I grab it before he can stop me.

"Who's this?" I point the whale's face at him.

"Dammit," he says. "I forgot to hide him."

I wiggle the whale's head. "Oh, so it's a him? Does he have a name?"

"I'm not telling you his name."

I hug the whale to my chest. "Please, Kai. He's so cute. He deserves a name."

"He's shy. He doesn't like meeting strangers."

"I'm not a stranger. I'm your *girlfriend*."

"Fine. His name . . ." Kai lets out a heavy sigh. "His name is Doctor Whaley." He chews on his bottom lip, looking up at me with eyes so miserable it's like I've physically wounded him.

"Wow." I laugh. "Whaley. Honestly, your creativity is astounding."

"Hey, I was five!"

"No, I love it. *And* he's got a PhD. Doctor Whaley went to college, Kai."

Kai lunges for me, trying to grab the stuffed animal out of my hands, but I dodge out of the way, laughing and screaming and holding Whaley out of reach. I jump into the air, bringing Whaley up as high as I can get him, and Kai jumps too, but I move my arm at the last second, and somehow I'm still in control, still have him in my clutches.

"He's mine now!" I let out a full-on cackle. "He's coming home with me."

"Whaley would never," Kai says, all mock offended.

"*Doctor* Whaley," I correct. "Don't insult his intelligence, Tanaka."

He laughs, lunging for me again, and then his arms are around my back, his hands find my stomach, and he's tickling me. I shriek and squirm in his arms, dropping Whaley onto the rug. There are tears in my eyes from laughing. "Okay, fine! You win!"

We're both breathing heavily, and he doesn't bend down to pick the stuffed animal up off the floor because his arms are still around me. My back is pressed up against his chest, the same way it was in the bunk bed, and again I have the same urge to turn around so we're facing each other. My heart is still racing from the tickling and from the laughing, and definitely not from anything else.

Slowly, the laughter subsides, and then Kai lifts his arms off me and I step away from him, making my way across his room, putting a good three feet between us. I don't know what just happened, how I keep finding myself in these positions where I forget for a brief moment that this is all supposed to be pretend.

Kai picks up Doctor Whaley, setting him gently back onto his pillow. Then he sits down on the bed. I sit in his desk chair, and I realize we're back in the same places we were only a month ago, the first time I came up here. Everything felt so different then.

"So, you like whales a lot, then, huh?" I ask, trying to pretend like everything is totally normal.

Kai nods. "Yup. They're fucking majestic."

"Yeah?"

"I had this book of whale facts I used to read all the time when I was a kid. Like, you could not get me to put that book down."

"That's kind of adorable," I say, and the sincerity in my voice startles me. Because Kai's story is making me feel all warm and fuzzy, and these are so not feelings I'm supposed to be having around him.

"Like, did you know beluga whales love music? They've done

studies where they play music for belugas in these underwater speakers and they start dancing, like in rhythm."

"Oh yeah?" I say, trying to hold back a smile. "What kind of music was it? Was it maybe . . ."

"Don't say it," Kay warns, laughing.

". . . a *whaletz*?"

"Wow." He sighs dramatically. "That was . . . really exceptionally terrible."

"Was it played by an . . . *orca*stra?"

"You're really trying so hard, though," he says, laughing. "That's the worst part."

"I'm really *fin*tastic at this, Kai. I've found my *porpoise*."

"I'm supposed to be the one who makes the awful jokes around here, Pen."

"Well . . . now you know how it feels." And then, because I feel like I've derailed the conversation, because I really liked the excited look on his face when he was talking earlier: "Tell me another whale fact."

"So you can make fun of it?"

"I'm not!" I put my hands up. "I'm into it. I'm into—" I cut myself off, because I was going to say the word *you*. *This is fake, you idiot*, I repeat to myself. *Fake, fake, fake.*

"Okay, well, did you know that *Moby-Dick* was based on a real story?" Kai's eyes light up, and he stands and wanders across the room over to his bookshelf. "This epic whale sunk this British ship in the eighteen hundreds. The crew swam to shore and then had to resort to cannibalism." He thumbs through the shelf and then slides a book out, facing it to me. *Moby-Dick*.

"It's like you're setting me up," I say, laughing. "There are so many puns I could make right now, it is actually painful."

"Fuck," Kai says. "You're right. I'm so off my game. This is a real low point for me." He tosses me the book and, surprisingly, I catch it. "You ever read it?"

I turn the book over in my hands, examining it. "Yeah, in English last year."

"I remember back when we were kids, you used to read all the time."

I tense up, my shoulders suddenly rigid.

"I used to notice you sometimes on the playground," he continues. "I thought it was awesome."

I look up at him, surprised. "I don't want to talk about it. I'm not . . . that's not me anymore."

"No, I thought it was so cool." He's smiling and I'm looking for something, *anything* sinister behind it, but it isn't there. He seems genuine. "You actually kinda got me into reading, you know that? Like, I'd see those books you were always reading at school and you looked so absorbed in them, and I wanted to read them too. So I'd go borrow them from the library when you were done. And then you got me that book *Lord of the Flies* for my birthday once. I loved that one."

I remember going to the store with my mom to pick out a present for Kai's party. I'd gotten him *Lord of the Flies* out of spite, because I'd thought he'd see himself in someone like Jack— would mount my head on a pike if he could. "I didn't really think you'd read it."

"Of course I did," he says. "Actually, um, I have something for you."

He turns and runs his hand along the spines of the books on the shelf, then finds one and pulls it out. It's small and worn, half the cover ripped away. *The Giver.* My book.

He holds it out to me. "I'm sorry I kept it for so long."

I set *Moby-Dick* down on the desk and walk toward him, taking the book gingerly out of his hands. "Thank you." I hug it to my chest. I know it's just a book, that it doesn't mean anything, but it feels like an apology. It feels like so much more.

"I read it right after you loaned it to me. And then I meant to give it back. I wanted to tell you how much I loved it, but then, I dunno . . . things happened . . . and then it was too late."

Pukey Penelope. The name hangs between us in the air, a silent horrible thing; the words I wish could be wiped clean.

"I'm sorry," Kai says, his voice low. "For everything."

"Thank you," I say. And I mean it. I clutch the book closer to my chest.

"You know," he says. "I really feel like you were the only one who actually saw me back then."

"What are you talking about?" I laugh at his actual ridiculousness. "You were friends with everybody like the second you moved here. It was always so easy for you."

Kai laughs. "You think picking up my whole life was easy? I had to leave my dad behind, all my friends, had to move across an ocean to a place where I didn't know anybody. Started a new school—which was mostly white kids, by the way—and I didn't know how I was supposed to act. Remember on that first day? I was so cold and my mom dressed me in this stupid snowsuit and everyone stared at me like I was an alien."

"I liked your snowsuit," I say.

"That's what I mean, though." He sits down on the bed, and I take a seat next to him, hesitant. "I was so sad back then, you know? So homesick, and everyone on that first day was already friends. Nobody even looked at me. And then I saw you reading, and you smiled at me, and it was that little smile that got me through it all. I was like, *This girl gets it.*"

"I felt the same way," I say, smiling now. "I mean, when you came over to talk to me. But then you became friends with Jordan and everybody else and you were so cool so fast without even having to try. They all wanted to be friends with you just because you were from Hawaii."

"Yeah," he says. "Exactly. They only wanted to be friends with me because I'm from Hawaii. You think that's a good thing? I mean, I took it. I ran with it because people were finally talking to me, thinking I had, like . . . merit all of a sudden. But, like . . . I'm way more than where I'm from, Pen. I wanted real friends, not people who thought I was cool because of whatever stereotypes they'd associated with me."

"Oh." It all makes so much sense now that he's said it. I can't believe it never occurred to me. I was so jealous back then of how the kids swarmed him at recess when they found out where he'd moved from. But I hadn't noticed that before that moment, he'd been just like me—someone lost and afraid and looking for a friend. That underneath it all, that's who he still is. "But everyone is real with you now, right? I mean, you and Jordan . . ."

"Jordan was the best back then." He runs a hand through his hair, like he's uncomfortable to be bringing Jordan into this. "I still remember Danny Scott asking some stupid fucking question about whether I surfed to school, some microaggression bullshit about whether my family lived in a grass hut on the beach, and Jordan schooled him. We started shooting hoops together and he never asked me about any of that stuff. He just asked me about *me.*" He laughs, shaking his head. "But that's how I felt about you too. I wanted to get to know you better, but you avoided me after those first few days. Like as soon as Jordan and I started hanging out, you disappeared."

"Well, Jordan made me so nervous back then, so that probably had something to do with it."

"Really, this has been a thing since then?" He bites his lip.

"Since forever." I sigh. "I do this thing when I like somebody where I can't even look at them. Like if I make eye contact and he sees me looking, suddenly he's going to know everything I'm thinking and if he knows I like him, that would be the worst thing." I don't know why I'm telling him all of this, giving him a glimpse into the tangled mess of my brain. I look away, my eyes flicking down to stare at the carpet.

"But why would it be the worst thing?" He's looking at me—I can feel his eyes on the top of my head, but I'm finding it extremely difficult to look up from the floor.

"If he doesn't know I like him, I can't get hurt." This is all too personal, even after everything we've been through.

"Sometimes it's worth the risk, Pen."

I pull my eyes from the carpet then, feeling my cheeks flush. Our eyes lock together and somehow he's a little bit closer than he was only moments before. And I realize suddenly that Kai and I are not friends. That's not what this is at all. Because more than anything, I want to close the gap between us and kiss him.

But kissing Kai was what got us into this whole mess in the first place. This was supposed to be pretend; just a way to get our friends to forgive us, a way to get back with our exes. This whole thing was only supposed to be temporary. Kai belongs with Olivia.

"I have to go." I jump up and walk to the door.

"Hold on," Kai says. "You don't have to leave."

"No, I do, actually." I remember the rules we made when this all started. *If either of us wants out at any time, we're done.* And I want out. If we wait until Disneyland, who knows how messed up things could get before then? But how can I tell him that without admitting my feelings? "Tell your mom thanks for me, okay?"

And then I'm down the stairs and out the door before Kai has a chance to call after me.

NOW

IT'S A FEW DAYS LATER, around two p.m.—almost the end of my shift—when Jordan walks into Scoops.

I look up at the little jingle of the bell as he pauses in the doorframe, almost like he can't decide if he wants to come all the way through. Then he shuffles inside and shuts the door behind him. He's still wearing his hairnet from the Upper Crust, so I know he must have walked over from next door. He pulls it off when he sees me.

"You want a banana split?" Sarah calls out, drumming her gloved fingernails on the counter. Jordan lingers for a minute on the welcome mat and then nods and walks toward us. My heart feels like it's beating a million miles a minute. I don't know what he could possibly be doing here in the store. Did he come to see *me*? He obviously didn't come for the ice cream—Jordan is lactose intolerant.

"Hey, Harris," he says.

Sarah rolls her eyes. "I'll let you take this one."

"Um, hey." My voice comes out scratchy, so I clear my throat and try again. "Hey, Jordan."

"I was on my break and I saw your car parked out front. Thought I'd come see how you were."

I look to Sarah. "Can I take my last ten?"

"Be my guest." She shoos me out from behind the counter. I strip off my plastic gloves and remove my Scoops hat (it makes my ears stick out horribly), smoothing my hair down. I don't know what's worse—the hat or the potential hat hair underneath. I feel so underdressed for whatever is about to happen.

I take a seat at one of the plastic tables, and Jordan sits next to me.

"You have to be a customer to use the tables," Sarah calls out, and I snap back at her.

"Come on, Sarah!" Sarah knows how important this is.

"Okay, sure," Jordan says. "Can I just get a coffee with almond milk?"

"You got it, Parker."

Sarah keeps surprising me, honestly. I don't get how she's so confident around Jordan, so assured, when at school she usually doesn't talk to anyone at all. Sarah doesn't seem to care that Jordan is, well, *Jordan*.

She brings him his coffee and he hands her a five, and then finally she's back behind the counter and we're ready for whatever this is. I don't know why Jordan's here, which way I want this conversation to go. All I can think about is my talk with Kai the other night, how I fled from his room when I realized the plan was starting to feel a little too real.

"So, did you have fun at the lake?" Jordan asks, taking a hesitant sip.

"Yeah," I say truthfully. "Kai and I had a good time." Before I can help it, my mind flashes back to the moment Kai and I kissed in the woods, me trying to cover his face with my red lipstick. Having these thoughts in front of Jordan feels so wrong.

"Yeah. About that." He fiddles with the lid on his cup. "So, are you guys, like, serious or something? I saw that pic you posted. You went to his house for dinner?"

I don't know what to say to Jordan. Is my relationship with Kai still a lie? Am I still trying to make Jordan jealous? "Oh, I mean, sure," I say, which is not a real answer. "I don't know. You know what they say—the best way to get over someone is to get under someone else." My face flushes with heat as soon as I've said it because *oh my god*, I can't believe I just implied to Jordan that Kai and I are sleeping together.

Luckily, Jordan seems to think I'm kidding, because he laughs. "*They* seem to know what they're talking about." He pauses, fiddling with the top of his cup. "But rebounds aren't the real thing usually, right?"

"No, they're not." Is he talking about me and Kai right now? Or himself and Olivia?

I feel weird about where this is headed. Kai and I put on a show at the lake—we told everyone we loved each other—and now it's all unraveling in a second with the word *rebound*. It feels dirty, like this conversation is a betrayal. But that's stupid. Getting Jordan back was the whole point.

"Listen, Penny," he says, and the seriousness of it makes my breath catch. "I don't know, I saw those pictures you guys took and it just got me thinking." He chews his lip. "*I'm* the one who's supposed to be in those pictures."

It's all wrong. I know these words are supposed to make me

happy, that they're words I've been waiting all summer to hear, but instead I feel a lurching pain in my stomach: guilt.

"What about Olivia?" I ask.

"Olivia means nothing," Jordan says.

"But—"

"Just let me say this." He takes a deep breath. "The way everyone's been, like . . . celebrating you and Kai getting together has been really fucking hard for me—all those dumbass comments our friends made about you and Kai while we were together, like I was just some placeholder till you two figured out your shit? And then it actually happened. They were right. You and Kai were *in love*."

The pain in my stomach gets worse at each word. I feel horrible for what I did, for twisting the knife in deeper after my first mistake. Why did I want to make Jordan jealous when I had already broken his heart? Because I thought he wanted Olivia? Am I really that selfish?

"That's not what happened," I say.

"Come on, Pen—"

"It's not," I insist. And then the words are out in a rush. "Kai and I aren't together."

Jordan rubs a hand down his face. "So it *is* a rebound, then?"

"No, I mean . . . this whole thing is fake. Kai and I were just pretending." I thought I would feel better after telling Jordan the truth, that suddenly I'd be absolved of all my sins, but I feel so much worse.

"What the hell, Harris?" Jordan is laughing, but it sounds forced.

"It was stupid. Myriah made some comment about how she

knew I wasn't a bad person and said I must have kissed Kai because I loved him. And then you and Olivia were kissing and we thought maybe you'd understand what you were missing out on if you saw us together." The more I say, the more ridiculous it sounds. How on earth did Kai and I ever think this would work? But then I realize—maybe it actually *did*. Jordan is here with me now, next to me at this plastic table, and he's hearing me out. That's more than I could say a few weeks ago.

And the worst part is that I don't know if I even want him back anymore.

"That's idiotic," he says. "This is the stupidest plan I've ever heard. Did you guys even think this through at all?" He's still laughing, and I can't tell if he's mad. "My best friend steals my girl and then says he's in love with her. I mean, even though he took you from me, I'm not gonna step on his toes and take you back. Not if he loves you."

I don't like what Jordan's implying here. You're supposed to fight for the people you love. You're not supposed to worry about stepping on anyone's toes.

"Kai doesn't love me."

"This is so twisted, Penny." Jordan stands up, and the plastic chair falls back behind him, hitting the floor. "I'm gonna go. My break is over anyway."

He scoops the chair up, flipping it back to its legs. Then he grabs the coffee and dunks it into the trash and walks out the door, the little bell jingling as he leaves.

All of a sudden, I feel like I'm going to cry, the reality of what I just said crashing down on me. I messed with Jordan's feelings, and Olivia's. And maybe Jordan was coming here to forgive me, but I messed that up too. Worst of all, I confessed about the plan, which means things with Kai will be probably be over once he finds out.

But that's what I wanted, right? I needed a way to get out of this mess with Kai—to make a clean break—and now I'm free.

"Holy shit." Sarah's voice startles me, and I flip around to face her. I completely forgot she was there this whole time, watching us. "Wow, Penny, there's a whole lot to unpack here."

We close up shop at four p.m., and then twenty minutes later I'm in the passenger seat of Sarah's Honda, headed toward McDonald's.

"A McFlurry always fixes everything," Sarah had said as she'd locked the Scoops door behind us. "You're coming with me. I am abducting you."

"We literally work at an ice-cream shop," I'd said, trying to walk to my own car. "Real local ice cream made from real local cows. Instead of mysterious lab-grown chemicals."

But she'd grabbed my arm. "People like chemicals, Harris. At least I'm not pushing LSD on you or something."

And so I'd gone with her, thoroughly abducted, to get a McFlurry. The truth is that having someone to talk things over with sounds nice. And Sarah Kozlowski seems like she'd be a good listener.

Her car is filthy—there are crumbs ground into the seat cushion, fast-food boxes scattered all over the floor, and it reeks of cigarettes. I have to step on a backpack when I climb in, and I wince as something cracks under my foot.

"It's not that bad," Sarah says. "Stop being dramatic."

"Do you live in here?" I mean it as a joke, but I realize when

I look around at all the items strewn everywhere that it might be true.

"No," she says. "Jesus. I just cart stuff to gigs a lot. Most of this is music shit. And my boyfriend keeps a lot of his stuff in here too."

"You have a boyfriend?"

"I thought we'd established by now that I'm not the social pariah you think I am."

I remember the text Olivia sent her last year pretending to be Kai; how Sarah had responded saying she had a boyfriend and we'd all laughed like it was preposterous.

"Sorry," I say. "Um, actually, wait—I need to tell you something." My heart is in my throat, my hands shaking. But I can't be here in Sarah's car letting her drive me around and trying to cheer me up without coming clean. I owe her that much.

"What now?" she asks. The lake passes us by on the left.

"Okay, so you know how Kai texted you last year? He said he thought you were hot." I take a deep breath. "That was us. I mean, it was Olivia. But it was my fault too."

"Wow," she says. And then she starts to laugh. "Wow, I'm actually so fucking surprised you just admitted that. Kudos, Harris."

"Wait, you're not mad? You can be mad."

"Thank you for your permission, dude. I know I can be mad. I already knew about it, though."

"You did? And you've been talking to me?"

"I know Olivia's handiwork," she says. "I'm not fucking stupid. I just think it's hilarious you guys thought you fooled me. That's so good."

"Well, I'm sorry," I say. "I don't know what we were thinking. I mean, there's no reason—"

"It's chill," she says. "Just don't fuck me over again."

"You have full permission to poison me with bananas." I grin.

"Noted."

"So tell me about your boyfriend. Who is he?"

"His name is Brian—I know, the most boring white guy name ever, right?—but he's cool. He lives over in Wentworth. I met him at band camp last summer."

"Isn't that what people say when they're making up a significant other? Oh, she lives in Canada. He's from band camp."

"You think I'm making this up?" Sarah turns to me, and then her face softens when she sees I'm laughing. "Oh, you're joking."

"I can make jokes, you know. People think I'm funny."

"Oh yeah, what people?"

The answer is *Kai*. I think back to the way we were laughing in his bedroom—all those stupid whale puns. Kai thinks I'm funny. But I don't want to tell her that.

"That's what I thought," she says when I don't answer. "Your friends aren't especially known for their humor."

"That's not fair." I'm suddenly defensive. "Just because you don't hang out with us doesn't mean we don't have fun."

"What kind of fun is that?" she asks, flat and sarcastic. "Throwing awesome parties and taking selfies and drinking so much you black out? Cheating on your boyfriend and waking up on the lawn? That's fun?"

Her words are like a slap in the face, and I feel like I'm going to cry again. If this car trip was supposed to be making me feel better, it's not working. "Pull over," I say. "I don't have to put up with this shit." I reach for the door handle like I might try to jump out of the moving vehicle.

"Hey," Sarah says. "No, sorry. I shouldn't have said that."

The MCDONALD's sign comes into view up ahead and Sarah pulls into the lot, parking the car instead of heading toward the drive-through. She switches off the ignition and turns to me. "I mean it, I'm sorry."

"How do you know all about that?" I press my palms hard into my eyes and take a deep breath, trying to keep my emotions under control. My first day at Scoops, Sarah alluded to knowing a bit about what had happened with Kai, but I didn't think she'd heard the whole story—thought maybe she was the one person who didn't know everything about my horrible mistake.

"I have Instagram. I know how to use the internet. Olivia was posting about it everywhere."

"I don't know why I did it. I had everything I've always wanted. I was the perfect girlfriend. I was *perfect.*"

"Perfect is boring," Sarah says. "And honestly, what happened happened. What's the big fucking deal?"

"What?" Her words are so absurd that I actually start laughing.

"People are assholes. Cheating is a dick move, but it's not the end of the world. You can't change what you did. Either people will get over it or they won't."

"The only reason my friends kept talking to me is because I got together with Kai," I say. "We just wanted everyone to forgive us. It was like you said: everyone forgives a good love story."

"Fuck them. You spent the night on the lawn and instead of asking whether or not you were okay, your friends posted shit about you. You could have, like, been assaulted or died or something. Why are you trying to get back together with them? They fucking suck."

"You don't know them like I do, okay? You've only seen one

side of them." I think about the time Olivia yelled at Gabe Pinkerton when he insulted my ass, the way she's always hyped me up and called me beautiful and tried to support me; And sweet, lovely Myriah, who always somehow gifts the best, most personalized birthday presents, who knows what you want better than you do; Katie, who is always the last one to get a joke but then laughs the hardest when she does; Romina, who makes the most badass playlists and is amazing on the cello, always quick with the most hilarious dirty jokes. Maybe, collectively, we've done bad things. But they're not bad people.

"Yeah," Sarah says. "The side of them that sends me mean text messages and pretends to pick their noses when I walk by. The side of Olivia that told me I was going to tip the school bus over because I was too fat. The side that called you Pukey Penelope for like two years before you mysteriously decided to forgive her."

"All I want is for everything to go back to normal. I just want everyone to like me, okay? Is that so horrible?"

"Don't spend so much energy trying to get people to like you that you forget how to like yourself." She turns the car back on and pulls up to the drive-through. "I used to think you were funny," she says. "Just FYI. Back when we hung out. Before Olivia ruined you. You were hilarious."

"Olivia didn't ruin me." Olivia was the one who rescued me—who asked me to sit with her at lunch that day after I'd loaned her my sweatshirt, who started Pukey Penelope— I don't know how I ever let myself forget that. "It's all Kai's fault," I tell her, my usual line.

"So now you're dating him," Sarah says. "Sorry, *fake* dating him. Or were you just bullshitting Jordan back there? I'd bullshit Jordan Parker too if I could get away with it."

"I wasn't bullshitting anyone," I say. "I thought you were supposed to be on my side."

"I'm not on anyone's side," Sarah says. "It's not my job to make you feel better for your own problems. You can't just use me for emotional labor."

"Fine," I say again. "Forget the McDonald's. I wouldn't want anyone to see us together in public anyway."

Sarah looks at me for a long time and then reaches across me and pushes open the passenger-side door. "Get out."

"Fine," I say, stepping out of the car and slamming the door. She drives away, leaving me in the McDonald's parking lot. I feel like I'm going to cry again. Sarah has no reason to be nice to me—not after I blew off her band's shows the other day. Not after the way I've ignored her since elementary school. Not after what I just said.

And the truth is, Sarah is probably right. These are my own problems to solve. But right now, I don't know what I can possibly do to make things better.

THEN

JUNIOR YEAR–MAY

I GO OVER TO OLIVIA'S house to study for finals. We've raided the bin candy aisle at the local grocery store so we're fully stocked with sugar for the miserable long hours ahead. There are mountains of Twizzlers on her dining room table, bags of Sour Patch Kids, sugar granules pressed into the pages of my biology textbook.

These finals are the most important yet. They'll impact my financial aid for college, whether I can apply to UCLA with Olivia. They're the last tests standing in the way of an entire beautiful summer—and then finally we're seniors and it will be the best year of our lives. It's so hard to focus on the cell cycle and mitosis when all I want to think about is Jordan and what will finally happen between us once this stupid bio final is done.

Because I've decided something. Jordan's parents are going out of town next weekend for some giant dental conference in Las Vegas and they're leaving him home alone. None of us can believe it, honestly. It's the first night of summer and we'll have so much to celebrate.

I've been thinking about maybe sleeping with Jordan for months, but I haven't been sure until this moment. But now with his parents leaving, everything is aligning perfectly. I can't wait to sleep over his house, wake up next to him in his bed, just like we're two regular people—no rules, no parents, *just us.*

I haven't told Olivia yet, and now that I've officially decided, it's killing me to keep it inside. I just want to shout it from the rooftops, make some cheesy proclamation on Twitter, text it to everybody I know. *Jordan and I are having sex!*

Olivia glances up from her textbook and looks at me, chewing on the end of her pen. "Why do you have that look on your face?"

"What look?"

"You're, like . . . drooling. Does the life cycle of the cell make you horny?" She laughs.

"Oh my god, no. It's Jordan. I mean, not that he makes me . . . I'm just thinking about him."

She sets down her pen. "Obviously."

I close my textbook, giving her my full attention. "Actually, I've decided something."

"You guys are going to get married and make beautiful babies together and move to his Christmas tree farm in Vermont?" She picks her pen back up and leans over her stack of flash cards again, writing something in her big loopy handwriting.

"Well . . . I mean, hopefully not the babies. Or the farm. But I'm going to sleep with him."

She doesn't look at me at first, just keeps working on her flash card. I watch as she finishes her sentence with a heavy exclamation point. Then she looks up, a smile stretched across her face. "Really? My little Penny is all grown-up."

"I mean . . . do you think I should?" I'm unsure now, even though I was so positive a few seconds ago. Maybe it's because she didn't answer me right away. The long moment she took to finish writing her sentence has made me hesitate.

Olivia grabs a Twizzler out of the bag and bites into it. "It's a big decision."

"Yeah, but we've been dating for almost six months. I don't know. I think I'm ready?"

She chews the Twizzler. Swallows. "Just remember. Once you have sex with him, you can't take it back."

I grab a Twizzler too, tapping it against my palm. "Okay. But . . . I don't think I'd want to take it back. I love him."

"Then you should totally have sex with him." She smiles. "But just because you love someone doesn't mean they can't hurt you." She grabs a handful of Sour Patch Kids and pops one into her mouth. "Actually, the people you love are the ones who can hurt you the most."

"Jordan wouldn't do that." What Jordan and I have is perfect. We're the couple all the other couples want to be.

"Of course he wouldn't." She sighs. "You guys are different. Jordan treats you like you're special."

NOW

IT TAKES TWO HOURS to walk back to my car from McDonald's, but I know I probably deserve it. My legs are aching by the time I get to Scoops, sweat dripping off me, but I barely even notice, because all I can focus on is everything that just went wrong.

Telling Jordan the truth felt like the right thing to do at the time, but now I'm not so sure.

And I feel terrible for what I just said to Sarah. Sarah has never been anything but straight up with me. In a summer of lies, she's the only person who has been fully honest, who hasn't played any games, has given me so many chances to prove I'm worth it.

But maybe I'm not.

When I get to my house, I pull the car into the driveway, braking a little too forcefully. There's another car here, and I'm immediately more on edge. It feels like I haven't seen my mom in weeks, and I really don't feel like dealing with Steve. I just want to go inside and take a shower, rinse all of today's fresh mistakes off me. It would have been nice to talk to my mom about everything going on. Except how can I possibly fill her in when there are just too many layers of history that she wouldn't understand? How can I have an honest conversation with her when Steve is here?

I quietly open the door, hoping I can sneak by and not have to talk anyone. But then my mom pops out from behind the door to the kitchen. She's all dressed up in her favorite purple date-night dress, dark hair long and flowing down her back. I'm not used to seeing her out of her scrubs. The house smells like garlic, Norah Jones playing quietly on the speakers.

"Penelope," she says. "There you are."

"I'm just gonna go upstairs to shower," I say, starting to turn away. And then a man walks up behind my mom. He's tall, broad-backed, with curly dark hair, a rumpled flannel shirt, and glasses. He is most definitely not Steve.

"This is Phil," she says. "We met at the grocery store."

I just look at her for a second. And suddenly I'm so angry. All the negative feelings I had for Steve are replaced in an instant with sympathy. Steve was nice and he was *trying*, and even Seb seemed to like him. But she pushed him away just like all the others, replaced him right when things were starting to feel a bit too real. "Are you kidding me?" I say, backing away from her.

Her smile falters. "Phil was just telling me all about the hotel he's opening up on the lake—your brother is on his way home too, and then I thought maybe we could all have dinner."

"*Why*, Mom?" It's a loaded question. Why did she end things with Steve? Why should we bother having dinner with this man, who we'll obviously never see again? Why, when I haven't seen her in days, does she want to invite this stranger to hang out with us when we could have spent the time as a family? "What about us, Mom? I mean, what about *Steve*?" I'm surprised that I feel the question in my gut.

"Penelope," she says, an embarrassed warning in her tone. Her hands are up, like she wants to reach out and hold me but she's scared I'll run.

"All I want is a little bit of time with you," I say. "That's all I've ever wanted. You're the only parent I have, and you . . . you care more about impressing some guy you met at the grocery store than you do about actually being here for us."

"Should I go?" The man—Phil—says, backing away from us slightly.

"No," I say, turning back around "No, I'll go." My mom tries to grab me then, to pull me to her chest, but I twist out of her grasp, and then I'm running out the front door and down the driveway, the screen door slamming behind me.

"Penelope, wait!" she calls out to me, but I don't turn around. I just keep running, putting as much distance between us as possible.

Our road is long and winding, trees towering on either side, sheltering me from the sun, and I run. I run until I can barely breathe, until my lungs feel like they're on fire. My phone vibrates a few times, and I know it must be my mom calling, but I ignore her.

I don't know how long it is before I stop, but at some point my wobbling legs slow down on me, and then I bend over, leaning my hands on my knees.

My mom calls again, and I press the button to ignore it, and then scroll through to find Kai's number before I have time to wonder what I'm doing. He picks up after the first ring. "Hi, my little cinnamon roll."

"*Kai*," I say, and I'm surprised to find that I'm crying. It comes out as a sob.

"Penny? Are you okay? What's wrong?"

"Can you come get me?"

"Yeah, of course. From where? Where are you?"

I tell him the cross streets, and then sit down on the curb to wait. For once, he's not late. His Jeep pulls up in fifteen minutes and I climb in. I'm emptied out, hollow, but seeing Kai makes me feel a little bit better.

He turns the Jeep left and heads toward the highway, and I know where he's taking me without having to ask. He flips on the stereo and finds us a playlist—something loud and angsty and intense—and then we drive the forty minutes it takes to get to the beach. It's foggy today, and cold—cold enough that we should probably close up the sides of the Jeep, but I don't care. I kind of like it. I like the smell of the ocean, the wind whipping through my hair, stinging my cheeks, making me feel like I'm alive.

It's not until we're parked that Kai turns down the music, looks at me, and finally speaks. "Do you want to talk about it?"

I press my hands to my eyes; they're puffy now, and probably streaked with mascara. The wind has dried my tears cold onto my cheeks. I know I should be embarrassed for Kai to see me like this, so weak and vulnerable and disheveled. But for some reason, I'm not. I mean, it's just Kai.

I don't answer for a minute, trying to keep my breathing steady as I form the words. "It's my mom."

Kai holds my gaze. "What did she do?"

"I came home today and there was another guy in the kitchen." I let out a bitter laugh. "Some new guy from the grocery store."

"But what about the pancake guy?"

"I'm just so mad at her," I say. "It's not even really about Steve. I just . . . want to have real conversations with her. Ugh, I'm sorry." I let out a strangled breath. "I shouldn't have called you. This is so embarrassing. I promise I'm not always this much of a mess."

Kai reaches out and takes my hand. "No, hey, babe. This isn't embarrassing. Life is messy sometimes."

His use of the word *babe* throws me. It doesn't sting like it did before. Instead, there's a fluttering in my chest, a sudden feeling like I might cry again, but in a good way. I hold his hand just a bit tighter. "Hey, remember—you're not supposed to call me that."

"Call you what?"

"Babe."

"Oh," he says, letting out a gust of air. "Oh, I guess I didn't realize that I said it."

"It's okay."

I reach out and tuck a strand of his hair behind his ear, and then for some reason, I leave my hand there on the side of his face. We're looking at each other, neither of us blinking, and strangely I'm finding it hard to breathe. I know I need to pull my hand back, or look away, or make some silly joke to get us laughing, but I can't stop staring at him.

And then he's leaning closer to me and I know I should pull back like I did in his room because this is dangerous, so dangerous, and will only make things more complicated. Except suddenly his face is so close to mine that I can feel little puffs of air on my lips from his breath. But that doesn't last long either, because then his lips touch mine and *oh, wow*, we're kissing.

This is different than our kiss back at the cabin, which was light and quick and meaningless. I know there's no one watching us, that we're all alone right now at this beach without an audience to fake this for, but I don't want to think about that. I don't want to think about anything, really, except for the feel of Kai's lips against mine, the fluttering feeling in my stomach, the pressure of his hands on my back. His tongue touches mine then, and the feel of it sends a jolt of electricity through me. I just want to move closer to him, to press myself against him so we're touching everywhere.

I know we've done this before, that this isn't the first time we've kissed like this. But that was messy and drunk and all wrong. This feels right. It feels like it's the first time. It feels brand-new.

The air is cold, the wind whipping my hair around us like a curtain, and I can't tell whether I'm shivering from the wind or the kiss. Probably both. I shudder, and Kai pulls away from me.

"Are you okay?" His forehead is resting against mine, and I can feel his words on my lips like a whisper.

I nod. "It's cold." But I kiss him again, because really that's the best way to stay warm.

A few minutes later, he pulls back again. "We should put the top back onto the Jeep. I have blankets and stuff."

At the word *blankets*, I'm sold. We break apart and he opens a hatch in the back and pulls out the tarp siding. Soon, we're cozied up inside on the back seat, warm and out of the wind.

It's awkward for a few seconds, because *what the hell are we doing?* We're quiet, cuddled up under a blanket, but then he leans over and kisses me again, and it's even better than before.

My phone vibrates in my pocket, and I pull away from Kai to look at it. It's my mom again. I turn the phone off and stuff it back out of sight.

"Do you think you should tell her where we are?" Kai asks, but I shake my head.

Then an idea comes to me. "Let's stay the night here."

Kai looks at me in surprise. "Really?"

"I mean, can we? Like, legally, can we leave the Jeep parked here all night, or . . ." I trail off, the look on Kai's face making me feel doubtful about everything.

"This beach is pretty hidden," he says. "I think we could probably get away with it."

"We don't have to," I backtrack, but Kai stops me with a smile.

"No, I want to. I'm just surprised. It's a very . . . un-Penny-like suggestion."

"Well, maybe I'm changing." I smile back. The truth is, I'm feeling very un-Penny-like at the moment. I know it sounds crazy, but I really, really want to stay here. Let my mom worry about where *I've* gone for once, instead of the other way around.

And there's another part of me that really doesn't want to stop kissing Kai. Something about this beach makes me feel removed from the real world, like maybe out here the rules don't count. Like I can get away with whatever I want.

I kiss him again, smiling against his mouth. "We're going to get in so much trouble for this." The idea of it is thrilling and terrifying all at once.

"I like trouble," Kai says, kissing me, and then he threads his fingers through my hair and pulls me closer. We stay like that for a while, and then his hand finds its way to the button of my shorts and tries to reach inside.

I pull back from him. "Wait. Not yet. I've never done this before."

He draws his hand back, his voice a whisper. "Really? But Jordan—"

"We never did."

He looks at me for a long time and his silence makes me nervous. "We were supposed to, actually," I continue. "The night that everything happened. But obviously, things didn't work out."

Kai pulls away, sitting up beside me. "Fuck. Really?"

I try to bring him to me, feeling the absence of his warmth deep in my bones. I need him on top of me again. I just want to go back to the part where we're kissing.

"Hey," I say softly, like I'm coaxing a spooked animal. "It's not your fault. We're equal-opportunity assholes, remember? And things with Jordan—"

I stop then, remember Jordan's visit to Scoops from earlier in the day. I can't believe I told him Kai and I were faking things. Thinking about Jordan right now seems wrong, in any capacity. I don't know whether I should tell Kai about what I said. Because if I tell him, we'll have to stop this thing between us, and he might be upset I ruined the plan. He might go right back to being that guy again, the one who thinks I'm stuck-up and selfish and fake. I don't want that to happen. Whatever this is, I like it.

"I think this is all working," I say instead. "Jordan came by to see me earlier today at work."

Kai bites his lip. "Oh. What did he say?"

"He saw the picture I posted of us at dinner . . . I think he was jealous."

"And . . ." Kai pauses, chewing still on his lip. ". . . is that something you still want? For Jordan to be jealous?"

No. The answer to the question comes so immediately and surely. But saying the word out loud feels like too big a risk. "I . . . I don't know."

"Penelope." My name is a sigh.

I look at him for a moment, too scared to say anything and break whatever this might be between us. But I have to. There's too much to say. "What about Olivia?"

"That wasn't real," he says. "*This* is. This thing between us isn't pretend anymore, and you know it."

"When did it stop being pretend, Kai?"

"Was it ever?" He cocks his head to the side, studying me, and I'm terrified. Fighting with Kai has been a part of my being for as long as I can remember—as true a part of me as my long hair and my blue eyes and my big ears. It's my identity. Kai Tanaka is the *worst*. I'm scared to let myself trust him.

"But we don't get along," I say softly. "We hate each other."

"Do we?" He runs a hand over his face. "What don't you like about me?"

"Kai," I say, a warning.

He takes my hand. "No, I want to know. I want you to tell me so I can do better."

I sigh. "Okay, you asked for this." I think for a moment, listening to the lapping of the waves on the shore. "You're late for everything." He grins, and I grab his cheeks with my hand so he'll stop. "No, I'm serious. It's rude. It means you don't value people's time." I look down at the faded blue fabric of the blanket because it's easier than looking right at him. "You always think everything is a joke. Even now. You've always been so condescending to me, and you don't care about anything. You're such . . . wasted potential."

"Wow," Kai says. "Don't hold back."

"Like, you don't even try, and the world still opens up for you because you're a guy and you're good-looking and apparently that's all that matters. I have to put in double the effort to get half the respect."

"Okay," he says, pulling away from me. "Yeah. I get that. I feel so terrible that I'm partly responsible, you know? That I was an idiot—that I've been an idiot for most of my life—and made your life even a little bit harder. I'm sorry I made up that nickname. I like making up nicknames and I thought it was funny and obviously it wasn't. But also, you're white, Pen. Sometimes I have to put in double the effort too. You just don't notice it."

"Oh," I say, my cheeks flushing. "I never thought about it that way."

"You know the kind of shit Asian guys have to deal with? There's always gonna be more doors open for you or for guys like Jordan. I mean, they had internment camps here less than a hundred years ago." He sighs. "I *love* being Japanese. I'm proud of it. But it's not always easy."

"I'm sorry," I say, chewing my lip. I remember then how difficult he'd said it was when he moved here, how out of place he'd felt in our mostly white school. Just because things haven't always been easy for me doesn't mean they've been any easier for Kai—he's been fighting our whole lives to climb over a barrier I can't even see. "You're right. I should have realized sooner."

"And just because I don't care about the same stuff as you," Kai continues, "doesn't mean I don't care. It doesn't mean I don't try."

"But . . . you just coast by at school," I say, hesitant. "You don't study and you still get good grades anyway. You don't even want to go to college."

"Yeah, and why do you want to go to college?"

"Because that's what you're supposed to do, right? That's what people do. They graduate high school and if they're privileged enough to go to college, they go."

"Yeah, and they get a bunch of loans they'll never be able to pay back and they make themselves miserable, all for what? Where's the passion in that? Do you love to study?"

"No, but I'm good at it. It's important—"

"What do you love?" Kai asks, pulling the blanket tighter around us. It's so weird that we were just kissing and now we're having this conversation.

"What?"

"What do you love? What makes you happy?"

I'm just looking at him, my mouth slightly parted, because I don't know what to say. I don't know how to answer. I guess it's just not a question I've ever thought to ask. I know what makes Jordan happy, what makes Olivia happy. I know that I care *so much* about being liked, about being respected, looking my best, presenting the right version of myself to the world. But underneath all that, what else is there?

"I like . . . making things. Like I told your mom. I like craft projects, and creating cool makeup looks." I'm embarrassed. I feel naked, exposed, my underbelly unprotected. I feel more vulnerable than I did when his hands were all over me only minutes before.

"Then that's what you should do."

"That's just for fun, though. That's not a career."

"Who says?" Kai shrugs. "Lots of people do makeup professionally. Somebody has to design costumes and build props for shows and stuff. You don't have to go to school where Olivia wants to go."

"It's not about Olivia," I say. "I want to go to a big city. There's something exciting about the idea of a crowded sidewalk—somewhere I can blend in." I need to start over somewhere fast and new. There's the vision again—me walking quickly across the UCLA campus headed to class.

"LA's not that urban," Kai says, and the vision pops. "It's all traffic and suburbs. People drive everywhere."

"I like to walk."

"I know you do," he says. "I pay attention. I do care, Pen. I care about my friends, and I would do anything for my family. I care about surfing, about my paintings, about, like . . . enjoying my life, making people laugh. I love my mom more than anything. I care about dogs, and tacos, and, like . . . fucking injustice in the world." He pauses for a second. "I care about you."

My cheeks flush pink. The truth is I care about Kai too. I like the way he always seems to make me laugh even when I'm trying my hardest not to. I even like his stupid nicknames for me, even though his stupid fucking nicknames got us into this whole mess in the first place. Somehow, despite all our planning for the contrary, everything changed.

"Just so you know," Kai says, "I never hated you."

"What? Yes, you did."

"I'm telling you that I didn't. I mean, did I think you were annoying sometimes? Obviously. But mostly I just ribbed on you because you always gave it back just as hard. I liked that. I kinda thought our whole vibe was . . . fun."

My mind flashes through our history then: Kai making fun of my excitement on spirit day, Kai telling me I'm exactly the same as everyone else, Kai annoying me in the boathouse on the freshman camping trip, just the two of us alone in the middle of the night. He made me miserable in all those moments, made mean comments, turned everything into a joke.

"It wasn't fun for me," I say. "You hurt my feelings. I don't like fighting with you. I don't want to fight anymore."

"Okay." He nods, then after a pause, "Sometimes it wasn't fun for me either. I mean, sometimes I think it went too far. I tried to mend the bridge so many times, and you just held so tightly to the idea that you hated me."

The memories in my head replay from a new angle: me yelling at Kai for wearing the wrong thing, me telling Kai he ruined my life, me taking all of his comments so literally, twisting them to fit my view of him as a horrible person. But he's not a horrible person. He's someone who has made mistakes, but who has been trying to make things right, trying to apologize for most of the years since. Maybe I've used Kai as a way to feel sorry for myself. It's so much easier to blame everything on someone else.

"I think . . ." I pause, trying to find the right words. "I think I never hated you either."

Kai smiles and leans into me and then we're kissing again, his hands sliding into my hair. And maybe this is crazy, maybe this is all wrong, but it doesn't feel like it. It feels like we're supposed to be here. Like that butterfly flapping its wings and causing a tornado across the world, all of the little moments between us for all the years we've known each other have been building up to this one. Now we're finally where we're supposed to be.

I pull back from him, wrinkling my nose. "I can't believe I'm kissing you. Twelve-year-old me would be so mad."

"Twelve-year-old me would be thrilled." He snuggles into me then, pulling me closer to him.

We stay like that for a while longer, side by side under the blanket. There's so much more I want to tell him, but I can't say any of it out loud. Not yet. All I know is that I never want to leave this car, this moment, and that scares me. Rule number one—I wasn't supposed to fall in love with him, and right now I'm terrified maybe I already have.

Once his breathing has slowed and we've been lying silently with each other for what feels like forever, I reach over and take his hand in mine. Then I squeeze three times.

I wait, heart beating in my throat, to see if he'll squeeze back, but he must have already fallen asleep. So I lie beside him, willing myself to sleep too.

THEN

JUNIOR YEAR–JUNE

"HERE." OLIVIA PUSHES a shot glass into my hand. "Take this." The world around me is swirling shapes and colors.

"I think I'm okay." I try to hand the glass back, but she shakes her head.

"It's the first day of summer! We're celebrating." She pours herself a shot too, and then we clink them together and throw them back. The alcohol burns my throat.

NOW

WE WAKE UP EARLY the next morning, the glamour of sleeping in the Jeep transformed overnight into aching backs and sore necks. The sun is still rising as we fold the blankets and move into the front seats.

The air is calm now, the morning sleepy and quiet, like the whole world is holding its breath. I can't stop thinking about everything that happened last night—kissing Kai, *for real this time*. Almost doing more than that. Squeezing his hand in the middle of the night, so caught between waking and dreams I almost don't remember doing it.

We drive back home in comfortable silence, listening to the radio, glancing at each other and looking quickly away. I don't know what this is yet; we never fully established if we were going to do this for real. But I think I might want to.

There are a few more missed calls from my mom, and I feel surprisingly guilty. What felt like rebellion last night—exciting and adventurous and worth the risk—just feels stupid in the light of day. And *mean*. I imagine her pacing around the kitchen, wringing her hands, calling my phone over and over and never getting through. As mad as I was with her, she doesn't deserve that. I shoot her a quick text and feel a bit better. On my way home now. Sorry.

We're almost back to my house when Kai turns down the music and looks at me, slowing the Jeep so we're at a crawl. "Are you feeling better?"

"Yeah," I say. "Thanks for being there when I was freaking out."

"Listen, Penny." He reaches out and grabs my hand and I'm reminded again of last night, of the moment I'm too scared to talk about. "There's something you should know." He turns left onto my street. "I should have told you last night when we were talking about everything, but I didn't want . . ."

He trails off as we pull into the driveway because we both notice the car that's parked there: a lime-green buggy.

"Why is Olivia here?" I ask, suddenly nervous. I hate how we've deteriorated this much—that we used to be best friends and now her presence sets me on edge. I open the car door, ready to step out, when Kai holds out an arm to stop me.

"Wait, Pen." He presses his lips into a thin line. "Before we go in there, I really want to talk to you. There are some things I haven't been—"

But he's cut off, because the front door flies open then and everyone streams out onto the front lawn—my mom, Seb, and behind him, Olivia.

"Oh, thank god you're all right!" my mom says. I jump down out of the car and she wraps me in a hug. It's weird—honestly, my mom and I don't usually hug like this. But I involuntarily sink into her arms, melting against her, enjoying the feeling of her worry.

"When you didn't answer last night, I called Olivia's parents. I assumed you went over there like you always do." She pulls back and looks at me. "Imagine my surprise when I was informed you hadn't been to her house once all summer."

"I'm sorry," Olivia says. "I didn't want to lie. She was too worried about where you were."

"I'm fine," I say. "I was . . ."

"It's my fault." Kai steps forward, putting his arm around me. "She was with me."

My mom tips her head to the side, studying him for a moment. "And who are you?"

My mom knows who Kai is. She drove me to his birthday party all those years ago, has sat through middle school graduations, and school auctions, and science fairs. Everyone knows everyone in this small town. But I know that's not what she's really asking. She means: *Who are you to my daughter?*

Kai knows it too. His arm tightens around me. "I'm her boyfriend."

He's said the words before, of course, but for the first time, it feels like he means them. It feels real. And even though my mom is looking at me like I'm going to be grounded until I'm eighty, I can't help the swoop in my stomach.

"Well," she says, hands on her hips. "It seems we have a lot of catching up to do."

"Yeah, I guess there's a lot you don't know," I say, accusatory.

"Because you've been lying to me! How am I supposed to know you're safe if I don't know where you are?"

"Well, maybe if you were around more, you would know!" It's

so infuriating that somehow this has all become my fault when my mom is the one who has been absent, the one who is flaky.

"Why don't you send your friends home," she says, taking a step back toward the house. "We should talk about this in private. Thank you, Olivia, for coming to help. Penelope, I'll be inside." She turns and walks back into the house, the door slamming just a little too hard behind her.

"I know you're mad at Mom," Seb says. "But she was freaking out all night."

"I know, okay?" I tell him. "This isn't about you."

"I'm just saying, maybe you shouldn't be so hard on her." And then he disappears inside the house.

"Wow," Olivia says. "Even Seb is mad at you."

"Liv," I say, turning to her. I'm embarrassed she had to see all this. "Why did you actually come here?"

"Believe it or not, I wanted to see if you were okay." She fiddles with the straps of her baby blue backpack.

"Really?" A small seed of hope blooms in my chest.

"Well, yeah, and also I want to talk to you about something."

"Olivia, what's going on?" Kai asks, hesitant, but she ignores him, keeping her focus on me.

"I talked to Jordan this morning, Penny. He told me what you said."

My stomach drops. Did Jordan tell her that Kai and I were faking this?

"Wait, what?" Kai asks. "What did Jordan say?"

"I should have known," she says. "I can't believe I didn't catch on, after everything."

"Olivia," Kai says, a warning in his tone.

There's a glint in Olivia's eyes, like she knows she's about to drop the grenade that will blow us to pieces, like she's happy she's won. "I've sat by the past few weeks watching you guys all over each other, and now I find out this whole thing was fake?"

"It's not fake," I say, because even if this started out that way, it isn't anymore.

Except that's not what I said to Jordan.

"Jordan and I got coffee this morning," Olivia says, her face growing redder. "He said he talked to Penny yesterday. Said she gave him hope or something—that she was only dating Kai to make him jealous." She shrugs. "Apparently it worked. Con-gra-tu-fucking-lations, Penny. You win."

"You told Jordan this was fake?" Kai takes his arm off me, stepping away. "You said that yesterday?"

"Oh, like you're one to talk," Olivia says to Kai. "You started this whole thing by kissing her at that party! You were supposed to wait until after we broke up, but you just couldn't resist. You had to go and make me look stupid."

"What?" I say, something horrible churning in my stomach. "What do you mean—wait until after?"

"She kissed *me*!" Kai says sharply. He rests his face in his hands so I can't see the expression in his eyes.

Olivia turns to me. "I know, and that's the worst part." Then she looks at Kai. "Or maybe the worst part is that you actually used my idea against me."

"Olivia, please let me tell her," Kai says again. He looks pained now, his face red, his forehead scrunched as he turns to me. "I fucked up, Pen. I'm sorry. This isn't even what I—"

"Oh my god," Olivia interrupts. "You're in love with her, aren't you?"

Kai's face crumples and he squeezes his eyes shut. I hold my breath, waiting for him to answer, but he doesn't. "This is actually hilarious," Olivia continues. "This is too good. Jordan loves Penny and Kai loves Penny and absolutely no one loves me. Wow, wow, wow." She's laughing now, like maybe she actually does think this is funny. But I know that she can't, not really.

"Olivia," I say, feeling the aching need to comfort her. There's still a part of her printed on my heart. "That's not true and you know it. Everyone is obsessed with you. You're Olivia Anderson. You're number one. You're number one and I'm only number two. That's how it works."

Olivia laughs again, a strangled sound like she's still trying to hold it together. "Don't you get it, Penny? People aren't freaking numbers. We're just people." Her words catch me off guard—I always thought Olivia cared the most of all of us. "Anyway," she continues. "I just wanted to show you." She flips her backpack and unzips it, rummaging around inside. Then she pulls out a folded sheet of paper. "I have receipts."

Kai lunges forward for a second like he might try to grab it, but then thinks better of it.

Olivia sighs, holding the paper out to me. "There's a reason I should have known you and Kai were faking it. Because the truth is he's had a lot of freaking practice."

She points the paper at me like a blade. I hesitate, then reach out and take it. Then she walks past me down the driveway. Her green buggy *chirp-chirps* and she climbs inside.

I watch her drive away, the paper still clenched in my hands. I'm too afraid to open it because as soon as I read it, there's no going back. You can't just force yourself to forget things once you know them.

"Just let me explain," Kai says.

I unfold the paper and recognize Olivia's loopy handwriting, Kai's scratchy signature below it.

And then I read:

The rules:

1. This is strictly business. Either party has a right to end this at any time.

2. If Jordan or Penny show any interest, we're done.

3. No kissing! Unless in front of Penny and Jordan.

4. Olivia must tell Penny how awesome Kai is whenever she can. Kai has to brag endlessly to Jordan about how Olivia is the hottest girl in school.

5. No matter what, we break up by summer.

6. If either of us catches feelings, we're done. No exceptions.

Signed,

Olivia Anderson & Kai Tanaka

THEN

JUNIOR YEAR–JUNE

IT'S SO LOUD, everyone's laughter thumping in my ears with the bass of the speakers, the sound like some terrible carnival music. There's a familiar roiling in my stomach, the ache in my chest that means I'm going to be sick.

There's a door in front of me. I lean against it, twisting the handle and tumbling through into the laundry room, running to the little bathroom off to the side. I crash down onto my knees, dimly registering the pain of it in the back of my mind, and then hurl into the bowl, a mess of snot and tears. All I can think as I slump there on the bathroom floor is how stupid I am. Tonight was supposed to be special, and now I've ruined everything.

There's a sound behind me, I register the feeling of someone's hands on the back of my neck, and then my hair is being pulled gently out of my face. Then smooth circles on my back, comforting noises as I keep crying, heaving into the toilet.

After what seems like forever, the clenching in my stomach subsides and I feel like the worst has passed. But when I turn around to see the owner of the soft, comforting hands, the sick feeling comes raging back. Because the witness to my misery is the worst possible person: Kai.

"What are you doing? Go away." I try to wobble to my feet, but only manage to tumble onto my butt. I see the bruises forming on my knees then and realize I must have crashed down on them harder than I thought.

"Shhhhh," Kai says. He pulls a long line of toilet paper off the roll and hands it to me. "Take this."

I bunch the toilet paper in my hands and wipe around my mouth, then drop the soiled paper into the toilet. Kai grabs another bunch of paper and then reaches up gently to dab the tears around my eyes. Even in my inebriation, I'm aware of how humiliating this is, Kai taking care of me in a moment like this one, all snot and tears and the acidic smell of vomit. *It's Pukey Penelope. Don't let her touch you.*

"I'm so stupid," I say. It's the only thing I can think to say, the phrase that keeps repeating itself over in my head. "I'm so stupid. I'm so stupid."

"You're a lot of things," Kai says. "But stupid isn't one of them. We've all been there." He holds the toilet paper up to my nose and I blow. Then he throws the tissue into the bowl, reaching across from me and flushing. "I've been there worse, to be honest," he says. "I got so drunk at Jordan's sister's grad party sophomore year I ended up puking on a tray of canapés in front of his whole family."

He laughs and I feel myself smiling too at the visual. But then I think about Jordan again and my smile turns back into tears. "Where's Jordan?"

"He's back there somewhere." Kai nods toward the living

room. I can still hear the thumping bass just behind the door. "Want me to go get him?" He starts to stand and I reach out and grab his arm, pulling him back down onto the floor next to me.

"No!" The only thing worse than Kai seeing me like this would be Jordan seeing me like this. "I'm disgusting."

Kai smiles. "I'm not going to argue with that. You smell like a dumpster fire."

"*You* smell like a dumpster fire," I say back, which I know is not the witty comeback I want it to be. Usually, I'm better than this.

"I bet we can fix that." He stands and opens the cabinet above the sink, rummaging around inside it. Then he pulls out a big bottle of mouthwash. "I was looking for a toothbrush, but this is even better."

Twisting off the cap, he takes a sip, his cheeks puffed up like a chipmunk, then spits it out into the sink. Then he pours a little bit into the cap and brings it down onto the floor to me. "Here, take this. Make sure you don't swallow it, okay? Just spit it back out into the toilet."

I swish the mouthwash around my teeth, and it burns, but in a good way. It feels like it's cleaning me from the inside out, erasing some of the humiliation of everything that just happened. I lean over and spit. Kai flushes again, sitting back down next to me on the tile floor.

"Nice job, Penelope. See? I bet you're feeling much better now."

"Now you smell like the dentist," I say. The world is still spinning, and I lean forward and collapse into Kai's shoulder. Somehow I'm crying again and I don't know why. There's a passing thought that it might be because Kai is being so nice to me.

I'm vaguely aware of the fact that I'm getting his T-shirt wet with my tears, but I can't seem to pull my head away. His hand is on my back again, rubbing it in smooth circles, and as I cry into his chest he makes little comforting sounds into my ear.

"Please don't tell anyone about this," I say, my voice muffled.

"That I'm actually helping you?" he says. "Wouldn't dream of it."

"I don't want to be Pukey Penelope anymore."

His hand on my back stops moving. "I know."

We're quiet for a while, or at least it feels like a while. I'm not so sure. I feel like I could fall asleep right here on the floor, my nose pressed into his shirt. In fact, I'm not so sure I'm even awake at all. Then he speaks again.

"Listen, Penelope. There's something I should probably say." I make a sound to indicate that I'm listening. "I'm really sorry about that, you know? About that name. I had this stupid crush on you back then and I didn't know how to handle it. I think I called you that because I wanted to get your attention. Classic fucking idiot kid behavior."

I pull my head off his chest. "You have a crush on me?"

"I had a crush on you in like fifth grade," he corrects. "Now I can't stand you."

"But I'm with Jordan," I say, crashing back into his armpit.

"I know." There are more soothing sounds in my ear. He moves his hand from my back and brings it to my arm, his fingers tracing light patterns down my skin. "You know, actually, when you and Jordan got together, Olivia and I got kinda jealous? We always thought it was supposed to be the other way around, you know? Like all those comments our friends always make. Olivia and Jordan, me and you."

I pull back to look at him. "Me and you?" I'm vaguely aware that I'm just repeating everything he's saying, but I can't get myself to say new words, can't connect my mind to my mouth.

"Me and you," he says.

"But . . . you don't like me," I say, and for some reason he smiles.

"That's what I thought. You're so frustrating. You drive me insane most of the time. But you got together with Jordan and I just . . ." He trails off and I tense, listening. "It didn't feel right. You know how much of my day I spend thinking about you? God, I lie awake at night thinking of ways I can get under your skin, ways I can make you laugh. You're exhausting."

"You stole my book."

"What? What book?"

I shake my head and then lean forward again, nuzzling my nose into his neck. Sitting up feels like too much work and it's nice to have a place to rest, somewhere comfy to close my eyes.

"Olivia came up with a plan," he says. He swallows and I feel it against my cheek. "She thought if we got together when you guys did, if we flaunted it in your face, you'd get jealous or something. You guys would realize you're all wrong together."

"Your neck smells good," I say in response.

"It was a dumb idea," he says. "But Olivia is my friend and I wanted to help her. I mean, that's what I told myself. I was just doing it to help her. People are always fake dating in the movies, right? It always works in the movies. But clearly it didn't work in real life."

"Fake dating?" I ask, pulling back to look at him again. "Who's fake dating?"

He sighs, running his hand behind my head and tucking a

strand of hair behind my ear. "You're too drunk for this."

I like the feeling of his hand in my hair. "Kai," I say. "Keep playing with my hair."

He does, running his fingers softly through the strands, and I feel like a little kid, like I did back when my mom used to brush my hair, when things between us were still good.

"I shouldn't be telling you any of this anyway," he says. "You're with Jordan. It's not my place to try to talk you out of that, especially when you're drunk. Fuck, I'm an asshole." He pulls away from me and starts to stand. "I should go. You're doing okay now?"

"Don't go," I say, trying to pull him back down to me.

"Pen," he says. "We should get back to the party." He takes my hand and pulls me to my feet. I notice then that my shoes are gone, and one of my socks.

He leads me out of the bathroom and back into the laundry room, but once we're almost to the door, I stop him. "I don't want to go back out there."

"Jordan will be wondering where you are."

I notice then that we're still holding hands and for some reason I don't want to let go. I like the way his fingers feel linked with mine. "Thanks for helping me."

"Of course."

And then using our clasped hands I tug him closer to me. I don't know why I do it. It's just that his presence is warm and comforting and I want to be here with him more than anything in the world. Something about what he just told me has ignited a spark in me, and even though my brain is foggy and I already can't remember the details, this quiet laundry room alone with

Kai feels like a bubble. I don't want it to pop and for the two of us to go back to fighting with each other. Fighting with Kai has always been so exhausting.

"Kai," I say. I like the sound of his name, like the way it feels on my tongue. "Kai Tanaka."

"Yeah?" He's grinning and so close to me. How did he get so close? Somehow his lips are just a few inches from mine, and it's so easy to close the distance between us. There's no reason his lips should be that close unless they're kissing mine.

So I do. I fall toward him, crashing my mouth to his, kissing him like it's the most natural thing in the world. My eyes are closed, and behind them I don't see darkness anymore, but vibrant colors. Kissing Kai feels like what a kiss is supposed to be, the way I imagined kissing to feel back before I'd ever tried it. I reach my arms behind his back and pull him closer because I need to be pressed against him, want to be as close to him as possible.

He opens his mouth and his tongue slides against mine, minty from mouthwash, and the feel of it sends a shiver down my whole body. I don't care where I am or how I got here because this kiss is the most important thing. Actually, I don't know where I am or how I got here. Where am I?

Kai pulls back from me. "Pen, we can't do this."

I open my eyes. We're in a laundry room, pressed up against the washing machine. It all looks vaguely familiar, but I can't place it. But it doesn't matter. I lean back toward Kai, back into the kiss, but he turns his head away from me. "This can't happen like this. You're too drunk."

"I'm not drunk," I say, kissing him again.

He kisses me back for a moment and then pulls away. "Yes, you are. God, this is killing me."

"Just a little more," I say, and then kiss him again.

That's when the door opens. I hear the burst of noise from the party and silence again when it closes. Then a voice speaks, loud and clear. "Well, this is quite the development."

I pull away from Kai and open my eyes again and see Olivia, arms folded. There's a sinking feeling in my gut as I take her in, as pieces come flying together. I know something about this is wrong, but I can't speak, can't figure out what the right words are to make things better.

"She wasn't feeling well," Kai is saying.

"So you were comforting her with your mouth?"

"What's going on?" I ask. Kai's arm is still wrapped around my waist, and it confuses me that he hasn't taken it off, hasn't jumped away from me.

"You couldn't even wait like ten more minutes till we broke up?" Olivia says.

"She kissed me," Kai says. "I wouldn't have . . ."

"Well, congratulations," Olivia says. "I guess you got what you wanted."

"Olivia," he says. "This isn't what I wanted—not like this."

"I get it," she says. "But I'm not letting her off this easy."

"Olivia, don't. She's your best friend."

"Yeah? And you're my boyfriend."

"I'm not really your boyfriend."

"And yet this betrayal still fucking hurts," she says.

"Please, Olivia," he says. "We were going to end things anyway. This doesn't have to be a big scene."

"If you think that's true," she says, reaching to open the door, "then you don't really know me at all."

And then she looks behind her into the party and back at us and screams, like she's only now just discovering us together. She screams like her heart is breaking.

And so I run.

NOW

"I DON'T UNDERSTAND," I say, although of course I
do. It's just that I don't want to understand. I want to go back to
this morning, to last night, back to when this game between Kai
and me was special. It was *our* thing—something stupid and silly
and maybe completely messed up, but something that belonged
to only us. Now it's ruined. Kai has already played this game with
Olivia. Of course I'm number two. I've always been number two.

"It wasn't supposed to be like this," he says. His body is tense,
coiled, his hands pressed into fists. He looks ready to flee or
fight—anything to keep from just standing still. "It was Olivia's
idea. She—"

"Don't"—I put my hands up—"blame this on Olivia. You're
not some innocent guy who things just happen to, Kai. I know
you better than that."

"I know, Penny. I'm sorry. I just . . . Olivia has been my friend
since I moved here—for like seven years she's been my friend.
All those years you hated me, or avoided me or whatever, Olivia

was there. I've heard her talk about Jordan forever. She's been asking me for help with him since like sixth grade."

"*No*," I say, shutting my eyes. "She knew I liked him. She's been trying to help *me*."

"*Pen*." His voice is soft. "Jordan and Olivia have had something for a while. You know they slept together on that freshman camping trip, right?"

"What?" The word rips out of me, and I'm choking on it. It's wrong—it's all wrong. *I liked Jordan, and Olivia liked Kai.* She wouldn't have done something like that. Except—at Kai's words, so many pieces are clicking into place in my head, all of my memories rearranging themselves so that everything lines up.

"That whole night was a setup," Kai says.

"Yeah, a setup for me and Jordan!"

"No." He lets out a heavy sigh. "No, it wasn't."

I let myself think of that night again, Olivia conveniently forgetting her sweatshirt, needing Jordan to go get it with her. They were gone for what felt like forever, leaving Kai and me alone, confused and waiting. Except maybe that had been the whole point. Suddenly, Jordan's assumption that I hooked up with Kai that night makes horrible sense.

Olivia was my best friend back then, someone I would have told anything to, and yet she'd lost her virginity to Jordan out in the woods somewhere and then hadn't even bothered to tell me about it the next morning. That's what hurts the most, even more than the betrayal of her feelings for Jordan. It's that I mattered so little to her I didn't even get to know about them.

I remember the story she told us only a few months later when we got back to school from winter break—that she'd slept with a guy she met on her family trip to the Bahamas. She'd come home sun-drenched and giddy, regaling us with stories of how they'd snuck out of the hotel in the middle of the night and done it on the beach, how since her first time was so romantic, she didn't mind all the sand.

Was that story all a lie? Was she talking about the beach from our camping trip—telling us about Jordan this whole time without actually telling us about Jordan?

"He moved on right after that," Kai says. "Started a thing with some girl he met at another school, and then just kinda . . . kept jumping from girl to girl. And Olivia was crushed. And then he started liking *you*."

"I don't want to hear this," I say.

"That's what this is." Kai takes the paper from my hands. "She had a plan and she needed my help. So I helped her."

"Just like you helped me," I say. "Guess you're just everybody's savior."

Kai unfolds the paper again and points to the line that says: *No matter what, we break up by summer.* "We were going to end it at Jordan's party anyway. She said she'd talked to you and it seemed like you and Jordan were stronger than ever, so clearly our plan wasn't working. She was going to back off, wave the white flag, and try to be happy for you. But then she caught us kissing and . . ."

"I betrayed her anyway." I feel sick at the thought. I remember Olivia telling me earlier in the night that she and Kai were having issues. She was just setting the stage for their breakup. She had been playing me, but I played her right back. She wasn't dating Kai for real. But I didn't know that.

How did we get to this point? When did our friendship turn so toxic?

"I tried to tell you all of this that night. I mean, I *did*. I thought I had come clean. I was excited to see you when you came over the next morning, and then you couldn't remember all the details of what happened, and you had just spent the night outside, and the whole thing was so fucked. You were so heartbroken. And then you told me on the beach that they all thought we were together, and I figured it made sense for us to become a team, to work together to get through this. You wanted my help—you asked me to help you, so I did."

"So you never actually wanted Olivia back," I say—a statement, not a question. "You just wanted to play a stupid game with me."

"It wasn't a game. I like you. I didn't want you back with Jordan, okay? But if that's what you wanted—if that's what it took to get people to forgive us, I was going to help. I just didn't expect . . ." He doesn't finish the sentence, but I know what he means. He didn't expect last night, kissing me, holding me as I fell asleep. He didn't expect all of this to feel so real. "I wasn't faking anything last night, Pen."

"How can I believe you?" I take in a gasping breath. "You lied about having feelings for Olivia. You pretended to date her and then you pretended to date me. You were trying to take me from Jordan this whole time. All of this is based on a lie!"

I just feel so stupid. My whole life I've been so worried about being left behind, the one out of the loop, the only person who doesn't understand an inside joke.

"I can't believe I . . . ugh, I actually started to *like* you. I trusted you—even though I knew better—and look where it got me. I thought we were finally being honest with each other, but you had this huge secret the whole time that you conveniently never mentioned!"

"I was going to tell you," Kai says. "In the car just now. I was going to tell you, but then it was too late."

"You had so many opportunities to tell me!" I say. "But you waited until the last possible second because that's what you do. This is such *classic* Kai behavior. I shouldn't even be surprised. Other people care about people's feelings. Other people actually *have* feelings. They actually have real relationships instead of just fake ones."

"This is a real relationship!" he says, crumpling the paper tightly in his hands. "Penny, please." There are tears in his eyes, which kills me. All I want to do is hold him closer, wrap him tightly in my arms and take some of that pain away. I hate that despite everything, my first inclination is to make him happy. "I'm so sorry, Pen. Please, look at me." He tries to reach for me and I duck away from his hand. "What about last night? We don't hate each other anymore, remember?"

I turn away from him. "I will never stop hating you."

NOW

WHEN I GET IN the house, I walk right up the stairs, past Seb and my mom, who are sitting at the kitchen table waiting for me. I am in no mood to talk to them about everything that just happened, to get into yet another fight.

I spend the next few days successfully avoiding everyone—telling my mom to go away every time she knocks on my door, ignoring calls from Kai, and feeling miserable for myself.

The thing is—Kai can tell me whatever he wants, but how am I supposed to believe his words when his actions show me just the opposite? This is probably for the best anyway. Whatever was blossoming between us—whatever stupid feelings made me kiss him for real in the Jeep—would never have worked. There's too much history, too much I just want to forget. But the memories keep replaying themselves, kisses looping over and over again in my head.

I hide in my room for as long as I can, scrolling through Pinterest and trying to let some DIY crafts distract me from thinking about anything at all. But it's not working. By Friday night, I'm exhausted from not doing anything and I feel disgusting.

So of course I open Instagram—the place where all dreams go to die. My last post has been taunting me. It's the picture of Kai kissing my cheek at dinner. There's the one of Kai and me at the lake too, smiling and cuddling against each other, our stupid matching red and white bathing suits. This was back when it all started, maybe—when I realized I kinda enjoyed the feeling of his arm around me, felt relieved on that boat to have someone in my corner. Turns out he was never actually in my corner at all.

Before I can think too hard about it, I swipe and delete both pictures.

I flip over to my feed and start mindlessly scrolling and feeling so stupidly alone. I hate that a whole month has gone by and I'm right back where I started. But this time it's worse. At least Kai was pretending to help me back then. Now I have no one.

I swipe to a picture Romina posted with Myriah, holding a bag from In-N-Out, arms around each other, matching grins. Who do I love more? the caption reads. My girlfriend or this burger? It hits me that in the midst of everything, I've forgotten to check in with them, and I feel the sharp guilt of it in my stomach. But it looks like they sorted everything out.

I'm so happy for you, I comment, knowing that once they find out I lied to them, they'll probably hate me just like everyone else.

The worst part is I know I brought this upon myself. Maybe Kai lied to me, but I was lying to everybody. I'm the one who betrayed her best friend, who faked a relationship to try to make things better, who pushed everyone away in the process.

I keep swiping and then my finger stops instinctively when I see a graphic of two cats flying through space. It looks like neon colors have thrown up all over it. The Disco Cats.

Sarah has a show tonight.

I remember the thoughtless comment I made to her the other day: *I wouldn't want anyone to see us together in public anyway.* Sarah has been there for me all summer, has treated me far better than I deserve, and still I pushed her away because it felt like she was getting too close to the truth of me, the ugly part I'm afraid to uncover.

But I need to be there for her too. Maybe it's too late to fix everything with Olivia, but I can still try to mend things with Sarah. The first step to setting all of this right is to start apologizing—for this summer but for everything that came before it too.

So I jump up from the bed and get dressed—a bright pink skirt and clear jelly shoes to match the vibe, purple swirls of glitter around my eyes—and run down the stairs, texting my mom to let her know where I'm going. And then I head into town to watch the Disco Cats.

The show is at this crunchy granola hippie coffee shop I tend to avoid because it always smells like weed. So I'm actually kinda surprised at how cool it looks when I walk in. There are twinkling fairy lights strung up over the windows, big leafy plants in all the corners, the walls covered in colorful posters and old maps. A platform stage in the corner is set up with a fog machine and purple lights, and I spot Sarah right away, her curly blue ponytail a beacon. She's with a few other people, bustling around, plugging in amps and testing microphones. I walk up to the counter and order a latte and then take a hesitant seat at a table on the sidelines, feeling uncomfortably out of place. I stopped at McDonald's on the way over to pick up a *please forgive me* present, and I set it down beside me, taking out my phone and scrolling through it so I don't look so alone.

"Holy shit," Sarah's voice calls loudly through the mic, startling me. "Is that Penelope Harris sitting over there at my show? Is that Penelope Harris being seen in public with me?"

I hunch over in my seat, embarrassed by the attention and the callout, even though I deserve it. Sarah jumps down off the stage and comes over to my table. "I thought you were busy every Friday for the rest of time."

"Well, I guess my plans changed."

"Good," she says.

"I'm so sorry about what I said," I say, my cheeks flaming. "I brought you something." I hold out the tray. "You said McFlurries always fix everything, so I was hoping . . ." I trail off, and Sarah peers at the assortment of choices—I got Oreo, M&M's, and Reese's Pieces because I wasn't sure—and then takes the Oreo.

"You're not supposed to bring outside food in here, you rebel." She picks at an Oreo with her spoon. "And you can't just bribe your way out of problems."

"I know," I say. "The thing is, you're the only person who has ever been totally honest with me. And I've been scared. I'm just . . . so scared all the time, and it's *exhausting*." I've always thought I wanted to be more like Olivia, but I realize now I wish I could be like Sarah too—someone who lets things roll off her, who doesn't give a damn what anyone else thinks. I'm so used to people who talk in circles, who whisper behind your back, whose language is sugared kindness laced with poison. It's all so much work.

"I like you, Penelope," she says. "There's a good person some-where in there. But you gotta give her a chance, okay? You can't keep her covered up by all these layers of bullshit."

"Why are you so nice to me?" I ask. "I don't deserve it."

"Pshhhh." Sarah blows some air out of her lips. "You think I'm nice? I am far from nice, Harris. I'm a raging bitch."

"I don't think that's true. If you were a raging bitch, you wouldn't be talking to me right now." I feel a pain in my chest then. "If anything, *I'm* the raging bitch."

She lets out a barking laugh. "Well, yeah. But we knew that already."

"I'm not . . . like . . . trying to be mean to anybody," I say. "I'm a good person." I fiddle with the lid of my drink. "Aren't I?"

"Dude, I don't know," she says. "Are any of us good people, really? I mean, you're not fundamentally one or the other. You just have to try to make the right choices, you know? And if you make a bad choice, you have to try to fix it. You have to put in the work to make things better. Like . . . you made a good choice in coming here tonight to listen to my astonishing, face-melting band. You made a bad choice in, well . . . pretty much every other choice you've ever made, actually."

"That's reassuring," I say flatly.

"Well, yeah, but now you're trying to fix it, so I'd say you're headed in a good direction."

"Why aren't you like this at school?" I ask. "I mean, why don't you stand up for yourself? Why do you just take it?"

"My life is outside of school," she says. "My life is this band and my camp friends and all that. These guys get me. I don't wanna waste my time fighting with Olivia when I'm at RHS. I just want to get through my day. I want to read my goddamn books in peace."

"But it would be so much easier for you if you just said something."

"Yeah, it would be so much easier for me if *you* said something too. Why does it have to be on me to get it to stop?"

I can't help my sinking feeling of guilt. "You're right. God, I really am the worst." The thought strikes me suddenly. "I've been so mad at Kai for calling me that stupid name, but we were doing the same thing to you the whole time, weren't we?"

"Pukey and the Nose Picker," she says. "We should form a band."

I grin, feeling a bit lighter. "Thank you."

"Just don't make me regret this. Got it?" She turns around and calls to this big guy on the stage. "Yo, Brian! Come meet my friend."

And something inside me breaks at her words. *Come meet my friend.*

"I'm your friend?" I ask, my voice small.

"Oh," Sarah says. She smooths her hands down the legs of her black ripped jeans. Her nails are painted a holographic pink. "Well. Yeah, I mean, I thought so."

"Yeah, I think so too," I say, and I realize I'm smiling.

She bites her lip. "Don't let it get to your head, Harris."

Brian comes over to us and throws an arm around Sarah, leaning against her with the kind of comfortable ease that I can tell means they've been dating forever. He's huge—like two heads taller than she is—with spiky black hair and a nose ring—and it feels like I should be terrified of him, but I'm not. It's his smile—something about it is so friendly and warm that when he flashes it at me, I feel like we're already buddies. He's got a guitar pick clenched between his teeth, and he keeps it there when he speaks. "Hey, dude."

"This is that bitch I was telling you about," Sarah says, grinning. I should probably be offended, but from what I know of Sarah, *bitch* is a term of endearment. "I love your outfit, by the way," she says. "You usually look a lot less cool than this. What the fuck is that glitter on your face? It's insane."

"Insane . . . good?" I ask, reaching a hand up to touch it but then pulling away at the last second. I don't want to smudge anything. I blended purple and blue shadow on my lids, using eyeliner to draw a wing shape and covering it with glitter so it looks like there are butterflies on my temples.

"Yeah," she says. "You should do more interesting makeup looks at school. You're always so basic in those photos Olivia takes."

"Well, she likes simple black-and-white stuff," I say. "Her aesthetic is minimalist." I love planning outfits for Olivia's Instagram series, but I'd be lying if I said I didn't wish I could get a bit more extra.

"You should do some looks for our next show," Sarah says. "That's how you can make it up to me. I want something with lots of disco shit, lots of sparkles, and lots of cats. Think you could handle that?"

Her words stir an excited flutter in my chest—the first positive feeling I've had in days. Immediately, I start designing something in my head. I could paint the solar system on Sarah's face, silver stars at her temples, and her blue hair would look incredible.

"Are you by yourself?" she continues. "Where are your two boyfriends?"

She must see the hurt on my face because she stops smiling and sits down across from me at the table. "Oh, shit. Which boyfriend do I have to kill?" She turns back to Brian. "Babe, we need some estrogen time over here. I'll meet you in five, okay? This is a no-bone zone."

He grins at her, chewing on the guitar pick. "But you love my bone."

"I will love your bone *after* the show." She narrows her eyes flirtatiously. "Right now, Penelope needs my help."

He shrugs and leans down to kiss her and then lumbers away back to the stage. It's still so weird to connect this version of Sarah to who I've always thought she was: the girl who sits alone at lunch, who hides in the band room during study hall, who always has her nose buried in a book. Back when I used to read on the playground, it was because I had no one to talk to. Maybe Sarah reads all day because she doesn't want anyone to talk to *her*. It's never occurred to me that other people could be happy in the place where I was so miserable.

"All right." She leans toward me. "We go on in five, so I don't have much time."

"I thought you said my problems were emotional labor."

"Yeah, yeah," she says. "I don't know. Sometimes it's fun to hear the details of your drama." She picks up my latte and takes a quick sip, like I offered to share. "We're friends now, right? Just hit me with it."

So I tell Sarah everything. About the fight with my mom,

spending the night in the Jeep with Kai, how I thought I might have been in love with him, but then I found out about his lies, his fake relationship with Olivia. It comes pouring out of me, and it's freeing to be so honest. It feels good to tell the truth when I've spent so long covering it up.

"Damn," Sarah says when I'm done. "Your life is like some Shakespeare shit."

I laugh and it feels good. It's the best I've felt since I stopped talking to Kai. I feel almost sort of a tiny bit human again.

There's a loud squeak from the microphone, the strum of an electric guitar, and Brian's voice is amplified across the café. "Babe, we gotta start."

"One sec!" Sarah shouts at him, then turns back to me. "You going on the Disney trip next week?"

"I wasn't planning on it," I say, fiddling with my now-empty cup.

"No fucking way," she says. "You're coming."

"I'm turning into an old man up here!" Brian shouts. "My hair is graying as I wait."

"Calm down, dude!" Sarah shouts, then to me: "My mom is forcing me. She has this idea that if I spend more time with people from school, we'll all magically fall in love and skip together through meadows holding hands and braiding each other's hair."

"My bones are decomposing!" Brian calls into the mic.

"I mean, okay, it's not like she's forcing me to stick needles into my eyeballs or something," Sarah continues. "But it's almost as bad. Disney is anti-Semitic, racist, misogynistic bullshit. Fuck that noise. If I have to go, you're coming with me."

I don't know if I want to. I don't know if I *can*. It's a five-hour bus ride full of people I don't want to talk to, and then an overnight in a hotel room. At this point, I think it might be too late to switch rooms, and I do not want to share with Olivia after everything that's happened.

And of course Kai will be there too.

"I don't know," I tell Sarah.

"Just think about it, okay?" She reaches her hand into the air to give me a high five, and I smack it. Then she turns and runs onto the stage, grabbing the mic from Brian. "We're the Disco Cats. Prepare to jump into a new dimension."

NOW

CAN WE TALK? Kai texts me a few nights later. How are things with your mom?

When I don't respond right away, he sends a picture wearing a sheet mask. To be honest, he does look a bit like he's from a horror movie. Sheet mask privileges are for friends, he says. And then a few minutes later: Wow my skin is luminous.

I resist the urge to text him back by throwing my phone to the other side of the room so it's lying on the rug in a place I can't reach. I hate that he's acting concerned for me after everything he did. The worst part is that I still care too, that every time he texts me some stupid joke I get a little flutter in my chest that won't go away.

I busy myself by packing for the Disney trip. The bus leaves tomorrow morning, and I still don't know if I want to go. It feels wrong to go on this trip I've been dreaming of for months if I'm not talking to any of the people I planned it with.

Still, I blast a Disney playlist from my phone and pull my little red suitcase out of the closet, setting items inside—shorts and tops and sneakers, all neatly folded and perfectly placed, because if there's one thing that can distract me it's finding the right outfit to make a statement. I open my Mrs. Potts backpack and throw in some things to keep me busy on the long bus ride: my headphones, a notebook and colored pens, a book of crossword puzzles. I pause for a second on the Mickey and Minnie ears I made months ago for Jordan and me, but decide to bring them. Then I make a quick pair for Sarah—purple and glittery and *so* disco, a cat in the middle of each ear.

At the last second, I pick up *The Giver*—the copy Kai just gave back to me—and toss it into my bag too before I can change my mind.

There's a knock on my door.

"Go away!" I say, because whether it's Seb or my mom doesn't matter. I don't want to talk to either of them. But the person on the other side doesn't listen and the door creaks open anyway.

"I know you're mad," Sebastian says. He takes a step into the room, his Pokémon socks just barely over the edge of my doorway, like he knows he's not invited inside. Like he's a vampire. "You should try to cut Mom some slack, though."

"I thought you liked Steve," I say. "Shouldn't you be defending him?"

"I did like Steve. I do like Steve! But we can't control Mom's emotions. She didn't do anything to us."

I know Mom's absence doesn't feel quite the same for Seb as it does for me, because they were never as close to begin with. "Yeah, that's the whole problem. She doesn't ever do anything."

I throw a pair of sunglasses into the suitcase using a little too much force.

He takes another step forward, running a hand through his hair. "Do you ever think . . . maybe . . . you look for reasons to be mad at people? Like maybe it's easier for you to be mad than to deal with your other emotions?"

I want to disagree with him—of course I do. It's instinct to want to tell him to leave, to shut him out again. But that would be what he expects me to do. Which means he has a point.

"You're too young to psychoanalyze me."

Seb comes fully into the room, sitting down in a pile of long limbs on the floor. "I took an intro psych class last quarter for my elective." He grins. "I psychoanalyze everyone."

"Ugh, don't tell me you want to be a scientist too."

"Yeah, maybe I do. I poked around the UCLA website, you know, because you're always talking about going there, and they actually have a really legit psych program. Could be cool. We could be there together."

I try to picture myself at UCLA next year, the image I've always been able to conjure so easily, but it doesn't come. California just doesn't feel like the right place anymore. *What do you love?* Kai asked me at the beach last week. *What makes you happy?*

"I think I might go to design school, actually." The thought comes to me like it was always in there somewhere, just waiting for me to uncover it. "Like, maybe I'll apply to Parsons or FIT or something?" I like the idea of New York, where I can walk purposefully down the sidewalk wrapped in a fashionable coat, taking in the vibrant hubbub of the city. I don't want to go somewhere just because it's what Olivia wants. I don't want to go somewhere as Olivia's *muse.* I want to go somewhere just for me.

"Yeah," he says. "That sounds cool." He points at my suitcase, the items carefully folded inside. "You're going on that trip tomorrow, right?"

"Oh, I don't know." I run a hand over the cover of Kai's book, sitting faceup in the center of everything. "It might be weird to room with Olivia."

"Because you stole her boyfriend."

"That's not what happened," I say, although of course, it is. The truth just feels so much more complicated than that. I'm waiting for him to make his typical comment, some joke about how hot Olivia is, how much he loves her, but he takes me by surprise.

"She probably did something bad to you first."

"Sort of," I say. "It's not that black-and-white. We both did something bad to each other."

"Olivia isn't very nice to you."

His words take me aback. "You just saying that because she won't date you?"

"Nah, she's definitely a smoke show. But your whole friendship is basically you guys telling each other how hot you are. You're always calling each other all these stupid pet names: the soup to my sandwich, the tea to my bag or whatever. Being friends with someone isn't just telling them how cool they are."

It all sounds so fake now when Seb says it. But it didn't feel fake while it was happening. I never realized what was so obvious to my little brother this whole time.

"Maybe you *should* be a psych major." I pick up the pair of sunglasses again, tapping them against my palm.

"You gotta go to Disney," he says. "Don't tell me I've had to suffer through the *Beauty and the Beast* soundtrack our entire lives for nothing. You'll regret it if you don't go."

And I know he's right. I've worked hard for this, have been daydreaming about it for months. I can't let my anger at Kai stop me from living my life. I should go on the Disney trip because Sarah asked me to, and because I *want* to, and isn't that enough? *This* is my Hawaii, it occurs to me suddenly, my heart beating madly in my chest. This is my Hawaii, and I won't ever let a guy take it from me.

NOW

IT'S STILL DARK OUT when my mom drops me off at the school parking lot on her way to work. It's a long drive to the parks, so we're supposed to be in the bus as early as possible to beat traffic. We'll be staying the night at a hotel in Anaheim and then hitting Disneyland the next day before riding back home. It's awkward to be in the car with her after spending the whole week in avoidance mode. We didn't talk the whole drive over, the dark roads and quiet morning a good excuse for both of us.

Now when I move to get out, my mom stops me. "Be safe, okay?" She hands me a thermos of coffee. "Text if anything happens."

"It's not like you'd even see my text," I say, and then feel terrible when her face crumples. I know by taking the time to drop me off this morning, she's making an effort. I think back to what Seb said to me last night: *Maybe it's easier for you to be mad than to deal with your other emotions.* He was right. And I don't want to be that person anymore. "I'm sorry. I don't know why I said that."

"No," my mom says. "I deserve it." She sighs. "I know I'm not always around, but I really am trying. It's tough being a single mom."

"We just never get to talk about stuff anymore," I say, my words hitching in my throat. "I miss you."

That's the truth of it. *I miss her.* I'm not angry with her, not really. It's just that I'm a little tiny bit heartbroken.

I think then of the two of us designing dresses for my stuffed animals with colorful markers when I was little, decorating holiday cookies, eating handfuls of buttery popcorn while I begged her to watch *The Little Mermaid* for the eighteenth time.

"I know. I miss you too." She takes my hand, squeezes, and I'm reminded of when she used to drive me to school and drop me off, before she worked mornings, before I started carpooling with Olivia. "There's no guidebook for being a mom. Sometimes I try, and I mess things up."

"You shouldn't need a guidebook to tell you to spend time with us."

She shuts her eyes. "I know, baby. But this goes both ways. When you were little, you were always home, and so *loving* and chatty about everything. You were interested in the world, always asking me questions, eager to learn. And then you grew up, and I was so happy that you found all those friends, but it's like you forgot yourself a bit in the process—forgot me a little bit too."

"That's not true."

"I'm not saying I haven't messed up. But . . . sometimes I want to talk about things too. It's hard to get a moment with you. I know you don't *need* me anymore, I know you're growing up, and that's wonderful, but sometimes that's hard for a mother to deal with. You're always out of the house on some adventure with your friends. Whenever there's a problem, you just run away from it. I want to be here for you when things get hard. You had a crush on that boy for so long, and when you broke up, you didn't want to talk to me about it."

"You knew about Jordan?" I ask, surprised.

"Of course." She gives a watery smile. "I'm your mother. I know everything. But I want to hear the details of your life from *you*. I want you to choose to share."

It never occurred to me that my mom could be feeling the loss of our relationship too.

"I thought you didn't want to know."

"Of course I do!" She pauses, then takes a breath. "I've de-cided I'm not going to date anyone for a little while, actually. I think I need to be alone for a bit. Spend my time with you both."

I should be relieved, but instead my stomach twists. "I don't want you to be unhappy because of my—"

"Oh no," she says. "This is what I need. I think . . . I think I never let myself properly heal from your dad. I'm just so angry with him for leaving us, but there's another part of me that's . . . always been keeping a spot in my heart open in case he comes back. And that's not fair to you. It's not fair to Steve, who has been nothing but wonderful. I think I push people away so I can't get hurt again. And I got so used to pushing everyone out that I pushed you and Sebastian away too."

Before I can help it, tears sting my eyes, her words breaking something open inside me. Maybe my mom and I are more simi-lar than I ever knew—because I've been pushing her away too, have turned into a destructive, selfish person that I don't like.

My mom smiles and rests her hand on the weird backpack I

made, the elephant-like face with the purple bonnet. "What is this? Is this Mrs. Potts?"

"Yeah." I'm embarrassed because of course I want her to like it. "It's part of a costume."

"Belle," she says. "You always did love that movie. You're so talented. I love all the things you make. You're so special, baby girl." Her words make me feel light and floaty—because they are finally the right ones.

"Thank you," I tell her, then take a deep breath and get out of the car, walking over to the bus. There are teachers standing around all over the place with clipboards, checking us in and looking through bags to make sure nobody is sneaking in any illegal contraband. I know people still will, though. If there's one thing my class seems to be good at, it's sneaking alcohol into places and then drinking too much of it. I should know.

I walk by a group of girls and hear them whispering, fragments of sentences following me as I pass: *I heard she and Kai broke up . . . it was all fake the whole time . . . Kai and Olivia . . .*

I turn away from them, trying not to listen. I scan the crowd for my friends, bracing myself for their reactions when they see me now that they know the truth. That's when I find Sarah. She's wearing a pair of noise-canceling headphones, nodding along to some music I can't hear. I don't know why I ever let my fear of what people might think hold me back from talking to her, because right now I have never been so relieved to see a friendly face in my life.

I walk over to her, and she tears the headphones off. "Penelope! Didn't think you would actually show."

"It's Disney," I say, grinning. "I wouldn't miss a trip to the happiest place on earth."

Sarah scoffs. "Any place where there's a high chance of getting puked on by a crying child can*not* be referred to as the happiest place on earth."

"I think you secretly love it," I say. "Oh, wait, actually . . ." I pause, spinning my backpack around and pulling out the ears I designed for her. "I made these for you."

She takes them from me tentatively, like she's afraid they might burn her skin, then turns them over, examining them. "There are cats on here."

"They're Disco Cats."

"I can see that. *Fuck*, Penelope." She sighs. "Are you really going to make me wear a symbol of an evil corporate empire on my head?"

"They sparkle," I point out.

She sighs dramatically and puts on the ears. "This is the worst thing you've ever done to me."

"You're welcome."

"I brought some snacks if you'd like to partake." Sarah holds a canvas bag in my direction. "We've got extra spicy Flamin' Hot Cheetos, some gummy worms for the pain, and La Croix if you want to be fancy."

I laugh because the image of Sarah with her big headphones and her loud mouth drinking a can of Pamplemousse just gets me. I reach into the bag and take a handful of gummy worms.

I'm midchew, worm dangling half out of my mouth like I'm a baby bird, when I hear a voice behind me. "Harris."

I turn and see Jordan, and quickly suck the rest of the worm into my mouth in a panic. He looks scruffy, like he just rolled out of bed, in a pair of RHS sweatpants and sweatshirt, his hood thrown over his head. It looks good on him. What is it about guys in sweatpants? I'm reminded again of how excited I used to be at the prospect of waking up next to him. Of seeing him just like this.

His hands are stuffed into his pockets, his shoulders hunched, and he seems . . . *nervous*. To talk to *me*?

I turn back to Sarah, and she nudges me forward with her elbow.

"Hey," I say to Jordan, tentative. "Um, what's up?"

He looks questioningly between Sarah and me, probably wondering why we're standing together. "Can we talk?"

I think back to the last time Jordan and I spoke—how I came clean about the plan and put into motion the series of events that ruined everything. But maybe it was all for the best. Because at least now everything is out in the open. Now I know Kai and Olivia's big secret.

"Yeah," I say. "We should talk."

He pulls his hood down and runs a hand over the top of his head. "Okay, cool. Well, you wanna sit together?"

I look back at Sarah. Did she want us to sit together? I don't want to leave her by herself. But I owe it to Jordan to explain everything to him. And I want to hear his side too.

"Don't let me hold you back from true love," she says, pushing Jordan and me together.

"Are you sure?" I ask her.

"Dude, Penny. It's fine," she says. "You two should figure out your shit."

"Okay," I tell Jordan, following him tentatively onto the bus. We find a seat toward the back, and I feel a little bit like I'm going to throw up as I scan the rest of the seats for Kai or Olivia. Luckily, neither of them are here yet.

But the others are. Myriah and Romina are sharing a pair of earbuds, their heads bent close together over someone's phone. They glance up at me, and I look away, too afraid to make eye contact. I'm not ready to face the disappointment I know will be in their gazes.

We slide into a seat in front of Danny and Katie. Jordan and Danny do some complicated fist bump, and I watch the emotions flit across Katie's face as she notices me there beside him—watch the internal struggle as she decides whether she's supposed to be my friend. Eventually, she smiles.

"Hey, Penny. I heard about you and Kai. That sucks."

"Yeah, well," I say, because they're the only words I can manage. The pain still feels so fresh, so new. It's weird, but walking down the aisle of the bus in front of everyone with Jordan, taking this seat beside him, back where I belong—it doesn't make me feel the same kind of powerful that it used to.

I sit by the window, and before I can stop myself, I'm scanning the parking lot looking for Kai. Jordan squeezes my knee and I turn back to him, startled.

"You know he's late for everything."

"Oh," I say. "I wasn't . . ." I trail off. I don't want Jordan thinking Kai is on my mind. Kai is done. He's over. And Jordan is right here.

"It's weird, huh?" He leans closer to me and gives me a reassuring smile. "Like, all the shit we went through this summer and now we're right back where we started."

"We are?" I don't feel like the same person I was a month ago.

Jordan sighs, then lowers his voice. "I ended things with Olivia. That's what I wanted to talk to you about."

And it's funny, because even though they're the words I've

been waiting all summer to hear—ever since I saw them kissing on the beach and felt like my world was ripping apart—when Jordan says them now, it just makes me feel *sad*. Not for me, but for Olivia.

"Oh," I say. "Is she okay?"

"I mean, it's kind of fucked up what they did to us, don't you think?"

"Yeah." I just don't know how everything got so complicated.

I remember the ears I made for Jordan then and pull them out of my bag. I made them back when we were still together, before everything this summer got so messed up, and I don't know if he'll still want them. But they feel like a peace offering. So I hand them to him. "I made these for you."

He takes them, turning them over in his hands. "Oh. Nice. You know, we should take a picture in these tomorrow at the park. You wanna meet up in front of the castle?"

I can see us in my mind like always—walking hand in hand down Main Street, posing for the perfect picture in front of the castle, the couple all other couples want to be. But then the vision is replaced with a new one: me pulling Kai onto Splash Mountain, staging a fight, and pretending to break up like we planned. It's the second image that makes me sad, that makes me feel like I've lost something. But Kai and I are done. And everything I went through this summer was to get back this moment in front of the castle with Jordan. It was the whole point.

Just then, Kai's Jeep pulls up outside the bus window. My pulse quickens, nerves tingling at the thought of seeing him. I watch as the Jeep doors open, and he tumbles out, one of his arms in a sweatshirt, the other half of which is flying behind him like a flag. He's pulling his beanie onto his head, his sandals sliding off his feet as he races toward the bus. My heart warms a bit at the sight, at how cute he looks all disheveled. But I push that thought away. He's not allowed to be cute when I'm this mad at him.

Then the other side of the Jeep opens, and I watch as Olivia climbs down from the passenger side. My stomach drops. I should've expected they'd be together. I mean, here I am sitting with Jordan. But the thought of them comforting each other makes me a little sick.

I watch as they walk onto the bus, preparing myself for what I'll say when they pass by, but they take a seat together at the front and don't even look my way at all.

"Okay," I tell Jordan. "Noon tomorrow in front of the castle."

NOW

JORDAN FALLS ASLEEP almost immediately after we leave, his head resting on my shoulder. I try to join him, squeezing my eyes shut, but I'm too anxious about everything to calm down enough to sleep. Instead, I stare at the scenery passing by outside the window and think about everything that went wrong.

When we get to the hotel, we all wait together in the lobby as the teachers get everything organized and check us into our rooms. It's warmer here, and brighter than at home, and it really feels like summer. There's an excited buzz in the air as everyone departs the bus, all the Disney-themed restaurants and billboards coming into sight. There's happy tinkling music playing from the speakers in the lobby. Even though I'm anxious about everything going on, it's hard to be that stressed when "A Whole New World" is playing.

I'm sitting in one of the lobby chairs waiting to check in

when Kai catches me off guard, sitting down in the chair next to me. "I saw you guys sitting together."

I flinch. "Yeah, well. I saw you guys sitting together too."

"Olivia really needs a friend right now," he says, which makes me feel terrible. "So are you and Jordan back together?"

"No," I tell him. "I don't know. But getting Jordan back was the whole point, wasn't it?" I'm only saying it to spite him, but when I see the hurt on his face, I immediately regret it.

"Yeah," he says, running a hand down his face. "Yeah, I guess it was. Is that what you want?" he asks, his voice low. "Because if it is, I'll leave you alone. Just tell me to back off and I will." He raises his arms. "Promise."

It's momentarily hard to breathe. I don't know what I want. Kai hurt me, and I don't know if I can ever let that go. And even though I don't think I want to get back with Jordan either, there's a part of me that's still too bruised.

And so I do what comes so naturally to me. I push him away. "That's what I want."

Kai looks at me for a beat longer and nods. "Okay."

Then he spins away from me and disappears out the front doors of the hotel.

Olivia and I both try our best to convince the chaperones to let us switch rooms, but the damage has already been done, the room placements all fixed. We're stuck with each other.

After we're all signed in and given our key cards, we have an hour to settle and get changed before we're all supposed to head to dinner at the Rainforest Cafe. Olivia and I walk to the room together in silence, pointedly Not Looking at each other. We wheel our suitcases into the elevator in silence, and both reach for the button to the fourth floor at the same time. She gets there first, and I pull my hand back as she pushes her finger aggressively into the button. We avoid each other's gazes as we walk silently down the hall and then stop in front of room 426.

"Do you have your key card?" Olivia asks, looking at me expectantly.

I dig through my bag and find it, then tap it lightly against the door. We walk silently into the room. It's disappointing to think back to how excited I once was about this moment—my first big overnight in a hotel, getting to share a room with Olivia. I remember how thrilled we were to try to sneak into the boys' room, to raid the vending machine for chips and cookies and come back here, staying up all night watching Disney movies. I can see it all before me as I enter the room and put my suitcase down on one of the beds.

But I couldn't be that girl again even if I wanted to. Things are different now. Still, I just hate this so much. I think about Sarah's words from the other night: *If you make a bad choice, you have to try to fix it. You have to put in the work to make things better.* I don't expect Olivia to forgive me anymore; I don't know if I even want her to. But I need her to know I'm sorry.

"Olivia," I say, unzipping my suitcase. "Can we talk?"

She pulls out her makeup bag. "I don't know what you could possibly have to say to me."

"I shouldn't have kissed Kai." I raise my hands as if in surrender. "I'm sorry."

She folds her arms. "Yes, obviously you shouldn't have kissed Kai."

Something in her tone prickles—because even though what I did was wrong, Olivia isn't totally innocent in this either. "I shouldn't have," I repeat. "But you spent the whole school year trying to get me to want him, and then when your plan actually worked, you got mad." I bring my toothbrush into the bathroom and set it down on top of a tissue.

"That's not fair," she says, following me into the bathroom with her makeup bag. She slams it down a little too hard on the counter in a way I know might damage an eye shadow palette. "You were supposed to break up with Jordan, not make out with my boyfriend."

"But he wasn't actually your boyfriend!"

"Yeah, but you didn't know that. You were my best friend, and you still kissed him even though you thought he was mine."

"You wanted Jordan the whole time we were together!"

I've seen so many movies where couples pretend to date each other for some silly reason or other—to win a bet, or earn an inheritance, or make someone jealous. In the movies, it's always fun and hilarious and full of lighthearted mishaps. But the truth is, in real life, messing with people's feelings isn't okay. Olivia and I were manipulating each other, toying with each other's emotions all for the sake of some stupid boys. That's not lighthearted or fun or cute. It's messed up.

Olivia presses her hands into her eyes, taking a gulping breath. "I was with Jordan first," she says, voice quiet. "I knew you had a crush on him. You wished for him on that stupid candle. I'm sorry, but you didn't actually even know him, Penny. Every time you'd try to talk to him, you'd just clam up. You'd been obsessed with him since first grade, but you didn't actually know him. I knew him. Jordan was my friend. And then when I started to like him, I was just supposed to back off because you'd staked some ridiculous claim on him? That wasn't fair. I'm not sorry I slept with him, Penny. I'm just sorry about how he treated me afterward."

"I don't think . . ." I try to interrupt, but Olivia holds up a hand to stop me.

"No, let me finish. Please."

"Okay." I take a seat on the edge of the sink.

"When Jordan was sleeping with other girls, it sucked, but I could deal with it. I'm tough. I'd hear rumors about all the girls he was with, but none of them lasted. And it was okay that you liked him too, because it didn't matter. It wasn't real. Your crush on him was harmless. But then he started showing interest in you back, and I couldn't handle it. He said things to you he never said to me. He bought you presents and held your hand in public. I mean, even after you cheated on him he still defended you at every possible moment. Still acted like I was the bad guy."

She takes a tube of highlighter out of her bag and dabs it on her cheeks. "You and Jordan started hanging out, and it sucked, but still I knew it was going to be okay because he was going to drop you too. Drop you like he dropped me. And maybe I would tell you then about everything between us and we could cry over it together. But then he *didn't*. You guys became official. And you weren't even sleeping together! You didn't sleep with him for months, and I had slept with him like it was nothing and he was done. But you were worth holding out for. I was furious. I *am* furious."

"Then be furious with Jordan!" It's just so typical. Girls always get mad at the other girl instead of taking things out on the boy who's wronged them.

"When you and Jordan got together," Olivia continues, "I knew Kai could help me. He's been my friend through all of it.

And I knew he had a thing for you—even if he claimed to hate you or whatever. I mean, all of us wanted you and Kai to get together. So he and I made a deal. If he said nice things about me to Jordan—talked me up—I would say nice things about Kai to you."

"So all that stuff you said about Kai. How he's the world's best kisser. All those things—"

"I made it all up. The only time Kai and I have ever kissed was during truth or dare."

"But you . . . I thought you guys . . ."

"It was never supposed to last this long. You guys were supposed to figure out you were with the wrong person. You were supposed to get jealous and break up. But you didn't. God, you just kept dating. For *months*. And then you told me you were going to sleep with him and I knew. I knew our plan was never going to work. We'd tried it and we'd failed. We were going to stage a big breakup at that party and move on with our lives. I was going to back off and let you have Jordan. And then I saw you kissing Kai. You don't get to have both of them, Penny. That's not how life works." Her eyes moisten with tears, and she dabs at them with the side of her pinkie, keeping them in. It's all wrong. Olivia isn't supposed to be this fragile. She doesn't cry, and she doesn't let down her guard, and she doesn't bother herself with petty emotions.

"Olivia," I say, meeting her steely gaze in the mirror. "Why do you want Jordan if he makes you feel like this?"

"Because nobody else wants me." Her eyes in the mirror soften, lose their hard edge for just a second, and my heart breaks for her. I think I get it for the first time. Olivia is human just like the rest of us. Maybe—just like me—she's always thought of herself as second best.

"But you're amazing," I say. "You're incredible. Why else do you think I've been your best friend for so many years? You contain multitudes. I loved you, Liv." The past tense just slips out, and I realize it's true. There's no getting back what we had. And it's probably for the best. I don't want to let guys get in between us, but this isn't about Jordan and Kai at all. Not really. Our friendship hasn't been healthy for a while. Real, true friends wouldn't do what we both did to each other. We always said we'd be best friends forever—we even had the necklaces to prove it—but sometimes you outgrow friendships. *Forever* is such a long time.

"If I was so *amazing*, we wouldn't be in this situation," she says, meeting my gaze in the mirror.

"I just think you deserve better—"

"I don't need your advice, Penny. I'm fine, actually." She spins away from me, setting the highlighter down on the counter. "I'm gonna go find Katie, okay?"

She leaves the hotel suite, slamming the door behind her. And I'm alone.

NOW

I DECIDE TO SKIP dinner and stay in my room, eating some chips from the vending machine, the gentle hum of the air conditioner a sad downgrade from the tropical thunderstorms of the Rainforest Cafe. Olivia gets back late, and I hear her stumbling around in the dark as she tries not to wake me.

The next morning we get up before the sun for the second time in a row. Olivia and I get packed for the day together in silence, put on our makeup in silence, get dressed in silence. I fill my Mrs. Potts backpack—my headphones, a water bottle, some granola bars in case I get hungry and don't want to spend a million dollars on a sandwich in the park. And then my hand lingers on Kai's book. I know it's stupid to bring it. It's just going to be extra weight I'll have to carry around. But I place it gently in my bag anyway.

We're all supposed to meet down in the lobby before walking over to the park together. I don't really want to hang around all the people who hate me, so I head toward the hotel café to get an iced coffee instead. I'm almost all the way in line before I notice Myriah and Romina standing together in front of me. Romina sees me and nudges Myriah's shoulder. I freeze, fighting the urge to back away.

"Do you hate us or something?" Romina asks, folding her arms.

"What?" I ask, caught off guard. "Why would I hate you?"

"Well, you've been straight up avoiding us this whole trip. It fucking sucks, Penny."

"But . . . I lied to you. I thought you hated *me*."

Myriah squeezes Romina's hand and lets go, taking a step closer to me. "We don't hate you." She fiddles with the end of her braid. "I mean yeah, you lied to us. But avoiding us doesn't fix anything. And I understand why you and Kai did it. I'm not even really that mad. I'm just . . . sad. I want you to trust me. We're supposed to be friends."

I know she's right. It's just like my mom said. All I've done this summer is run from my problems. And instead of owning up to my mistakes, I've just created more of them, piling lies on top of lies. But I don't want to be the type of person who cheats, who betrays her friends, who lies to cover it up. I don't want to trick everyone into thinking I'm a better person. I just want to be one.

"I'm sorry. Myriah, you're just *so great* and . . . I didn't want to let you down. You all wanted Kai and me to be together and it was easier to just go with it than admit the truth."

"Well, I'm sorry too," she says. "That was kind of unfair of us. You were with Jordan. We should have respected that."

"Well, if we're all saying sorry," Romina says, clearing her throat, "then I'm sorry about that video. I mean, you shouldn't have cheated or lied, but I shouldn't have posted something like that. I was just caught up in the moment and I—"

"It's okay," I say. "I get it."

"Olivia just has a way of pulling you in and making you do stupid shit," she continues. "But it's always about her, you know? You remember when we were at the cabin and it was raining and Olivia wanted us to drink my parents' wine? We all just did it. I had to find someone to buy us some replacement bottles and paid them all my money from cello lessons, and I was so terrified my parents would find out. Like, my parents are *so* strict, and you know things have gotten even trickier since I came out. And I'd already gone out on a limb having you all stay there. It's just stuff like that."

"Maybe we all kind of suck in our own ways," I say, and Myriah snorts. And even though I'm just joking, I realize it's kind of true. None of us are perfect. We've all made mistakes. But being friends with someone means knowing all the ugly, messed-up parts of them too. What all of us had before wasn't friendship—not exactly. It was like we were *pretending* to be friends. It was all fake.

"I would have still liked you," Myriah says. "If you had told me the truth."

We head back to the lobby and I find Sarah, sitting beside her while we wait for the chaperones to take attendance. She's mid-rant about the racist stereotypes in *Dumbo* when the elevator dings and Kai emerges. My breath catches—an involuntary reaction—because he's wearing a pair of homemade Mickey Mouse ears. He glances over at me and our eyes meet for just a second and I can tell my cheeks are pink.

I know it's a gesture for me—Kai, who thinks dressing up is pointless, who has been teasing me mercilessly the past month about my love of Disney. Sarah knows it too because she nudges me a little too aggressively with her elbow.

When we get to the park, we scan our tickets and walk through the main gates together as a class, greeted by cheerful tinkling music. I recognize my favorite song from *The Little Mermaid* played on a shimmering flute. It's a beautiful sunny day, happy laughing people all around us. It's so freaking whimsical.

And even though I'm happy about making up with Myriah and Romina and I'm dressed like a literal Disney princess, everything still feels off. We all kind of walk as a group down Main Street until the guys break off and head toward the Star Wars area, Danny practically skipping with joy, all six feet of him vibrating with excitement. He's wearing one of his favorite Star Wars shirts: PALPATINE FOR PRESIDENT. Kai and Jordan follow on either side, and I know they're just trying to be good friends to Danny, but it's weird to see them together.

The castle stands tall before us, sun glinting off its blue turrets, and I remember I'm supposed to meet up with Jordan there later, a plan that feels a little more lackluster than I expected.

We walk by an ice-cream parlor, a candy store, a line of children waiting to meet Pluto, who is signing autographs and jumping around like a real dog. There's a cart selling twenty-five-dollar mouse ears. I nudge Sarah with my shoulder. "See? And those ones aren't even Disco Cats–themed."

She touches the sparkly mouse ears on her head, which she is graciously wearing just for me. "You're right. Your crafting skills have saved me a whole twenty-five dollars I was definitely going to spend."

There's a surprising shriek then and we all stop, turning to watch as Katie runs straight for Pluto. Even Olivia gapes at her in confusion as she cuts the line of children and waves at him. He looks at her, crawling away from the kids he's supposed to be taking pictures with. He waves and then taps his wrist, like he's indicating a watch, and then turns and scampers through an alley between buildings and is gone.

"Did . . . Katie just scare away Pluto?" Romina asks.

"I think you traumatized him," Myriah says.

Katie turns back to all of us. "It's Matt!"

"What?" I ask.

"You mean like . . . Matt the ghost?" Olivia asks. "Matt who doesn't exist?"

"I told you guys he worked at Disney!" Katie says.

"You for sure never told us that," Romina says.

A minute later, Pluto comes back out to greet the line, and behind him is a tall, skinny white boy with brown hair and glasses. His face is flushed red from the heat. He runs to Katie and wraps his arms around her.

"I'm not allowed to break character," he says. "I had to send out my replacement."

They make kissy faces at each other, and it's actually kind of sweet. I make eye contact with Olivia for just a second before she looks away, but I know we're both feeling the impact of this moment the same way. Of course Matt was real all along. Why did we ever doubt her?

Sarah and I break off from the crowd together then. There are still several hours until I'm supposed to meet up with Jordan at noon, so I pull her onto the rides I've been dreaming about since I was a kid: Pirates of the Caribbean, which smells like the chlorine of the local pool; Indiana Jones, fast and bumpy and stomach-flipping. We eat popcorn from the vendor in front of New Orleans, climb through Tarzan's Treehouse. She even lets me take her onto It's a Small World, despite the fact that she tells me the dolls will place a curse upon my entire family for generations.

At one point, we bump into Myriah and Romina, and they join us too. I keep waiting for something to go wrong—for Romina to take a joke too far, for Sarah to snap back at her—but it doesn't happen. It feels like we're all building a bridge to a tentative friendship, something brittle, too flimsy to walk across, but something that might become magical.

"What are you listening to?" Myriah asks as we're waiting in the weirdly long line for Peter Pan's Flight, pointing to the head-phones hanging around Sarah's neck.

Sarah's face lights up in excitement—her *music* face. "It's my boyfriend's SoundCloud, actually." She pulls the headphones from around her neck and hands them to Myriah. "I know that's super embarrassing to listen to your own boyfriend's music, but he's so talented. He writes all the songs for our band."

"You have a boyfriend?" Myriah asks, taking the headphones.

"You're in a band?" Romina asks, her eyes lighting up. "You have to send me the info. I make fucking baller playlists. I'm put-ting you guys on one."

Romina makes plans to check out the next Disco Cats show, and Myriah gets excited because she loves to dance more than any of us. And it's fun. It's different than I imagined the day go-ing, but in the end it actually doesn't matter. It feels amazing not to overanalyze everything I say, not to be on constant alert from someone's judgment.

But I can't stop my mind from wandering back to Kai. Every time the peak of Splash Mountain appears in the distance, I'm reminded of him. The thing is, ignoring Kai is starting to make me feel just as miserable as fighting with him used to.

"You should just text him and put me out of my misery," Sarah says at one point when she catches me staring off into space during the show in the Enchanted Tiki Room, instead of the appropriate reaction to that attraction, which is, of course, sheer terror.

"Text who?" I ask her.

"You know he's staring sadly at all the Baby Yoda dolls over in the Star Wars area, feeling all wounded and alone," Romina says.

"He's probably pretending to date the Baby Yoda dolls and then breaking their hearts."

"Did Kai break your heart, Penny?" Sarah asks. "Or did you break his?"

I turn away from the animatronic bird singing in front of us and look at her. "What are you talking about? Kai manipulated me. He doesn't deserve my forgiveness."

"Yeah, just like you manipulated Jordan," Sarah says.

"Some things are unforgivable," Myriah says, voice soft. "But there's a difference between forgiving someone who doesn't deserve it, and letting someone learn and grow from their mistakes. Your bad decisions don't have to define you forever."

"Personally, I've had enough of this hetero nonsense," Romina says, and Myriah elbows her.

"Kai has seen all the worst sides of you and somehow he still wants to be with you," Sarah says. "That's worth something."

• • • • • •

It's almost noon when we cross paths with Olivia and Katie by the entrance to the Jungle Cruise. They're sharing a Dole Whip, passing the spoon back and forth, and they stop walking when they see us. In a park filled with thousands of people, somehow fate is pulling us together in the meanest way.

Olivia crumples her napkin, looking back and forth between Sarah and me. "So you're all just fully hanging out with Sarah now, I guess?"

"Yup," Sarah says, crossing her arms.

"Yeah," I say. "We are."

"Are you guys going on Jungle Cruise?" Katie asks, licking a bit of juice that's dribbling down her arm.

"Obviously, Sarah wants to go on the ride for middle schoolers." Olivia smirks. And I know now that Olivia's comments must come from a place of insecurity, that inside she has a heart somewhere and she's hurting. But that doesn't give her an excuse to constantly treat Sarah like shit. I've had enough of it.

"Can we not do this?" I ask, taking a step closer.

Olivia takes a step closer too. "Oh, so now you're concerned about Sarah?"

"Whoa," Romina says. "Maybe we should go check out the Haunted Mansion or something. Or get some popcorn?"

"I am dying for a churro." Myriah grabs gently on to my arm as if to pull me away. But I shrug her off, still focused right on Olivia.

"This whole place is for middle schoolers," I say. "*And* high schoolers, and kids, and adults, and literally everyone! Just let people live. Is that so hard? Sarah is my friend."

"You know what?" Olivia says. "You're the world's biggest hypocrite, Penny. You've laughed right along with every joke

I've ever made. You let other people do your dirty work so you can still feel good about yourself. But you're not perfect. And you're not a good friend."

I stare at her for a second, let her words wash over me, and for the first time I don't feel crushed by them. Because I agree with her. "You're right."

"What?" She tilts her head to the side, her body still rigid, like she's expecting a fight.

"You're right, Olivia."

I'm not perfect—because no one is. People aren't absolutes. We are all layered: mean sometimes, and flawed, but also funny, and caring, and happy, and in love. We are all so many different things at once. And I can have love in my heart for Olivia—can feel horrible for breaking her trust—while also not condoning everything she says.

I remember what Sarah told me the other night at her show. People aren't fundamentally good or bad. It's all about the choices you make. You have to choose to be a good person over and over. You can't change the past; you can't fix the mistakes you've made. You just have to choose to be better.

And then it hits me. Being a better person means standing up for Sarah—but it means standing up for Olivia too. It means not dragging things out with Jordan when I don't even want to be with him anymore. All I've wanted this whole summer is for Jordan to take me back, for Olivia and all the rest of my friends to forgive the horrible mistake I made. But I never thought about how my actions were hurting Olivia even *more*.

"I've got to go," I tell them. Then I turn and run away through the crowd, heading in the direction of Sleeping Beauty Castle.

NOW

IT'S 11:55 WHEN I get to the castle, and I text Jordan letting him know I'm here. Then I take a seat on one of the benches to wait. The sun is shining, the air warm on my arms, a nice flowery scent on the breeze. I look through my bag for my water bottle, and my hand catches on the book I slipped in there—the book I only took with me today because I wanted a piece of Kai with me. I take it carefully out of my bag and look at it for a second.

"Why'd you bring a book?" Jordan asks, and I startle, looking up at him. He's leaning over me, all broad shoulders and arms, and he looks perfect against the outline of the castle.

"What?"

"That book," Jordan says. "Why are you carrying that around with you?"

"Oh," I say. I know I should drop it back into my bag and move on, but I'm still holding it like it's a precious thing. I don't want to let it go. "I just thought . . . maybe if the lines were long or something, it would be good to have something to read."

Jordan cocks his head to the side, studying me like he's never seen me before. "I didn't know you were so into books."

"Well, I mean . . . yeah . . ." I trail off, unsure what to say. All my memories of reading on the playground are tainted by how lonely I felt back then. I've been trying to push that side of me away, too worried that if anyone knew the real me, they wouldn't like her. But I do love books. I've always loved to read. My heart breaks at the fact that I've kept that part of myself hidden.

"I've just never seen you with a book," he says, shrugging. And it hits me that maybe Jordan doesn't even remember who I used to be as a kid. All those days I spent staring at him, longing for him, obsessing over him . . . well, he didn't notice me at all.

Jordan points to the Mickey Mouse ears on his head. "You ready to take that picture?"

"Why did you want to meet me here?" I ask, instead of answering.

He looks taken aback. "I thought you wanted this."

"But what about Olivia?"

"Olivia and I are done. I told you, rebounds aren't ever the real thing."

"But she's not a rebound!" I jump up from the bench. "You've led her on for years. You slept with her, and then you pursued *me*, her best friend, like it didn't even matter!"

Jordan's eyes narrow. "I wasn't ready for a girlfriend back then." He runs a hand down his face. "I mean, I was only fifteen. I just wanted to have a little fun."

I'm furious then on Olivia's behalf. I've spent too long idolizing Jordan, too long putting his needs over those of my best friend. I can't believe I always thought Jordan was so *nice*. Maybe I just saw what I wanted to see. I've been so absorbed in my own daydreams—my silly fantasy of him—that I couldn't see Olivia's true heartbreaking feelings right in front of my face. I've twisted that memory from the camping trip around in my head so many times, warped it to represent what I wanted it to mean instead of coming to the obvious conclusion.

"Why *me*, then?" I ask. "Why did you want to be with me?"

He laughs then, a nervous chuckle. "Why do you think?"

I back away. "That's not an answer."

He smiles—the full grin that once made me giddy—and takes a step closer. "Well, you're beautiful."

I clutch Kai's book tightly in my arms. "Is that it?"

"Of course not," Jordan says, but I think we both know he's lying. And maybe his words should hurt, but they don't. Because the truth is, I think the only reason I wanted to be with Jordan was because I thought he was beautiful too. I don't think I ever loved him. I loved the idea of him.

And maybe he only loved the idea of me too.

"Well, what changed? I mean, why did you ask me to go get Popsicles last year?"

I think about the Lady Gaga candle again, my wish about Jordan that seemed to change everything.

"Um," he says, and his face turns bright red. "Well, I heard Romina that day at the pep rally. *Penny is madly in love with Jordan. Are you mad? Don't be mad.*"

"Oh," I say, internally dying just a little bit. Because of course that's what it was. It wasn't the magic of some candle. It wasn't the fact that I learned how to do my makeup better over the summer, that I came into junior year with a newfound confidence. It wasn't that he found out I liked musicals, or that he thought it was cute I couldn't parallel park. It was the fact that Jordan knew he could get with me if he tried.

Jordan doesn't even know me.

"Did I ever tell you about my dad?" I ask him abruptly.

"What about him?" He's understandably confused.

"We dated for six months and I never brought him up at all." I let out a laugh, feeling strangely free.

"You could have told me whatever," he says. But I know it's not true.

"I'm so sorry I kissed Kai at that party," I say honestly. "I'm sorry I lied. But I think I finally get it, you know?" It all makes sense now, everything that has felt so extraordinarily messed up all summer. "I think I was so sick of trying so hard to be perfect, and I just . . . wanted to feel what it was like to make a mistake."

"Well, how did it feel?" Jordan asks. "You made a pretty fucking big one."

"It felt . . . *amazing*," I say, laughing still. It occurs to me that maybe I drank too much at that party because I was too scared to be the real me—to be wild or spontaneous, someone who takes risks. And drinking made that person a little less harsh, dimmed her around the edges, made her more willing to act out, less self-conscious about what others thought of her. But I don't need to drink to be that girl.

And I know then what I have to do.

"I'm gonna go, okay?" I pat Jordan's knee and stand up from the bench. "There's somewhere I have to be."

Then I walk away, leaving Jordan in my memories, where he belongs. As I disappear into the crowd, I'm surprised by how free I feel. I was so terrified of being left alone at Disneyland, but being by myself right now doesn't feel like loneliness—it feels like potential. I don't have to play by anyone else's rules. I don't have to be the girl I think everyone wants, the one who looks put together all the time, who is too scared to get her hair wet because of how it might look.

Earlier this summer, when everything happened, I could have dealt with it on my own, but I'd gone to Kai for help. I'd used Kai for protection—had pretended to date him instead of being on my own, because the idea of being someone's girlfriend made me feel more powerful than being alone.

But depending on someone else isn't power. Using someone to make yourself feel less alone isn't strength. I don't need anyone's approval—not Jordan's, or Olivia's, or Kai's.

I start speed-walking through the crowd, toward the pulsing drums of Adventureland. The sun is hot on the back of my neck, but right now I don't mind. Because I know what's coming.

I move through the crowds of people, pushing until I'm in Frontierland, and then I see it up ahead, the brown peak towering over the rest of the skyline: Splash Mountain. I'm running now, toward the excited screams, toward the splash of the boats as they crash down into the waves. I hop into the single-rider line, and it's short enough that pretty soon I'm right at the front.

I realize then that I still have Kai's book in my hands, that in my hurry to run over here, I never stuffed it back into my bag. I run my hand over the worn cover, flip through the torn pages turned yellow over the years from the sun.

"Penelope!"

At first I think I must be imagining his voice, that I've conjured him into being, but then I turn and see Kai running up the single-rider line behind me. I spin back around, away from him.

I hate that my heart jumps when I see him, that I feel an excited flutter in my stomach.

"I'm not talking to you," I say.

"I saw you running over here," he says. "Why were you running? Why are you alone?"

"Because I want to be alone," I say.

"Okay." He backs away, accidentally stepping on the foot of a man who has entered the line behind us. "Oh, sorry," he says to the man, then turns back to me. "Sorry. I thought something was wrong. I'll go."

"No, wait." I don't know why I say it. It's just that suddenly I don't want him to leave. "Jordan and I are done. For good."

"You are?" Kai takes a step closer. "Wait, why?"

The woman in front of me gets into the back of a log boat and it drifts away, and then moments later I'm first in line. I open my bag to stuff the book back inside so it won't get wet.

"You brought my book," Kai says, pointing at it.

"Technically it's *my* book," I say, zipping it up safely.

Another boat pulls up.

"I need two single riders!" the cast member in front of us calls out, pointing to me and then to Kai. I climb into the second to last seat and then Kai follows and climbs in behind me.

"Wait, what are you doing?" I twist around to face him. "Kai, this is a log flume. There's a drop." The boat jerks forward, and then we're moving along the track, water splashing our feet. There's a mom and daughter in matching Pixar T-shirts sitting in front of us, and the mom wraps her arms protectively around her kid as we start to move faster.

"I don't care," Kai says. "What happened with Jordan?"

Our boat begins to climb. "I just . . . don't think I ever actually loved him."

Kai's cheeks have gone red, beads of sweat gathering at his brow. He looks . . . not well. Like he might pass out right here in this log. I remember how nervous he got about the top bunk, which was only about five feet off the ground. We reach the top of the crest and then shoot down, only a small drop. I know this is just the warm-up.

"Pen," Kai says. He's clutching the back of my seat so hard his knuckles are turning white. "I kinda can't breathe right now. But I just want to—"

"It's okay," I say. "You don't have to say anything."

"No," he says, his voice breathy. We round a bend and the boat starts climbing—up and up and up. "I just want to get this out," he says. "I had no right to do any of that stuff I did. I was selfish and stupid, but I don't want to be those things anymore. I know you think I don't take anything seriously, but that's not true. I take this seriously. I am serious about *you*. I want to be better for you, Pen."

I think of Sarah then—how she's given me so many chances when I didn't deserve them. I think of my mom, who is trying her best, but still sometimes messes up. I think of myself, who kissed her best friend's boyfriend and spent the next few weeks trying to cover it all up. People make stupid mistakes. They cheat, they lie, they leave.

Right now, I have all the power I've ever wanted. Whatever I do isn't weakness—it's strength. This whole summer, I've tried to blame everything on everyone else because admitting I wanted to kiss Kai that night would turn me into the kind of person who would do a thing like that. But there was some part of me that *wanted* to kiss him, that has always wanted to kiss him. I'm the one who cheated on Jordan. I can't put that blame on anyone else, as much as I want to. Maybe Kai has made some bad choices, but so have I. And when we put aside our egos and our anger and actually *listen*—I think Kai and I make each other stronger.

"I want to be better for you too," I tell him.

We're almost at the top of the peak now, and I can feel Kai's panic behind me. It's rolling off him in waves. I reach out and take his hand, gripping it firmly.

"It'll be over before you know it," I say. "We're almost there. Just hold on tight, okay? It's three . . . two . . . one . . ."

Right as our boat tips over the edge, right when we're airborne, I squeeze his hand three times. Seconds later, we crash into a wave and it's done—the water soaking us, drenching our clothes and hair. I'm laughing, giddy from the drop, and when I turn around in the boat and see his shell-shocked face, I lean forward and kiss him. It takes him just a second, and then he kisses me back, his hands threading through my soaking-wet hair.

"Did you mean it?" he asks, pulling away. "When you squeezed my hand."

"I think so. I think . . . sometime during this mixed-up summer you became my best friend."

"You're my best friend too," he says, laughing. "I think you might be my favorite person in the whole world."

The woman and child in front of us are turned around in their seats too, staring, but I don't care. Our boat comes to a stop at the exit, and we all climb out. Kai's legs are still shaking, and once we're on dry land, I wrap my arms around him, pulling him into a tight hug.

"Weren't we supposed to break up here?" Kai asks.

"I've had enough breakups for one summer," I say into his chest. "I'm sorry I hated you all these years." I squeeze him just a bit tighter. "You really did deserve it, though."

He laughs, pulling back. "It was kind of fun. You're cute when you're mean. But I like you even better when you're nice, Sweet Bread."

"Do you know what sweetbreads are?"

"What? Like dinner rolls. The fluffy, delicious kind."

"I'm pretty sure sweetbreads are animal organs."

"I've *got* to take you to Hawaii," he says. "Because that is some nonsense." He places a quick kiss to the top of my head. "But I like you either way. Now let's get you dried off. You look like a Jackson Pollock."

I dig through my backpack and pull out a little compact, checking my reflection in the mirror. Kai is right—I look like a splatter painting. There are black mascara tracks down my cheeks, my hair frizzing wildly around my head.

And I couldn't be happier.

NOW

THE FIRST DAY OF school is bright and sunny, crisp air that smells like promises. Olivia and I planned matching spirit day outfits months ago—bright red mini dresses and devil horns—but when I see it all laid out on my floor this morning, I don't want to put it on. The girl who picked out those clothes feels like a different person.

I rummage through my dresser and choose something else—jeans and the soft yellow T-shirt I wore to Disney. It smells a little bit like chlorine, like the moment on Splash Mountain when I squeezed Kai's hand three times. I know I'll catch hell for wearing a yellow shirt on spirit day, but I don't actually care. The thing is, if I wear the wrong thing, the world won't end. And there are so many other projects I want to spend my time on—so many other beautiful things I'm making just for me, because they make me happy.

I've spent the last few weeks designing and sewing costumes for Sarah's band. I made an iridescent purple jumpsuit for her, a giant matching tank top for Brian. We're meeting up after school tonight and I'm going to surprise her with a cape I made—it's soft and shiny and bright blue to match her hair. I made a scarf for Romina too, just in case. She's been saving up for an electric cello, and I know she and Sarah have talked about her potentially joining the band.

As I get dressed, I actually start laughing a little at the madness of it all. *You're the most stubborn person I've ever met*, Kai said to me once. *Don't see you changing your mind anytime soon.* I'm so glad to prove him wrong.

My mom is in the kitchen when I get downstairs, pouring coffee into three thermoses. "Oh," I say when I see her, stopping short in the doorframe. "Why aren't you at work?"

She sets down the coffeepot. "I called in. Going in late today. It's my baby's first day of senior year. Thought I could drop you off."

Before I can stop myself, I slide across the floor in my socks and throw my arms around her. I'm still not completely over everything that happened, but if there's one thing I'm trying to get better at, it's this: I don't want to be so hung up on the idea of being angry that I don't let myself forgive. And right now, my mom's arms around me, squeezing me tight, the smell of coffee, and the chirping of birds outside the window—isn't this the whole point?

And then Seb is there too. "I want in," he says, his strong arms wrapped around my back so I'm in the middle of a tight Harris sandwich. It's so crazy how big he's gotten—that his arms are strong now instead of scrawny, that his head is almost a full head above mine and my mom's as we hug. He's our little man now, and I'm proud of who he's become. We don't need my dad. We have each other. And I love our family just the way it is.

"Okay, okay." My mom pulls back and there are tears in her eyes. "We're going to be late. Let's get out of here!" She's laughing and handing us our thermoses of coffee, and we gather our lunches and backpacks and hustle out to the car.

We drive to school, pulling up to the parent drop-off. I know I should probably be embarrassed to be here—there are tiny green freshmen pouring out of all the other cars around us, and I feel like a giant. Seb gets out first, throwing a peace sign and slamming the back door behind him. Immediately, he's swept into the crowd. I know I should get out of the car, but I can't help but hesitate. It's strange to be here with the babies and the school buses instead of catching a ride in Olivia's green buggy. But my mom reaches over and squeezes my knee, and finally this feels so right. "I'm proud of you, baby girl. I mean it." She tucks a strand of hair behind my ear and I pull it back out because my big ears aren't going anywhere. "I'm going to do this more often, okay? I want to be here for you when you need me."

"Me too," I say. "I was thinking maybe I could work some extra hours at Scoops too." I run my hand along the hem of my jeans. "Help out a bit."

"You don't have to do that. You're still a kid. I want you to enjoy it."

"But I want to, Mom. I don't want you to be so stressed out all the time."

She smiles. "Then whatever you want to do, you can do. But for now, school." She pats my knee. "I'll try to be home for dinner tonight, okay? So you can tell me all about it."

"Okay." I open the car door. "I love you." The words still feel new in my mouth, like I'm learning to speak a foreign language. But I like the way they feel. I want to practice saying them, want to get to the point where they're comfortable.

"Love you too, Penelope." I can tell they're still a little hard for my mom too, but I think that's what's so great about love: it's something worth putting in the extra effort for. We're both still learning how to be the kind of mother and daughter we've always wanted to be. And I actually kind of like the sound of my name when my mom says it. Penelope, the name she gave me when I was born, the name I've been trying to shed ever since Kai was an idiot and ruined it for me. But maybe now that I've forgiven Kai, the name can be mine again. It belongs to me. And when my mom says it, I don't think of elementary school taunts, of leaving birthday parties early, of hiding myself in the spine of a book. When my mom says *Penelope*, it sounds like a song.

I get out of the car, and then she drives away and I'm all alone. Scanning the parking lot, I find Olivia's car parked in its usual spot, and feel a slight ache from the loss—the fact that it's the last first day of high school we'll ever have and we're not together.

Before I can change my mind, I turn away from the school entrance, walking across the field toward the tennis courts.

Olivia is there with Katie, both wearing the red dresses and devil horns that were supposed to be mine. They're taking pictures and laughing, posing in silly ways for the camera. Olivia sees me, and before I can turn away, our eyes meet. She stops laughing, the smile fades from her face, and her eyes narrow. She nudges Katie with her elbow, and then they're both staring at me. So, fine, Olivia and I are never going to be best friends again. But maybe we don't have to be enemies either. We can start fresh, be real with each other for the very first time.

So instead of fleeing, or ignoring them, or pretending they don't exist, I wave and walk forward onto the tennis courts. "It didn't feel right not to help with the first-day-of-school pictures." I chew my lip. "I mean, if you want my help?"

Olivia studies me for a second. "You're not dressed like you."

I look down at my shirt, a representation of one of my favorite moments. "Actually, I really am."

Olivia nods in Katie's direction. "All right, get in there."

"Or . . . do you want me to take a picture of you two?"

Olivia clutches her camera—her baby—tightly in her hands, but then sighs and hands it to me. It's this little moment that makes me feel like maybe, potentially, things might get better. Olivia may not trust me completely anymore, but she trusts me enough for this.

She moves beside Katie, and I take some pictures of the two of them, arms around each other like it's the most natural thing in the world.

"You were right about Jordan," Olivia says, when I hand the camera back to her.

"Oh yeah?" The relief I feel at her words is instantaneous.

"Yeah," she says. "I'm fucking awesome, and I deserve a guy who knows it." She chews her bottom lip, studies me for a second. "Maybe you could help me with my eyeliner sometime? I mean, now that I'm a single woman, I'm officially on the prowl."

"I'd like that." I smile, turning away from them. "I'll see you guys later, okay?"

There are still a few minutes before class, so I leave them on the tennis courts and take a seat on the bench outside the senior section. I scan the parking lot and entryway for Kai, but I know he's probably not here yet. Kai is late for everything—why wouldn't he be late for the first day of senior year? I pull out my phone and send him a quick text. Late on your first day, Tanaka?

He types back right away. Forgot my alarm. Fuck! You know me so well.

> I'm always early and you're always late.
> Maybe one day we can meet right in the middle.

I think we already have, he answers. I have a surprise for you.

Then he sends me a picture. He's dressed all in red—a red soccer jersey, red hearts painted onto his cheeks, a bright red senior spirit day top hat. I look down at my own faded yellow T-shirt and can't help but laugh.

I love it, I tell him. I start to type I love you, but then delete it. I'm not ready yet, and there's too much to say. I told Jordan I loved him before it was real. I don't want to make that mistake again. But I know it will come out eventually, the layers of meaning behind the phrase *I love you*, and they won't just be empty words when I say them. But for now, I settle on this:

> Want to go swimming? Drive me to our spot after school?

> Skinny dipping????!!!

> Sure . . . why not? Let's go skinny dipping

Kai sends me a long row of exclamation points then, and I laugh and tuck my phone away in my pocket. The air is getting even warmer, so I lean back and close my eyes, letting the sun heat my face. And it's peaceful, being here by myself, listening to the hustle and bustle of everyone else around me.

I know I must look weird, but I don't really care anymore. I'm comfortable right here in this moment. I'm happy. And the thing is—I'm not really alone at all. I have Kai, once he actually shows up. I know we're going to be that annoying couple who is always making out against the lockers, but I also know I'm not going to worry too much about it, because making out with Kai is the greatest freaking thing in the entire world. I have Romina and Myriah, who I can't wait to double-date with. I have Olivia— the *real* Olivia—who might be mine again someday, after we've both healed.

But there are new friends too—friendships that don't exist yet, friends who are still waiting to be discovered. There's Sarah, who I'll drag to the pep rally with me in a few minutes. There are those art classes I've been meaning to take, the school musical if I'm brave enough to try out this year.

And there are the possibilities I haven't even thought of yet— friends down the line, next year wherever I end up for college: friends in the dorms, on the quad, on vacation, in my future office at my future job. There's an endless amount of birthdays, happy hours, brunches, weddings, trips to Thailand, or Australia, or France—future memories unfolding before me, waiting for me to reach out and grab them.

The truth is that high school is such a small blip on my timeline. Life is too short to waste the whole thing worrying. Kai taught me that. And he's right. Who cares if people are staring?

The fact is, they probably aren't even looking my way at all. No one else really gives a shit about what I'm doing but me.

I know eventually I'll have to get up. I have to find my locker, face my future, make senior year my bitch. This bench will always be here to return to when I need a minute to think. Maybe it will be my new spot, somewhere I can bring Kai to show him a little bit more of myself, someplace we can take sandwiches and eat our lunch, or just another spot to make out and drive ourselves crazy.

But right now, it's just for me.

I reach into my backpack and pull out the book Kai gave me. *The Giver*. My book. *Our* book. I run my hand over the torn cover. And then I open to the first page and I start to read.

ACKNOWLEDGMENTS

They say your second book is the hardest to write—and that's before dealing with a worldwide pandemic. This book will always remind me of the coronavirus, an amalgamation of all my hopes, fears, anxieties, and struggles during these wild months of 2020.

While you might think being stuck alone in lockdown would make for good writing conditions (Fewer distractions! More time to work! No friends pressuring you to hang out!), it was incredibly difficult to get into a creative headspace while the world around me was falling apart. How do I write about these silly, privileged, mean little characters and their insignificant problems when there is so much else to worry about? How can I write about romance when there are truckloads of bodies, protests against the systemic racism in our country, a corrupt government that is actively standing in the way of progress?

My answer to this is that art has always been a way to fight injustice, a way to bring attention to a cause, to disrupt and engage and delight. Art will always be important. So I tried to take my doubts and my anxieties at the state of the world and channel them into making my own art—creating in the way that makes me happy. And if I can bring a seed of hope, a few hours of escapism to just one reader, then this will all have been worth it.

I truly could not have gotten through this year without the help and support of those around me. Even though I only got to speak to all of you through the screen of my computer, it meant so much.

Thank you to my parents for listening to all my worries over the phone. I can't wait to celebrate with you in person once we're allowed. Thanks once again to Shirin Yim Leos and the rest of the Uninventables, especially those who helped me through early drafts of this book: Cady, Cassia, Chris, Jenn, Julie, and Leata. Thanks to the 2020 Visionaries for letting me vent and being my support system through this year, filling my life with laughter and memes and gifs and frondship from a safe distance away: Amanda, Irene, Jessica, and Remi. To the Roaring '20s Debut group who were here for me through the wild and unexpected path of debuting during a pandemic when all the bookstores were closed. We did it!

Thank you of course to my brilliant editor, Julie Rosenberg; my agent, Taylor Haggerty; my publicist, Olivia Russo; and the rest of the team at Razorbill/Penguin Teen: Felicity Vallence, Shannon Spann, and James Akinaka, as well as my cover designer, Kristin Boyle, and illustrator, Carolina Melis.

Thank you, Justin. I could not have made it through quarantine without you.

And thank you so much to my readers for making this all possible. The messages I got from you were the only thing that made being a published author feel real while being stuck in lockdown. To go full LotR nerd, I will end by saying that in this hellish year, you have all been *a light in dark places when all other lights go out.*

Thank you.